About the Author

Marlene. South African-born Swiss citizen, lives in Geneva, Switzerland, where she writes and practices as a therapist. Prize-winning poet and author of *The Magic of Africa, Campfire Tales and Stories, The Thrill of Africa, The Curse, There is Only One of Us – We are All One,* and various poetry collections she continues to write. An active participant in writers' workshops, she encourages others to try their hand at creative writing. She has travelled far and wide, delving into various cultures, religions, traditions, and beliefs. Her curiosity expands her imagination, daring her to explore different genres.

Impact

Marlene Jeanrenaud

Impact

Vanguard Press

VANGUARD PAPERBACK

© Copyright 2025
Marlene Jeanrenaud

A CIP catalogue record for this title is available from the British Library.

ISBN 978-1-83794-631-0

Vanguard Press is an imprint of
Pegasus Elliot Mackenzie Publishers Ltd.
www.pegasuspublishers.com

First Published in 2025

Vanguard Press
Sheraton House Castle Park
Cambridge England

Printed & Bound in Great Britain

Dedication

To Pierre, for the tremendous gift.

Acknowledgements

I wish to acknowledge the support of the members of Library In English, Geneva, Writer's group for their support and especially Rose Yarom, who encouraged and gave up valuable time to go through my first draft.

Other works by Marlene Jeanrenaud:

Memoire: (PublishAmerica)
The Magic of Africa *– ISBN: 1-4137-7675-2*
The Thrill of Africa *– ISBN: 978-0-20-61521-1*

Novel:
The Curse *– ISBN: 978-1-68222-642-1 (Bookbaby)*

Self-help – Spiritual: (Greece)
There is only one of Us – We are one *– ISBN 978-960-6744-95-2*
Il n'y en a Qu'un – Nous sommes tous Un *–*
    ISBN 978-618-5565-00-8
Poetry and short works; (Cloverleaf Press)
Ebb and Flow *– ISBN: 0-9543175-0-5*
Watermarks *– ISBN: 0-9543175-1-3*
Shifting Sands *– ISBN: 0-9543175-3-X*
Traces *– IISBN: 978-0-9543175-2-2*
Mountains of the Moon: *ISBN: 978-0-9543175-5-3*

For orders or information contact:
Email: **marlenejeanrenaud@gmail.com**
jeanrenaud.m@sunrise.ch

PROLOGUE

Alexandra experienced a deep panic. White and blue lights still pulsated against the walls of her apartment. At least the high-pitched scream of the police sirens had stopped. She didn't want the police here; they brought back bad and terrifying memories.

Her skin crawled every time she thought of the scene in the street earlier. Hours have passed since the two plain clothes policemen had left the scene. Their presence seemed imprinted all over the street. She couldn't close her eyes when the scenario repeated itself. Sleep was out of the question.

*

She had entered her bedroom to close the curtains before turning on lights as late afternoon quickly turned into the dusk of evening, when she heard the shot. Feet pounded the street as the few bystanders and pedestrians scattered in different directions, clearing the area.

Balmy air, soft against the skin, came in through the open window and carried flavours of summer barbecues and geraniums. The pleasant summer air belied what she saw down in the street.

He lay there, bleeding, his blond hair disappearing into the dark stain of blood. The patch on the grey road surface grew, giving the impression of him lying on a black, uneven rug. The dark-haired girl with him stood there, immobile. Then she turned her head in the direction of a slamming car door. Tyres screeched as it drove away. The sounds shocked the girl, forcing her eyes to the sight at her feet. As if coming out of a dream, the girl became aware of blood spatter on her face and pink dress. Hysterically, she tried to swat the drops away like insects invading her physical space. Alex watched the girl look down, then left and right.

She began to scream from shock. The sound of her own voice brought her back from hysteria. The event finally registered. After slight hesitation the girl pulled out her phone. She knelt next to the fallen young man.

Sobbing, she stayed on her knees next to her companion. A man approached, offering help, she swatted him away.

Time stood still until police sirens broke into the neighbourhood. An unmarked car with flashing lights slid to a stop 15 metres from the body. Two plainclothes policemen, guns drawn, got out, scanning the surroundings. Besides distant traffic sounds, it was quiet; nothing seemed to move. Satisfied the shooter long gone, they approached the body. The shorter one pulled the girl to her feet. Uniformed officers arrived. The taller, lanky policeman gave orders, and yellow crime tape went up, cordoning virtually the whole block. He inspected the body and spoke on his radio while the other led the girl to their car. The curious steadily filled the ranks of onlookers. The uniforms took names and statements from the crowd, advising possible witnesses to contact the two detectives working the case. Other officers milled around, trying to keep the curious at bay.

CHAPTER ONE

Blood spatters caked her clothes and stuck to her raven hair. With distaste, she looked down at her dress, deciding to burn it as soon as possible, even though it was her favourite. What an untenable situation! Cynthia swiped a drop of congealed blood from her cheek and pushed her hair back behind her ears as she paced the floor.

The memory of Marcus lying in his own blood made her feel faint. It could have been her lying there. If he hadn't turned to pull her close at that moment for a kiss, the bullet would've hit her square between the eyes! Instead, it found a target in his heart.

With a shiver, she tried to sit down, but as soon as her body touched the chair, she jumped up as if the seat was on fire. She wanted to forget it ever happened. She wanted nothing to do with it. She wanted to go home and have a shower. She wanted a lot of things – and the most pressing one – to distance herself from this situation.

Her mind raced, convinced the police had other ideas. They forcibly held her, like a prisoner! They treated her as a suspect! The shock of the event had turned into disgust for authority. Fury consumed her. She'd never talk. And the place smelled funny; even the faint fresh-paint smell didn't hide the nervous sweat that clung to the walls. And that stupid fat policeman kept attacking her with questions, trying to trip her up. For heaven's sake she had reported the shooting! She didn't ask for any of this. Impatiently, she stamped her foot – her Latin temperament beginning to show.

What more could she tell them? Why ask why they were there? Why did they want to know who she dated before Marcus? What was it to them where they went for early dinner? To explain again what brought them to Paquis was ridiculous! She had repeated the gist of what happened three times, and that's all she'd say. The police now have the description of the car, and the fact that she didn't see the shooter or the vehicle's registration number. Three times! That's enough, isn't it? She only dated Marcus; she wasn't attached to his hip. Everyone liked him, and she found him handsome and fun – the 'in' jock at Uni. He got all the perks of the position as captain of the hockey team, and why shouldn't she cash in as his girlfriend? He was tall and blond, and she short with the olive skin of her ancestors. She looked good next to him. Why not go out with him? But that was all. He had his uses, so what else could she say – not the love of her life, just a means to an end. Why didn't they believe her?

Cynthia had enough, she wanted to leave. She looked around her. What's with this colour scheme? Light grey walls with charcoal up to waist level? It gave her the creeps, and she needed to get out, and soon. The longer they kept her, the more difficult it became to remember what she had said in her limited statement.

'Come on! Anyone there? I want to go home. Now!' Her voice sounded shrill in the confined space. No panic was present in her attitude, just anger and disdain. 'You must let me go! I've done nothing! Wait till my father hears of this!'

The policeman at a desk facing the room had enough of the noise. He opened the door and, as calmly as possible, said: 'please be quiet Miss Gonzales. Someone will be with you in a moment.' Cynthia didn't take this lightly, rushed to the door as he closed it behind him. She banged her fists against it, screaming insults at anyone who might be listening.

The officer shook his head and returned to his desk. 'I wish someone could deal with that spoilt brat in there or shut her up,' he said to no one in particular. An experienced officer, he had dealt with many different types of people, but found young people of today spoilt, tiring and above all, disrespectful. If he had his way, he'll let them spend a night in jail just to teach them a lesson. In his opinion, the fault lay with the parents. They indulged their offspring to the extent of creating egotistical monsters who demanded the right to do as they pleased. In short, they had no regard for others, no compassion, and were never concerned if anyone got hurt as a result of their actions.

As the minutes ticked by, Cynthia's temper rose even more. Her voice had become hoarse when finally, the door opened. The duty sergeant came in with paperwork in his hands.

'What took you so long? I need to get out of here. You can't keep me. I'm only a witness and I want to go home. NOW!'

'Young lady, please calm down. Yes, as our only witness, we had to keep you here to make sure we get all the facts clearly – before you forget details.' He gestured for her to sit down. She ignored him.

He repeated his request. 'Please sit down for a minute. We had your statement typed out and have it here. You need to sign it before you go.'

'Give it to me! And your pen, can't sign with my nail now, can I? Or do you want a fingerprint?'

'Here you go. Do you need someone to take you home or do you want to call your father to pick you up?' It was getting difficult for the sergeant to keep calm, not to mention remain polite and non-committal.

'No, just let me out of here, I'll find my own way home.'

*

The recurring sight of all that blood would not leave Alex. Transfixed, the scene continued to unfold. She couldn't breathe. Glued to the spot, terrified that she'd be spotted, she was thrown back into past fears. Caught in that moment of panic and terror, with darkness surrounding her, she forced herself to find the resolve to break out of it. With escape from this trap foremost in her mind, she knew she had to work through the panic she now found herself in. Push it from her mind. Except, it kept coming back, again, and again.

Her childhood determination to not allow anything which could bring her down or destroy her optimism, no matter how difficult it was, had made her shake off her fear. Slowly moving back from the window, she sat on the bed in the fast-growing dark. Alex had no idea how long she stayed in that position. It must have been at least an hour. Once convinced no one had seen her, she quietly moved to the kitchen without switching on the lights. The illumination of the streetlight guided her through the apartment, where she made herself a couple of slices of toast and a cup of tea. Comforted by the smell of butter melting on the toast, she moved to the living room. She sat in heavy silence on the sofa and munched the toast, sipping the tea. She resisted turning on the TV.

In the darkness, raw emotions from her childhood came to the fore. She always felt as if her family excluded her – as if they put her in a dark room, deliberately shutting the door behind them. This exclusion created a nightmare from which she had no way out. With no glimmer of light to be seen anywhere, the dark became tangible. She always felt surrounded and consumed by it. Uncontrollable trembling inevitably followed this sensation of abandonment. With nowhere to go, no escape, no way out, and every call for help unanswered, it had made the isolation real. Incomprehensible to her – it made no sense how or why a parent would treat one of their own children in such a way. The physical separation made her feel small, alone, and shunned for no reason. Though, deep down she knew there must be more to life and continued to ignore her parents' efforts to break her spirit.

For Alex, each day began filled with optimism and an inner joy. Even as a baby and young child, she had woken at four every morning, singing. But as the day progressed, the disillusionment of life brought her to tears. By four in the afternoon, she would cry uncontrollably. Only her uncle could calm her and bring a new perspective on the world around her. Now, as an adult, she still awoke with a song in her heart and positive attitude. Petite and fair, this positive attitude masked an inner insecurity.

She had found it odd that her sisters never went on trips or visits without their parents but were always kept close to home. However, now for the first time, she realised the various school outings they had allowed her to take, and frequent visits to her grandparents on the farm were a respite for them. Not as a special treat which she deserved. She finally understood that being allowed, and able to leave home to attend university in the city, stemmed from this fact. It all fell into place – clarity at last! Unbeknownst to her parents, they had given her a tremendous gift, the gift of independence and free thinking. Although she doubted their intentions stretched to giving her an insatiable love of travel, she nevertheless, relied only on herself, her optimism and perseverance carried her through many difficult and sad moments.

Pounding on the door brought her back from her reverie. Revisiting her past always resulted in conflict, as fear tended to make her overly cautious. Alex didn't move.

'Police! Is anyone home? This is the police.' She could hear them talking amongst themselves. She stayed silent, pulled her knees up to her chest, and hunched her shoulders. Convinced that if she made herself small and stayed in the dark, they'd move on. She knew they'd come again during the next couple of days. Only then would she be prepared. Yes, she'd be prepared when they came again. It was too late to speak to them tonight. Sure enough, they moved on and pounded on her neighbour's door, calling out as they had at her door.

She heard Mrs Ginet greet them. True to form, she invited them in for coffee. The officer declined, took her name, and asked her to come to Servette Police Station as soon as was convenient. They told her to ask for Detective Favre or Garcia, obviously assuming her to be a busybody. Alex let out her breath and relaxed. They were gone. For now.

*

'Your husband's playing with fire.' A raspy voice whispered. *'We know your name, where you live, where your children go to school. We know everything. He must back off. If he doesn't, we'll slit your children's throats, one by one, then yours. He can watch.'*

Her smile froze.

In that instant her pleasant day, her whole life shattered.

A click. The sound of the dial tone reverberated in her ear. The click sounded like a gunshot followed by loud continuous thunder.

What? She looked at the small screen on the phone. No caller ID. On impulse, she wanted to throw the phone against the wall, to rid herself of the threat. Then fear took hold.

Maria let out a long, slow breath. She replaced the menacing receiver onto the cradle, forcing her emotions down. She had to regain composure – act as if nothing had happened. What was unusual was that her hands started to shake. Then the trembling overtook her whole body. The ice in the calm voice reverberated in her mind, sending cold shivers through her whole being, it multiplied into a complete freeze. Imprisoned in this frozen fear, her mind blanked. She sank into the chair next to the telephone table, unable to move.

What just happened?

Slowly, she took in the familiar things around her, found strength in her surroundings: the warm colour of the parquet, the cut-glass bowl next to the phone, and near the entrance, the children's parkas on pegs. These things grounded her, brought her back from the brink of her inner terror.

She breathed deeply.

She had to think clearly.

Who just called?

How did they know her name?

Where did they get their number?

How did they know everything about them?

27

Why the warning?

Were the children safe?

There was no time to react or ask who was on the line.

José always accused her of overreacting. Only there was no doubt in the message.

How would she tell him?

He needed to know.

He won't believe her.

It had to be something to do with his work, but what?

Where was José? He should've been home by now.

Her mind a trapeze artist tumbling into a jumble of fear, anger, thoughts of escape, and protection for her family.

CHAPTER TWO

'This is chaos! We live in the centre of a storm which began as a whirlwind,' Paul Favre felt on the point of being swept up in recent events.

'Everyone only talks about crime against humanity! I suppose it's inevitable with the current migrant crisis. Then, a close second, comes global warming and the environmental destruction going on around us, with animal cruelty third. I agree to a great extent, but people downplay gun-violence and murder! The impact of any kind of crime is far-reaching and unacceptable.'

Paul Favre shook his head, mumbling into the empty interior of the vehicle. His partner's day-old sweat still clung to every part of the passenger seat in their squad car. Convinced that their perspiration, which kicked off every time they left the precinct, carried their fear, anxiety, and apprehension, he rolled down the window. Yes, they ventured out not knowing what awaited them outside that fortress, forcing them to think about daily survival. It felt like an eternity had passed since he took this job, twelve years, in fact. Nevertheless, his heart rate rose every time he set off to the scene of a crime.

In the academy, they concentrated on how to defend themselves, how to approach a dangerous situation, and of course, how to handle a firearm, but what about actual life out here? No one could've warned him about the real danger on the streets. They were not prepared.

Attached to the Serious Crime Unit, Paul instinctively straightened his shoulders. The unit dealt with cases whenever gun violence is involved, and the rate of avoiding injury was perhaps lower than any other unit. He should be used to it by now. And what about reality? There were other, more subtle dangers – not the importance of the uniform, but the various emotions the uniform elicited in people. So much hate had been aimed at them that he frequently marvelled at how he, himself, managed not to commit murder because of hurled abuse. This attitude had raised its head repeatedly in the last couple of years.

He had begun to doubt his true feelings. Every time he received a case,

29

fear, apprehension, or perhaps excitement, filled him. Which one was it? The most gruesome cases became an obsession with him. Could it be that he wanted to right the cruel world? Or did he subconsciously feed on the threat of violence? Or did he play roulette with his life? Either way, it worried him. He needed to get home at night. The day getting home in one piece was not his priority, he would quit the force. No, he said to himself, he must stop doubting, for the sake of his daughter and those he worked with. Divorced, he saw his daughter rarely. But he knew it would be hard on her if something happened to him.

Paul jolted his mind back to focus on the present. The traffic had hardly moved in the last ten minutes, and he speculated they wasted much of their time being stuck in traffic instead of catching culprits. All he wanted was to get home and relax. Unencumbered by a seatbelt, he moved his lanky form in the seat.

Their current case had also given him and José Garcia, his partner, headaches – at a loss as to how to find witnesses to the crime. Even though the young man met his death on the street in the light of late afternoon; no pedestrians or any resident in the apartments around the scene claimed to have seen anything. It was crucial to get information within a few hours of an event, but still nothing had come to their attention. None of the bystanders had anything to say: saw nothing; heard nothing; arrived after hearing the shot. Already in the early days of the investigation, frustration had set in.

Various windows look down on the very spot of the crime, and the lack of witnesses or information was odd. In this neighbourhood of Geneva, during the heatwave virtually everyone had windows wide open. Often, some would hang out of their windows to find relief from the heat and for a breath of cooler air. However, no one admitted having seen anything. He had decided to repeat the door-to-door questioning in the morning hoping someone with courage would come forward after a good night's sleep.

He ran through the hard facts they had.
- Young man, Marcus Stephens, aged twenty, with GSW in chest.
- No drugs or firearms found on him.
- Initial tox screen clear.
- No apparent gang affiliation or tattoos.
- a 117 call by girlfriend, Cynthia Gonzales, found at his side.
- No obvious motive at site.

José maintained – no, remained convinced – that it had something to do with the girlfriend. A jealous ex or a stalker, someone obsessed with the girl. From other preliminary information they've gleaned so far, Cynthia, the girlfriend, aggressively pursued the victim from the day he became captain of the university's hockey team and selectors' first choice for the national team. She chose him as a perfect replacement for the neighbouring university's football goalkeeper, Antonio, who lost his position because of a knee injury in a freak accident. Therefore, she – despite his popularity – dropped him as he had no clout or attraction left. José felt the girl needed the limelight, and in this case, that which reflected onto her from whomever she dated at that moment. She craved the attention.

Paul had read and re-read her statement, certain she had left something out. The only indisputable fact he found was that she couldn't be bothered to get involved. But he still held out hope that she could remember part of, or the whole, registration plate of the car. However, he now doubted her willingness to dig into her memory. The image that she dated the victim only for attention had now become crystal clear. Her selfishness astounded him. He could not shake the feeling she was hiding something more than the ability to remember.

Paul heard the police radio crackle into action. Off duty, he indifferently listened and ignored the message. His thoughts went back to the young man lying in a pool of blood on the sidewalk. Clean-shaven, neatly dressed, and after speaking to the parents, confirmed Paul's first impression. The victim appeared well brought up and obviously serious about life. What made Marcus fall for someone so shallow and completely different? Obviously, her powers of seduction had played a role. Hopefully, his teammates could shed some light on their relationship. What a loss! Tonight, sleep would elude him. He knew it would until he found a plan to go forward on this case. Tomorrow, tomorrow they could tackle the individual team members.

Thirty minutes later, Paul pulled up in the reserved parking spot in the basement of his apartment building. He took the stairs to the second floor, much more reliable than the old Schindler elevator which served the six floors of the building. He paused in front of the door to his apartment, looking left then right before he inserted his key in the lock. With a quick turn, he entered the dark apartment. Again, he took his time, all his senses on high alert as if sniffing the air to check if all was in order. When no alarm

31

bells went off in his head, he stepped deeper into the space and switched on the light.

He pulled open the drawer of the sideboard, unclipped his shield and radio from his belt placed them in the drawer. He removed his cell phone from the inside jacket pocket, placing it on top of the sideboard, and took off the jacket, throwing it over the chair next to the door. He slipped off his holster, released the safety tab holding the gun in place, and pulled it out. Again, he looked around, saw, and heard nothing untoward. Satisfied, he checked and secured his firearm putting everything in the same drawer. With a low, tuneless whistle he moved to the kitchen.

On the way, he saw the impatient blink of his answering machine. Tempted to not respond, he walked past – then realised that the irritating light would not go away without his interference. He grabbed a beer from the half-empty fridge and turned back to listen to the message. With a swish the beer breathed as Paul pulled the ring on the can. He pushed the button on the answering system.

'Drop this case. Write it off as a gang-related drive-by. If you don't, your loved ones could disappear. You have now received your last, and only warning.'

The message ended, and Paul stood staring at the instrument, stunned, the beer forgotten in his hand. What case? The one with the young lad? It must be that. How did this person get his private number, and for what reason? He put down the can and grabbed his cell phone. Immediately he tapped in his partner's number. José answered after two rings. *'Wow, that was quick. You expecting my call?'* The quick response surprised Paul.

'What a coincidence. I wanted to call you. The strangest thing just happened. Maria is in a terrible state. She took a call just before I came home, and a guy just said, "Back off! You've been warned." She's taking the children to her sister's in Fribourg. Do you know why?

'It freaked her out. But you know she is always a bit of a worrywart so, I'm sure it's not serious. I said I'd look into it, but I'm not going to waste our time.'

'Garcia, drop everything and meet me at the station. Now!'

'No, I just got home, and now, tiredness and hunger take precedence over creepy phone calls and your desire to see me. Maria's already pissed with me.'

'Garcia! No joking, this is serious! There must be more to that call.

Meet me there immediately. There's something we're missing. That girl Cynthia knows more than she's saying. Something about this case disturbs me and puts all those around us in danger.' Paul's insistence gave him a dry throat.

'Okay, man. But I don't like it. And I can tell you, I'll never hear the end of it from Maria if I leave her alone after that call. She'll also insist I don't leave without eating.'

'Get the children to help her pack and tell her you're following up on the call. But get here now!'

'She'll make me pay! Fine, see you in fifteen under protest.'

Paul quickly downed the beer and grabbed everything he had just placed into the sideboard. Out of habit, he checked his gun, making sure it was loaded with the safety on, slipped it back into its holster before pulling it over his shoulder. As he turned toward his front door, he switched off the light, his mind already in overdrive, anticipating the road back to the station. Going in the opposite direction, the traffic no longer at a peak, would allow him to get back to his destination in roughly the expected time he told José.

The usual chaos in the office had also died down; only a few old-timers manned their desks, trying to complete paperwork or avoid going home. Well, better than propping up a bar, Paul thought. He moved through to his desk and sat down. While waiting for José's arrival, he looked through the current file. Again, the fact that crime against humanity and the destruction of the environment occupied most people filled his mind. However, this real death seemed cruel. He dealt with this every day, though, a youth with such talent and his life ahead was a double tragedy. Here a seemingly innocent, clean-living young man was killed. And for what? And why had they been threatened? What could be behind all this?

José walked in gulping down a sandwich.

'Good, you've arrived. Did Maria and the kids leave?'

'Yeah, in quite a hurry, she didn't argue.'

'Garcia, I received the same warning.'

'What? Now you tell me. So, Maria didn't make it up.'

'No. I presume it was the same person who left a message on my answering machine.'

'What on earth could all this mean? Who do you think called?'

'I don't know, but they didn't waste any time to send out warnings.'

'Strange. Maria couldn't describe the voice – she was too freaked out.'

33

'I would like to know where and how they got our home numbers.'

Paul ignored José's further questions and didn't waste time. 'Let's go over everything again, and this time let's concentrate on your hypothesis that the girl and her ex-boyfriend have something to do with the crime.' He took a breath and continued before José could interrupt. 'Teammates of Marcus gave us some low-down on her ex. What did you say his name was, Antonio Vicario? Sounds Italian to me. Could he be the culprit? Let's see if there's a connection between him and the ex-girlfriend that could've had an impact on the victim.'

'Right, I definitely agree! I haven't got a lot to go on, but let's see. Here we are: the ex, Antonio Vicario, studies law, in his second year, and received a scholarship based on his talent as a goalkeeper. Let me check him out on Google.' José fired up his computer. It whirred into action and the screen emblazoned with the Police Emblem ready for José to type in the full name. 'Wait a minute, this could be interesting. It shows his mother as the only parent listed in his bio, nothing about his father. So, unless something metaphysical happened or it involved a test tube, we're missing a few facts.'

'Could you Google the mother? According to his details, her name is Manuela Juanita Vicario. Her bio might be useful.'

José typed in the name. 'That's interesting, informative, but not giving us much. She was born in Valais, but it doesn't give us the name of the town or the year. Her parents aren't mentioned, and neither is it clear if she's an only child. No date of a marriage, just one child listed, Antonio. The school and university she attended are also not mentioned.' José slapped the desk in excitement. 'This initial search with its non-information gives us more than we could ever have wished for! I'll look in the police database next.' He rubbed his hands together and flexed his fingers.

'Okay, let's get to work. Obviously, there are many gaps to fill. We'll concentrate on finding out more about this family. After getting a clearer picture of the mother, we might have an idea on who the father could be.' Paul knew they were clutching at straws, but what else could they do?

'The father might be the one who tried to strong-arm us. Or maybe Antonio's mother didn't want us to look deeper into the situation, worried that her son's connection with the girl might uncover something. Perhaps she found a man to do her bidding by warning us off. In the meantime, I've already put in a request to find out where the calls originated from. Have we got a photo of this ex-boyfriend?' Paul reached over to the additional information, regarded as irrelevant to the initial investigation, flipped through pages of typed up statements. *'Voila!'* In a group photo taken the night of last season's final match celebration, Antonio stood next to Cynthia. 'Do you really think it's basic jealousy and that the ex is involved?'

'If we run this image through facial recognition for an eighty percent match, we might just find a family member, perhaps even the father. What do you think?' José's enthusiasm to involve technology as much as possible came to the fore.

'A bit far-fetched. Still, it's worth a try.' Paul was convinced it was another of José's hair-brained schemes. Nevertheless, he decided it at least gave them something to investigate, a starting point other than the scene of the crime and decided to go along. It's better than doing nothing. They settled in for a long night. 'Did you bring me a sandwich as well?' Paul realised he was starving, but José found the suggestion humorous.

'Go get your own.'

At the dispenser in the corridor, Paul found only one very doubtful tuna sandwich remaining, the only other edible offering, a Mars bar. He inserted the coins, selected the candy bar, and thumped the side of the machine. With a mechanical cackle and ding, the bar fell into the tray with a thud.

Two hours later, and nearly midnight, their eyes burning from scanning the information streaming on the computer, a beep brought them to the present. 'What?' they said in unison. Both spun around on their chairs to the computer on the desk behind them. Paul continued, 'Well, it looks as if we have a near match on the preliminary facial recognition search. Did we get DNA from this Antonio?'

'When the officer spoke to Antonio you mean? Nah, it didn't seem relevant; he's only the ex-boyfriend.'

'Well, I think we should go ask him.'

'What for? We found no DNA at the scene.'

'No, my friend, the DNA would show that he could be related to this jolly fellow whose DNA we have on file.' Paul grabbed his jacket off the back of his chair. 'Come on, let's go see.'

'Wait! At midnight? Why go at this time of night?'

'Students don't go to sleep before two a.m., so we'll catch him nice and mellow. Move, I'll even let you drive, no time to waste!'

In contrast to the homes and other buildings in the area, light shone from windows of the student hostel. Due to his popularity, although waning, they easily found Antonio's dorm room. He languished on his bed, smoking as if he didn't have a care in the world. The smoke didn't disguise the smell of stale gym bags. He casually turned his head and glanced in their direction.

'Hi, you're Antonio Vicario, aren't you?' Paul asked after introductions.

'You've heard of me: the best goalkeeper in recent University football history. My reputation precedes me! That is until I busted my knee. But that's only temporary; I'll be back on the field and on top before the end of season.'

'We only wondered,' José began. 'You used to date Cynthia, didn't you?'

'Yeah, well what of it? It's been over for more than a month. She went for that wimp on our competitor's hockey team. Go figure!'

'Forensics is going over Cynthia's dorm with a fine toothcomb, and as you were obviously there before the breakup, your DNA will be all over the place. We're taking swabs of every possible donor to eliminate her regular visitors. Would you donate a sample?' José sounded apologetic.

'Don't you need a warrant for that?'

Paul took over. 'Well, yes, but that means you'll have to very publicly come down to the station for an official statement. However, as it is for elimination purposes it would be much better and less traumatic to do it in private. What do you say?'

Antonio looked from one to the other, suspicion clear in his eyes. Then he lazily unfolded his athletic body, stood up and limped towards them. 'Aw, what the heck, go ahead. You can't say I was uncooperative, now can you.' Antonio's attitude of superiority slightly surpassed his arrogance.

'Right, open up.' José, with swab in hand and satisfied grin, approached the smug young man. 'Done. Beddy-byes, Romeo. See you soon!' The two policemen turned and left without another word, smiling inwardly, DNA sample in hand. Impatient to get back to the station, silence prevailed until the car doors closed and they moved off.

They delivered the DNA swab directly to the night shift at the precinct's lab, putting a rush on the test. With controlled excitement and anticipation, they completed their report. Sighs of satisfaction escaped as both closed desk drawers and switched off their desk lamps. They walked out together, calling it a day – ready to fight again tomorrow.

*

Alexandra woke in the morning in a much better mood. The sun streaming into her room gave her a calm and positive feeling, her panic of yesterday virtually gone. The whole situation much clearer and less threatening.

Her calm remained as she watched from her window as uniformed police arrived, repeating their door-to-door enquiries of the previous day. They meticulously moved from apartment block to apartment block. Four went in – two remained standing guard at the entrance of the building they scouted. The four officers inside, paired up, and each pair took alternate floors knocking on doors.

She felt her equilibrium being tested as they approached, and had to decide very soon – could she risk it? She didn't want to get involved. Did duty call? But how do we describe duty? Confusion consumed her, threatening her calm demeanour. What to do; tell the police what she saw? Come to think of it, though upsetting, she didn't see much: just the blood, the girl and the car speeding away. With the confidence which arrived after a good night's sleep she knew she could do it. But fear overtook her renewed resolve. To get entangled in someone else's story could expose her to the shooter. He might come after her. But she didn't see him. Still, he's not to know that is he? He could seek her out.

The anticipated knock came. With slight hesitation, she forced herself to take a few determined steps towards the flat's entrance, stopped, and with final resolve, strode to the door and opened it.

'*Bonjour, Madame.* We're canvassing all residents with a view over the street to enquire if they saw anything concerning the shooting yesterday afternoon. Anything strange before or after the event will be of interest to us,' the older of the two officers said. The younger one pulled out a notebook, asking her name, if and where she was employed. Alex politely answered all their questions. He hurriedly began making notes. She could feel their analytical scrutiny, exactly as she tried to get a feel for them and the threat they posed. Her defences rose, but knew she had to be co-operative not to raise suspicions. She wanted them to leave and not come back.

'You were home yesterday? Could you tell us what you saw, please?'

'Yes, I was home, but no, I didn't see anything.'

'Are you sure you didn't see what happened?'

'Yes, not really, officer, it was already done. I only saw the girl standing over the body and a car leaving suddenly. I'm not even sure the car had anything to do with the girl or the boy who got shot.'

'When we called yesterday early evening, you didn't respond. Could you tell us why?'

'Well…. Well, I don't know, fear, I think. It could've been anyone at the door.'

'*Madame,* we identified ourselves. You have a duty to report a crime.'

'But I didn't see anything.' Alex began to lose her resolve, unsure of what the officers wanted her to say. 'You could've been anyone posing as police officers.

'What exactly did you see?'

'Nothing, I told you. I saw the young man lying on the ground bleeding, the girl standing next to him and a car leaving.'

'What kind of car? The colour, make, model. Did you see the number plate?'

'I think it looked either dark blue, or black. But I don't know anything about cars, so I can't tell you much except it had a silver bumper. I couldn't see the number – it all happened so fast. Do you know how something like that could be scary?'

'Why scary? You stood up here safely in your apartment, not in the street. Did you know the young man or the girl? Have you seen them before?'

'Why ask me all these stupid questions? I live alone, and who knows what could happen if any one of those involved saw me at the window? And no, I don't know them, and I've never seen either of them before.' Annoyed, Alex continued, 'and if the shooter saw me, what then? I could be his next target. I doubt the local police force would give me protection in that case.'

'You stood exactly where when the shooting took place?'

'Nowhere. I came from the hall to the bedroom when I heard the shot. At first, I didn't know what had happened. Then, when I reached the window to draw the curtains, I saw the boy lying there and surmised that it must have been a shot I heard. But it had already happened. I only saw him on the ground bleeding, and the girl kneeling next to him.' Alex found the officer irritating. This interrogation needed to end.

'And the car speeding away, you said.'

'Yes, I told you!'

'So, not a local university sports fan, I take it?' The younger policeman interrupted.

'What? What are you talking about, what has being a sports fan to do with the shooting?'

'Oh, never mind.'

'I really think you should leave now: I've told you everything I know. In fact, I'm beginning to think that I should have kept my mouth shut. I should never have answered the door.'

'Well, last night you did exactly that, didn't you? You ignored our knock. You have a duty to cooperate with the police. Unless you want to be brought up on charges.'

'What do you mean, "knock"? Whoever came pounded on the door, nearly broke the door off its hinges and out of its frame! It scared me to death! So, now I'll repeat myself: I think you should leave. Thank you and goodbye.' Alex ushered both towards the door and virtually pushed them out.

'Well, one more thing. You need to come to the station to make an official statement.'

'What for? I told you everything, which boils down to nothing. Now please leave.'

'Then we'll expect you at the station tomorrow at the latest. Don't forget what we said – it's an offence to withhold information. The detectives in charge of the case will want to talk to you as well.' They turned and left. With a sigh of relief, she closed and locked the door behind them.

The ordeal of the police and the effort of dealing with them, completely drained her. Relief, as well as apprehension, flooded her. Why would the detectives want to talk to her? Finally, she saw the folly of her earlier attitude, it's only routine. She grimaced and questioned if she would be able to put aside her fear to face the police one day. She assured herself that she had nothing to worry about – the crime happened outside on the street. No one saw her at the window.

CHAPTER THREE

Two days later, Paul and José received and studied all the statements collected by the door-to-door calls. Disappointed that very few people had the courage to talk to the officers, and those who did had nothing that shed further light on the event, frustrated both men. But they persevered. They rearranged their notes several times in case something jumped out giving a clue which they previously missed.

Tired of juggling what they had over and over, relief flooded them when the general outline of the DNA test arrived a bit later. At least it was a new piece of information which might just prove useful. José frowned, and his face seemed to fold into itself with concentration, then it smoothed out. A satisfied smiled replaced the frown, and he passed the report to Paul. It definitely peaked their excitement.

'José, do you realise that this could be our first real connection? I can't believe we have a seventy percent match! Your hunch paid off. Together with the facial recognition, I think we could pin down a starting point.' The fact that they would only have the full report in another twelve days didn't dim their excitement. They had enough to work with for the time being.

José came around to Paul's desk and bent over to scrutinise other pages in the file open in front of Paul. 'Unbelievable! Hey, look at this. I think I can name the possible father!'

'Who? Do you see something that I don't?' Clarity still evaded Paul.

'Yes! Paul look!' José insisted, poking his finger excitedly on the typed words on the report. 'This could explain everything and the threatening calls. What a father won't do to protect his offspring, and a father such as this, without a doubt.' José thumped Paul on his back, his excitement lighting up his eyes.

'I still don't see it. Antonio wasn't the victim. So why would his father want to do away with his son's ex-girlfriend's boyfriend?'

'There must be a connection somewhere. We only have to find it.'

'I think that is wishful thinking, but let's run with it – we don't have anything else.'

'Why would anyone besides this type warn us off? Think about it. There must be something they want to hide. Perhaps they wanted to rig the outcome of the next hockey match, and this Marcus – boy scout that he was – didn't want to play along. I am sure if we dig deep enough, we'll find it.'

Paul looked at the photos and the DNA report again. 'So, his father is Georgio Antonio Bescutti, that alleged organised crime boss? I now understand why Antonio enrolled under and used his mother's maiden name throughout his life. Could it be for protection, or as camouflage to his real identity?'

'Yeah. It would be interesting to know who came up with this ruse – I mean, keeping it all under wraps.' José scratched his head. 'That could change our way of tackling the matter and everything else. Those involved and the reasons. It would definitely throw a different light on the shooting.'

'I suppose keeping the son's identity secret would be the father's premier objective. I wonder what else could be their driving force. Or dare I ask?' Paul mentally tried to connect the dots.

'Well, then we have jealousy amongst that family. The second and strongest genetic trait of the Bescutti family, and no one messes with the "grandfather" in waiting!'

'I can imagine – their desire to eliminate competition of course.' Paul shook his head. 'But again, Antonio wasn't the victim. Do you think it's a case of old information or mistaken identity?'

'It could be that the father or mother felt their son should not have to compete with someone like Marcus for the affection of the girl.'

'That's really screwed up. If you're right, it means wielding unbelievable control over the son's life by either or both parents.'

'If so, it's a real tragedy.'

'This is real crime.'

'What do you mean? Oh, never mind. Come on Garcia, we have work to do.'

*

Cynthia's cell phone beeped with the arrival of a text message. Despite the heat, she lay curled up on her bed with the duvet pulled up to her chin. She felt safe this way, except now it was more a hiding place from the world outside. She picked up the phone and looked at the screen. With disdain, she read the message and threw the phone back on the bed.

When she came home, she appreciated her mother's attention. The incident with Marcus left her feeling fragile. It drew the kind of attention which she preferred not to be part of, and these messages only made it worse.

'What does he want that could be so urgent now?' This third text from Antonio aggravated her even more than the first two, which went unanswered. At first, he wanted to know how she felt after the tragedy. 'Bozo! How does he think I felt? I saw Marcus gunned down and die in front of me! Such an idiot! Why does he want to talk this instant?'

Her irritation spilled over into anger, and she grabbed the cell. She hesitated between responding with a text or phoning him, finally deciding on a short text: '*Very upset not up to seeing you just yet. What's so urgent to talk about?*'

The reply came immediately. '*Need to see you, very important about the shooting.*'

With a sigh of resignation, Cynthia arranged to meet later that afternoon. Tears of frustration veiled her eyes. She threw the phone down as if red-hot coals had touched her skin. Memories of their relationship flooded back, and her heartbeat increased. The excitement and adventure with a touch of danger still aroused her.

Antonio had no fear, loved to drive as fast as possible, and test all limits. He was her adrenaline, and she revelled in it! Yet, now thinking back on their relationship, she couldn't explain why she always felt an underlying sense of being trapped. Perhaps because of his addictive presence – she could never refuse him or distance herself from him. A power emanated from him that elicited politeness, even from figures of authority. His charisma seduced all around him, which sometimes brought out the green dragon of jealousy, but oh, how she loved the attention he drew.

With mixed feelings, Cynthia pulled a short, sun-yellow shift dress over her head. She slipped on flat, thin-soled sandals. Though, dressed to turn heads, the sense of reticence to meet Antonio at Starbucks in Plainpalais remained. After two days of hiding, she felt exposed as she left her home, looking left, then right for anything out of order.

Humidity hung heavy in the heat of the day. The cool interior of Starbucks provided relief. Cynthia took a seat in the far corner. A few minutes later, Antonio limped in on crutches. Dressed in denim shorts and a white sleeveless tee-shirt, his tanned body rippled with each step. The knee brace and crutches took nothing away from his athletic form.

She felt her stomach lurch. Even after all this time his smile still brought on an adrenalin rush. Irresistible, but she noticed his smile seemed slightly forced and wondered again why this meet meant so much to him.

'Hi, Babe.' With clumsy movements, Antonio took a seat opposite Cynthia.

'Hi, how's the knee?'

'Okay, it hurts, but not too bad now.'

'So, what's so important that you have to talk to me in person?'

'It's about the shooting.'

'Well, you said that. What has it got to do with you?'

'I care about you.'

'Okay. Now, what about it? Marcus died in front of me, I couldn't do a thing. And the police have been interrogating me. And that's it.'

'You mean asking you questions?'

'No, it didn't feel like asking questions! It was an interrogation, for heaven's sake!'

'What did you tell them? Did they ask about me?'

'They knew we used to date!'

'I know, but what did you tell them?'

'Why on earth would they ask about you? Marcus was shot, not you - unless you did the shooting. Was it out of jealousy?'

'Don't be absurd! Why would I shoot him? And no, I wasn't jealous. I knew you would come back to me. He filled an interim position, that's all.'

'Gosh, what an ego! Get over yourself and get on with it! Tell me what you wanted to know and why.'

'Well, what did you tell the police?'

'What I saw. Marcus was gunned down, a car sped away, and that's all. Now tell me why it is so important for you to know.'

Antonio moved in his seat to find a more comfortable position. He looked around and over his shoulder, making sure they were alone in the corner. He leaned forward and lowered his voice.

'My mother wanted the details. She's worried it would affect my chances of getting a scholarship.'

'What has that got to do with the shooting? And why is your mother

43

involved in this?'

'Well, she said it was more about the family.'

'What family? I thought you said it was only you and your mother. Are you trying to tell me there are some other members who are interested in your future career? Where did they come from?'

'There are some others. I think I might have an uncle or aunt and some cousins as well, but I don't have any contact with any of them. My mother keeps in touch with them, I think. I've never even met any one of them.'

'Why not? Why does she keep them away from you?' Cynthia shook her head, wanting to get up and leave. 'I don't like this, it's bizarre. Out of the blue, your mother inserts "your family" into my life. We're not even dating anymore!'

'Please, I don't like this any more than you do. But according to my mom, we must give them all the information, especially whatever you told the police.'

Cynthia was losing her temper. 'We broke up, remember? That should mean something to them.'

'I know, I know, but what can I do? They're pressuring her.'

'Why? They aren't my family! I'm not going to do what they want. It's got nothing to do with them.' Cynthia got up. 'Goodbye, Antonio. Please just leave me alone, the experience was traumatic enough.'

'Wait, please wait. What do I tell my mom?'

'Tell her whatever you want. It's got nothing to do with me.' Cynthia got up to leave, then turned around. 'No, tell her to leave me alone. Goodbye Antonio.'

Antonio watched as Cynthia stomped out of Starbucks and thought, 'jeez, she's hot! Why did I ever let her go out with that loser Marcus?' Unfortunately, his thoughts immediately jumped back to his mother.

*

'How in the world could you do this to me?' Antonio's mother ranted, pacing the kitchen floor as she berated her son.

'What did I do? Jeez, Mom, calm down!'

'I told you to tell Cynthia to keep her mouth shut! Your whole life I've protected you from your father's family, and this stupid act has brought them all into our home!'

'But Mom, how could you accuse me of this? I had nothing to do with the shooting. I was holed up in my dorm room with my knee. Also, I broke up with Cynthia long before this happened.' Frustrated, Antonio wanted to escape the restrictive hold of his mother. He could not understand why the death of Marcus posed such a problem for him, his mother, and his so-called family.

He only ever wanted to play football, nothing else. He practiced endlessly, blocking goals until he perfected his technique. He kept his eye not only on the ball but on the kicker as well. You could tell a lot from the player's body language and his eye movement. He told everyone who showed any interest that even from a distance, if you practiced long enough, you could read volumes in a player's eyes. He became adept at anticipating and reading this language, achieving a ninety-five per cent average in blocking goals. His grades didn't match, but they weren't too bad either.

His whole life revolved around his sport, and luckily, his mother wanted him to follow his dream. She pushed him towards a sports scholarship. So, why was she now involving herself in what happened to his ex-girlfriend? How could it interfere with his sports career? And what about his father, he thought they were estranged. How come she never told him about his father? Who is he? Why did she keep him away from him? Was he a pervert, a paedophile, a murderer? Lately, you hear so many stories – was he one of them? Possibilities crowded his mind.

None of this made any sense. His father apparently left before Antonio's birth and, according to her didn't feature in their lives. So, why suddenly, and what has it got to do with Cynthia? It couldn't be Marcus, he is – or rather was – such a whoosh. Antonio found the whole situation very strange, and the questions running through his mind didn't stop.

At this moment, more than anything, he wanted his mother to calm down and stop shouting. Her agitation only brought on more questions. He had done what she asked, he met with Cynthia. Even though he didn't understand why she told him to find out what Cynthia told the police. And not to say anything to anybody – what's that all about? Why has she lost her cool?

'Tell me again, what exactly did she tell the police?'

'Please, Mom! I told you. She couldn't say much because she didn't see who did the shooting, who drove the car, or what kind it was. Let it go!'

'How can I if I'm getting calls insisting that I clear up this matter.'

45

'But what matter? You keep on saying that they want the "matter" cleared up. Are they talking about the shooting? If so, what has it got to do with us, and why are they so interested? I don't understand. It's weird beyond weird.'

Even though Antonio's mother now sat down, her hands still belied her apparent calm. He saw a haunted look in her eyes, shaking his head, he tried to find an explanation. He found the whole situation disconcerting. Things didn't add up. This unexpected interest from that side of his "family" was weird. But something else didn't make sense. Suddenly what bothered him became clear. 'Did they say how they found out about the shooting?'

'What does that matter? I want you to keep away from them.'

'No worries there, Mom, I don't know them.' He turned to the fridge, took out the carton of milk and poured a glass as he continued. 'I reckon that anyone of them, even my father, could stand right in front of me and I wouldn't know! As you say, you made sure of that.'

Then his curiosity peaked; he turned towards his mother again. 'By the way, what does my father look like? Am I the spitting image of him, or do I take after you?' Now, more excited with the idea of seeing if he resembled his father, he needed to know. 'Do you have a photo of him stashed away?'

'I kept in touch with him, that's all. I'm sorry!' His mother's tone had changed completely, her voice dropped with defensiveness mixed with regret and shame.

'What? Why did you keep me in the dark? Did it never occur to you that I needed or wanted to know my own father?'

'I thought I protected you. He agreed, but he did pay us a generous monthly sum, also took care of your tuition. You know we would never have managed on our own.'

'I know you never had a job. But didn't you inherit your family's money?'

'No, my family weren't rich. When they died, they left even less than they had in life.'

'So, we lived off my father's money, who, by the way, I never knew existed. Still, you haven't answered my question. Do you have a photo of him that I can see?' his earlier excitement turned into anger which consumed him. 'Never mind, I'll look him up on Google.'

'You won't find him. He doesn't have the same name as you.'

'What do you mean?'

'I never took on his name, you were registered under my maiden-name, and we thought it best to leave it like that.'

'So, I don't even have his name! What is it? Now, on top of all this, you expect me to do what you say, I mean: what he says. No, I want nothing to do with this and will not answer to any of the "family's" requests!'

'But Antonio, they won't like that!'

'You reckon?'

*

'Did you see that suspicious black SUV parked across the street?' Alex's elderly neighbour's whisper overflowed with conspiracy. 'There are two men inside.' Mrs Ginet, affectionately known as the building's information centre, kept herself – and others who cared to listen – up to date about everyone and everything that happened in the vicinity. She regarded herself as the guardian of peace and justice, not to mention morality, of those who lived in Paquis. Alex knew not to get on her wrong side.

'Why are you whispering? No one can hear you. Did you say they are suspicious?'

'They have been there since the police made their rounds the day after the shooting.'

'Are they not from the neighbourhood? You know, those people who moved in last month into number fifty-two?'

'Oh no! They have a silver car. This one is black. You know, like gangsters drive. Only criminals drive black cars – they like to hide behind the blacked-out windows.'

'Does this car have blacked-out, I mean, tinted windows?'

'Yes, come and have a look.' Mrs Ginet took Alex's arm and led her to the window. 'Look. You see? You can see better from my apartment. Do you see the two men inside? They haven't moved since last night, when they took the place of the other two who were there the whole of yesterday.' She turned and looked deep into Alex's eyes, 'We must do something. They look dangerous!'

'Did you tell the police?'

'Oh no, not yet! I thought you could call them.'

'Mrs Ginet, please. I don't really like to do that. You're the one who saw them from the beginning. They'll ask questions that I wouldn't know the answers to. It would be much better if you call. If you want, I'll be with you when you do.'

'What questions?'

'Well, like when did you first see them? You know, they'll ask from when they were there; what time did they come; what did the first two men look like; when did the next two arrive, etc… Those type of questions to which I wouldn't know what to say.'

'*D'accord,* but only if you are with me.'

'Did you make notes? I know you are always very thorough about security. The police would appreciate your attention to detail.'

'You think so?' The old lady puffed up with pride.

The last thing Alexandra wanted was the police asking questions again. Her panic rose as she carefully peeped out the window. Sure enough, the black SUV parked with two men inside had not moved since Mrs Ginet pointed it out. She herself never noticed anything different since the shooting. However, she had made a point of staying away from the windows. Paranoia returned, slowly creeping up her spine. Were those men here for her? How long will it be before they knocked on her door, or more likely breach? She never saw anything, but will they believe her? Do they employ methods of torture to extract information from their targets? Again, her emotions ran wild, and it unsettled her completely.

To take her mind off the possibility and types of torture racing through her mind, she went to the kitchen to fill the kettle. '*Madame,* could I offer you a cup of tea or coffee?'

'*Volontiers. Un thé, merci.*' Age had slipped off her face, excited to share her information with the authorities. 'Should we phone them now?'

'Let's have our tea first and then we'll phone from your place. We'll tell them we have information and go down to the station, better than if the police come back here.' As far as Alex was concerned, the call could wait.

'But that'll take time, and they won't see the car.'

'No, I'm sure they'll see us as soon as possible, and send a patrol car around to have a look. Don't worry; it'll be all right if we go there.'

*

The Serious Crime Unit had put out an urgent request for anyone who had information to come forward. They used a specific number to call with assurance that the caller would remain anonymous. So far, most were crank calls or reporting crimes in a different part of the city.

Towards the end of the morning, Paul Favre took the call from a Mrs Ginet, who asked for a meeting. At first, he wanted to get rid of her as politely as possible, assuming her to be someone looking for attention, until he asked from where she was telephoning. His senses heightened. Also, the call didn't come from the tip line; it was to their direct line. Suddenly, he straightened up, clicked his fingers in front of Garcia's face, and pointed to the receiver. He mouthed the words, 'pick up the phone, it's a lead!' A younger voice came on the line.

'Hello, we were told to come to the station to make a statement. We have information which you might want to know about.'

'Good. Who am I speaking to and how soon can you get here?'

'My name is Alexandra Labelle. But everyone calls me Alex, and we – that is my neighbour Mrs Ines Ginet – and I could be there in twenty minutes. Who should we ask for please?'

'Detectives Paul Favre or José Garcia, we'll both be here. You know where we are?' Alex assured him they knew where the Servette Police Station was. Favre confirmed the address and added the office number.

He didn't waste time asking if their information was real or not. Obviously, from the address given, they had to have seen or heard something of importance. On the other hand, it could be that these are two lonely women who would like male company and should be ignored. His instinct told him not to lose a possible lead and follow up.

As they put the receivers back in their respective cradles, the two detectives silently looked at each other and sighed. Was this what they were waiting for? Had someone from the neighbourhood finally find the courage to talk?

'Well, let's see, they'll be here in twenty. Let's go over what we might have missed and see if they can fill us in.' Paul rubbed his hands together ready for the interview. José wanted to get something to eat and a coffee before they arrived.

'You can eat after they've been. Let's put them in interview room three when they arrive.'

*

49

Alex replaced the receiver at Ines Ginet's apartment. The excitement showing in Ines completely contradicted her own mood. A cautious peep through the curtains confirmed the black SUV still guarded the road. Unsure if the vehicle posed a threat, Alex felt prudence would be best. Through eyes clouded by doubt, she regarded her neighbour.

'Mrs Ginet, when we go to the police station, we should take our shopping baskets with us.' Her voice trembled slightly.

'But we are not going to do shopping.'

'I know, but we might stop after and pick something up for dinner.'

'No, I don't think so. I'll be far too tired.'

'Well, I think it would also make those men in the car think that we are only out for nothing else except our usual shopping at the Migros.'

'Oh, I see. You think it would be better?'

'Until we know who they are or why they are here, it would be better. They might not take much notice when we leave.'

'You think they will follow us?'

'I really don't know.'

'But you think we shouldn't take the chance, is that it?'

'Yes. If they have bad intentions, it'll be better if they don't know that we'll be at the police station giving a statement.' The necessity to convince her neighbour of the ruse, brought all her insecurities and fears back. But the commitment of Mrs Ginet to do "the right thing" could not be ignored.

'Mrs Ginet, get your coat and basket. I'll pick up mine and meet you in front of the elevator. We'll go down together.'

'You are making me nervous.'

'Please, don't be. We'll just walk calmly to the tram stop and get the tram.'

'But we usually walk to the shops.'

'I don't think they know that. Today we could make as if we are going downtown.'

'Good! That's a good idea, let's do it.'

'See you in a minute Mrs Ginet.'

Alex turned on her heel and let herself out to collect her purse and shopping basket. She entered her flat, looking around, then checked each room to establish that all was still the way she had left it – she couldn't shake the feeling of unease and panic. She grabbed her handbag and basket, locked up, checking that the door was firmly closed, and saw Mrs Ginet already waiting. With a forced smile of reassurance, more for herself than Ines, she called the elevator.

'Alex, do you think the Police will think our information important?'

'All you can do is to tell them what you saw. I'm sure they will be able to use it.'

'I brought my notes.'

'That's good. It will come in useful.' The elevator arrived and Alex let Mrs Ginet enter in front of her.

'What a beautiful day! Pity we have to go to the police and not the park.'

Mrs Ginet's excited chatter floated around Alex, but nothing stuck. She smiled and nodded when appropriate, right up to the tram stop. Relieved when the tram quietly slid to a halt in front of it, they got on and found a seat.

Two stops later, with Mrs Ginet still chatting, Alexandra pressed the button to request a stop. The Servette Police Station, virtually opposite the stop, unobtrusively occupied the ground floor of an apartment block on Route de Meyrin. The chemin, or path, next to it led up to another apartment block. A small patch of green separated the two blocks of flats. They walked back the fifty metres to reach the entrance of the Station.

At the reception desk, which blocked further entry into the property, Alex gave their names and asked for either Detective Favre or Detective Garcia. The duty officer asked them to wait a moment as she telephoned the two detectives. Within minutes, a short, stocky man with obvious Portuguese ancestry, appeared behind the counter. He lifted the end part of the counter-top and pulled back the lower part, gesturing for them to come through while introducing himself.

'*Bonjour, Mesdames, suivez-moi s'il vous plaît.*' I'm Detective Garcia, please follow me.' He led them through a corridor with offices on their right and rooms on their left marked "Interview Room1", "Interview Room 2", and stopped in front of "Interview Room 3". He opened the door and showed them in. 'Please take a seat, we'll be with you in a second. Would either of you like something to drink, coffee, tea, soft drink or water?'

Mrs Ginet smiled and said she would like a coffee. Alex declined; already as tight as a spring about to jump out of a box, caffeine would only increase her nervousness. It struck her that on the tram she had watched every passenger with suspicion. Every other second, her glance

51

alternatively went over her shoulder or out the window. She had to be sure that they weren't being followed: a strange person watching them, or a vehicle pursuing them.

The room was sparse, with neutral grey colours, a table and four chairs. It looked more like an interrogation room than an interview room. Alex's unease mounted, and various scenarios rushed through her mind, convincing her she had made a big mistake in accompanying her neighbour. She should have kept quiet and out of it, as was her intention all along. Luckily, for her state of mind, they didn't wait long before Detective Garcia arrived with two coffees – one for Mrs Ginet and one for himself. A taller lanky man, who introduced himself as Detective Favre, followed on his heels. They pulled out the chairs opposite the women and took their seats. Detective Favre cleared his throat.

'It is good of you to come. We've been struggling to get witnesses to come forward and have received no information, except what we have collected from the scene of the shooting.' The detective's voice, filled with kindness, inspired Mrs Ginet to immediately begin her account of the day of the crime.

'Look, here are the notes I took. You see, I make a note of all the movements in the street.' She smiled, puffed up with pride to show the detectives her attitude of community service and safety. 'We cannot be careful enough with all these terrorists running about, now can we?'

'You are absolutely correct, *Madame.* We appreciate your contribution.'

'Look, if you look at the notes from the day before, you'll see there was nothing strange going on, except for the people opposite who always leave their car parked half in the road and half on the pavement. Surely that is illegal. You must give them a fine!'

'Yes, we'll see to that. Now, let's look at the day of the shooting, please. You noted here that the street was clear with no traffic at 4 pm. Did you see the young people arrive?'

'There! Look for yourself. I saw them coming down the street from the direction of Place de la Navigation. Perhaps they had lunch at that Indian restaurant, 'Bollywood'. You know they serve you from about eleven in the morning right through until late at night. Or they could have come off the bus. I didn't see.'

'No problem. So, were they arguing or laughing?'

'I noticed her because she looked so pretty in that little pink dress, so terribly short. Ready for a party, I thought, but it was too early. And the young man with her, so handsome!'

'To come back to how they appeared: happy, nervous, or annoyed?

'They seemed happy, just walking along when this car came around the corner. I thought it backfired, but then I saw the young man fall. I realised it was a gunshot, we don't often hear them, but, well, it must have been.'

'So, you saw him being gunned down?'

'Well, no. I didn't know he was shot. He fell down. Blood only came a second or two later. It was horrible seeing it so black and shiny on the surface of the road. You know there the road looks grey, not black. It was then that I knew he must've been shot.'

'Yes, I understand. But did you notice anything else?'

'Like what? Look at my notes!'

'Like who shot at him, or if there were anyone else on the road.' Favre perused the notes, pushing them back towards Mrs Ginet. For a moment, everyone's eyes were on the notebook now in the centre of the table. Obvious that he needed to resume his questioning with patience and delicate phrasing, he tried not to put words in her mouth or lead her to say what they wished to hear.

'No, they were alone except for the car that came past and left very quickly. It sped away like an arrow out of a bow!'

'Did you manage to get the colour, make, model, and registration of the vehicle?'

With impatience, Mrs Ginet pushed her notes back towards him. 'Didn't you see? It's all there. It happened so fast. I'm not sure if the car was dark blue or black. No, I'm sure it was black, and I got the first part of the plate. It was a Japanese car, but I know it was a SUV. Like the one parked outside our building right now.'

'What do you mean, like the one outside your building now?'

Alex watched the word exchange with trepidation. An occasional peek at Detective Garcia to gauge his reaction to the information only gave the impression of impatience as he periodically stroked his paisley-patterned tie. Terrified that they would turn their attention to her, she made herself as small and insignificant as possible. She counted on Mrs Ginet to keep them busy with all her notes. But Garcia shifted forward in his chair and looked at his partner. Their attention was now not only on Ines, but also on Alex as they looked from one to the other for answers.

'I asked what you meant by: like the car outside your building now.' It seemed as if Detective Favre's antennae were on full alert. He turned to Alex. 'Perhaps you can clarify. You've been very quiet so far. Please explain.'

'I, uh, well, uh, I don't know. You have to ask Mrs Ginet, she pointed the car out to me.' Alex stumbled over her words, panic constricting her throat.

'Look, I told you I made notes!' Mrs Ginet, losing her patience, again tapped the notebook with her finger. 'If you'll just look, you'll see when they came and the details of the car. Why don't you read all my notes?'

'Sorry, Mrs Ginet, we acted a bit abruptly, we are pressed for time. We will look at everything carefully. Thank you for your diligence. However, we're afraid this recent development changes things. The event might pose a direct threat to you both. Could you remain here for a little longer until we have this vehicle in front of your building checked out, please?' Favre picked up Mrs Ginet's notes.

'Where are you going with my notebook?'

'We will be taking your notes to go through them carefully and make copies. You'll have to remain here for a while.'

'I need to go home. I'm not young anymore, I get tired, and I need to have my lunch.'

'Don't you worry about that. We'll arrange for some lunch for both of you. Then, if all is well, we'll take you home.'

'I would want my notes back, please.'

'We'll bring them back. In the meantime, could I bring you ladies something to drink? Another coffee, *Madame* Ginet? Perhaps Miss Labelle, you prefer a tea?' Besides asking if they would like something to drink, this was the first time Garcia spoke. Alex wondered if he sat in only to observe their reactions. She regarded Garcia with suspicion as he got up and opened the door. But relaxed when he called through to another officer to bring the lunch list and arrange for whatever the two women would like. At that, both detectives thanked them and left the room.

'What do you think, Alex? I suppose they were pleased that I could give them my notes. But they said things are dangerous. Do you think that's true? Will they protect us?'

'Well, with a shooting in our street, I think we should treat the situation as dangerous. All we can do is trust them to find out what it is all about and wait until they come back with news.' Her voice did not betray her deep unease.

'What do you mean?'

'I mean that we have nothing more to add, and that perhaps there's nothing strange about the SUV. I'm sure it will then be safe for us to go home.'

'Good. I wonder what they will offer for lunch.' Mrs Ginet had already moved on.

*

'At last, we have something.' Garcia tapped Favre on the back and moved around to his desk. While his partner got a junior officer to make copies of Mrs Ginet's notebook, Garcia picked up the phone to get the name of the parked SUV's owner. He recited the registration number into the phone and replaced the receiver. 'He'll come back to us in a couple of minutes.'

'Thank heaven for busybodies?' Garcia couldn't believe their luck.

'You can also call it neighbourhood watch. Sure, it has its uses. So, let's use it.'

Garcia turned when his desk telephone rang. *'Garcia.'* He listened as the correspondent spoke. *'Good, I've got it. No further information?'* He nodded his head. *'Fine, see what more you can find. We'll work on what you've got so far.'*

'You have a name?'

'The vehicle is registered to a company: Synergy Trading. He'll try to find out who owns it – so far that info is obscure, obviously a shell company. We'll see. So how do you propose we check on the vehicle in front of their building without arising suspicion?'

'You still have that friend in the *Service du Stationnement?*

'I have a friend in the Municipal Police.'

'I'm not sure where though, sorry.' Favre ran his hand over his face.

'Perhaps you mean Joe Monnier, my bowling partner?'

'Yeah, that's the one.'

'He is in the Police Department, not in the Parking Violation Section.'

'You think he'll do us a favour and send someone to check on our parked couple? It would be best if he sent someone with authority and not just the SdS.'

'Yes, you're right, the MP's have more authority and it'll be easier for them to check.'

'I agree it won't look odd if he, by chance, happens to control that area. Definitely less strange than if a policeman approaches the SUV.'

'Okay, let me ask. It depends if he's on duty and where he is at present.'

'Two MPs on their beat passing to either give them a fine for loitering or ask them to move on would be less obvious. They are a normal sight on the streets.' The junior officer approached and put a pile of photocopies with the notebook on Favre's desk. He took a seat and began looking through them page by page while Garcia pulled out his mobile phone to call his friend.

'*Salut, Monnier.*' He nodded. '*Yeah, Yeah, it's me, ... no, I'm not cancelling. I know we're playing in Gland this weekend. It's nothing to do with bowling.*' He laughed, '*No Maria hasn't kicked me out. Well, not yet! ... No this is a completely unrelated matter. We need your help, Joe.*' Garcia gestured that yes, it is unusual. '*Yes, I know, the powerful Serious Crime Unit of the Canton of Geneva's Police Force, requests the help from the Geneva's lowly Municipal Police,*' he laughed and continued.

'*Are you on duty now? And if so, where are you beating the pavement at this very instant...?*' Garcia nodded. '*Great, that suits us perfectly.*' He looked at Favre and, lowering the phone, pressing it to his chest, told him that Joe is on duty in Paquis, a few streets further up from where they would want him to check. '*Good, there is an SUV parked in front of a building, apparently for more than a day, with two men inside. We need to be very careful not to let these guys know that we are on to them, but we need their names.*' He gave full details to his friend and asked for a response as soon as possible with details. '*You think you can do it...? Oh, okay, I owe you!*'

'How long do you think it'll take?' Favre asked.

'Well, as they are on patrol not too far away from the relevant spot, I estimate about forty minutes at the most.'

'Not sooner?'

'Well, not if they want to appear to be executing their daily duties following a routine.'

'Okay. It might mean that the ladies need to stay here longer. I do not want them to distrust us even more than they – especially the young one –

do already.' Favre gave the notebook to his partner. 'Take this through to the old lady and see if they're ready to place their lunch order. If they ask how long they must wait here or, what we have done so far, reassure them that the vehicle and the men inside are being investigated. As for how long they need to stay put, we'll tell them it'll give them time to have a good lunch.'

'What do you want me to do in the meantime? I've exhausted all the leads we had.'

'Do you mind looking at the notes, as she has written them down, please? You might see something that I've missed by only glancing over them. Combined with our interview, something might jump out at you.'

'Well, I was wondering... No, perhaps it will only confuse the issue.'

'What? Let's hear it.'

'Well, a thought crossed my mind as I watched the old lady insist that you look at her notes. I discarded it as it's ridiculous.'

'Come on, spill, what was it? Anything, even if it is way out of the ballpark, would be worthwhile looking at. Seeing we have zilch!'

'But now, thinking about those men in the SUV who seem to be on a stake out in front of the building, I'm considering it again.'

'What are you thinking?'

'It's way out, I know, but well...'

'I can tell you; I'm prepared to look at anything to narrow down a motive. That'll help us find the shooter.'

'Well, here goes. What we are considering might be limited by her information – seen from her perspective of course. What if the car speeding away was only there by coincidence? We might be giving it too much credence. It might be insignificant.'

'But what about the phone calls? They were specific – they strongly suggested or rather insisted; we treat this as a drive-by. Oh, by-the-way have we received response on tracing the calls to our private numbers yet?'

'Well, that could also be a misdirect.'

'You mean we might overlook another possibility, such as the shot coming not from the car, but from elsewhere.' Favre scratched his head. 'It's possible of course.'

He didn't like the direction in which this case was going.

*

Manuela Vicario paced the floor, phone in hand. Dark chocolate eyes flicked from the device to her surroundings. She dreaded the call, knew it would be coming. Her son's questions have merit. She had no answers. It worried her as well. Why?

The sun filling the front room of the apartment went unnoticed. Normally, this time of day in summer, she let the shutters down until mid-afternoon to keep the heat out. Today this didn't happen. The vase filled with roses on a small table in front of the window caught the rays. The petals, illuminated by the light, caused the colour to bleed into the space around. The room's built-up heat brought out the perfume of the flowers. The smell swelled, reaching every corner. The colours patterning the oriental carpet, separating two perfectly matched ivory leather sofas, faded in the light. The pattern would only be in full depth again later in the day.

Totally unaware of these changes, she forced herself into routine: preparing lunch for Antonio, the first step. It would keep her mind off her husband and his family. Just concentrate on that, she told herself.

Without warning, and with a dizzy force, Manuela fell back into the anxiety of earlier. Her son's voice reverberated in her head. Why the concern? Antonio wasn't involved. Why the interest in Cynthia? She's his ex-girlfriend. Why was it important to know what she told the police? When she demanded what their preoccupation with the matter could be, she was rudely ordered to just get the answers and not argue! Resolved to ask the questions and not be brushed off again, pushed the anxiety aside. Manuela looked at the phone's screen.

If only she could speak directly to her husband and not his assistant. Frustrating is not the word for it. He hides behind that horrible man. Calls to her husband were completely prohibited; she had to wait for his office to contact her. Never before had she realised how ridiculous this arrangement was. She wondered if it was the Bescutti family's requirement or his. Well, in any case, his henchman asked irrelevant questions – nothing to do with them. She realised that speculating like this would get her nowhere.

Even though they had been separated since before Antonio was born, they were still legally married. The "family" don't believe in divorce. She could never understand why they wouldn't allow them to annul the marriage. Their moral compass remained a mystery. The situation bound her to him forever.

Is this because of their son? In that case, why didn't he want Antonio to meet him? It was his choice; she was for it, but he was so adamant it made her wonder. At first, she was sad and disappointed that her son wouldn't know his own father, though over the years she got used to having Antonio all to herself. Could it be that Georgio has not produced another son – out of wedlock, of course – meaning Antonio remained the son and heir to the Bescutti Dynasty? Again, an illegitimate child would never be accepted into that clan, so why not rectify the situation? There's no reason as to what drives them or their ideas.

Now she must exercise her rights, and serious explanations are called for: insistence the key. He'll have to meet her face to face with the motive for this harassment or ….

Or what?

She swears that if his family has anything to do with this, she will ….

Do what?

It was all useless. Powerless, Manuela paced, periodically hesitated, pushed her hair back behind her ears, turned and paced again. A splitting headache overwhelmed her. All this angst was unhealthy, for her and for her son. And the "family" created it. A way needed to be found for her to get them through this.

Why involve Antonio? Why phone her for what Cynthia saw or said? Didn't they know that they weren't even together? They broke up weeks ago. It's not of her son's making. They should ask Cynthia directly if it's so important. It has nothing at all to do with them and was unnecessary. Her thoughts ran rampant.

Thankful that Antonio had returned to his dorm last night, she went back to thinking about his lunch. For him to see her like this when he arrived would be upsetting. They had better not phone when he is around!

*

The sight of Antonio in Starbucks overlaid the vision of Marcus in a pool of blood. Then the scene shifted – it was Marcus in Starbucks and Antonio in the street, bleeding out.

Danger surrounded them. She shouted for them to run, but her voice disappeared in the scream of tyres speeding away. It chilled her skin.

She tasted blood. It covered her face and body. Where did it come from?

The sun reflected on the lake, turning each diamond into a shard of glass penetrating her skin. *Lac Leman,* always so serene, was now tempestuous. She couldn't understand why shattered glass lay at her feet. In the middle of each glass shard, Antonio dribbled a football. A yellow hockey jersey floated above the lake, and each reflected shard stuck into the shirt, drawing blood.

The shards turned, aiming for her. She had to run. Powerless, her legs jelly.

Back in Starbucks, both young men chatting, laughing. How can they be so nonchalant? Look, they are coming for me. Look what's happening to you. They giggled. What's so funny?

Again, the young men's faces superimposed on each other, becoming one, which morphed into a grotesque and bloody skeletal mask with hollowed-out eyes and toothy grin. The face provoked, teased. But the face looking back at her was her own.

Marcus and Antonio turned toward her. They laughed, they found her a joke.

Then Antonio's phone rang. He ignored it. Why not answer? It must be his mother. It kept on ringing. Insistent.

As if unstoppable, the ringing continued.

Someone will answer.

Please make it stop.

The ringtone finally broke through. Cynthia turned over. Bathed in perspiration, her head felt stuffed. She lifted her head from the pillow, stretched out an arm and finger-touched the bedside tabletop for her mobile. Sleepily, she brought it to her ear.

'Hello?' She croaked and fell back onto the pillow and closed her eyes.

'Cynthia? You sound out of it. Are you sleeping?'

'Not anymore, you creep. You woke me. Go away!' with the phone to her ear she turned onto her side, eyes still shut.

'I wondered if...'

'What do you want? I don't want to talk to you.'

'I just wanted to check that you're okay.'

'I'm not! I said go away!'

'But since we met the other day, I can't get you out of my mind. Can we meet?'

'Not if you're going to pepper me with questions.'

'No, I promise. I only want to see you. I've missed you.'

'You've got a cheek. You think I should drop everything and meet you! Why?'

'Well, you're the one that dropped me, remember? I'm still me even though hobbling about for the time being, won't be for long. Soon I'll be back to my old self.'

'Then what?'

'I thought we could date again. What do you think?'

'Will think about it.'

'But can we meet? Please, Cynthia.'

'Okay, when?'

'Half an hour at Starbucks?'

'No can do. I need at least an hour and have to ask my mom first.'

'Since when do you need permission from your mom?'

'Since you harassed me, you asshole. She told me to stay away from you.'

'Not cool. What is it with our mothers?'

'Your mom still on at you to find out what I told the police?'

'Get this, apparently, I have a father! He's alive and in contact with her all these years. I don't even know what he looks like. I thought he was dead. But no! Oh no, he demanded to know what was happening. Also, there is his FAMILY!'

'What do you mean a "family"?'

'Jeez! What do I know! Decide for yourself. Could be anything – like a commune, or sect like where the head honcho decides for everyone, or the mafia, in the style of the 'Godfather'. You know, like rules the roost.'

'Well, I don't want to hear about it. The less I know, the less trouble I'm in with my mom. You know she'll ask what we talked about.'

'You don't have to tell her, do you?'

'Could you avoid your mother's questions?'

'Good point. So, I'll see you in an hour?'

'Yeah, okay, see you then.'

Reluctantly, Cynthia rolled out of bed, plodded heavily to the bathroom, and turned on the shower. Her dream resurfaced, and the same powerlessness and insecurity forced her down onto the toilet seat. Finally, her breathing became regular. She stripped and stepped under the warm,

61

relaxing water. True, water washes away a lot of things. That's what her mother always says. Does that include bad dreams? What about bad memories? She decided to stay under the pelting water a bit longer to test the theory. After a while, she turned off the taps. Well, it must be real because she feels much better. Cool.

Though still not sure if she was ready to face her mother, she dreaded asking if she could meet with Antonio. With no compulsory classes to attend ten days before end of the last semester, her time was her own. No objection on that score.

So far, so good.

What about her mother's objection to her seeing Antonio? That didn't make sense. He was her boyfriend before he had that freak accident on the field. She didn't object then. What's different now?

Nothing's different.

That was the problem. Her mother seemed to think that everything had changed since the death of Marcus. She regarded everyone as a possible threat. That's not fair! It was a freak event, just like Antonio's accident. It must be some gang or someone wanting to prove themselves, or an initiation or something.

Oh, all this was giving her a headache. She'd have to have another shower, but no time for that now – she had to get ready.

She wanted to see Antonio. He's still her first love, but she won't let on. He'd take advantage if he knew that she thought him hot. Well, first things first, wrapping herself in a towel, she padded back to her bedroom and pulled out undies, selecting a pair of shorts and tee.

Yes, today a pair of shorts – pale blue stripe on white with a white top – would do. It'd show off the tan she had so painstaking built up on the terrace.

'Hey, Mom, you here?' Skipping down the staircase and through to the kitchen where she probably would find her mother. In fact, she hoped her mother had left to do shopping. But that was wishful thinking as the response came immediately.

'*Bonjour, ma chérie. Comment ça va?* I'm watering the plants on the terrace.'

'Oh good, I'm going out for a while.'

'How did you sleep? Did you have another nightmare?'

'Oh, Mom leave it alone please!'

'I want to know if you are okay.'

'Well, just a little one, I'm fine, Mom, don't nag.'

'Have you cleaned your room?'

'Well, it was clean.'

'Where are you going?'

'Just to meet some friends.'

'Which friends? Will Antonio be there?'

'I suppose.'

'You know how I feel and what I said. I don't want you to hang around him.'

'Okay, Mom, but it's just to say 'Hi' and talk about college. Nothing else, I promise.'

'Good. But as soon as he starts asking questions again, you come straight home. That was an ordeal best forgotten. Every time it is dredged up, it makes it more real.'

'But Mom, it was real!'

'Exactly, how could you ever get over a thing like that if you keep harping on it? Best to forget and move on. Put it behind you. So, don't let him drag you back there. Why does he want to know, anyhow?'

'I don't know.'

'Well, mark my words; he can only bring you heartache.'

'Fine, I heard you. Can I go now?'

'I told your dad, and he was furious. He agreed with me. No more Antonio!'

'I won't be alone – I'll be with my other friends.'

'Can I trust you to do what I say?'

'Of course, Mom. I'll do what you say, I'll stay away from him.' With downcast eyes, Cynthia kept her fingers crossed behind her. 'Can I go?'

'Yes, but mind what I said. And remember, your father will freak out if he finds out you saw that boy behind our backs.'

'Mom, I said I won't!' She sighed, shrugged on her small backpack.

'Your father wants you to stay away from him. He doesn't see eye to eye with that family, and therefore they are to be avoided!'

'See you later!' Cynthia waited no longer, turned on her heels, and sped out the front door. *Enough was enough,* she thought.

*

Two Municipal Police officers emerged from behind a row of parked cars and casually traversed the street. To any onlooker, it would seem as if the two crossed only to find some shade while patrolling on this very hot day. One pulled out his mobile phone and checked messages. He nodded slightly to his partner.

The two continued their walk until they reached the rear end of a black SUV, where they stopped. The one with the phone checked the registration plate again while the other bent slightly, trying to look inside the vehicle. From that vantage point the tinted windows provided minimal visibility, except for two shadowy figures. Both officers took out notebooks and carefully walked forward towards the driver's window.

With two sharp raps on the window, the elder officer indicated he required it to be rolled down. A second's hesitation – when the two men inside the SUV looked at one another – before complying, gave the officer the required time to assess the situation. The window whirred down. Empty coffee and Coca-Cola paper cups, with burger wrappers and plastic sandwich containers, covered the dash. Obviously, the occupants have been in the car for a while without moving.

'Good day to you both. I'm Officer Monnier, and this is my partner, Officer Jaccaud. We hope your day has been pleasant.'

The two men again looked at each other, uncertain if they should interact with the MPs. The driver grunted as the passenger leaned forward to look around him at Monnier. The driver recovered.

'Sorry, yes, good day to you too. Can we help you, officer?'

'Well, yes, sir. If you would be so kind as to show us your identity documents and the registration papers of the vehicle.' While Monnier busied himself with the occupants of the car, Jaccaud radioed the situation and their position to headquarters, asking for a check on the owner of the vehicle.

Suspicion crossed the eyes of the driver, then a flash like that of a snake recoiling ready to strike. Slowly, he settled with a forced smile, locking eyes with Monnier for a few more seconds, daring. Reluctantly, he reached over and took the registration papers from the glove compartment, handing them over. Monnier took the grey card and without a beat or a show of emotion, held out his hand for the rest.

'And the ID cards, please?' Jaccaud took the grey card for the SUV from his partner and holding it open, took a photo of it on his phone. When the IDs were handed over, he did the same. Without waiting, he sent all the photos on to HQ and, as pre-arranged, to Garcia.

'Could we ask you what you are doing here?'

'We're waiting for a friend. We arranged to pick him up here.'

'When do you expect this friend to arrive?'

'Oh, we don't know, he seems to be late.'

'How long have you been waiting?'

'Well, not long, just about thirty minutes.'

'From the state of the inside of your vehicle, it looks as if you have been here much longer. I would guess a couple of days. What will the results be if we ask the neighbours how long you have been parked?'

'They'll say nothing.'

'Why is that? You threatened anyone?'

'Not at all. But they know it's no good being busybodies.'

'We are sure that if we asked around, they would say that you used this spot as a camping ground. We'll have to ask you to move on, as staying here as long as you have would amount to loitering, and I doubt you would want to be arrested for that.'

'You're right. We'll wait for another five minutes, then move. Will that be acceptable?'

'Unfortunately, not. You must leave immediately, please. And please fasten your seatbelts before moving off.' Monnier and Jaccaud waited. No one budged or made an effort to leave. Seconds turned into minutes, and still no reaction from the two loiterers.

The two inside the SUV whispered amongst themselves and concluded that their orders to stake out the street until witnesses to the shooting were found, overruled the MP's request. Fear of their boss by far overshadowed that of being arrested. Their unwillingness to leave became clear.

'No, I think we'll wait a while longer. Thank you very much, Officer.'

'Fine, you're both under arrest and will need to come to the police station.'

'We'll pay the fine and be out in less than an hour.'

'That may be so, but in the meantime, you will be answering some questions.'

During the exchange of words, Jaccaud had turned away from the SUV and radioed in the situation. He called the Geneva police for assistance giving their location. Within minutes uniformed police arrived taking the two men into custody with instructions to take them directly to La Servette where Favre and Garcia waited.

*

Ines Ginet smacked her lips. She ran a piece of bread along the plate, wiping the last drop of gravy left from her meal.

'I knew *fonctionnaires* have a good cafeteria in situ no matter which section they work for, but this meal was excellent. I was also very hungry.'

'It is true, government employees do have good benefits, and I agree this was really good.' Despite the excellent lunch and cordial treatment, they had received since their arrival, Alex felt uneasy. How long do they still have to wait before they could go home?

'You know that tall detective, Detective Favre, reminds me of your ex-fiancé. He has the same eyes, and the way he walks reminds me of him.'

'Ines, what are you on about? Why are you talking about Denis? He's long gone. I haven't thought about him for ages.'

'But you made such a good couple. I remember when you broke off the engagement. You never told me the reason. Did he cheat on you?'

'I don't think this is the right time to talk about this. In any case it's private.'

'Oh, my dear, you know I care about you, and I think it troubled you more than you wish to admit. And I do think this is not a bad time, since we must wait for them to come back with news before they let us go home.'

'Well, they won't let us leave until they know it's safe. You know that, and it could be anytime now.' The last thing Alex wanted was to talk about her ex-fiancé or the reason why they ended it.

For at least six years, Denis had taken centre stage in her world. Their love affair grew over time and in importance. Then it imploded: The End. Why bring it up now – it serves no purpose. No matter how Alexandra tried, her mind would not let it go.

It began when Denis had reached out at the same time as she did. Their hands closed over the same book at the Library in English Autumn book sale. The unexpected touch sent an electric shock through her. The force with which she pulled back, toppled her over and nearly upset a whole table of books. But he caught her before catastrophe hit the entire book display.

The bond between them took shape that day in their mutual love of books and literature in all its forms. They spent many happy hours attending book readings, book launches and sales. Concerts and the cinema were also among their interests.

His attentiveness and proclamation of love six months after they had met took her by surprise at first. Though, after a while, she realised that she felt the same and relaxed, giving herself completely over to him. Idyllic days grew into weeks, months followed and became years. With his UNHCR work schedule, which often sent him all over the world, they treasured each moment together. His life, he explained, resembled the stream of refugees which never ended and refused to stay in one place. Therefore, each spare moment needed to be treated as precious. She appreciated that sentiment.

That was until eighteen months ago when she discovered he led a double life. Conveniently, for him that is, he had a whole support system in Ethiopia: a family with a wife of fifteen years which included three children. His deceit crippled her initially. However, because of her inherent attitude of surmounting obstacles, she recovered. Though, it dented her faith in the male species.

Why dredge it all up now? The whole experience was best forgotten. She had moved on. The reminder of her foolishness only embarrassed her.

'I only mentioned there is something that reminds me of him. I do not think he is the same type of person.' Ines broke into Alex's reverie.

'Oh, it's not important. I'm over his dishonesty and learnt my lesson.'

'The Detective looks very dependable, and I'm sure he is an honest man. Don't forget, he is a policeman.' Mrs Ginet tried her best to rectify her faux pas.

'But that doesn't mean he is an honest man. Police deal with so many bad things that I'm sure they must hide most of their true feelings. They keep secrets.'

'Their secrets are there to protect us, not to hurt. I know you were very upset when you broke off your engagement, but isn't it time to forget all that and find a new beau?'

'That remains to be seen. No one can control when, and if, I'll meet the right person.'

'Well, Detective Favre doesn't seem married. Why not him?'

'Now come on...!' At that precise moment, the door opened, and

Garcia walked in. The audible sigh of relief Alex let out made him turn to her.

'Is everything okay in here?'

'Oh yes, thank you.' Alex recovered quickly and looked sharply at her friend, warning her not to discuss the latest subject any further.

'I only came in to find out if either of you needed anything.' With mumbled thanks and a negative to anything further, he continued. 'In any case, I'll bring in some more coffee.'

'How long do you think we still need to be here?' Alex asked.

'We are busy checking out that SUV, and until we know who they are, and what they are doing there, we want you to be safe when you go home.'

'Do you think they were watching us?' Fear crept back into Alex replacing her uneasiness.

'Miss Labelle, of that we are not sure and until we have a clearer idea of what they had in mind, we do not want to speculate. But as we said, in the meantime, we want to keep you, and everyone else on that street, safe.'

'So, there's a definite danger?' Mrs Ginet wanted reassurance.

'That we don't know yet. It could be nothing. They could be ordinary loiterers who have nothing better to do, or they could be the lookout for a team of burglars operating in the area. We've had various reports of burglaries in a four-block range. So, as I said, it could be nothing, but better safe than sorry, hey?'

'Oh good, so we've "fingered" the thieves' lookout!' Ever the neighbourhood watch, Mrs Ginet concluded and convinced herself that spotting the parked vehicle had solved many crimes. Further, that her assistance was essential to the wellbeing of the whole community. Proud as a peacock, she obviously enjoyed the attention and special treatment she had received at the station.

'In any case, we will be leaving a presence in the area just to keep an eye, so sit tight until we can take you home.' With that, he turned and left.

'Isn't he nice? I feel so much better and confident that we've made the right decision in coming here.' Excitement bubbled through Ines.

'Oh, yes, so do I.' Distracted, Alex reluctantly agreed.

CHAPTER FOUR

The duty officer intercepted José Garcia on his way back to his desk and handed him a note. José glanced at it and turned to the young man.

'Why didn't you phone it through to Detective Favre?'

'The line was busy, and the visitors didn't want to wait. They insisted I interrupt him.'

'Fine, give me five minutes and bring our visitors through to the waiting room. We'll talk to them there. Arrange for coffee, please.'

'How many will be having coffee, sir?'

'Detective Favre, our visitors and I.'

'No problem, *chef.'*

Garcia turned and rushed to show Favre the visitors' names on the note. 'Favre, finish off, they're waiting for us. Perhaps they have information.'

Paul Favre held his hand over the mouthpiece of the phone. 'Wishful thinking, I'm sure. Okay, let's stay positive.'

He turned back to his call. *'Thank you for the information, we'll follow that up and keep you updated. Are you going to impound the SUV? ... Fine, let us know. In any case, we'll check on those two goons. Good day to you.'* He replaced the receiver, got up, and followed his partner to speak to their visitors.

'Good afternoon, Mr and Mrs Stephens. This is my partner, Detective Garcia, and I am Detective Favre.' The room always surprised him. It looked more like a doctor's waiting room, than a room in a police station. The couple he greeted got up from easy chairs and shook hands in way of greeting to both. Their overall grey demeanour permeated the room. If sorrow could seep from pores like perspiration, both would be completely soaked. Their brows were etched with lines, and bracket creases enclosed their mouths. Desolation surrounded them.

'We hope you didn't have to wait too long. Again, we would like to say how sorry we are for your loss. We know nothing compares to the loss of a child. Please accept our condolences.' Garcia gestured for them to sit down, and the two detectives took seats opposite the parents of Marcus, the victim.

'At this moment, we are completely occupied by your son's case.'

'Well, that is why we're here. We want to know what progress you've made. Why is it taking so long? We need to know. Why did this befall our son? Who did it? What exactly happened?' The questions flowed in an anguished stream from the bereaved father. His wife looked on with such distress, the fine linen handkerchief in her hands already a twisted rope. Paul wanted to reach out, relieve this couple's suffering. Impossible, he knew.

'We are very sorry for your loss. Unfortunately, we cannot discuss the case. However, please be assured we are doing our utmost to solve this murder and bring the criminals to justice' Paul's voice soothed but didn't satisfy either parent.

'Please don't patronise us! This was our son who was murdered! We demand justice without delay and without fail. If you are incapable of doing that, make no mistake – I will not rest until I have found and put that son-of-a-bitch in the ground!' The sudden anger Mr Stephens showed, transformed him. Yet, as quickly and violently it had raised its head, it dissolved, and he crumpled back into the chair. He buried his head in his hands, covering his face, trying to hide the tears wetting his cheeks. His wife stretched out, putting a hand on his back.

'Dad, they are doing their best. They will find who did this.' She tried to calm her husband, looked back at Paul. 'You will find who killed our son, won't you.'

'Be assured, we will not rest until that is done *Madame.*'

'Oh... I... I apologise. I'm sorry for my outburst. Yes, I know. It is just so hard and frustrating. I couldn't stop it from happening. You know a father's duty is to protect the family, especially your children. Only, look what happened. Our Marcus; gunned down like a lowly gangster. My hands are tied, even if I knew who's responsible, I can't even go after the man! It's too much to bear.'

'We understand your frustration completely. We beg you, please don't take matters into your own hands. It could only lead to more heartache. Leave it to the professionals. That's why we are here: not only to protect our citizens as much as possible, but to bring to justice those who are responsible for crime.' Paul breathed deeply and hoped there wouldn't be any illegal action leaving a mess for them to clean up later.

Both detectives had a deep understanding of the anguish the loss of a child caused. They had seen it often enough. In front of them, they again had indisputable proof. It was also evident that this couple's grief altered their attitudes and behaviour. No doubt they were decent people tested to the limit. Both Paul and José resolved to catch and bring the offenders up on the charge of murder in the first degree.

At that moment, the young officer brought the coffee, holding the tray for Mrs Stephens to add cream and sugar, then to her husband. Soft mumbles of *merci* followed his movements. He placed the tray on the small coffee table in the centre of the group and let the two detectives serve themselves. As he left, the silence broken only by teaspoons and cups rattling in saucers, gave all a moment to regain their equilibrium.

'This is the first time we have ever been in a police station.' Mrs Stephens brought all back to the present. Her husband nodded in agreement.

'Is that so?' Garcia responded, 'I only wish it was for a different reason.'

'Amen to that. We hope the next time you visit us would be when we have finalised this terribly sad case. Obviously, we have to cover all bases, and would like to ask a few further questions.' Favre took a deep breath, knowing this would be difficult, still it had to be done. 'We know he lived at home, which makes it easier for us. Can you recall if Marcus made any new friends, and if so, do you know who they were?'

'No, he always kept to his fellow teammates. As far as we know, the only new person in his life was that Cynthia girl. We thought she would bring trouble. We didn't like her and told him so. You know youngsters, you can't tell them what to do. It was his choice to go out with her.' Mr Stephens lowered his head.

'Yes, we know about her and understand your apprehension,' Paul continued. 'He never received any hate mail or threats of any kind?'

'Not that we know of. No, nowadays they do those things on the internet, don't they? The youngsters attack each other and threaten in cyberspace, so they tell us.'

'We are looking into that. So far, we haven't found anything bad. He seemed to be well-liked and admired for his abilities on the ice – a great sportsman.'

'Yes, that he is. I mean… was.'

'We understand, Mr Stephens. Another thing: did his routine change in any way, or did you notice a change in his attitude or demeanour?'

'No, he kept pretty much to his classes and practice routine. He went out a bit more often after practice, you know, to meet this girl. Other than that, no, nothing changed.'

'He didn't seem scared or nervous?'

'No, not at all, he was his usual smiling, kind self.' At this, both parents broke down again. They turned in their chairs towards each other and awkwardly held on, heads resting on the shoulder of the other, trying the impossible task of consoling one another.

The two detectives could only look on in sympathy and give the bereaved parents a moment in their shared agony. Paul ran his hands along his thighs and looked at José, as to say, 'let's wrap this up.' Garcia nodded.

'Mr and Mrs Stephens, we think this is all for today. If we need anything further, we'll contact you. Would you like a lift home, or did you bring your own car?'

'We didn't trust ourselves driving across town with the state we are in, so we came by taxi. It would be nice if you could take us home, please. Thank you.' The father, having managed to compose himself to a degree, stood up, holding out a hand to his wife.

'Come on, Mother, let's go home. We have to make arrangements.'

'This is the first time we've been inside a police station,' the dazed mother said, unaware that she repeated her statement of earlier.

'They know, Mother. Now come on, let's go.'

'I'll call the young officer to drive you home.' Garcia left to give the address in Vandoeuvre to the young man. Paul watched as the two slouched figures slowly shuffled their way to the entrance. It crossed his mind that this couple, in their early fifties, looked like a pair of seventy plus.

*

Starbucks was reasonably empty. The cool interior welcome after the heat, which was climbing as noon approached. Only three other people were there having something to drink, one munched on a muffin.

Antonio looked around, found a table in the corner, pulled out a chair, balanced his crutches against the wall, and sat down to wait for Cynthia. He felt confident that he could win her over. His heart raced just thinking of her. Gosh, how he missed her!

She stepped through the door, and he felt warmth flood his whole body. He couldn't repress the smile, which he knew was virtually ear to ear – the pain in his knee forgotten. He stood up and pulled out the chair opposite his.

'Hi' was all he could say. She was breath-taking. Immediately, he felt embarrassed. If she knew the effect she had on him, he'd look like a loser. Better to cool it.

'Hi. I'm here as you wanted. Now what?'

Her nonchalance threw him even more at her feet. And oh, that pout when she was fed-up. Irresistible! His good knee buckled, and he sat down quickly to hide his body's reaction to the effect she had on him. His mother completely forgotten, and her voice in his head, disappeared behind the Alps.

'I told you. I'm not talking about what happened to Marcus.'

'No, I know, you said.' Antonio was at a loss for words as she sat in front of him, only the table separating them. How he wanted to lean over and take her hand, pull her towards him for a lingering kiss. He shook off the feeling.

'So, what do you want?'

'Let me get you something. What would you like to drink? Do you want something with it?' He could see her eyes flit on and back off his own. Perhaps she was also nervous.

'I'll have an Iced Caramel Macchiato, please. Oh, no, I think a Berry Boost Smoothie and a brownie, please.'

'You sure you don't want a salad and a sandwich? I'm having a sandwich and an Iced Caffé Latte.'

'Yes, I'm sure. Just a brownie will do, I'm not staying long.'

'Fair enough. Hold on, I'll be back.' He could feel Cynthia's eyes on him as he limped over to the counter and placed the order. It didn't take long for it to be ready. During the wait, he glanced over his shoulder, noting the sudden movement of her head away from him towards the window. He felt encouraged. He collected their tray and, with a smile, took it to the table. So far, so good.

Without a word he placed the smoothie and brownie in front of her, taking his sandwich and latte. Silently, they opened their snacks, each concentrating on what was in front of them. He swallowed the last bit of the bread, took a swig from his paper cup latte; crumpled the serviette and threw it on the tray.

'I'm so pleased you came,' he began hesitantly. He didn't know why it was so important to speak to her, except that he wanted to see her. 'I don't want to talk about Marcus, even though my mom is still on at me for information. I only want to talk, talk about us. And I wanted to ask if we could go out again.'

'Well, I don't know, perhaps later, but not now – there's too much going on with the police and everything.'

'The first semester of the year will begin in about a month.'

'I know. We'll see each other in class. I'll come watch you practice when you're back on the field.'

'I'm hoping that'll be soon. I have to see the "ortho" next week.'

'Good luck. I've got to go.' Cynthia pushed the chair back, ready to go.

'Can't you stay a little longer?'

'What for? Was there something else you wanted to say?'

'No, just to hang out a bit. Don't really want to go home, you know.'

'I can imagine, if your mom's nagging is as bad as mine, it must be unbearable. I really don't want to hear another word from her or what my father wants.' Cynthia could see her mother waving her finger at her.

'But what are your mother's complaints? I thought it was mine that has innumerable questions that drive you mad.'

'My mother keeps on telling me that my father doesn't want me near you. I have no idea why. But that is what they want – for me to stay far away from you. Something about your family.'

'What? I don't believe this! What about my family? How come your parents know more about my family than I do? How could they prevent us from seeing each other because of something or someone I know nothing about?' Antonio was becoming frustrated and felt anger well up.

'Calm down. I don't think my mother knows them, just my father.'

'I have nothing to do with anyone who says they're my family!'

'Shoosh, surely it's not that serious?' Cynthia reached across the table and took his hand, but he pulled away, moved in his chair.

'What's your father got to do with my father? What's this all about? My life is ruined!'

'I don't know, please lower your voice, people are beginning to stare.'

'Okay, okay, but I didn't even know I had family, except of course for

74

my mother. Suddenly, a family pops up, and to crown it all: I have a father! Apparently, he has been paying for everything. But why haven't I heard of him or met him? Why did my mother hide him from me?'

'Weren't you curious about who or where he was? Or even if he was alive?'

'My mother never mentioned him and always told me that we didn't need anyone else, that we were complete, just the two of us.' He shook his head, thinking back to all the times he saw his teammates' parents at games. Invariably, there were more mothers present than fathers, so it didn't seem strange that he didn't have a father.

'I wonder why my parents are so adamant about staying away because of them. What does your family do?'

'I don't even know their surname – she only now told me that I have been using her maiden name.'

'What? Surely, she must have said something. Why didn't she at least tell you what your father's name was?'

'Your guess is as good as mine! When I asked my mom, she didn't give it to me, so I don't know. It sounds like they had a big family blow-up or something and broke off contact. It must have been about me. Perhaps they're one of those snooty families who think they're better than anyone else. I don't think they accepted my mom getting pregnant. It must have shocked their pants off!'

'I just thought of something else. Why didn't they object when we dated before? But now, suddenly, I'm to stay away from you. Why?'

'Yes, that is strange – must have something to do with the death of Marcus. But what? Did either of your parents say anything about Marcus before?'

'No, never. Even now they don't mention him, except to say that the event must have been traumatic for me and that I should see a therapist.'

'As if that's going to help. I'm not standing for it. I'm going to get to the bottom of this! I want them to leave me alone. No, leave us alone!' Antonio saw his agitation began to rub off on Cynthia.

'Don't go and do anything stupid, Antonio!'

With force, his chair scraped back. He grabbed his crutches and pushed on them to get up. Cynthia rose with him. Furious, because once again this incident interfered with his life, he stepped past her. It was not how he envisaged this meeting would have gone. He wanted to rekindle what they had or at least elicit a promise that they could date again – perhaps even hook up. Everything was out of hand. Nothing went according to plan, and now this: her father knows his father and family.

How does he ask his mother about this? Could he speak directly to his own father? Would his mother be prepared to put him in touch with his father? Oh no, from her earlier reaction she'd hate it. She'll flip!

*

'That was quick!' Paul Favre took the faxed copy from José Garcia. 'I didn't expect any response until tomorrow afternoon.'

'I asked Monnier to push our request through as fast as possible. In any case, there is no one at home with Maria and the children gone, and it's only seven pm. Shall we get a take-out?'

'It never fails! The first thing you think of is your stomach.'

'Well, no one can live on love alone – you should know that. Oh sorry – you don't know, seeing you've avoided that connection for the last six years.'

'It looks like we have the vehicle's owners and the names of the two gents. At least now we'll be able to check them out.' Paul rolled his chair closer to the desk and began typing the name of the company under which the vehicle was registered. 'Let's see who's behind this Synergy SLC.' He searched the companies register and waited for the information.

José took the fax and moved over to his desk, where he entered the name of one of the SUV's occupants on the paper. The computer hummed and blazed into an identity photo with details. He scrolled down, and a list of misdemeanours and infractions appeared. The seriousness of the crimes escalated from one incident of petit theft as a youth, to aggravated assault, leading to short incarcerations on three different occasions. José sent the document to the printer and typed in the second name. The second man's information was even more interesting: a violent streak with various disturbances of the peace and assaults. A couple of assaults with a deadly weapon appeared to have sent him to the *Prison du Champ-Dollon* for two stretches, one of three and the other of five years.

'Hey Paul, we struck gold with these two! Their mothers would be proud! Between these two, I cannot make up my mind who is the most upstanding citizen! They're adept in the art of being interrogated by our lot.

But who knows, they might just let slip something about who they're working for. They don't seem to be the sharpest tools in the box.'

'Great!' Encouraged, Paul turned back to his search. *'Merde! Trois fois merde!* I've not had the same luck in finding those behind this company.' He shook his head. 'Synergy SLC is owned by Geoman, which in turn is owned by another company in Lichtenstein, which is owned by one in Hong Kong, which in turn is owned by a company in Belize and finally by a holding company in the Cayman Islands. It will virtually be impossible to find out exactly who is behind Synergy or Geoman. These tax havens have their bank secrecy regulations, which extend to company ownership that is more impenetrable than our Swiss system. And here, with Synergy, we have various secrecy systems to crack.'

'Don't get discouraged, we'll get there. I have no doubt. You always manage the impossible. And together we make an awesome team!' Garcia, the eternal optimist, said.

'Now, not so fast, you always pat yourself on the back. I don't like it – you might just blow our chances to get this bastard.'

'You know, Favre, from what you've said about the ownership, it sounds like there could be much more involved than we first realised, not as innocent or straightforward as we thought. Don't you think it could be the Mafia or a drug cartel? First impressions are usually ninety percent correct.'

'Yeah, I remember you mentioned it might be. Let's keep an open mind and if necessary, we'll contact Europol and Interpol.'

'Though, first things first; I'll get uniforms to pick up those two beauties first thing in the morning, bring them here before they're out on bail and we'll have a go at them. See where it leads us.'

'Well Garcia, who knows, we might be lucky. They might have replacements who would be camped out in front of Mrs Ginet's block again. That'll be a gift.'

'It's a good place to start – gives us the opportunity to go home for a snack and some much-deserved sleep.'

'Again, your stomach! Okay, let's call it a day.' Paul shut off the computer and gathered his things. He shrugged on his jacket. 'See you in the morning.'

*

The way he left her at Starbucks frightened her. Cynthia had never seen Antonio that upset, angry even. She crawled deeper under the duvet. If only she could forget it all, hide away from her thoughts as well as her surroundings. She had tried blocking it all out with her phone's playlist at full blast, then she tried Ed Sheeran on YouTube – nothing worked. Ed only accentuated her aloneness, making her miss Marcus more acutely. Though, every time she thought of him, Antonio's face floated up – confusion increased with each breath she took.

She buried her head in her pillow, then changed her mind and pulled it over her head. Sounds still penetrated despite all efforts.

From the minute she got home, her mother had kept on asking how her day went. Avoidance could only be carried so far, but at least she could – with confidence – say that they did not discuss the shooting. She didn't lie. The fact that their conversation revolved around the effects the incident provoked, was definitely not reliving the sight of Marcus prostrate in the road.

Her unease increased the more she thought about the concern her parents showed, and the proclaimed interest of Antonio's mother and his 'family'. She felt as if her world had been turned upside down. She had no confidence in either of her parents ever telling her the truth. Then there's Antonio's mother. Before, when she dated him, his mother was cool, but now, not so much.

Her mother came to check on her a couple of times. She ignored her – let her think she was asleep. Her father had not yet come home. He was always late, and when he did arrive, he usually only patted her on the head with a 'my beauty', going off to his study with business calls as the excuse. Her mother's explanation that his business interests all over the world with different time zones, did not allow him regular hours. Fine, she didn't need him anyway.

She heard the front door open and close. Hushed whispers between her parents continued for a while. Then her mother tiptoed to their bedroom. Cynthia could hear her in the bathroom, getting ready for bed. From downstairs, she heard her father's voice. The urgency in his tone made her listen more carefully. Except, the sounds reached her muffled, making it impossible to make out what he said or discussed.

Exhausted, she finally fell asleep.

Downstairs, Arthur Gonzales had called his partner, Eric Pichat. He put the phone on speaker as he paced up and down in the den. Arthur's insistence that their Colombian suppliers deliver the product as soon as possible, seemed to have escaped the attention of their overseas representative. The shipping agent was standing by. However, the delay was damaging their reputation in this market.

Their various business competitors based here in Geneva also worried him. Since he and his family arrived in Switzerland, he had established a good base and made progress. The market he and his partner controlled enlarged every day. The fact that they had a better and cheaper product, mainly because they dealt directly with the producers, helped. Of course, he realised their gains would not go down well with those he pushed out, but that's business.

This incident with his daughter also concerned him greatly. He objected when she dated that Antonio Vicario, and now, he's been contacting her again. They've been meeting up, and he couldn't stop it without them uncovering what he knew, or what his project here in Switzerland entailed. She needed to keep away from that Antonio!

The not so well-known fact that Antonio was the son of Bescutti, his possible main competitor, disturbed him as well. He found out about the hidden son by accident when he had a drink with a cute brunette in a bar. She happened to be the secretary to Georgio Bescutti's assistant. Slighted by the boss himself, she couldn't stop talking. He heard later, when he tried to meet up with her again, that she had left town. Now, that phrase "left town" could mean anything. That's why he felt, to say the least, greatly relieved when Cynthia moved on to the hockey player. Now he realised that the relief turned out to be short-lived.

How could he get through to his daughter? Involvement with that Antonio could implicate her and his wife in the enterprise. They have a good life here; they lived in a spacious and comfortable house, though not ostentatious. He needed to be inconspicuous, not draw attention to himself, his family, or his business. At the same time, he wanted them to have all the comforts he could afford. That's what he thought he had managed: a house in Conches, within easy reach of the town centre, where his wife and daughter could spend to their heart's content. Yes, all the comforts, including a domestic servant from Colombia.

This shooting made no sense. They would have to get to the bottom of it. Did it have anything to do with them? Were they targeted? Why did it happen? Was it a warning? If it was connected to them, who was behind it, and if so, why and how? Did the person or persons stumble upon their operation?

'Eric, we need to find out as soon as possible who was involved and if this will impact on us. Also, if this was a warning directed at us.'

'I'll do so, and discreetly find out if there are any whispers amongst our competitors as well. Someone must know something.' On the other end of the line, Eric drew deeply on his cigarette, never a good sign.

'Good, but as you say, do it quietly.' Without a further word, Arthur ended the call.

*

Paul enjoyed the dusk as he drove home. Admittedly, they had not achieved much, but what they uncovered during the last two and a half hours could lead to something. Satisfied, the slight progress gave him hope. He kept on reminding himself to keep an open mind.

At nine-thirty, the hint of night ahead brought a thin veil to the sky. Even though the traffic had eased, it never really thinned before midnight in summer. As he crossed the Mont Blanc Bridge, he looked out over the Rhône on his right and the lake to his left, during one of the many forced stops due to traffic flow. The *Jet d'Eau* reached high – a familiar and comforting sight – a slight smile emerged. It represented home.

Yes, he looked forward to putting his feet up with a beer as soon as he got home. The whole day turned out better than expected, in fact, interesting. Without a doubt the two women brightened the whole station.

At first, the precise note-taking by the elder of the two – and brought to the table – irritated him. Finally, he found the value in it, which of course gave them their first opening. The younger, Miss Labelle, reflected her name. She was damn good-looking, though a bit nervous and "anti" police, apparently. Moreover, it did not detract from the fact that he found her very attractive. What really struck him was the way she wore practically no make-up – she looked so natural.

80

He dragged his thoughts away from Miss Labelle, and back to the pair of them. He acknowledged both women's contribution to the improvement of his mood. The talkativeness and sunny disposition of Mrs Ginet carried over, even after the ambiance clouded due to the visit of Marcus's parents.

The grieving couple had moved him; they touched his heart in a way he never thought it would. It was impossible for him to imagine how a parent could surmount such a loss, and the hardship of facing life without their child. Not to see them become an adult, find their way in the world, or form their own family, would be the most difficult. What do they say? A parent should not outlive their child. He had seen it before, always the same. Often the marriage broke down due to the oppressive burden grief loaded on a couple. Though, he had the impression that this couple would stay together. Their sorrow would put them both in the grave much sooner than expected for their age.

Surprised by the extent to which their son's death affected him, he asked himself question after question. Why this loss? Because Marcus was an only child? Why this young man? Because he had a bright future ahead of him? Why this couple? Because they appeared to be honest and generous people? Why this shooting? What was different about this crime? Something had changed, not sure what, except he couldn't stop examining not only the case, but his surfacing emotions. Why now?

His thoughts meandered through the day and the people which featured therein, until he realised with a shock that he was in front of his apartment block. At the last minute, he turned into the parking garage, parked, locked the car, and with his mind still in the office, went up to his flat, taking the stairs two at a time. The usual routine of checking the corridor before unlocking his front door, entering with caution, removing his shield, radio, jacket, gun, and putting them away followed. He whistled under his breath as he grabbed a beer, flopped down on the couch, and clicked on the television.

'This is the life!' he said to himself, breathing deeply. If he could only put this case aside for one evening, he would feel vindicated.

His euphoria lasted exactly fifteen minutes when the ring of his phone shattered the peace. With a sigh, he decided to let the answering machine pick up the call. And it did.

'*You were warned. Now live with the consequences,*' the hoarse voice whispered. Without another word, the call ended.

For a second, silence engulfed Paul. Then he snapped bolt upright. Incredulous, he recovered, reached for his phone, and tapped in his partner's number.

'*Garcia, I just had another call.*' Further explanation unnecessary.

'*What do we do? See you back at the station?*'

'*As soon as possible, yes.*' Paul took another sip of beer and switched off the TV. With a sigh, he returned to the coatrack, slipped on his holster, and from the sideboard took out his gun, badge, and radio. Finally, he put his jacket on, checked everything behind him in the flat, and stepped out into the corridor. He took the stairs down to his car.

The drive back to Servette didn't take too long with thinning traffic. He parked, then before going in, walked back the way he came and ordered a takeaway pizza from the restaurant. With small talk, he waited the ten minutes for his order to be ready, hoping it would clear his mind before tackling the case again.

As Favre entered the bullpen, he found Garcia rifling through the file on his desk, a worried look on his face. The pizza box warmed Favre's already hot hands, though, just the change of expression on his partners face to an appreciative look, gave him sufficient gratification.

'Thank you. I thought I would've had to settle for another dubious dinner from the dispenser.'

'No, couldn't do that to my so-valued partner!' But Garcia didn't react to the sarcasm the way Favre expected. 'What's wrong? Have you heard from Maria?'

'When you phoned, I thought you found something important, and therefore didn't ask any questions. However, as soon as I put the phone down, I had a call as well.'

'Let me guess – deep-throat, whispering sweet nothings. That's why I called – this second threat.'

'Yes, he said, "We know where Maria and the kids are hiding." Then the call clicked off. I contacted her immediately and told her to move to my brother's this evening, as quietly and as quickly, as possible. She didn't know how to explain it to the children, but I am sure she'll find a way. She knows the danger seeing she was the one who received the first threatening call.'

'I hope you're right. Oh, I have other bad news – our two friends posted bail and they're home.'

'*Merde!* I had hoped they could sweat a bit in the cell for us to pick at their story. Now we'll have to wait till tomorrow,' Garcia said.

'I don't think we should wait until tomorrow morning. Let's make a surprise call to pick up Tweedle Dee and Tweedle Dum immediately. We'll send a wagon and six uniforms over to their pad. I don't want to take any chances on any score.' As he spoke, Paul Favre picked up the phone to brief, as well as getting their superior's permission to bring the two men in.

'Good, before they can get to Maria and the kids. And hopefully, with a show of force, there won't be any violence when they are brought in.'

'Thank you. Let us know when you've got them.' Paul put the phone down. 'Good. All organised. Let's get working. It's going to be a long night.'

'But where do we start?'

'We'll have to look at the origin of the calls again. I know we didn't get anywhere before, but this time we'll dig a bit deeper. Also, there must be a connection to someone between our two prize citizens. Let's begin with pulling their backgrounds to pieces.'

'Good call. I would also like to look a bit deeper into the Bescutti/Vicario connection, just to make sure that we're not missing a Mafia or Cartel link.'

'Fine, your instincts always prove to have merit. I want to investigate the girl again – Cynthia. I'm sure she saw something and holding back.' They both settled behind their desks, pulling and opening file folders while their computer screens blazed with the official site of the Geneva's Cantonal Police logo.

*

'They're here.' Paul Favre replaced the phone. Both detectives got up, each with a notepad in hand, and moved through to the interrogation rooms. 'You take one and I'll take the other and see where we go from there. I'll take the big guy. Let's say twenty minutes?' They nodded, separated, and entered the respective rooms.

Dramatically, Favre slapped down his notepad onto the steel table and slipped into the chair opposite the suspect. The bulk of the man made the room look inadequate. The table and chairs were bolted to the floor for safety. The duty officer handed Paul a sheet of paper. 'Shall we begin? Your name, date of birth, and place of residence please.'

'You already have it from my ID.'

'We need you to repeat it verbally. So, what is it?' Favre compared it with the information given by the officer. 'Now, Xavier, who do you work for? I see you have quite a bit of history here. You've done some impressive stuff in your life. So, I'm wondering who your boss is, who gives you orders.'

'What do you mean? I work for myself, obviously.'

'Obviously? So, you are responsible for everything you do?'

'Of course. I'm my own boss.'

'And what does your partner say, does he work for you, or does he also work for himself? Don't forget if your statements don't correspond, you'll be in bigger trouble than what you are in now.'

'What are you talking about? You still haven't told me why you brought us in. What kind of trouble am I in?'

'Illicit loitering for one. The charges might expand to include various other crimes, but for the moment we are beginning with that. You must know that we are all very conscious of terrorism now, and any person or persons acting suspiciously will be questioned.' Favre looked down to the sheet in front of him and back up. He saw the man's eyes follow his every movement. 'So, I repeat – who do you work for? Who's your boss?'

'I'm not a terrorist!'

'Why were you hanging around in front of that apartment block?'

'What apartment block?'

'You know perfectly well. The Municipal Police asked you to move on and then reported your activities to us.'

'What activities? We were just waiting for a friend.'

'What friend? What's this friend's name and where does he/she live?'

'It's my business.'

'So, what is your business? Is it terrorism?'

'Definitely not! We don't involve ourselves with that type of thing.'

'But everything points to you and your pal next door being terrorists.'

'Can you prove it?' Favre made a show of writing on the notepad, periodically looking up at Xavier. He let the silence drag on. Xavier moved his bulk in the chair, but nothing relieved the pressure he was beginning to feel.

'What are you writing? Why am I here?'

Favre ignored the question. 'I'll ask you again: who do you work for? and don't tell me you work for yourself because I don't believe you.'

'I told you, nobody.'

'So, what were you doing outside that building?'

'Nothing.'

'Nothing? But you were there for a long time. Who asked you to case out that specific building? Surely you didn't just pick the address out of the telephone book. There must be a reason why you were there.'

'I told you; we were waiting for a friend.'

'I'm sorry Xavier, that doesn't wash with me. No one waits for a friend the whole day and night. So, we are going to book you for suspected terrorism.'

Beads of perspiration appeared on Xavier's forehead as he jumped to his feet, shaking the table on its bolted legs, shouting that he was not a terrorist. Paul ignored the outburst and left the room. As arranged, Garcia exited the other interrogation room at the same time.

'Did you get anywhere?' Garcia shook his head, no information forthcoming from the other man. 'They're experts at being questioned. Though, the terrorism aspect seems to rattle. Let's give them the rest of the night in the cells and tackle them again in the morning.'

CHAPTER FIVE

A new day – for the first time, Alexandra felt relaxed. She had slept well with pleasant dreams, the nightmare of a few days ago far from her mind.

Their visit to the police station had given her a sense of closure. With her duty done, she breathed a sigh of relief. Though, at the back of her mind, she knew the end of the story was far from over.

She had checked around ten p.m., and there had been no unknown vehicle parked in the road, only a police cruiser slowly driving by. In fact, when they came back from the station, the SUV was gone. At least now she knew the police would do their job, serve and protect. They're not all bad. One thing was certain; the disappearance of the black SUV had a lot to do with her lighter mood.

As of yesterday, her admiration for Mrs Ginet had risen. Alex always held her in high esteem because of all the difficulties she had overcome in her life. But this! That woman showed courage and would not let anyone browbeat her! The way she kept insisting the detectives look at her notes, and more importantly, take them seriously. Just like those little terriers: when they got their teeth into something, they held on! She had them wrapped around her little finger, especially Detective Garcia, who succumbed to her beguiling charm by the end of their visit – and she, his.

Her neighbour had touched a raw spot when she compared Detective Favre with Denis. In her effort to put his betrayal and the dispirited period which followed behind her, she had busied herself with various hobbies. Yoga became an escape, and painting classes gave her a completely new view of the world. However, as soon as Mrs Ginet compared the detective with Denis, it all came rushing back. The humiliation and the shame of having a relationship with a married man nearly broke her, which was completely against her values. But the fact that he had kept this from her, gave back some of her dignity and, in a strange way, consoled her.

It was true. The detective physically resembled Denis, and despite the bad memories which that conjured up; he seemed like a good man. Alex didn't envy him his career. All those crimes and violent people he had to deal with day to day, must give him sleepless nights. How could he do it and still believe in humanity? He obviously had the safety and wellbeing of the citizens of Geneva foremost in mind. What would they do without men like him?

She hoped this current case would soon be solved. She didn't want to think about that scene in the street. It made no sense; a young man being shot down in such a manner. At the police station, she listened to the questions the detectives asked. From the gist of the questions, she wondered if the speeding car had anything to do with the death. Perhaps it was only a bystander who panicked because he didn't want to be involved, and who might have something else to hide. Oh, it had all just become more complicated, and she wondered if the police had thought about that possibility. Surely, they must have. It would be better to put it all out of her mind.

Mrs Ginet had invited her for a light lunch today. She declined with the excuse that her yoga class and chores would keep her busy practically the whole day. She dreaded going as the conversation would surely involve the crime, the SUV, and their visit to the police station. She needed to concentrate on other things, such as the new day which the weather channel predicted would again be hot and sunny. She could also take a walk along the lake and breathe in different energies. That would change everything and improve the day even more.

With breakfast and a shower behind her, she dressed for yoga. With this weather she knew she could, in fact, take that walk along the lake without having to change, everyone wore very casual and light summer clothing during the heatwave. She grabbed her purse, phone, yoga mat, and a shopping bag, locking her apartment door as she left with a spring in her step. This really was a good day.

Mid-afternoon, Alex arrived home, all the chores done and feeling good after the yoga session. As she neared her building, a police vehicle cruised by re-enforcing her assurance. A smile formed on her face as she entered and bounded up the stairs to her floor, where Mrs Ginet waited at her open door.

'Good, you're back. Hope you had a good day. Come in, I have the coffee on, a cup of Nespresso, just as you like it.' No escape – Alex said she'd be there in a few minutes, as she needed to put the shopping away. 'No problem. I'm here.' With a big smile, the older woman turned into her flat and left the door open for Alex to follow.

It took Alex only a few minutes to put everything away, with a visit to the bathroom to freshen up. As she grabbed her keys, her glance fell on the window from which she had seen the young man lying in a pool of blood. A flash penetrated the corner of her mind. She shook her head and turned to leave, pulling the door closed behind her.

After small talk and recounting the day's events, Alex got up and moved over to the window from where Mrs Ginet saw the dark SUV. The road was clear. No strange vehicles filled the parking spots. She couldn't shake the feeling that she had missed something but couldn't pull it out of her mind's fog. She needed to separate and sort out all her thoughts to find the missing piece.

*

The feel of the carpet began to irritate her bare feet. Alex had been pacing the whole afternoon since she had come back from her short visit to Mrs Ginet.

She struggled to draw the thought from the corner of her mind. What did she miss? The nagging feeling from earlier didn't go away, but it didn't get clearer either. If only she could remember what that flash meant, it might be the information the police needed. She also felt confused about whether she should talk to the detectives. But what to say if she couldn't put her finger on this elusive idea? This was turning into a nightmare.

*

Georgio Bescutti stared out of the window of his third-floor office in the WTC building next to the airport. He loved to see planes take off and come in to land – it confirmed his sense of being an international trader. The taller than average reflection in the window showed Roman features with dark hair and eyes to match. As his reflected image – in the centre of the action – was where he liked to be. Though, he would've preferred if his business involved less of his family's illegal trading. He accepted the part that he controlled, but for the rest, to which he was not privy to, unsure. He pulled his attention away from the runways to the problem at hand. His assistant stood in the middle of the room with a file in his hands.

'So, what have we got?' Georgio trusted Emilio with most things in his life. However, not being a trusting person, he had long ago convinced himself that his assistant always kept something from him. Then again, he had kept Emilio in the dark about various things, especially concerning this shooting. Emilio could very easily slip something when he spoke to his wife. Who could he trust completely? He could throttle those idiots who bungled his orders.

'Apparently, two of our foot soldiers are being questioned,' Emilio offered.

'Is it about that shooting in Paquis?'

'I asked someone to look into it.'

'I didn't know you sent someone to the area.'

'What can you tell me about it?' Bescutti turned back to his desk.

'So far, nothing. In any case, they couldn't find out a thing. Our police contacts say the two were taken in for questioning. No one seems to know who this young man was, except, that he was a star hockey player at the University.' Emilio's long fingers adjusted his glasses and consulted the file.

'What? How come?'

'Well, apparently, our two went to the spot where the shooting took place hoping to find out more or if they saw someone suspicious.'

'And?' Bescutti felt getting information out of Emilio was like pulling teeth.

'They were spotted by the Municipal Police and asked to move on. Apparently, a neighbour reported a vehicle with two occupants in the same place for nearly twenty-four hours.'

'Good, then there's no problem, I suppose they complied and moved on.'

'Well, yes, but their explanation on why they were there didn't convince the MPs. The police picked them up last night. As per my latest information, they are still there being questioned.'

'What? For what reason?'

'I am told they have not been charged but have been pulled in on an illicit loitering charge which as you know can be used as a basis for many crimes,' Emilio explained.

'Are these two trustworthy? Will they talk?'

'If you mean: will they tell the police who they report to? The answer to that is no, they are seasoned. In any case, there are so many foot soldiers between them and you, that they most probably would never work it out. They're brawn, not brains.'

'Do they know what our business is all about?'

'No, as far as they are concerned, they are bodyguards to an important politician.'

Georgio smiled for the first time this morning. 'That's good, there's real scope there! It covers a whole bag full of sins. Let's keep it that way.'

'They are far removed from us and the nature of our business.'

'Okay, I'll take your word for it.'

'These two chaps were hanging around specifically to see if anyone might know something. There's really no reason why anyone could think it has anything to do with our business. Besides the young man being the latest conquest of your son's ex-girlfriend, there is absolutely no connection.'

'What do you mean my son's ex-girlfriend? I thought they were still thick as thieves and dating. When did this happen?'

'I don't have all the details, but apparently she dropped your son when he lost his spot on the team due to his knee injury.'

'Cold, that is. I didn't know. You should've kept me informed.' Sometimes, Emilio irritated Georgio because of the way he filtered information, and this was one of those times. 'You have spoken to his mother again, haven't you?' He dreaded the idea of having to speak directly to Manuela concerning their son.

'I did as you requested. She couldn't understand why you were interested, but I insisted. So far, she has not managed to uncover anything. In fact, she gave me less information than our contact in the police. Your son is apparently incapable of getting the girl to talk about the event. She seems not to know anything or is reluctant to discuss what she told the police. Or there may be another consideration, which is that she's just too traumatised to discuss it.'

'Is there anything else you could use to make my wife understand the urgency of the matter for us to get what we need?'

'At the moment, she's insisting on speaking to you directly.'

'That's not happening.'

'She's already very nervous. I threatened her with the ire of the family; perhaps the wrath would've been better – it sounds stronger. But she seems to grasp the problem. I mentioned she might have to disclose that you are alive and that a paternal family exists.'

'That'll be unfortunate. Under no circumstance do I want him involved in the family business. He must be kept out of it at all costs.'

'That may turn out to be impossible.' Emilio pushed his glasses back up his nose. He had always been thin but was convinced that this job caused him to lose even more weight. Now, the conversation had turned to a dangerous subject: family. The Bescutti family terrified him. Even though most of their dealings were illegal, the business dealings Georgio concluded have been legitimate and profitable. He could live with that. Nevertheless, the way the rest of the family dealt with opposition, and those who crossed them, made his skin crawl. He could put up working for Georgio, but wanted nothing to do with the brother or any of the cousins. They were ruthless.

'Did anyone in the organisation talk about this?'

'No. I haven't heard a thing. I can't think why it happened. Unless someone in our organisation held a grudge.'

'Keep me informed. Let's see where this goes.' Georgio turned back to the window, dismissal clear.

*

Favre reached over the stack of files on his desk to his ringing phone. *'Favre,'* he listened for a moment, then pushed the computer keyboard and a couple of files out of the way, looking for his notepad. *'Hold on. Miss Labelle? Repeat that please.'* He beckoned to Garcia. *'Could you come in?'* He waited for her reply and then said; *'of course. ... When? Well, as soon as possible, please.'* He finished the call and looked up at his partner.

'I thought she didn't know anything or liked us – found the police terrifying.' Garcia, who heard Favre's side of the conversation showed his incredibility.

'Well, Garcia, you wouldn't believe this. She wants to talk. She wasn't very clear, so I thought it better if she came in,' Favre replied.

'When we interviewed them, she hardly said a word. What do you think this could be about? She repeatedly said she never saw anything.'

'We'll find out when she arrives, won't we?'

'And when will that be?'

'Now. She's on her way.'

'It gives us about twenty minutes to see if our two loiterers have changed their tune and are prepared to tell us something interesting.'

'I hope we get something, as we can't hold them much longer without a charge.'

'Oh, I mean to charge them officially.'

'With what? Loitering?' Garcia scratched his head.

'Exactly, that will give us a couple more days: Loitering under Suspicious Circumstances.'

Neither detective managed to get anything more out of the two men by the time the duty officer knocked on the respective doors to announce Miss Labelle's arrival and awaited them in the interview room. They sent the two men back to the cells with a warning of them being formally charged within the hour.

'Good afternoon, Miss Labelle. Pleased to see you.' Favre shook her hand and gestured for her to take a seat. She nodded a greeting.

'*Salut*' Garcia's eyes couldn't resist flicking up and down her body as he pulled the door closed behind him. He noted how the pastel-blue blouse and white skirt accentuated her attractiveness. He took a seat after offering his hand in greeting. Alex tugged her skirt over her knees and looked at Favre.

'We were surprised to hear from you. When we spoke last you didn't have anything to add to Mrs Ginet's statement. We are eager for any information you might have. Did you remember something?'

'Well, I … I'm not sure you see. It's more like a feeling.'

'A feeling? What do you mean – a feeling? Didn't you see something?' The pen hovered over Favre's notebook as he looked up. He had difficulty locking his eyes onto hers. She moved in the chair. Paul found it surprising that her discomfort concerned him.

'Yes, I mean no. I mean I think I saw something.'

'I don't understand. Did you, or didn't you?'

'I forgot all about it. But having coffee with Mrs Ginet earlier today, I thought back on the events of the night.' She took a deep breath, her eyes flicked from one to the other. 'I remember hearing the shot. I then went to the window and saw the car speeding away, but in the corner of my eye a movement registered. A person, I think a man, who slowly turned and walked away.' Her fingers intertwined then uncurled before twining again.

'Yes, I am sure it was a man, too big for a woman. But my attention stayed on the girl, and I lost the movement.'

'Can you recall in which direction the person went?' Garcia asked.

'He must have gone to the left, from where I stood, as he disappeared from my line of vision pretty quickly.' She hesitated, then continued. 'Well, thinking back, it struck me as strange that someone would calmly leave and not try to help, or at least phone the police. Only, I forgot all about it until just a little while ago. That was when I realised I had to mention it.'

'Do you think you might be able to give a better description of the person?'

'No, it was so fleeting, and it was dusk.'

'So, you can't give us an idea? You're sure it was a man?' Garcia pressed.

'All I can say is that the shape was not skinny or fat – he seemed a bit bigger than medium size. I... I don't know.' She fidgeted. For Paul, it was clear that they wouldn't get any further.

'Fine, at least we have another angle to work on now. Thank you for coming in, your information was extremely helpful.' Paul closed his notebook and got up, holding out a hand to Alex.

'Oh, okay, thanks. I'll go now.' She got up, looked from one to the other. With a slight hesitation, she took Paul's hand. 'If there's anything else I remember, I'll contact you.' Nervous embarrassment replaced her discomfort.

Garcia unfolded from his chair. 'Thank you for the information. I'll walk you out.'

Paul watched the woman walk down the corridor. He could still feel the touch of her hand. Deep inside, he wanted to savour the feel of her soft skin as his hand folded around hers. Not sure why she elicited this reaction in him, he tried to shake it off. He turned and walked back to his desk, determined to put her out of his mind. He needed to concentrate on the case.

Garcia found Paul busying himself shuffling papers. 'You trying to look busy, or is something worrying you?'

'Oh no, just thinking. It could mean we've been on a wrong track completely. I mean what she said: seeing someone walk away.'

'So far, anything would be welcome to shove us in the right direction. But what did the ballistics say? Have they matched the bullet to a gun yet?'

'Inconclusive.'

'Now that's really helpful! What exactly does "inconclusive" mean on a ballistic test? Surely there is something it could be matched to?'

'Well, seems the bullet deformed when it scraped the tarmac on exit. There could be a match with a previous crime, but not a definite match. It would've helped if we had found the shell. There might have been fingerprints on that, which could point us to the shooter.' Favre looked at the papers in his hand, shook them into to a neat pile, inserted them into a temporary file, and sat down.

'Let's look at what she said,' Favre continued. 'If the pedestrian was the shooter and not the occupants of the car, it throws a completely different light on the matter. So far, we have no registration or other details of the vehicle. Further, it might have sped away afraid of being the next target. It's only natural to avoid a bullet. Anyone would disappear as fast, and as far away, as his wheels could take him.'

'Well, the same goes for the pedestrian. Why not run away as fast as possible? Instead, according to Miss Labelle, he calmly walked away.' A slight smile crossed Garcia's face.

'What do you find so amusing?'

'Nothing. I was just thinking how the young lady never took her eyes off you for the entire time we talked.'

'You're joking, right? Get serious, of course she would look at me, I spoke to her. You hardly said a word besides the two questions you threw at her.'

'What do you mean "threw at her"?'

'You pressed her for a description while it was clear she couldn't give us more than she already did.' Irritated by his embarrassment, Favre picked up the file again, and with two hands tapped the narrow edge on the desk, as if to even up all the corners. 'Now, let's get back to work. We can't afford to ignore this pedestrian. Are there any cameras in that direction?'

'As far as we know, there aren't any where the shooting happened, but I'll check the traffic camera further along. Now that we know which direction the person went; we could look at those in Navigation Square again. This time, concentrate on those on foot from a couple of minutes after the crime.'

'I think we should check up to thirty minutes after, he might have hung around out of direct sight, just to see how things unfolded.'

'That's cold.'

'I agree. Well, let's get on it, perhaps we'll pick something up.'

*

Alex couldn't get out of the station fast enough, stood for a moment on the sidewalk breathing deeply. In a way, she felt relieved; in another, she wanted distance from it all. Oh, she shouldn't have gone to the police! Now she did it, right or wrong, no going back. Her fear of getting involved made her doubt again. Too late now, not sure of what she saw. She had convinced herself it was the right thing to do, and now it was done. Why couldn't she be as brave as Mrs Ginet?

With head bowed, she made her way to the tram, not knowing if she felt desperate or embarrassed. The detectives affected her in different ways. Garcia made her uncomfortable – the way he looked her up and down. She had heard that a woman could feel like being undressed by a man just looking at her. Well, that was the way Garcia made her feel. Favre, on the other hand, made her nervous and awakened long-buried feelings; he made her realise that she was lonely. And she did not want to be reminded. How could two such different men work together effectively?

The heatwave was getting her down as well. The sun beat down, burning her skin. The strength of the sun's rays never felt this strong in all the years she could remember. Global warming could not be ignored anymore. With warnings of the danger of skin cancer on everyone's mind for these last ten years, she realised she hadn't put any sunblock on before leaving home. She craned her neck in the direction of Meyrin, wondering if the tram would be long in coming. The idea of the air-conditioned interior sounded very inviting. Though, even with her discomfort, her thoughts drifted back to Favre.

Amazing how much Detective Favre reminded her of Denis. Thinking back to the time they shared together brought a smile, warmth flooded her body. But as quickly as it came, a sadness clouded her mind; she would never be able to forgive his betrayal. True, as Mrs Ginet said, the detective is not the same as Denis, but could she take a chance? To believe again, to trust again, might be impossible. Eighteen months had passed, and her faith in men had not returned.

She couldn't understand why her thoughts took this direction. It was not her intention. Why would he be interested in her? Who knows, he might be married or attached? She couldn't go through it all again. In any case, it's got nothing to do with her. There's nothing going on, and nothing will be going on! Adamant that it's not in her future, she stepped forward and boarded the tram as it arrived, saving her from further ruminations.

*

'I gave you a simple task, and you couldn't even do that! You are all imbeciles.'

'Yes, Boss, sorry.' The alpha male, military straight, pulled his shoulders back even more, prepared to take the browbeating.

He stood squarely in front of two others, both sets of eyes downcast. Despite the air-conditioning turning the room into a butcher's cold room, perspiration showed on their foreheads. They dared not face the Boss. They were only the lookouts, tracking the comings and goings of the girl, but obviously responsible for what played out at that moment.

'Your intel was up the spout! How could you be so stupid?'

'Sorry, Boss.' The alpha's stare stuck to the wall just above the boss, it didn't waver.

'Explain yourself.'

'I had the target well in sight when they decided to kiss.'

'And you let that derail your mission?'

'I'm sorry, Boss.'

'Don't be sorry, tell me how you are going to set things right.'

'We'll find another opportunity.'

'There won't be a "we". It was clear that your team could not meet their objective. You will be alone for the next effort. Which, I wish to add, must not and will not fail. It is imperative that you follow through. Our future dealings depend on it, not to mention the future of the business.' The Boss turned back to the desk.

'Yes, Boss, I will not fail next time.'

'You had better not. I'm sure you know what I mean by the expression: cessation of our future dealings. No future on the cards for you. As for these two, let me know what your plans are with them.'

'Yes, Boss.'

'Dismissed! Now get out of my sight and make sure I never lay eyes on these two idiots ever again.'

The two idiots, well scolded, shuffled towards the door as fast as safety would allow. Alpha turned on his heels and briskly strode out. He didn't appreciate the dressing down in front of his foot soldiers. In fact, they were the reason this mission failed. Now his headache became even worse as he had to think of how to get rid of them as well.

He had another problem. The police were still investigating the shooting as an organised hit and not a random gang drive-by. At least his team did a reasonable job with the car speeding off. It gave him time to calmly walk away. But there was a hesitation before they took off. That could throw doubt on the whole scenario.

And what about that little old lady walking her dog? She had looked straight at him as he fired. She grabbed the excuse for a dog, covered his eyes, protecting him from unseen terror. He only whimpered and squirmed in her arms. She hurried away so quickly and disappeared into one of the buildings. He couldn't follow her. He expected the foot soldiers to have found her by now. He had given them a full description and the direction in which she ran. But nothing on that score either.

Further, both detectives have ignored his warnings. He would get them to take him seriously. Perhaps if he put the experience of what he had learnt in the army to use? That'd be a bit extreme, but such fun. No, using explosives should be his last resort, but it's oh so tempting. It need not be a grand gesture, just something small. A touch of fireworks could be exactly the change he was looking for. And if he did, how would that change the situation? It might even be exciting. He had already put things in motion, now he only needed to wait. At least he got through to the wife, except she didn't completely warn off her husband. Garcia's wife and children are holed up somewhere. He thought he had traced them, only they left again. Now they were off grid, and so far, he couldn't find them. They seemed to be constantly on the move. On the other hand, Favre showed absolutely no sign of heeding the warnings. Clearly, Garcia was the weak link with his family on the line. Except, where were they?

They weren't taking him seriously. His next step must be impeccable and impressive. He'd have to move fast with follow-up action on these warnings. He must avoid being regarded as a blowhard. Alpha scratched his chin.

Paul Favre looked at the still photos received from the traffic department again, hoping to see something he missed previously. He felt it worth looking at each with fresh eyes and from a different angle. With the street cordoned off, he hoped the nearby camera picked up something useful. None registered the vehicle speeding away. Most probably, it did not exceed the speed limit of 50km/h in range of the camera. If the event happened one block over, it would have been in a 30km/h zone and caught on camera.

This time he looked for a person on foot. Time stamps on the various prints had registered thirty minutes before the incident to two hours after. From the different views, the time showed three people walking towards the square, and away from the scene before the event. During the same period, two went towards the scene.

Favre selected certain prints and arranged them in order. He then scrutinised the photos after the shooting. He found none for fifteen minutes. Then, one photo showed a car going in the direction of the scene, but without pedestrians leaving, though, several hurrying towards it. The cameras registered a couple of photos when the first police vehicle arrived, though not their own sometime later. Neither of these proved useful as most on foot were interested in what had happened, and when they lost interest in the spectacle, slowly began filtering back to their respective destinations.

At that moment, his computer announced the arrival of an e-mail. He opened the mail as he called his partner. 'At last! Garcia, we've received the videos from Traffic and the Commune.'

'Good, let's have a look. These are all the movements in and around Navigation? How many are there?'

'Quite a few from various security cameras in the area. They sent four over. One from the ATM, another from outside the restaurant, the other two from the official municipal cameras covering the two bus stops. Hang on; I'm forwarding the mail to you.'

'Okay, you take the first two and I'll take the others.'

'We still have not connected the gunman with the car leaving or confirmed if the SUV driven by our two friends in lockup, are the same. The description of the vehicle at the scene was so sketchy, impossible to even make a guess. We need more independent witnesses.'

'But we've got nothing! No one gave us anything worthwhile.' Garcia rolled his chair towards his desk and opened the file Favre sent.

'Well, perhaps we can match the vehicle from the tapes.'

Both began watching, amazed at what people do when they do not realise they are being watched. A middle-aged man waiting for the bus continuously picked his nose and inspected his findings, as if hoping a diamond hid in the mucus. A teenager pulled his pants up, then readjusted them for the crotch to hang just above his knees – he repeated this process three or four times, never really satisfied. A young woman used her reflection in the restaurant window to apply makeup, moving her head in all directions to see if the eyeshadow and mascara were evenly applied. But the most amusing was the way she shaped her mouth while, and after, putting on lipstick. Some time passed while the young woman admired the face looking back at her, before moving fifty metres further along, where a friend joined her. Together they entered the Bollywood restaurant. An elderly woman, also waiting on the bus, but in the opposite direction of the man, had made a makeshift fan from the *20 Minutes* to find respite from the heat.

Both Detectives concentrated on the different videos, scrolling faster when necessary and pausing to replay other parts. They noted every vehicle registration number that appeared, irrespective of the direction in which it travelled. Those leading to or from the scene were highlighted. Every frame where pedestrians seemed possible persons of interest, were copied on to a separate file, and a hardcopy printed. Facial recognition would be applied later.

After two hours, they had covered every possible aspect of the tapes, sorted the notes, prints, and highlighted timestamps. Favre threw his pen down, stretched, and pushed his chair back.

'How are you doing? You think we can make sense of this?' Garcia rubbed his eyes.

'The only thing to do, is to try.'

'Gosh, this made me hungry. You want something? We could order a pizza, as it looks like we're going to be here for a while.'

'For once, I won't comment on your constant need to eat. I'm starving, and a pizza sounds just perfect. Go ahead and order.' He got up and turned the crime board over, which covered the wall behind their desks. They now had a clear surface to work on. He looked over his shoulder. 'Hey, ask for extra pepperoni and mushrooms.'

Paul stared at the blank surface, with a deep breath, took his time to select a marker. Time well spent, allowing him to collect his thoughts. Then, meticulously, frequently consulting the notes and prints, he began a sequential record of both vehicle and pedestrian movements. A pattern emerged – a flow mapped out.

José Garcia studied the prints laid out, deep in concentration when his phone rang. Still comparing one photo to the other, he responded:

'Garcia.' He jumped up, out of his chair. 'When, where? ... Okay, okay! ... Maria, calm down and start from the beginning.' He slowly sat down again, hand in his hair, 'tell me exactly when you saw him last, what he said. What happened when you saw him?'

Favre realised Garcia's attention had slipped from their task at hand to the phone conversation and moved over. Garcia made some notes.

'Chérie, I'll be there in forty-five minutes. Call the local police and report it immediately. I'll get Favre to see what we can do from here and follow up. Have you spoken to his mates?' He listened for a moment. Favre could hear her panicked voice squeaking over the ether from where he stood.

'Weren't they with him? ... okay chérie, ... chérie, please, I'm coming. I'll speak to them myself. See you soon.' With that, he shrugged on his jacket with one hand and continued to calm his wife without success. 'I'm coming, yes, chérie, don't worry, we'll find him. I'm coming.' He looked up at Favre as he banged down the receiver.

'What's happened?'

'My son Phillippe is gone. Maria can't find him. She thinks he's been taken.'

'What? By whom? Did she receive a warning note or message?'

'No, she didn't say anything. So far, she's heard nothing, but he's nowhere to be found. I've got to go. I've got to find my son.' He grabbed his mobile phone, tapped his pockets to make sure he had everything needed.

'When last did she see him?'

'This morning when she dropped him at the recreation centre. Sorry, I have to go, can't hang around, must find my son.' They talked while Garcia moved to the exit.

'Who was he with last?'

'Some mates, she said they told her he left with a man who interrupted their basketball game and called him over.'

'Did they know this man?'

'She didn't say, that's what I want to find out. Sorry, must go!'

'Okay, go. Let me know what you find out and what I can do from here.' With that, a whirlwind of air confirmed José's departure.

Garcia ran out, and Favre walked over to the window. He saw Garcia fumble for his keys as he hurried to his car in the outside parking area behind the building. He watched him get in. Garcia turned the key in the ignition before he even closed the door. Favre could hear his unsuccessful attempt in starting the motor. Garcia tried again. Then an explosion lifted the vehicle off the ground. It rocked the building. Windowpanes shattered; others shuddered.

CHAPTER SIX

Alexandra languished in bed – just a few minutes more, she told herself. The night had been with her tossing and turning. Her visit to the station running roughshod through her mind. She still wondered if she had exposed herself to danger and, more importantly, shown her insecurities. The other problem she encountered was the recurring thoughts about Detective Favre. He began to fill her mind with possibilities. All in all, a disaster. In the end, she got up and splashed water on her face, ridding herself of all the disturbing thoughts. With her mind going in all directions for hours, she finally fell asleep from exhaustion.

Pleased that she still had one month of vacation, she stretched and turned over to reach for the radio. As usual, her first action of the day was listening to the news as she slowly woke, readying for the day. But this morning, she jumped up with a start, startled by the news. As her feet touched the floor, the announcer told listeners of an explosion at the Servette Police Station the night before.

Her thoughts immediately flew to Paul Favre. Was he involved in the explosion? The report said that fatalities were not known, except, a police officer sustained serious injuries. Did he get hurt? How did it happen? Was it inside the station? She hardly heard the rest of the report as her mind spun out of control. 'Calm down,' she told herself.

Furthermore, all the questions flooding her consciousness muddled her feelings even more. She grabbed her phone – wanted to call him – knew she should not. What would he think if he got a call from her? What would he think of her? She threw it down again. She needed to know that he was okay! Then again, it was too early to call. She'd wait an hour. It'd give her time to calm down before talking to him.

Yes, she would have her breakfast and bath before phoning. She'd call his private number. She remembered he had written it down on the card he gave her. No, perhaps it would be better to phone the station. Would he take her call? In fact, why should he? He would be busy with the cause and reason of the explosion, with no time to talk to her. She's not important during this disaster's investigation. She would only impede their efforts, couldn't throw any light on it. She didn't want to distract him – she'd phone the station. Then again, they might be very busy or on lockdown. What to do? She wracked her brain. Another thing, she also didn't want him to realise that his well-being interested her. Except, if she called the general switchboard, everyone would know that she wanted to speak to him personally. No, calling his private number would be best. Now that the decision was finally made, she set to her morning routine and ran a bath.

Even with her mind set on doing first things first, her body had absorbed her nervousness. A slight tremble in her hands made her spill tea on the countertop. A quick swipe with the dishcloth and refilling her cup, gave her the opportunity to breathe and pull herself together. She went to the bathroom, checked the bathwater, and closed the taps. Not to waste any more time, she returned to the kitchen, sat down for a light breakfast of fruit and tea.

Steam vapoured around her as she emerged from the bathroom, cheeks glowing rosy. She smelled of toothpaste and verbena body oil. With careful consideration, she selected her outfit for the day. If he wanted to see her after her call, she'd be ready.

A rap on the door made her stop midway through dressing. She called out for whoever it could be to wait a minute, rushed to finish. At the door, through the peephole, she saw Mrs Ginet waiting patiently.

'Did you hear the news?' Without preamble or a good morning, Mrs Ginet came straight to the point of her visit.

'*Bonjour, Mme Ginet.* Please come in. How are you?'

'*Ah, oui, bonjour ma chérie.* Did you hear about the explosion at the police station? It was over the radio. Then I put on the TV, and they showed all the pictures. It's terrible, and to think we were there! Do you think it's because of the shooting? We might be next.' She walked right past Alex into the apartment. 'Do you have any coffee?'

'I'll make some, but I do have tea ready in the teapot.'

'Oh, thank you, tea will be fine. I need something. Can we talk?'

'Well, yes, I was going to phone the Detective to find out what happened.'

'Oh dear, do you think they were injured? Such nice detectives. They were so helpful and kind. I hope they're okay.'

'That's why I wanted to phone.'

'Do it now, while I'm here. I want to know if they're still alive.'

'We won't think negatively. Let me phone and find out what is going on.' With that Alex went through to the bedroom to fetch her mobile phone. She got the card with the number and touched the green receiver icon.

'Can you put it so that I can hear what he says?'

'You mean on speaker? Yes, of course.' She touched the appropriate icon. Together they listened to the call going through, with the ringtone on the other side. It didn't take long before the voice mail announcement came on, asking her to leave a message with her number, which she did, and ended the call.

'Why doesn't he answer? If he doesn't answer, he could've been in that explosion. Does that mean he's dead?'

'No! No, Mrs Ginet, it doesn't mean he's dead, he might just be on another call or busy. Let's just wait and give him time to call back. Let's have that tea.'

'Oh, you think so? That's a relief. Good, we'll wait. I wonder if the two nice detectives spoke to Mrs Marx and Dasher?'

'What's that? Why would they speak to her?'

'Well, I saw her walking her dog when that boy was shot.'

'Oh, you're talking about the shooting. I didn't see her. Was she there?'

'Oh yes, I was watching Dasher doing his business and wanted to see if she would pick up after him when it happened. She disappeared very quickly into her building. And she didn't pick up after him! It's an offence, you know.'

'Why didn't you tell the Detectives she might be a witness when we were there?'

'They didn't ask if we saw her! They only wanted to know about the SUV. That's what we went to the station for. You think I should've told them that she left his business right there on the pavement?'

'No, not about that, but they should know about everyone who was in the street at that time. She might have seen the person who shot the young man.'

'Oh, you think so. It's important then?'

'Why wasn't that in your notes?'

'Well, the shooting interrupted me. I simply forgot to note down her offence.'

'I'm not talking about the offence.'

'Oh, you mean that she was there in the street with Dasher?'

'Yes, it's very important. It also gives us a good reason to speak to one of them.' The relief Alex felt had nothing to do with the possibility of a witness to the shooting, only about disguising her real concern.

'You know, Alex, I haven't seen her walking Dasher for the last two or three days – in fact not since the shooting.'

'What do you mean, she hasn't been around? Her routine has always been walking her dog at the same time every day: in the morning and then in the evening.'

'Exactly. Then I saw Jerome with Dasher. You know he doesn't have patience with animals. At least he waited until Dasher did his business, and he picked up after him.'

'Do you think something happened to her?'

'You mean that she also died?'

'Stop that! Why do you say that? Nobody's dead! She might only be off colour, ill, or scared.'

'Well, it must be something serious if she let Jerome look after Dasher. You know she considers him her baby, and Jerome is such a ne'er-do-well.'

'I think it's good of him to help out, whatever problem Mrs Marx has.' She picked up her phone, tried the Detective again. 'Hang on. It's ringing. I'll put it on speaker.'

'Favre,'

'Good morning, Alex Labelle speaking.'

'Good morning, Miss Labelle. I saw you phoned earlier.'

'Yes, two things really. Just to let you know, you are on speaker. Mrs Ginet is here with me.'

'Fine, no problem. You have some information for us?'

'Yes, but firstly, we heard about the explosion, are you okay? And Detective Garcia? What on earth happened?'

'Did anyone die?' Mrs Ginet didn't hide her curiosity.

'I'm fine, thank you. You do realise I cannot give out any information. This is an ongoing investigation.'

'Oh yes, we do, but we needed to make sure that you were not hurt.'

'I was not in the vicinity of the blast. I cannot say anything further.'

'Okay. The reason for this call is also to let you know that Mrs Ginet remembered that one our neighbours, Mrs Marx – in fact, she lives two buildings along from ours – was on the street when the shooting happened.

She was walking her little dog.'

'You mean she could be a witness?'

'Well, yes, definitely as she saw the shooter, Then, grabbed Dasher and hurried off.'

'Dasher is the dog, I take it.'

'Yes, and she never picked up after him! You're supposed to clean up after your pet!' Mrs Ginet's interjection caused a slight pause in the conversation.

'Okay, be that as it may, let us get on with this information. Could you give us her exact address? And tell me exactly what you saw.' Alex could imagine Favre's pen hovering over his notebook.

As Alex gave Mrs Marx's full address, Mrs Ginet echoed it word for word just in case Favre didn't exactly hear the first time.

'We will contact Mrs Marx directly, thank you. It would be necessary for Mrs Ginet to come to the Station to make a revised statement whenever convenient.'

'Oh, I can come this afternoon, detective!'

'That won't be possible as we will be with Mrs Marx. But during the next couple of days would suit best. Thank you, we will be in touch.'

'Thank you, Detective Favre. Have a good day.' Favre had already cut the call before Alex or Mrs Ginet could say another word.

'He put the phone down without saying goodbye.' Either shock or disappointment made Mrs Ginet look enquiringly at Alex.

'Obviously, he is very busy, and now with having to contact Mrs Marx, and basically start all over, must be a bit disappointing for him. Don't worry, all will be well, and we'll get the information about the explosion.'

'At least we know that he is not dead or injured.'

'Obviously.'

'But what about that lovely other one, Garcia?'

'He couldn't say, so we should leave it at that.' Alex poured Mrs Ginet another cup of tea. She pushed some biscuits towards her hoping that her curiosity would abate, at least for the day.

*

Exhaustion seeped from every pore of Paul Favre. The evening before's events had rattled him. Very unlike him to be so unhinged. He could still feel the impact that had lifted Garcia's car a metre off the ground. His mind went back to that moment.

*

None of them could believe what had just happened. It took them a few seconds to recover and react. The duty officer immediately phoned the Fire Department and Ambulance. The others rushed out to assess the damage and help whoever needed help.

'*Mon Dieu! Ce n'est pas possible!* No, no, this can't be happening!' Favre shouted into the room. Without regard for himself he ran to the site and found Garcia bloodied and unconscious, half under the car next to his destroyed vehicle. He was bleeding from his ears and eyes. Paul bent down over Jose's body but couldn't detect any breathing.

'Where's that ambulance?' he shouted over his shoulder. 'Garcia, Garcia, wake up, look at me, I'm here mate. Help's on its way. Hang in there, old man.' Favre desperately tried to get his partner to respond but got no reaction from the inert form. Frantic, he groped for a pulse; placed two fingers against his partner's throat. He felt a faint throb. That meant hope. He breathed out with relief. He patted the body to see if there were any obvious broken bones but couldn't find any. The danger of internal bleeding from the blast could decide the fate of Garcia. To save his life, he needed medical attention immediately.

The deafening whoop and wail of sirens pushed everything else out of his consciousness. Very quickly the area around the station teemed with First Responders. Medics rushed over to where Garcia lay, while firemen tended to others with minor cuts and bruises. Soon Garcia was lifted into the Ambulance, which sped off, sirens blaring, to the University Hospital of the Canton of Geneva.

Favre followed, and on the way brought their superintendent, Captain Leonard, up to date by phone. They arrived at the hospital's emergency department at the same time, demanding a progress report. The nurse in charge told them to wait as Garcia was rushed to the operating theatre for emergency surgery. It would take a while, but they could go to the main waiting area, and will be called when information was available. Obviously, this didn't sit well with the superintendent, who told her in no uncertain terms who he was, and the power he had. But no headway could be made with the charge nurse, who had authority over all – this was her domain, and she could not be shaken. Not in a position to argue any further, both men reluctantly retreated to the waiting area where they were joined by other colleagues.

'Have you contacted his wife, or would you prefer that I do? I believe you know her quite well,' Favre's superior asked as they settled in for the wait.

Favre slapped his head as he suddenly realised that they had another serious problem. In the confusion of the events, he had completely forgotten about Phillippe, Garcia's son.

'Oh no! It slipped my mind! Garcia was on his way to her when his car exploded. She called to say that their son was missing, probably taken.'

'What? Why do they think he was taken?'

'They received a threatening phone call at home and thought it best she left town with the children to an undisclosed location.'

'Why wasn't I told? Who's on it?'

'Well, no one as yet. We didn't have time to advise anyone. Apparently, he was playing basket with some friends, when a man called him over and he left with this bloke. We don't know any more. Garcia was going to speak to these friends for more information.'

'I see. Get hold of Bachelet from Missing Persons. Tell him to get on it immediately. He's our best man for this.'

'Only one problem, she was in hiding. All I know is that she's somewhere in Vaud with the children.'

'Where's his phone, surely we can get the info from there.'

'It was smashed in the blast.'

'Send it over to Tech. they could most probably pull the info off it. Ask them to trace where her call came from.'

'No, wait. Yes, I mean that would help, except I just realised when she phoned, it was on the landline directly to his extension.'

'That means we have the number she called from.'

'Yes, I'll get tech to do both and pinpoint her location. Perhaps she still has her phone on – I'm sure she wouldn't switch off; in case he calls.'

'Try her number you have in the meantime. I would imagine she kept her original phone.'

'I'll get Bachelet first; then I'll tell her to expect him. She'll want to be here. What do I say to her?'

'Convince her that her husband is in good hands and that we will stay with him and keep her informed. Her priority, now, is to find her son. Tell her our best man will be there to help find the boy.' Leonard shook his head.

'My God, Favre, it's amazing that he is in one piece! How come we didn't scrape pieces of him from all over the parking lot?'

'Well, Sir, I watched him, and he hadn't closed the car door completely when the blast happened.' Both men looked at each other. 'Perhaps that's what saved his life?'

It took Favre only ten minutes to organise the Missing Persons section to take the case, with the request of being kept informed of each step. Then he made the call to Maria, which ended up in hysterical tears on the other end. A lot of crying, then screaming, and again crying, which changed into blaming, some more crying which ended in worrying, came towards Paul. It took a long time to calm her down and get the information through about Detective Bachelet's arrival. Finally, she understood and accepted that Favre would not leave Garcia's side until Phillippe was found, and she and the children could be at her husband's bedside in person.

With everything arranged, nothing more could be done. Alternatively between jumping up, pacing, and sitting to await news, both Favre and his superior were anxious for information, which seemed to take an eternity to arrive. Three hours after their arrival, a doctor made an appearance. Everyone jumped up simultaneously asking the same questions. 'What's the news? How's Garcia?'

'Touch and go. We can't say more than that for now. He came through the surgery. Unfortunately, he arrested twice - massive internal bleeding and damage to his spleen and liver. We managed to save the greater part of the liver and hope the rest will rejuvenate, but we had to remove the spleen. His lungs were also damaged, but we don't think there will be a problem. It's amazing that he actually made it so far. However, keep hoping, that's all we have at this moment.' With that, the doctor turned to go but a chorus stopped him.

'Can we see him?'

'Not yet, he's in ICU. We expect in about an hour you may go in to see him, but one at a time. He won't be awake, but at least you can see him, and talk to him. Everything will help at this moment to make sure he fights. He needs to fight. I have to go, will keep you informed.'

'Thank you, Doctor.' Again, said in unison, as they watched him leave and together turned back to the seating arrangement.

'Favre, I'll wait here with you until we can go in to see him. Once I've seen him, I'll leave to brief the Federal Police. I presume the Duty Officer followed protocol and that a High Alert has been issued. They'll most probably check all the Diplomatic and UN buildings.' Leonard scratched his head. 'Be prepared to hand over whatever you've been working on.'

'No! Then the investigation will be out of our hands.'

'We have no choice. Any car bomb is regarded as a possible act of terrorism, and once they've ruled that out, they look at the criminal aspect.'

'I highly doubt this is terrorism, I am sure it's connected to our case. We have both been warned repeatedly.'

'You began to tell me about it. You didn't mention that both of you received warnings. So, I want to know why I wasn't informed? You do realise that is a serious breach of protocol? All threats, no matter how vague or minor must be reported and logged. These don't sound minor to me.'

'Yes, Sir, at first, we thought it was a prank as both calls were to our private home numbers concerning a case. There were no specifics. I mean, none to which case they referred to. Then, we have just been so overrun with details, or the lack thereof, on the shooting in Paquis, that it slipped our minds.'

'Okay, I understand that. Still, all threats should be taken seriously, I should have been brought into the loop. Let's presume the warnings were about the shooting, who do you think was behind them?'

'We've not been able to find out where the calls originated from. We've also had trouble locating witnesses to steer us in the right direction. Therefore, the threats could've been connected to some other crime.

'Be that as it may, you'll have to log everything. The Federal Police will have to be informed of the threats, what they'll do with it, is anyone's guess. I'll oversee the investigation of the explosion from our side, and the disappearance of Garcia's son.' He turned toward the other officers in the room.

'Did any of you receive any threats?' He looked at each in turn, everyone shook their head and murmured in the negative. 'Fine, the rest of you should go back to your posts or go home and get some rest. We're going to have a difficult day tomorrow.

'I want to be in on this.' Favre looked his superior squarely in the eyes, daring him to refuse the request.

'That'll be up to the FP. As far as I'm concerned, you will be. First, we need to make sure your partner knows that you are there for him, handling his son's disappearance, and have not abandoned your current investigation. Further, I need you to re-examine all the information on this current case. We should not jump to conclusions that these events are connected. We cannot minimise their importance or, discard them either. The possibility exists, that it could be terrorism.'

'Yes, sir, I agree. The disappearance of Garcia's son is suspect, and then the explosion seems just too convenient to be true. While we wait, I'll pop over to the station and get the file and our notes. I can look over everything as I sit at his bedside.'

'Good idea. If you need fresh eyes on it, let me know.'

'At this moment, we're still sorting a lot of information and possible clues.'

'Fine, go now, rest assured I'll be here until you get back.'

The station was on lockdown. The bomb squad had arrived. Fire trucks surrounded the building. Favre was told a secondary device might be in one of the other vehicles, they were taking necessary precautions. He looked for familiar faces, yet the uniformed officers sorting through the rubble, were unknown to him. With some persuasion, Paul managed to get inside, retrieved the file with his notes, before he rushed back to the hospital.

'Any news?'

'Actually, the charge nurse came a minute ago to say that we could see him. She mentioned that he was showing signs of stabilising. Though, she put her foot down, yes, again, ONLY ONE AT A TIME can go in to see him.'

'Yes, I can just imagine. She scares the daylights out of me!'

'She definitely has the knack of making you feel like a clumsy schoolboy. Whenever my School Principal spoke it came over in CAPITAL LETTERS, and this woman has the same ability! They don't shout, it's just the way they manage to say things with force.'

'Well, we won't cross her. She is really scary! You go in first, sir. I'll stand vigil through the night and give you regular updates.'

'Good night then Favre, and if I hear anything, I'll let you know.'

Later, Paul had listened to the rhythmic beep of the machines his partner was hooked up to as he perused the paperwork. At six in the morning, a change in the machine's regular sound made him jump up and press the call button. He tried to collect the paperwork, which he had spread out on every surface possible, as well as on the foot of the bed.

A nurse came in, catching Paul with half the papers still all over the place, the other half haphazardly held against his chest. She checked Garcia's vitals, adjusted the machines, checked the drip, and advised the doctor would be in presently.

'What's going on?' Favre insisted.

'You'll have to wait for Doctor.'

Garcia showed signs of agitation. His eyelids fluttered, he tossed, turned his head from side to side and flailed his arms.

'Is he waking up?'

'Please leave, let us do our jobs.' The doctor said as he hurried in adjusting his stethoscope. 'Leave now, please.'

Reluctantly, Paul moved away, far enough not to be in the way. All he could do was watch the medical staff tend to his partner. The doctor listened to Garcia's heartbeat, his lungs, and shone a light in his eyes as he lifted one eyelid after the other. Garcia's pupils reacted. With visible relief, the staff settled into doing a thorough examination. The doctor gave treatment instructions to the nurses, turned towards Favre.

Favre's phone rang, He ignored it, paying attention to what the doctor had to say.

'His internal injuries are severe, and he'll need time to recover. I've decided to put him in an induced coma to help the healing process.'

'For how long?'

'That depends, but for the moment at least one day. After that we'll see how he responds. His body needs rest, and agitation is contrary to this. Now if you would excuse me, I have other patients to attend to.'

'Thank you, Doctor.' For a moment Favre felt completely at a loss as he watched him go. Why did this happen? Where to begin? What will he find behind it all?

During the night he had matched certain earlier photo printouts and thought they had a starting point. However, looking at the inert body of José, he doubted his previous findings. He'd have to go back and look at them from a different angle. At that moment, his phone rang again, this time he took the call.

'Favre speaking.' He heard the greeting of Miss Labelle saying she's with Mrs Ginet and that she's putting him on speaker.

Panic had long since turned into a state of constant hysteria. Where was José? He was supposed to be here last night. Maria's inability to reach José drove her to distraction. Perhaps she overreacted? Phillippe knew she was going to collect him. So, why wasn't he there? Why did he leave with a man? They were taught never to talk to strangers and never, ever go with someone they didn't know. Maybe it was something simple, or a misunderstanding. He could've forgotten that she was to pick him up. Then again, if he just lost track of time, why didn't he come home? If he wasn't taken, something must have happened. No, this was wrong! These things didn't happen to them. However, what about that phone call warning them. Does this have to do with that? Did they find where she and the children went to hide?

Where was José? For heaven's sake, their son was missing, and he's not answering her calls. His absence annoyed her. Again, the blame fell on his job. It wasn't the first time he'd let her and the family down. His lack of concern for his son was unacceptable. Her mind went in circles, and her agitation rose as the minutes passed.

The phone broke in on Maria thoughts. Paul's voice annoyed her even more – why didn't José call? Immediately, she reproached them both for not taking the kidnapping of her son seriously. It took time before she registered that a detective Bachelet of the Missing Persons Division would be arriving to look for Phillippe. Then, as if a bucket of ice water was thrown over her, she heard him say that José had been injured in an explosion and taken to hospital. For a moment, she couldn't find her voice, then incredulity set in. She asked him to repeat what he had said. No way could that be true, she had just spoken to him earlier – no, it was nearly four hours ago.

She didn't know what to do, where to be: her son was missing, her husband fighting for his life in hospital. Paul said he'd stay with José and give her updates as and when the doctors gave them news. As she finished her call, still completely confused, detective Bachelet added to her distress by calling to say he'll only be with her around eight in the morning. Further, could she in the meantime, find the boys' names and contact numbers who were with her son at the time of his disappearance?

From her sister-in-law's guest room, her two other children came running, asking what was going on, whether she had found their brother, and why didn't their father phone them as he usually did. Unable to control her emotions at that moment, she turned and rushed to the bathroom with a mumbled, "sorry". Her sister-in-law, Lena, stepped into the fray and replied to the children's questions in a typical vague parental way, which seemed to satisfy them as they rushed back to play video games.

'Maria?' Lena whispered through the bathroom door. 'Are you okay? What can I do? What's happening? Was that call about Phillippe? Where is José?'

'Are the children gone?' Maria stammered through sobs.

'Yes, they're safely in the room playing video games.'

'Oh Lena, you've got no idea. Everything is wrong!' With that, Maria opened the door and told her that José was clinging to life after an explosion and that someone, whom she had never met, will be coming to look for Phillippe, who's missing.

'Does that have anything to do with why you're hiding out here with me?'

'They warned me that they'll cut our throats.'

'What do you mean? Who warned you? When did this happen? Oh gosh, I've so many questions. You'll have to explain. Tell me everything.'

'I can't. José said not to discuss it with anyone. It could put you in danger as well.'

'Too late for that, I think. You being here has done that already.'

'Oh no! I never thought they'd find us.'

'Okay, let's see. We must deal with this. Do you think Phillippe's disappearance has anything to do with the warning or the case José is working on?'

'Maybe. No. Oh, I don't know. I suppose everything's possible.'

'Well, let's see what happens when this detective arrives tomorrow morning, then you can go back, and see José in the hospital. I'll stay here and oversee the children. I'll keep you up to date with the progress the detective makes. Now, let's get everything you could think of which he might want.'

'I have a photo of Phillippe which we should copy; here are some of the names of the boys he was with. I don't know them all.'

'Well, it's a start. If this detective is as good as José's partner says he

114

is, he'll find all other relevant information himself.'

'Thank you, you made me feel better. Unfortunately, I can't stop being worried.'

CHAPTER SEVEN

They had made a big mistake in dismissing the warnings and underestimating him. The warnings couldn't have been clearer. Last night proved it.

Alpha had made all the arrangements for the next step. He gave his foot soldiers one last task, which he hoped they would execute perfectly. Their ability to complete his demands would determine the country to which they would be banished. He chose to ignore the Boss's request, exporting them rather than permanently getting rid of them. They might come in handy when the time came to take over. Now, he only had to wait for everything to fall in place.

Yesterday, Alpha had taken his chosen spot at the tram stop for the Servette Police Station. He waited there – direction downtown, facing the police station. He portrayed the usual commuter. A tram arrived, stopped then pulled away. Alpha remained without moving. No one took any notice. He didn't expect anything to happen immediately but knew it would within the next thirty minutes. He lit a cigarette.

It had not taken thirty minutes.

Exactly twelve minutes later, an explosion rocked the building which housed the police station, and the air thumped his ears. A millisecond later, everyone heard the deafening blast.

Time stood still for a minute.

The noise settled.

A couple of car alarms screamed, and the station broke out in activity. Sirens went off, and three minutes later, the Fire Department's wail punched the air. Alpha watched as a red fire truck came as if from nowhere and sped down Route de Meyrin to the site. Seconds later, a 144 ambulance and two medical assistance vehicles arrived. Officers spilled onto the pavement, looking up and down the street for anything suspicious. Others moved along both directions of the building blocking off the area with crime tape.

Still, Alpha didn't move. Pedestrians joined him to watch the commotion. A tram arrived, stopped, then pulled away. Bystanders remained gawking. An officer came over to collect names and contact information of possible witnesses. Needless to say, no one saw anything. Alpha gave his name as Jean Jonas, a common name.

'What happened, Officer?' Alpha couldn't resist.

'Please, clear the area. Please go home, there is nothing to see.'

'But Officer, was it a bomb?' An elderly lady joined Alpha in demanding information.

'We have no information at present. Please move along. Do not stay here. You are restricting our work and the work of our colleagues,' the officer insisted.

'But I'm waiting for the tram.' A young man chipped in.

'Sorry, public transport on this line has been interrupted for the rest of the day between the previous and the next stop. Please go down to the stop at the corner of Route de Meyrin/Rue de la Servette and Ave Wendt/Rue Hoffman. From there, you can find alternate transport. For the time being, this stop is closed.' The officer ignored everyone's grumbles. 'Thank you and good day. Now move along!'

Alpha hovered for a moment longer. With a nod of satisfaction, he turned and walked away. He checked his mobile phone. No messages. So far, so good. Now let's see if they'd heed these warnings and get out of the way. This little bang should do it.

Before going home, he made a stop in Paquis to pick up some company. Satisfaction mellowed him further. After kicking out the prostitute, he fell asleep quickly – his other plans on the back burner for the day. He wanted to revel in this last success.

Now, after a deep, uninterrupted sleep, he had woken early, full of energy. That's what it feels like when a job is well done, he thought. With a coffee in hand, he switched on his computer. It took a moment for him to get on the internet. He called up the *Tribune de Genève* website. Disappointingly, the story featured third in importance with vague references to the cause, number of fatalities, and injuries. Typically, of the Swiss, they downplay any act which could be regarded as terrorism or even real crime. They refuse to give the media the names of those involved or any undue attention, to avoid notoriety or to create martyrs.

'Well, they will know about me one way or another,' he told himself.

*

'Detective! Good morning, you look rough. Have you've been home?' the duty officer asked Paul as he picked his way through the various cartons, cases, and obstacles the forensic team had set up for their evidence collection.

'What's all this? Clear the area, please.'

'It's Forensic, they needed space indoors.'

'When will these guys be finished? We need to work.' Paul ignored the officer's initial question. He suspected his day-old growth and crumpled suit told it all.

'Soon, they're packing up now.'

'Good, get rid of them as soon as possible.'

'I'll bring you some coffee.'

'I'll get my own coffee, thank you.'

Paul's irritation stemmed not only from lack of sleep, but concern over José's condition, and the call from Miss Labelle. He found it frustrating that evidence and witnesses in the current case were so elusive. If only they had all the information from the beginning, they might have been further along. This Mrs Marx needed to be brought in immediately, and they had to ascertain why she never came forward.

On the way to his desk, he put a Nespresso capsule in the machine and waited for the cup to fill. His mind wandered to Miss Labelle and Mrs Ginet. They seemed to be a mine of information without even knowing it. Before completely in his chair, he picked up the phone and requested Uniforms to find Mrs Marx and bring her in without delay for questioning.

His next call was to Maria, informing her of her husband's condition: no significant changes since he had been put in an induced coma. He assured her that there was nothing she could do besides watching him sleep. It would be best if she concentrated on finding her son. Tearful and scared, she stammered she had had to tell her brother and sister-in-law of the threats. Paul marvelled at how José managed to keep his volatile wife calm. So, he changed tactics and asked for news from her side. The information was scant as Bachelet had arrived at her brother's home only half-an-hour earlier, and she was still giving him the little detail she had. With Bachelet, a law enforcement officer, she wanted permission to tell him about the threats.

'Yes, Maria, you can tell him everything. I have informed Leonard, so the Department knows that we had received numerous threats which have to be dealt with. Don't you worry, it is all in hand, and we are going to get through this in one piece.' Still tearful, Maria thanked him. They ended the call with mutual reassurances of continuous contact.

While waiting for Mrs Marx, Favre shuffled through all the papers which he had collected in haste at the hospital, re-organising the information. It took another thirty minutes before the uniformed officers arrived with the diminutive Mrs Marx and waited at the entrance of the bullpen.

One of the officers came to Paul's desk and advised they had trouble getting her to come in, as they found her in a terrified state.

His colleague took her to interview room two. With that in mind, he requested a female Detective, Dominique Bender, to join them there. They found Mrs Marx trembling, her eyes darted in all directions.

'Good morning, Mrs Marx, could we get you some coffee?' She nodded, evading his eyes. Favre signalled to the officer, who left to get the coffee. Both he and Bender pulled out chairs and sat down at the table.

'What's this? Why am I here?'

'Mrs Marx, there is nothing to worry about. Only a few questions. It has come to our attention that you were witness to the shooting in Paquis. Apparently, you were seen walking your dog at the time.' Paul said as gently as he could.

'Who told you that? I saw nothing!' Her fear rose to terror.

'You are completely safe here. I repeat, there's nothing to worry about.'

'Perhaps, but when I go home, I won't be.'

'What do you mean? Did someone threaten you?'

'They didn't have to. I could see it in his eyes.'

'So, you saw the person who shot the young man.'

'I'm not saying anything anymore. I want to go home.'

'We understand you haven't left your apartment since the shooting. Why is that?'

'My sister's grandson, Stephen, lives with me, and he said it wasn't safe. He has been helping me and walking Dasher.'

'Why does he think it's not safe? Does he know something about the shooting?'

'No, he doesn't, but he's sure they have been watching the street.'

'Did he see someone watching the street?'

'He said there is a black car with two men. Also, another man asked him about Dasher and who he belonged to.' The coffee came in, and with a trembling hand, she brought the cup to her mouth. Favre gave her a moment to calm.

'Well, *Madame,* you can rest assured that you are now safe. We have those two men in custody. They won't be bothering you or, anyone on that street again for a very long time.'

'Good. What about what I saw?'

'That's what we would like to talk to you about. Do you think you could tell us exactly what happened and describe the person who had the gun and shot the boy?' Mrs Marx began trembling violently again.

Bender put her hand out to the old woman. 'Don't worry, you are safe here. You can tell us, and we will have another policeman keeping you secure.' For the first time Mrs Marx looked either of them straight in the eye.

'Really? You sure Dasher and I will be safe?'

'Yes, really.' Bender's reassurance hit home.

'*D'accord.* I was walking Dasher when this car came down the street and stopped. I wondered if it was my neighbour's son arriving, but a man got out. Then the car slowly moved off again. As it rolled away, this man, the one that got out, lifted his hand, and I saw he was holding something.'

'You're doing very well, Mrs Marx. What happened next?' Paul gently coaxed her.

'Before I could do anything, a flash came from his hand and a shot rang out. I didn't even see the boy fall down. I just saw the man. Then he saw me. He looked straight at me and turned his aim towards me. I grabbed Dasher and left as fast as I could. You know, I'm not that young anymore and move slower than I wanted to. He didn't shoot me. I don't know why. I think he liked it more that I am afraid than dead.'

'I think you are right. He seems to be a real psychopath – wanting people to be afraid of what he could do to them, rather than afraid of him.' Paul Favre paused. 'Now, could you perhaps describe him?'

'I'll never forget him. You see, it's his eyes. They're blue. I always like blue eyes, but his were like ice and piercing right through me.'

'Good, blue eyes. Now, was he tall or short? Thin or fat? What colour was his hair?'

'He was about the same as Stephen, except his hair was very blond where Stephen's is brown.' Mrs Marx seemed to have found her confidence and rhythm. 'Stephen is such a nice boy, helping me like that. He said he would come with me to see you if I wanted to, but when you came, he was out doing the shopping.'

'That's good, we'll talk to him later.'

'A man stopped him, asking about Dasher.'

'We'll see what he has to say about the man who asked questions about your dog.'

'But it wasn't the same man who did the shooting!' she insisted.

'Really? Okay, what else can you tell us about the shooter? For instance, what he was wearing? Could you see if he had any tattoos or distinguishing marks? Did you see in which direction he went, after he shot the boy? '

'You ask so many questions!' Mrs Marx became flustered but continued. 'I did look over my shoulder to see if he followed me. Luckily, he was gone. He either went into the side street or into one of the buildings. Though, I don't think he would do that because we all know one another here.'

'So, let's go back to what he was wearing.'

'He had a white t-shirt and khaki long pants.'

'The t-shirt had short sleeves, I suppose. Could you see his arms?'

'Oh yes! He was quite tanned. It contrasted with his very blond hair. And he did have a tattoo on his arm, two in fact: one on his biceps, half covered by the sleeve, and the other on his forearm. The one on the forearm looked like an eagle or something.' She blushed. 'I notice these things as Stephen wants tattoos and I don't like them.'

'You've been very helpful, Mrs Marx. Do you think you could sit down with our sketch artist to give us an idea of what he looks like?'

'I'll try my best. Will I then be able to go home?'

'Oh, just one other thing; can you remember what kind of car the man got out of?'

'Like what?'

'Like the colour, the make, the registration number. Was it a new car or an old one?'

'I'm not very good with cars, but it was very similar to the car Stephen's father drives. He can tell you. Only the colour was black, and Stephen's father's is silver.'

'And did you perhaps see the registration plate?'

'It was a Geneva plate and had two sixes and a three in it, but I can't remember the whole number. I'm sorry, it happened so quickly. But I remember those numbers as I always add the numbers on car plates to keep my mind active. You know, they say you must exercise your mind to avoid Alzheimer's disease. But this time I was distracted by the shooting and couldn't finish adding all the numbers.'

'It is a good practice you have. Thank you. It gives us something to work on. We'll ask Stephen about the make and model of his father's car. Thank you again.'

'Is that all then? Are you sure we'll be safe?'

'Yes, and we will give you a protective detail to take you home, then ask Stephen to come in. Will that be okay with you?'

'Will the officer be with me all the time?'

'He will walk you to your door and make sure that your apartment is secure. Then he will join the other officers we have placed in your street. They are in an unmarked car. Does that set your mind at rest?'

'Yes, a little. Thank you. Can I go now?'

'Yes, as soon as you have described the man to the police sketch artist.'

'Oh yes. Okay, where is he?'

They all got up, and Detective Bender accompanied Mrs Marx to meet with the artist. Paul couldn't get back to his desk fast enough to combine this new information with what they already had. He only hoped that the sketch would give them enough to run through facial recognition software. It might not be exact but at least give them some potential suspects. For Favre, at least a picture began to emerge. The shooter leaving the vehicle definitely had an important role, and he looked again at the photo printouts, this time with more interest. He missed discussing everything he had just learnt with his partner. Well, he'd need patience for that, and in the meantime do as much as possible.

The phone rang. The duty officer advised that a Mr Stephen Jacobson had arrived and asked for him. Elated, Favre requested he be brought to the same interview room. Without a moment to lose, he jumped up and was at the door waiting.

'Mr Stephen Jacobson? The grandson of Mrs Marx's sister?'

'Yes, that's me.'

'Good morning, Detective Favre.' Paul held out his hand in greeting. 'I am pleased to meet you, let's sit down and have some coffee as we chat.'

'Good morning, how do you do. Yes, a coffee will be great, thank you. I don't really know what my Great-Aunt told you, but I didn't see anything. I wasn't even there when it happened. So, why is it you want to speak to me?'

'Well, there are a couple of things that we think you might be able to clear up for us. Your Great-Aunt gave us a lot of information. Unfortunately, lacking detail.'

'What do you mean, lacking detail? As I said, I wasn't there and never saw anything.'

'We understand that, but she compared certain aspects of what she saw with you and what you know.'

'I still don't understand how I could help.'

'Okay, let's begin with: how tall are you and how much do you weigh?'

'What's that got to do with anything? Are you suggesting that I had something to do with the shooting? Do I need a lawyer?'

'Oh, definitely not! Sorry to make you uncomfortable. It's only that your Great-Aunt described the shooter as the same size as you.'

'That's a relief, I thought I was in real trouble here!'

'Could you give us your details, please?'

'Of course; I'm 1.85m and weigh 98kg.'

'Good, so I'd say tall and muscular. In other words: slender, but athletic and well-built.'

'Yes, I suppose if you say so. I work out, you know.'

'Then, the other detail you could help us with is the make and model of your father's car. Mrs Marx described the vehicle that left the scene as the same as your father's. Except, that it was black. Could you help us with that, please?'

'Oh, definitely, he has a 2015 Honda CRV. Is that all?'

'No not really. Perhaps she said something else to you about what happened?'

'No, not that I can recall. Although she was so terrified, she wouldn't leave the apartment at all. I had to take over walking the dog, as well as doing the shopping.'

'Then the other thing. Apparently, a man approached you asking questions about Dasher, your Great-Aunt's dog.'

'Oh yes, that's right, I thought it strange. A stranger on foot asked me about Dasher. Also, I saw a SUV parked on the street a few times while walking the dog. It seemed not to have moved from the same place for a couple of days.'

'This man on foot, did he ask specific questions?'

'He mainly wanted to know about Dasher and if he belonged to me. When I said no, he belonged to my Great-Aunt, he seemed interested in knowing how to contact her. When I asked why, he said that he liked the breed and would like more information on them.'

'Did you give him anything?'

'Well, no. At that moment, some traffic police showed up a little further along and he said that we'll talk again.'

'Did you see him again?'

'No. Later on, when I walked Dasher again, the car wasn't there. Do you think he was connected go those in the SUV?'

'We are not sure. But we picked up those two gents in the car. They're here under caution. In fact, we've replaced their vigil with our own. There is a police presence in your street, and it will remain there until we're certain that we have apprehended all the suspects.'

'That's a real relief. My Great-Aunt can't take much more of this tension. She's scared out of her mind,'

'I believe that. She seemed really rattled. Perhaps she'll calm down now. The main thing is that you gave no information to that man; therefore, they had nothing to report back. You will all be safe now, although we think, to be prudent, she shouldn't venture out alone. So, it'll be best if you still take Dasher for his walks and accompany her on shopping trips and other visits. You can take her and collect her, but please don't leave her on her own in the street, especially not when Dasher is there.'

'Why can't she accompany me on Dasher's walks?'

'Well, Dasher is the one known item the killer has and if he connects Dasher to her, she might be followed and in danger.'

'I see. No problem. She's an interesting person with many stories to tell. She has lived an eventful life, so I can put up with the situation. Dasher is also a well-behaved little dog.'

'As I said, there will be a police presence nearby – unobtrusive that is, however, there at all times, which you will be able to call on if needed.'

'Thank you. You know where you can contact me if necessary. Goodbye and have a good day.'

'Thanks again for coming in. We'll be in touch. Have a good day.'

Paul immediately returned to his desk where he found the sketch artist likeness as given by Mrs Marx. He moved over to Garcia's desk, fired up the computer, and scanned the sketch, added the physical description of the man according to Stephen. He pressed the enter key and, while he waited, went on his own computer to match up all 2013 to 2015 black Honda CRVs with registration containing two sixes and a three. His search yielded four over the period. He printed out the list matched with owners and their contact details. He thumped the desk with satisfaction. They're getting somewhere. His eagerness to share what came to light with José made him forget his exhaustion. He couldn't wait for José to come out of his coma. This was good news.

*

Alex still felt slighted by Detective Favre's abrupt ending of her call. He sounded cold, not at all as amicable as before. She thought he would at least be appreciative that she called with information of a potential witness. Except, he hardly reacted. He didn't even say goodbye, just put the phone down. It put a damper on her day. She couldn't shake her disappointment, even with a brisk walk along the lake. Yoga didn't help either.

She rebuked herself for feeling like this. Why he had this reaction on her was quite unsettling. It clearly made her act like a stupid schoolgirl in his presence. Sure, its roots lay deeper than the experience with Denis. Although she admitted what she had lived through with her old flame, certainly made her wary of men and reticent of going into any relationship. She became distrustful. Only there was more to it.

With Detective Favre around, a strange panic crept in as well. She didn't want it to; she liked him and maybe even trusted him. However, she knew that her deep-seated panic which bordered on terror, came from much further back.

Memories at the root of her fear needed to be pushed even further into the background. She wanted to forget that time of her life: dark days, fearful nights, and uncertain moments. Her family's attitude towards her – someone to be tolerated, but invisible most of the time – forced her to hide behind a mask of self-sufficiency. In fact, it became her coat of armour. This armour enabled her to cope with that terribly toxic time. Yes, that was the best way to describe it: toxic. It poisoned the essence of her soul, tainted every cell in her body. Unless she has a complete purge or essence transfusion, some of that toxicity will always be there to remind her. She hated the power it had over her.

She shook off her emotions; they were counterproductive – getting her nowhere.

Afternoon had already settled in, and her mood hadn't improved. For that reason, when her phone rang, she wanted to ignore it, yet reluctantly answered. She hoped her lack lustre '*Bonjour*' would put any caller off, especially if it's a telemarketer. At the sound of the voice responding to her greeting, her eyes popped wide open, and she pulled back her shoulders.

'*Detective Favre?*' She stammered. '*Nice of you to call, how can I help you?*'

'*Yes, sorry Miss Labelle, I only wanted to call to apologise for being abrupt this morning and, of course to thank you for pointing us in the direction of Mrs Marx.*'

'*Oh, but that wasn't me. Mrs Ginet remembered seeing her walking her dog at the time of the shooting.*'

'*In any event, we need to thank you and Mrs Ginet. I apologise again, I was exhausted. Detective Garcia was seriously injured yesterday, and I spent the whole night at the hospital.*'

'*I'm so sorry. Will he be all right?*'

'*We hope so. He's in an induced coma for today.*'

'*Please wish him well when you see him.*'

'*Will do. Thank you for your concern. The other thing I would like to ask is regarding what you personally saw. You remembered seeing a person walking away. If we show you the sketch made up from the description given by Mrs Marx, do you think you might recognise him as the person you saw?*'

'*Well as I said, it was so fleeting and only from the corner of my eye.*'

'*But you would be prepared to look? It may be confirmation. Not that we really need it, but it'll strengthen our case.*'

'*Do you know who the man is?*'

'*I'm still waiting for facial recognition to give us some information.*'

So, if I may, would you be prepared to come in or, do you prefer me to pass by your apartment.'

'Oh?'

'I mean, it's on my way home. It won't take a minute and save you time and effort coming all the way to Servette.'

'That'll be fine. You have my address, don't you?'

'Yes, no problem. I'm leaving early today. I need to get home and freshen up. If I leave right away; I could be with you in about ten to fifteen minutes.'

'Okay, will you have a moment to have coffee?' She decided to make an extra effort to make him feel at home.

'That'll be great, I need as much help as possible to keep going.'

*

It took Paul the ten minutes he had estimated to reach Paquis, but finding a parking spot, took another ten. He walked the twenty metres back to the appropriate street number and punched in the security code to Alex's building. Earlier when he spoke to her, he preferred to omit explaining that if she came to the station, she would see the destruction caused by the explosion. There was no need to scare her. He had to gain her confidence.

In front of her door, Paul combed his hair with his fingers, smoothed out his jacket, hoping to improve his appearance. He took a deep breath and rang Miss Labelle's doorbell. He glanced in the direction of Mrs Ginet's apartment next door, sighed. He couldn't hear any movement from there, and relief flooded him. His state of exhaustion could not withstand the energy of the intrepid Mrs Ginet. Yet, he refused to admit that his motive could be something else. No, he needed to show her the sketch, that was all. Further he convinced himself that it would be more likely that she would open up if they were alone. And it won't be so bad to spend a moment alone with Miss Labelle. He heard the bell echo in the apartment.

Alex opened the door virtually immediately. 'Hello! Do come in.' She stepped aside, allowing him to enter her domain. Everything changed for Paul. As if he walked into a cool, harmonious bubble. He suddenly felt calm and refreshed. He immediately relaxed and felt how his exhaustion cloaked him.

'Good to see you, Miss Labelle.'

'Please, call me Alex and take a seat.'

'Thank you, Alex. You're very kind. Please, call me Paul. There's such a calm energy here. How do you manage to maintain that sense of harmony in the middle of Geneva?'

'Thank you. I'm not sure, I don't always feel calm. I use colour which helps to create a mellow atmosphere. We need all the help we can get, don't we? Life is, in general, a challenge. I suppose it could also be because I feel the need to meditate as often as possible to chase away demons.'

'Demons? You have demons?'

'Doesn't everyone? We all have something that's haunting our daily existence. I believe it only depends how we deal with it which gives it the power to take control over our lives. Our perception of the problem allows us to accept it for what it is, and that makes it easier to cope.'

'But you showed a lot of fear or rather discomfort during our interview at the station.'

'Well, as I said we all have our demons.'

'Though, you now seem more confident, or shall I say, relaxed in my presence, I'm happy to say.' He looked around the apartment. His eye caught two bookcases filled with neatly arranged books covering the far wall, personal touches of photos, paintings, and ornaments – nothing overdone. He found it stylish and comfortable at the same time. 'Perhaps it's because I personally feel relaxed here. Or because we are not in the authoritative atmosphere of the police station.' Paul realised that he rambled trying to explain his own feelings.

'I'm pleased you feel you can relax here.' She indicated for him to take a seat. 'Let me get the coffee. I did promise coffee, didn't I?'

'That'd be great, thank you. Do you mind if I take off my jacket? This heatwave doesn't seem to abate.'

'Not at all, make yourself comfortable.'

As she disappeared into the kitchen, he perused the surroundings further. He noticed the books ranged from biographies to popular novelists with various books on poetry and Astro-archaeology. Very few of the photos displayed contained people, and he presumed those which did, were of family. Most photos were of animals or landscapes, many of the latter taken either at sunrise or sunset. They were all excellent – clear that the photographer had a good eye for compilation. The paintings also created interest as to their provenance. His curiosity peaked – who and exactly what, made up Miss Labelle? He could see her reach for a tray through the serving hatch which connected the kitchen with the living room. She returned with the coffee and a plate of biscuits.

'Oh, thank you, seeing those biscuits I realise that I've not eaten since yesterday! Unless numerous cups of coffee count as nourishment.'

'Gosh Paul, let me make you an omelette. It won't take long.' She placed the tray on the coffee table in front of him.

'Oh, sorry, that was not my intention. I mean, I wasn't hinting, I'm sorry. Thank you, Alex, it won't be necessary. I'll be home shortly and have something to eat then.'

'No, don't be silly. You have the coffee while I quickly whip up that omelette. Then you can really relax, and we'll be able to talk about why you came.'

'Well, you've now put me on the spot,' He wondered himself why he came – no, he had to get a grip. His purpose: to show the sketch, and only talk about the sketch. That's the single most important thing. He must win her over – for the case. 'It'll be rude to refuse. Thank you. It would be really good to eat something, and especially not something I've prepared or to eat alone.'

'Good, that's settled then. Would you like some cheese in it?'

'That'll be grand, and perhaps we could talk while you make it.' He got up, picked up his coffee as she entered the kitchen.

'Perfect. You install yourself on one of those barstools at that side of the hatch and we're set.' She donned an apron. It hit him that the last time he saw a woman put on an apron was ten years ago – his mother, just before she had died.

Alex bent down and pulled out a frying pan, then stretched for a bowl in the overhead cupboard and unhooked the whisk from the side of the cupboard. Every time she stretched, something in him moved. He found it hard to concentrate.

'Two or three eggs?'

'Three if you have them, thank you. I'm really hungry!' He watched her put the pan on the stove, dash a bit of olive oil into it, and turn on the heat. Without taking his eyes off her, they followed her taking the eggs from the carton, cheese, and milk from the fridge. She grated the cheese into a small plate, setting it aside. Into the bowl, she broke the eggs, added a bit of milk with a dash of salt and pepper before she whisked it into a foamy mixture. She poured the liquid into the hot pan; it hit the hot surface with a soft hiss. She turned to him.

'May I ask if you have any news of Detective Garcia's condition?'

'No change, I'm afraid. Although they did add that he has stabilised under the coma.'

'That's a relief, isn't it?'

'Definitely, but I would prefer if he came round and was finally on the mend.'

'What happened? Was he shot in the line of duty?'

'You know I cannot give out any information. All I can say is, no, he wasn't shot.'

'Wait a minute. I read in the *Tribune* this morning about an explosion. Was it at your station? The report was vague, and it didn't give details. Was it that? Please tell me.'

'Yes, it happened at our station, in the parking lot behind the building. We're still investigating. We have no idea what the cause could be. So, I cannot really discuss it any further, except to say that, yes, my partner was seriously injured in the blast.'

'Oh, I am so sorry, Paul. You're okay. You weren't near?'

'No. Thank you for your concern, Alex. I was inside the building when the blast occurred. I could feel its force hitting the building.'

She turned back to the stove and lifted the edge of the omelette with a spatula to check its progress. 'Nearly done,' she said, pulling out a plate setting it next to the stove. She placed a table mat and napkin in front of him, then got a knife and fork from the drawer and placed those on each side of where the plate would be. On a side plate she placed a fresh bread roll. Again, she turned to the stove, and with a satisfied nod, she sprinkled the grated cheese on the eggs and folded it over into a half-moon. She picked up the pan, and with the spatula, guided the prepared omelette to slide easily onto the plate, which she then placed in front of him.

'*Voila!* One cheese omelette as ordered! Now eat up.'

'Thank you. This is super; I feel quite guilty eating while you are not.'

'Don't think twice about that. I ate at one o'clock. With all that's happened, I doubt you realise that it's nearly three in the afternoon.'

'No wonder I'm so hungry! The last time I ate was breakfast yesterday, and that was on the run.'

'I'm making more coffee, you want some?'

'This is great, you make a great omelette, and yes, I would love some more of that good coffee.'

'Pleased you like it.' Alex watched him finish the plate. 'Let's have the coffee around the coffee table.' With that he wiped his mouth with the napkin and slid off the stool.

'Before we go any further, I need to show you that sketch.' He stepped over to where he had been seated before and picked up his jacket. From the inside pocket he pulled out an envelope. 'Take a look at this and tell me if there is anything familiar about the person. There is also a description of his build and body type, which might help.'

She took the sketch from him and carefully studied it, turning it this way and that. 'It could be the person I saw, definitely the same build; the face I couldn't be sure of. Although, I have to add that it feels familiar.'

'That could be it then. The subconscious registers details that our conscious quite often fails to. Therefore, if you have a feeling the face seems familiar, it most probably is the person you saw – fleetingly or not.'

'I'm very pleased that at least you have a face to put to the shooter. Did you find a connection with him and the car that left? Could you get the number plate? Where will you go from here?'

'Slow down! So many questions – which I understand. Yet, as I said before, I cannot discuss the case or how far we've got. Just be assured that it is in hand, and you are safe. The unmarked police vehicle will not leave this street until we have those responsible securely out of the way.'

'Thank you. That is reassuring. Mrs Ginet keeps on asking me if we are safe, and I don't know what else I can say except that you are looking after us.'

'Good tactic, but it is true. Did you tell her about my partner being injured?'

'Oh no, I haven't spoken to her since we telephoned you this morning. Also, I didn't know the newspaper report referred to your station.'

'Good, leave it at that. The less she knows the better at this moment.'

'I agree. She has a bit of a soft spot for Detective Garcia!'

'Amusing. She is really something.' He chuckled. 'However, something has been worrying me since the first time we met. You came in with her, though only on her insistence, isn't that so? She wouldn't come in unless you came as well. You didn't want to come at all. She knew that, so she insisted you accompany her. I got the impression you wished to be anywhere but there at the station. Or, perhaps even on another planet, as if you could avoid being near a policeman. It concerns the demons you mentioned earlier. Am I wrong?'

Alex hesitated. Her face reddened. She fidgeted. 'Well, I think that's my problem. Let's just leave it at that.'

'Alex, I would like to know. Maybe I could even help with whatever is bothering you so much. Why don't you want to talk about it?'

'It's got nothing to do with you.'

'But surely it would be easier if you shared what frightens you with someone?'

'As I said, it's my problem and I don't want to talk about it. Please leave it be.'

'I feel it's my duty to help you with this.'

'It's nobody's business!' Her whole body had stiffened.

'True. I'm sorry. I shouldn't have insisted. You don't have to tell me about it. If you do change your mind, I'm here if you need someone to listen.'

'Thank you for the offer, Detective. I think we have covered everything and am pleased I could help with identifying the shooter. Will you let Mrs Ginet know how Detective Garcia is progressing please?'

Paul felt the previous calm turn into cold tension. He chastised himself for mentioning her obvious distrust. It certainly wasn't the time to try and get to the bottom of it. Why did he destroy this very agreeable and happy moment he shared with her? He could kick himself for being so insensitive. Well, he'd have to repair the damage he did another day. He only hoped that it could be repaired.

'Oh, yes, fine. I've overstayed my welcome. Thank you again for the lunch, it's greatly appreciated. Rest assured I will keep you informed not only about the case but of Detective Garcia's condition.' He got up, threw his jacket over his arm, and held out his hand to her. 'You've been very kind and helpful. Thank you.'

'No problem. Goodbye, detective.' She shook his hand, holding open the door with the other, making sure there could be no mistake in her wanting him to leave.

As the door closed behind him, he mumbled to himself, *'Mince!'* Dash it all! How could he be so stupid? Why did he have to push the point? He knew that this incident would worry him for the rest of the day and most probably rob him of sleep which he so desperately needed to function properly. He thought back to his mother's warning not to act like a bull in a China shop. His ex-wife also had something to say about him always digging for information. Well, if she saw him now, she would have said that he should have heeded her words. He should be more careful in future, especially when meeting Miss Labelle again.

CHAPTER EIGHT

'*Paul, where have you been? I've been calling you the whole morning!*' Maria virtually shouted over the phone. '*I've left message after message on your phone and at the station.*'

'*Sorry, Maria, my phone was off. I'm exhausted, only just got home. I had to interview a couple of important witnesses.*' He unlocked his front door and, as he spoke, checked that all was in order and followed his usual routine.

'*In connection with José?*'

'*Not directly, but it could be relevant. I'm hoping to find something. We are looking at all angles. We don't know anything yet.*'

'*Well, at least I have good news. Phillippe is back!*'

'*What? Great news! When did he get back? Where was he? What happened?*'

'*He got back about ten-thirty this morning. A teacher at his previous school dropped him off.*' Evident that Maria's elation had relieved him of a great burden.

'*Why didn't he get home last night?*' Completely depleted he sank onto his sofa.

'*Apparently, the teacher saw him shooting hoops with his friends and went over to say hello. Phillippe had been one of his favourite pupils, and they wanted to catch up, so they decided to go to the Bistro for a juice. They got talking and didn't realise the time. At quarter-to-ten, my son remembered that I was due to pick him up at four-thirty.*'

'*So why didn't he come home then?*'

'*Well, in his panic of being so late and missing me, he couldn't remember my new phone number, my brother's number, or home address.*'

'*I don't understand. How did he then come home today?*'

'*Well, it's a long story. Last night, the teacher drove him around for about an hour to see if he found anything familiar or remembered more. Needless to say, the more he tried, the more panic took over. He said his mind went blank. The teacher wanted to take him back to our home in*

Geneva. Phillippe insisted that he couldn't go there, as it's under construction. That was the reason I gave the children for us to leave our home.' She hardly took a breath as she recounted the events, clearing her throat to steady her voice. He supposed she felt guilty for hiding the truth from her children.

'The teacher thought it best if he stayed with him for the night while they tried to find me.' Maria took a breath before continuing. 'They phoned around until after eleven o'clock and began again at eight this morning. They even phoned the station, but no one could give them any information, and they couldn't reach you. They only said that everyone was busy and couldn't take the call.'

'Who managed to give them the address?'

'In his frustration, the teacher contacted a colleague to commiserate. This was the breakthrough! Apparently, the colleague is a friend of my sister-in-law's and gave them her address. It took them only fifteen minutes to get Phillippe back to me. There are no words to describe how relieved and happy I am.'

'I am elated! You cannot imagine how pleased I am that he got home unharmed. Have you spoken to Detective Bachelet? He has been advised of the situation?'

'I phoned him as soon as my son arrived. Oh Paul, I had all these scenarios in my head. Everything that could've happened to my boy terrified me.'

'I think you need to put your new phone number on a tag attached to a string for each of them. You know, like a lanyard. Ensure that they don't take it off unless absolutely necessary. That way you're sure they can contact you.' He knew Bachelet would've told Leonard of the development. At least it was one thing he need not do.

'Good idea. I'll do that right away. Now, I need to know how my husband is doing and unless you are preventing me, for security reasons, from doing so, I'm going to the hospital.'

'Fine, you can go to the hospital, but leave the children where they are. Since we're still not sure where the warnings came from, we cannot let our guard down. At least we now know that Phillippe's disappearance had nothing to do with the threats. However, we're not taking chances.'

'I understand. I'll stay under the radar. Thanks for everything. Bye for now.'

'Oh, by the way, I'll let the officer guarding José's hospital room know that you're coming. See you at the hospital. Bonne route!' Paul clicked off his phone, visibly relieved with the news that the disappearance of José's son had been an innocent misunderstanding. It could've been so much more. He also didn't like the fact that Tweedle-Dee and Tweedle-Dum were again loose on bail. He stopped himself from looking for trouble where none existed. He sat in comfort for a moment, then unfolded his body and dragged himself to the bathroom for a much-deserved long, hot shower and shave.

The hot water pelted his body. He enjoyed every drop, which, as it hit him, massaged his tired muscles. With this, relaxation came. His mind automatically reverted to Miss Labelle. He reproached himself again for insisting that she share her fears with him. He realised that he wanted to know everything about her, especially on a personal level. But he pushed that thought away. It was unethical, getting involved with a witness.

*

Alpha took the call from one of his foot soldiers. He put the phone on speaker as he poured himself a cognac.

'What have you got?'

'No sign of anything.'

'What do you mean?'

'We haven't seen any old lady with any dog. Some old ladies, but no dog. Some dogs, but no old ladies.'

'Did you patrol as I asked you to?'

'Yeah. We walked up and down the street. First, I walked from one end to the other. Then he went from the other end to the one end. We swapped like that every half hour. As you told us, we never walked together.'

'Okay. Now, what did you see?'

'As I said: no old lady, no dog.'

'What do you mean? You said you saw some dogs?'

'Yeah. We saw some dogs.'

'Well, knucklehead, what kind of dogs?'

'Ah, Boss I don't know. Big ones and small ones.'

'Do I have to drag everything out of you? What did these dogs look like?'

'Well, there was one white one with many black spots, like in that movie.'

'You mean a Dalmatian?'

'Yeah! That's it, that's the name of the movie! It was a good movie that! With Cruella. She was some crazy broad!'

'Get back to the point, you bozo! What did the other dogs look like?'

'There was one with long hair – oh, like Lassie!'

'What's with you and movies?'

'I like movies.' Alpha could just imagine him pushing out his hands, palms up.

'Okay. Now, tell me about the others you saw. And please describe them, especially the small ones.' Alpha couldn't tolerate this stupidity much longer.

'You mean the other dogs? Yeah, okay. There was a small white one with a black patch over one of his eyes, like a pirate.'

'Okay, okay, carry on!'

'I saw another white one with curly hair – also small, but not too small. That dog walks funny, as if on its toes. Then one brownish-grey one with in-between long hair.'

'It's called a coat on a dog.'

'What's called a coat?'

'The hair you idiot! The dog's hair!'

'Oh, I didn't know. That's funny, a dog with a coat! Do they have buttons also?'

'For heaven's sake, get on with it.' Exasperated, Alpha wanted to hit something.

'Oh, that brownish-grey one was really small with short legs and a bow in his hair – I mean his coat. You know, on top of his head.'

'Who walked that one?'

'The one with the bow? Ah, let's see. Oh yes, a young man. The guy was about your height and build, but younger.'

'Did you see which building he came from and went back to?'

'No, we didn't see the beginning or the end of his walk because it was in between our patrols. We didn't hang around. You said we should always move while on patrol. We only stayed in one place in between our walks.'

'Where were you then? In other words, where did the two of you wait between patrols?'

'At a café from where we could see part of the street. He would wait while I walked and then I waited when he patrolled.'

'Did anyone see you?'

'Well, the owner and some of the regulars. They're all very friendly.'

'What did I tell you? Be unobtrusive!'

'Yes Boss.'

'You do know what unobtrusive means, don't you?'

'You told us it what it means.'

'So, repeat what I said.'

'It means that we should be quiet. And I assure you we didn't shout or make noise.'

'You idiots! You drew attention to yourselves by being in the same place for too long a period, on a regular basis, and too often. You might as well have walked up and down the street all day long and looked into the various buildings and asked neighbours who the old lady was!'

'You think we should've done that? But you said we shouldn't.'

At that, Alpha punched the red button with force to end the call, in no uncertain terms. He threw the phone against the wall. The back cover flew off and the battery slithered across the floor. Fools they were, he now doubted employing them, and his earlier decision not to permanently get rid of them. Does the world really need two like them? He needed to cool off before he spoke to either of them again.

His mind scrolled back to the two. He still couldn't believe that his intelligence could've been so wrong. He cannot rely on anyone except himself. At least, because of his philosophy, no one understood the extent of the operation he put into play. In any case, he needed to rectify the situation.

He accepted the setback, but refused to give in. Okay, fine. The first attempt backfired, but it won't be the last. He'd continue until they turn and run with their tail between their legs. Yes, that's for sure - they will run. He'll gather the intelligence himself of where and when the pigs could be found.

That old lady saw him. At the time, he thought it fun to let her squirm in fear. Old ladies are such easy targets. Though, it would be better to know where she lived and track her movements, in case she became a threat that had to be dealt with.

At least his little fireworks display went off well. The lack of an audience was a bit disappointing. Nevertheless, it made an impact. He still waited to hear if it eliminated his target. Well, either way, fatal for the target or serious injuries, it carried the threat to the next level. He nodded with satisfaction. He'd have to think about the next step. In fact, he was looking forward to the fun he would have in thinking up something special.

*

Why did she react like that? Alex could kick herself! She regretted her reaction when Paul Favre asked her about her fears. It was a legitimate question. Was it because he wanted to know more? Why, why, oh why did she do that?

She needed to control her emotions much better in future. It was feasible that a remark or something else could test her at any time. She had to guard against a similar reaction she had earlier. In fact, her sensitivity was becoming detrimental to her daily life. She would have to cope better.

She liked Paul. Not since Denis had she felt like this. His presence made her feel relaxed – well, not at first, but now that she knew him a bit better. Why destroy the only chance of friendship which might become something more? He was kind and a gentleman. Who knew, perhaps she could open up to him. No, not yet. Too soon, yes it was too soon.

Everything was going fine, very pleasant even, and then only the mention of her state the day before at the station set her off. It was as if he caged her. Then by insisting, he poured cold water over her. Yes, she literally froze.

All those questions threw her back into the past. That was just it, her fears and panic attacks rooted in authority, always examining her every move. Police interrogation had terrified her. She should go easy on him. She didn't do anything wrong, and his questioning had nothing to do with her actions. He deserved the benefit of the doubt – he was an investigator, for heaven's sake! He was trying to solve a case. To ask questions was second nature to him, nothing personal. Of all the people she would be able to confide in, it should be this man. They definitely had a connection.

Surely, she could explain what had happened so long ago. Then again, how would she ever be able to tell him without breaking down? Another thing, would he believe her? Would he judge her like so many had at the time? Would he condemn her? How would it impact her life now? She needed help, but she had promised herself she'd never go there again.

And if she did come clean, she was afraid it'd all come back with a vengeance. It was ancient history – or so everyone told her. Except it wouldn't be so if she revealed everything. She'd relive each moment and every emotion as if it occurred yesterday. No, it was all too much. It had to stay buried deep in her memory and only with those who knew at the time.

Alex paced the floor. What to do? To revisit that time would bring heartache and complicate her life. In fact, the last person she would want to see was the only one she could discuss this with. She wished there was someone else. Even talking to her psychiatrist was out of the question. Not that she saw the doctor on a regular basis – in fact it had been at least three years since her last appointment.

Besides her latest panic and rising fear, she was doing well – moving to Switzerland so many years ago had helped. A complete change of scene gave her a new lease on life. At the time, the only thing which had made her think twice about the move was leaving her family behind and starting a new life. But then again, no matter what she did for them, or helped them wherever she could, they were quite happy without her. They wouldn't really miss her. They always excluded her from their lives, so why would they include her now? She learnt that long ago. They would automatically think she could take care of herself, and her independence spoke for itself. Therefore, they wouldn't care about her well-being. Though, it would be nice to discuss this with one of her siblings.

She stopped in full stride and immediately put the thought out of her mind – there wouldn't be any understanding, only recriminations. She didn't look for sympathy, only discernment. A bit of perspective would have been welcome rather than accusations. However, they couldn't give her that before, so how could she expect it now? Even with the passing of time, she doubted they would ever accept her side of how the events unfolded. They had never forgiven her for shining the spotlight on them. Even more so for her being held and interviewed by the police for forty-eight hours. As far as they were concerned, the whole affair became a stigma on the family name, irrespective of her being innocent and completely cleared. Even the apology from official authorities, the Dutch Police Department, made no difference to them.

A knock on the door startled her and disrupted her thoughts. It took a minute before she collected herself to shake off her ruminations. Then, breathing deeply, she opened the door. Unsurprisingly, Mrs Ginet stood in front of her with a plate of biscuits.

'Oh, *bonjour Madame Ginet,* how are you?

'I baked some biscuits this morning and brought you some. Have you had your afternoon coffee yet? If not, here you are, we can have it together. What do you think?'

'Ah, well, no, I mean yes, come in, you know you're always welcome.' She stood aside for her to enter. 'I'll make some coffee.' Alex felt that she already had too much caffeine today, though couldn't refuse, and took a chance. 'Or would you prefer tea?'

'Whatever you feel like my dear. Tea will also be fine.'

'Good, I've had too much coffee already.' As soon as she said it, she realised that she had opened the door to Mrs Ginet's inquisitive mind.

'Oh really? Why do you say that? What have you been doing the whole day, my dear? The last time I saw you, we phoned that nice Detective Favre.'

'Yes, well I did my usual things, but then just after lunch he phoned, and came over to show me a sketch they had put together from the description Mrs Marx gave them.' She switched the kettle on, readied the teapot, spooning in loose tea leaves, ready for the hot water.

'So that was good that we told them about her? Why didn't you call me over when he was here? I could've helped.'

'Well, not really. You didn't see anything, remember.'

'Oh, yes, that's right. Either way, I would've liked to be here when he came.'

'Don't worry. Next time he comes, I'll call you over.' Alex busied herself with setting the cups and saucers out on a tray. The water boiled. Alexandra poured it into the teapot, replaced the lid, and waited for it to brew. To gain time and composure, she carefully placed the pot on the tray and brought it through to the living area, placing it on the coffee table.

'What did you tell him? Did you recognise the man?'

'I could only tell him that I had a feeling it could be the same person. Because I only saw him fleetingly; I couldn't be absolutely certain.'

'Surely, he wanted a more definite answer.'

'No, he felt it was confirmation enough, so he didn't need anything further.'

'I'm pleased. But you like him, don't you? I think he likes you as well.'

'That's beside the point I think.' She placed the strainer on the cup and poured Mrs Ginet's tea, handing it over to her. Alex realised that her neighbour most probably knew that he stayed much longer than just to show a sketch, so she continued. 'He hadn't eaten since yesterday, so I made him an omelette.'

'Really, why on earth doesn't he look after himself? You see, he needs a woman to make sure he eats regularly and well.'

'I suppose so. However, that won't be me.'

'Don't say that! You can never discard the possibility.'

'No, I doubt it very much.'

'Please don't be negative. You also need someone in your life.'

'As I said, be that as it may, it won't be possible.'

'Why ever not? You are both young and unmarried.' Mrs Ginet replaced the cup on the saucer – ready for a second cup.

'Mrs Ginet, take it from me, it won't happen.'

'Oh, why didn't he eat since yesterday?'

'What?'

'You said he hadn't eaten since yesterday.'

'Oh, yes, that's what he said. The case has kept them all very busy and the lack of witnesses and clues made them double their efforts. It was only when they got the information from Mrs Marx that they could relax and do their work properly.'

'How is Detective Garcia?'

'As far as I know, doing well.' Alex hoped that her evasive reply was enough.

'Oh good, he is really nice.'

Alexandra put her cup down, hoping Mrs Ginet would get the hint, but she didn't move. 'I'm sorry I must run. I still have various things to do. Do you mind? I'll let you know if anything comes up again.'

'Oh, my dear, of course, I don't want to keep you. Just know that I'm here for you.'

'Thank you so much, you are such a good friend. I'm running out to do some shopping now. Do you need me to pick something up for you?'

'No, thank you, I've everything I need.'

'Fine. Thank you again for the biscuits. Homemade cookies are always the best.'

'I agree, my dear. Okay, goodbye. Enjoy the rest of the day.

'I'll most probably see you tomorrow. Goodbye.' Alex walked with her to the door and held it open.

The last time she held open the door for someone, it was for Paul. Her feelings disturbed her much more than just the slight annoyance she had at this moment. In a strange way, it brought a certain balance and calm back to her. Life, she thought, goes on. It was just a matter of how we look at it and if we accept it for what it is: life. Her only solution for leading a reasonable life, would be to accept the events she had gone through, and her subsequent fears. These fears were only as strong or as destructive as she allowed them to affect her. Perhaps if she faced them head on and shared them with Paul Favre, they would lose their hold on her.

She shook her head, no, perhaps not, not yet. But soon, yes. Every day from now on she'd work on her courage. Find a way to explain what had happened. Then, when ready, approach the subject with him.

*

Georgio Bescutti stood at his office window as he always did when thinking, his hands clasped behind his back. He rocked gently to-and-fro on the balls of his feet. The view of planes landing and taking off calmed him like nothing else did. His eyes focused closer, unable to resist seeing his tall frame mirrored in the glass – reassuring.

An hour ago, the lawyer he had sent to arrange for the release of his two employees had advised that they would be there for a while and be charged with illicit loitering. Previously, this – on its own – was not serious. But with the global terrorism threat, the gravity of such a transgression had changed to a felony and had a stiff punishment attached to it; this due to Geneva being the European seat of the UN and many Diplomatic envoys. The lawyer warned that posting bail for the two might be difficult. Though, he assured Bescutti that they would not talk as they had been given an incentive they could not refuse. At least he could rely on his lawyer – expensive, nevertheless discreet and worth every cent. If he said they'd not talk, they wouldn't.

He turned, now back to business. He buzzed for his assistant, Emilio.

'What is the status of our shipment?'

'Dispatched and due in two days,' Emilio replied as he entered and closed the door behind him, cognisant of the fact that his boss didn't like to waste time.

'Any hiccups? Problems?'

'None so far, Sir. I expect a clean and clear arrival.'

'Good, so everything is arranged.'

'Yes, I'll oversee the arrival myself, check it and hand it over to our distributors.'

'Our inside man with their outfit is reliable and still reporting back as required?'

'Definitely. He's been constant in sending information back, so far very dependable.'

'You have a backup plan I presume if things go south?'

'Yes, our contact in customs will tip us off if there's a problem, and the goods will be diverted elsewhere from where we can collect them later.'

'You sure that'll work? There is no connection to us with this other site?'

'Definitely, the alternate paperwork is ready and will be swapped with the originals when and if necessary, without any scrutiny from other customs agents.'

'Good, let's hope the interception will not be necessary.'

'Yes, Sir, I agree, but I am confident that all will run smoothly.'

'Thank you. You may go.' Bescutti turned back to the window. It's better that Emilio remain unaware of the full extent of the business.

His father had the philosophy that work should be divided and no person in his employ should know about, understand, or be able to fill every position in the enterprise. Each aspect of their activities should be unitary. This way he had overall control. No one could take over, as none knew the whole business. A good and sound credo, which he planned to carry on. Except, he would do it legally. In any case, this would be the last shipment in which his family would be involved. From now on, the importation of these type of goods would be done strictly for his own company.

The competition strengthened and took over certain areas of the business which he thought were secure. The smaller distributors did not concern them. They had shared the market with them for years – a happy understanding where they even bought from the same distributors. This new group seemed to have clout behind them. Besides money, they had manpower and had infiltrated the market. Moreover, they seemed to know Bescutti's every move. Further, this group's product reached the market at lower prices, and analysis had proven the quality to be exceptional. Where and who were their suppliers?

More importantly, where were they getting their information from? Did the family have a traitor in their midst? If there was a spy, they'd skin him alive. The brutal example they would make of the spy would result in no one ever going against the family again. He needed to find out before they took steps. Or, before the competition took over completely. His fight concerned not only the family, but he had to secure his own existence. The question now was: who could he trust?

Only this forced him to speak to his wife personally, which he had tried to avoid for the last eighteen years. It might involve Antonio, but if he played his cards right, he could minimise his exposure.

He watched his reflection turn away from the window as he moved to stand behind the desk. He turned to the window again: straightened his tie, popped the cuffs from his jacket sleeves and with both hands, took hold of the hem of each side of the jacket, tugged it down. Satisfied that the suit sat perfectly on his form, he made a slight turn to the left then the right. His reflection confirmed his station and his readiness to speak to his wife.

He returned to his desk, picked up the receiver and dialled a number.

'It's me. Meet me at Le Carnivore in half-an-hour.' Without identification or any greeting, he finished the call. He expected her to be there on time, he's a busy man.

*

Manuela Vicario arrived at the restaurant five minutes ahead of the arranged rendezvous, not knowing what to expect.

Manuela, born in Valais, Switzerland, grew up under the guidance of an uncle after the death of her parents. As her only remaining family member, he had taken her, at the age of four, to Sicily. His home, on the outskirts of a village, nestled at the foot of the mountains.

She had received her education from the Sisters of Mercy Convent; the only educational institution in the village where everyone she knew went. Her uncle, a quiet man, had set the trend, and her life became a calm, tranquil existence as well. The usual fiery Sicilian temperament never came to the fore due to her uncle's example, the Sisters, and her secluded childhood.

Manuela's serene personality had been the main attraction when, at a chance meeting, Georgio seduced her on sight more than two decades ago. Debonair, he dressed accordingly. An impulsive romantic, he would show up without advance notice, and take her to places she had never dreamt her humble childhood would take her. Through him she saw what life in a city could be and learnt how to dress smartly and be ready to go out at a moment's notice.

After their six-week whirlwind romance, they had married, and she left Sicily, the only home she knew, for Switzerland, to begin a new life with her beloved. A dream even further from any she could've imagined. During their life as a married couple, he expected her to accept his work schedule, which took him away from their nest more often than she would've liked. At first, without friends and being a stranger in the country she had difficulty adjusting without speaking French. He insisted she learn the language and even hired a private tutor. Time went by, and on discovering that she was pregnant two years later, they were ecstatic, planning their new future as a complete family.

Though, throughout their time together he had never introduced her to his family; he kept finding excuses. As an expectant mother, Manuela's need for a connection to family became stronger. In the end, he admitted that his business, and his family's business, were the same and complicated. They were heavily involved in many things, though import and export were their main activities. He also laid down a rule that she refrained from wanting any connection with them as it would not be in her best interest. Confused, she found this unacceptable and argued the point, but he was adamant: there would never, ever be contact with the family. Saddened, her loneliness increased, but he didn't relent. He showered her with gifts; but she only wanted him, and a perfect family. At the birth of their son, the axe fell. He registered the birth under her maiden name and entered 'unknown' as the father on the birth certificate.

Secretly, he had bought a luxury duplex in the best part of town. He collected her from the hospital and moved her and their son, into the duplex. With everything furnished and all her belongings arranged, he showed her the nursery and handed over the deed and keys for the property. Elated, thinking this was their new beginning, she hugged him and tried to kiss him. Only, he pulled away. He coolly sat her down and explained that, from now on, she would live alone with their son and have no further contact with him. He would provide for all her needs and his son's. However, there would never be further direct contact between them. He expected her to provide photographs, and a short progress report of their son on a regular basis, at least twice a year, posted to an address he would provide.

Devastated, she had demanded an explanation. His only reply: 'It is business, nothing personal.' He assured her that he loved her and that it would never change; their love was forever. Furthermore, the safety of her and their son demanded this move. He insisted that she keep up appearances, live a life as a single mother. When she said she would give him a divorce, even if it was against her strict Catholic upbringing, he assured her that he would never divorce her, as in his eyes, she was and would always be his wife. He added that his family would not allow a divorce either. Also, he'd never share his life with another, and that she should be prepared to do the same. He repeated that contact between them would be through his assistant and that she should always be ready to do as requested.

While married to Georgio, she had also learnt never to be late or keep him waiting. So here she sat, waiting and even though he told her he would be there in person, she remained unsure if he would really come, and unsure if she would recognise her husband after all these years.

The waiter broke into her ruminations, asking if he could take her order. She waved him away. The young man left her repeatedly looking at the entrance. Her nervousness showed. She chewed her bottom lip, something he hated. And on remembering that, she stopped, took out a hankie, and dabbed her lips. Would she know him when he walked through the door? On the other hand, she was sure that he knew exactly what she looked like after eighteen years. He had a myriad of people keeping him informed of her every move.

In a blink of her eye, he stood there. She never saw him enter. He appeared as if out of nowhere. Her heart stopped. The reaction she had had the first time she laid eyes on him occurred again; spreading heat throughout her body. Her legs felt heavy and paralyzed. He looked around – handsome, dapper, and seductive; exactly as she remembered. When his eyes met hers, she had to look away to recover. He moved over in such an elegant and graceful way that she melted inside.

He reached the table, bent down, and greeted her with the usual three cheek kisses before sitting down opposite her. His cologne, the same as she remembered, enveloped her like a gentle caress. She couldn't move. Her eyes locked on him. She drank in his every move.

'Manuela, you look good. It's really nice to see you.'

'Oh, … oh thank you, Georgio.' She managed to recover. 'You haven't changed – slightly older, yet – the same.' Living alone for so long, she had managed to thicken her skin. Though, she could feel the blush creeping up from her neck to her cheeks. If it wasn't there before, it was now double the depth of colour.

'Thank you. Time has been good to both of us. You really are as beautiful as when I first saw you. I often wish the situation could've been different.'

'Too late for that now, it was what you wanted, and I had no choice but to agree.'

'Yes, I know. I was so convinced being apart would guarantee your and our son's safety. If I had a different family, we might have had our own perfect family, like you always wanted. The only way I could assure you of not getting embroiled in the family's dealings, was to keep you far away from them.'

'Why didn't you tell me about them before we got married?'

'Well, I had mistakenly thought that I could distance myself from them and make my own way in life. It was only when Antonio was on the way that the importance of an heir to them became clear. They got their hands on me, forcing me to take over. I knew that would mean my son would also become part of the family. I couldn't do that to you or our child. Then, no matter how hard I tried, I couldn't get out from under their hold.'

'We could've gone to another country.'

'They have business and people in every country. And the last thing I wanted was for our son to follow in my footsteps.'

'But who said he would've?'

'I didn't want to put him in the same position I was at the time. Also, I never wanted him to feel obliged or be forced into this life I must live.'

'I realise what you do is not always legal, but is it that bad?'

'Let's just say, I still insist that you and Antonio stay far away from the family. My dealings are mainly legal – only by association their illegal business rubs off on me.'

'Okay, but shouldn't he know his father? I know he wants to; he has asked many questions since the shooting of that boy. And you demanding information about his ex-girlfriend made him even more curious. He wonders who you are.'

'Out of the question. I refuse to meet with him. You can tell him … oh, I don't know what to tell him. Just make sure he understands that it is in his best interest not to contact or mix with his paternal family.'

'Fine, so why are we here? A personal meeting after all these years spells "serious".'

'Yes. It is serious. That shooting could bring the attention of the family to your doorstep and involve Antonio. While he's involved with that girl, he will be a target because her father has connections to the Colombians.'

'What do you mean, Colombians? Normally, that translated as problems.'

'His business is in direct opposition to a section of ours.'

'Answer me. I am not completely ignorant. I know they do illegal business and sometimes even exert criminal actions.' Suddenly, her eyes widened as she looked up at him. 'Wait, are you telling me you're involved with drugs? That's what Colombians are known for, aren't they?'

'No, I'm definitely not! All you need to know is that the family's interest in this matter is to eliminate the opposition.'

'What! What do you mean by "eliminate"? You're not serious, are you? They couldn't possibly mean killing, could they?'

'Look, all you need to know is that Antonio should stay clear of that girl. He must not and cannot get involved with her, until we know more.'

'That's an order, is it?'

'It's for his own safety. I don't want anything to happen to my son.'

'You mean like that young man that was killed?'

'If you want to look at it like that, yes. Well, this was what I wanted to press on you – the seriousness of the matter. And now that I've done that, I need to leave.'

'That's it? Nothing else? No further orders to issue?'

'Manuela, please don't. This is also difficult for me.' He got up to go.

'Oh, I see, difficult for you! How could I ever control my son and his feelings? You do remember feelings, don't you? They can run away from you and take you hostage forever. That happened to us, do you recall? We thought we could change the world. And where are we now? The father of my son. The son who doesn't even know what his father looks like, trying to control his son's emotions. Who he likes or falls in love with, is out of our control!' Her Sicilian temperament finally showed its face.

'Live with it.' With that, Manuela got up and pushed past Georgio with such force that he nearly lost his balance and had to grab hold of the chair.

*

His eyes clouded over. The emotion that upset his demeanour could not be ignored. In life, he sacrificed much in the name of the family. But watching her walk out became too much. This sensation confirmed his choice not to have direct contact with her over the years. The passion which bound them could not emotionally be tolerated on a regular basis without destroying him completely, both physically and mentally.

The certainty he had lost the best part of himself and, further, the possibility he had orchestrated the cause of the danger to his son brought on such a sense of sadness and regret that he felt he could not continue. He fell back into the chair, and when the waiter came over, he ordered a whisky. Real life awaited him, if he wanted it or not.

*

After his shower and forty winks on the sofa, the clock showed six-thirty. Paul couldn't believe how time had passed. As he made a cup of coffee, his mind wandered back and forth through the earlier hours and Alex Labelle's reaction. He hoped that she would one day trust him enough to take him into her confidence. Oh well, he'd tread carefully, wait, be patient, and hope to understand what disturbed her. He would like to help.

First, he wanted to go to the station to check if facial recognition had come up with a possible name. From the printed photos he compared to the sketch, he found one which could be a match, putting a name to the person would give them a great advantage. The explosion at the station pushed the case to the fore, not only for the Serious Crimes Unit but also for the Intelligence and Terrorism Units. It resulted in the SCU having to step aside, which he didn't appreciate. With the investigation in the hands of the Federal Police, Paul was anxious to get information on their progress. This would not be easy. For all intents and purposes, Paul Favre and his colleagues at the SCU couldn't actively be involved. Nevertheless, nothing would stand in his way to find the person or persons who planned the

150

explosion.

Officially, Paul would only be investigating the shooting, not the blast. Although the telephone threats were directed at the two detectives, the Federal Police looked at it and the explosion as connected to terrorism. Therefore, as far as the various units of the FP were concerned, until the connection to the case was disproved, they were looking at the blast as a separate incident connected only to the threats. At least the disappearance of Phillippe, Garcia's son, had turned out to be an innocent act.

This reasoning brought Paul back to his second planned stop, the hospital. He sincerely hoped his partner's condition had improved or at least stabilised. He assumed that Maria would've arrived by now. He cursed under his breath. The traffic was virtually at a standstill, not unheard of at that time of day. He told himself to keep calm and use the time to mentally go over the facts gathered so far.

He pushed into the station forty-five minutes later; the earlier chaos virtually a memory. Besides remnants of crime tape around the blast site in the rear parking lot, nothing else remained. The late-shift duty officer greeted him, handing over his messages, and advised that Superintendent Leonard awaited him at Garcia's desk. Apparently, he had been working there since mid-day.

'Thank you. I'd better not keep him waiting.' Favre said, anxious to get to his desk.

'*Bonjour, chef.* I see you've already begun.'

'Good, Favre, you're here.' Leonard briefly glanced up before returning his concentration to the file in front of him.

'I think I matched up the sketch with a pedestrian in Navigation Square. His image, well, only his profile, was caught on the ATM camera. But it looks pretty much like the same man. He appears in the background on the photo – here, have a look. It seems as if he was opening a car door. To get in? Could it be the same car which left the scene?'

'Let me have a look.'

'Has the result of the facial recognition search come through?' Favre immediately walked over to the computer to check the results.

'Yes, a certain Gustave Olivier, aka Jacques du Pont, aka Paul Senath, aka Sebastian Swartz, aka Benoit Bernard. And the list goes on. There are at least ten aliases, perhaps even more that we don't know of. One thing seems clear, and that is he is ex-Foreign Legion with a dangerous history.'

'It could be the same person. Do we have an address for him?'

'No fixed address. He's wanted in various countries and Europol and Interpol have an active warrant out for him. But he is a chameleon; changes his appearance completely as and when necessary – a master of disguise. He speaks eight languages, which, besides the European ones, include Mandarin and Cantonese.'

'What else does it say about him – his crimes or his preferred modus operandi?'

'Violence seems to be his middle name. Apparently, he has three favourites. He would just as easily break your neck with his bare hands as he would use a .45 to put a bullet between your eyes. He also loves to cut his victims. So, there you have a triad! His expertise in the Foreign Legion is listed as explosives. Therefore, to answer your question – for him, anything goes.' Leonard flipped over the pages.

'Does he work for himself or on commission?'

'You mean: as an assassin for hire?'

'Exactly, if he was, who hired him? Who gave the order, and why?' Favre had many questions and most of what they've found only made the list longer.

'These are questions we need answers to, and quickly. I will have to pass this on to the FP as soon as possible. They would be very interested in this gentleman.'

'Oh no! If we hand the info over to them, they'll take over our murder case. We'd have to tell them how we came about this facial recognition.'

'We must prioritise. Ask ourselves which case carries more importance. The shooting of the young man or Garcia's car being blown up.'

'What if the two are connected? If we solve the murder, we solve the blast, and it'd have nothing to do with terrorism. We need to make sure we don't lose our grip on the shooting, because I'm sure there was much more behind it than what we see at this moment.'

'Doesn't that mean it would be better if we have the FP working on it?' Leonard preferred to follow protocol.

'Okay, *chef*. I agree they could help, but if we were out of the loop, it would take much longer to solve this. They'd have to start at the beginning, where we've already interviewed all the witnesses, gathered and sifted through everything, and now have valuable information.' Favre shook his head but continued.

'I'd prefer if we keep on investigating the shooting, with this chap as our prime suspect. When we find there was a National or an International connection, we could then ask for their help or hand it over. It'll be a feather in our cap if we could steer them in the direction of such a connection. Don't you think?'

Leonard nodded, his brow furrowed. 'You're right. Let's get on with it then. I'll hold them off as long as possible and wait to see what they come up with. Perhaps by now they have the signature of the person who set the explosives. And if by chance it's the same person, we stand a good chance of ruling out terrorism and get on with our case.'

'I agree. I'm going to speak to those two we had in lockup before they leave town. I'll get uniforms to bring them in again. They might know this chap.'

'Good idea, shall I come with?'

'Feel free, you might get something out of them that I couldn't when they came in the first time.' Favre pulled out another file and handed it over.'

'This is all you have on them?'

'Yes, they weren't very forthcoming. They gave us their names, which checked out. They have various misdemeanours under their belts, nothing as violent as killing or previous reports of using explosives. We baptised them Tweedle Dee and Tweedle Dum as they really seem to be at the bottom of the barrel in respect of IQ.'

'I presume they are foot soldiers in their bosses' operation. Well, maybe we can convince them that they are only regarded as cannon fodder by the one who gave the order and have no chance of surviving our investigation. I'm sure we will be able to persuade them that their bosses will throw them on our mercy.'

'Doubt that. I heard they had a lawyer who arranged for bail.'

'Is our case not based on Illicit Loitering?'

'Yes. In fact, that charge gave us the right to hold them for a while longer than usual, which is what we wanted, until they were bailed out.'

'Well, can't we add suspicion of terrorism to the IL charge? Then we could keep them here until FP Security is completely satisfied that they were not planning a terrorist act. Do you think these two could prove their innocence?'

'With their level of intelligence, I doubt they could convince even themselves that they're here. We're only interested in knowing who they were waiting for. Why were they at the scene of the shooting and who were they working for.'

'I agree. We need to get to the bottom of why they were there.'

'Have you come across this lawyer before?'

'No.' Leonard paged through the file.

'I wonder if another detective at the station knows anything about him. It'd be interesting to know who sent him. And who will be footing the bill.'

'That's for sure, if we know who pays for his services, we might get nearer to who is behind the whole crime.'

'My thoughts exactly. Shall we give it a try with these two?'

'Good, Favre, lead the way.'

*

Anna Gonzales stood outside her daughter's bedroom door and called out to her.

'*Ma chérie,* please come downstairs and have dinner with us. Your Dad will be arriving in a minute.' She didn't like the fact that Cynthia had been unusually quiet since her meeting with friends – she suspected Antonio – two days before.

'Come on, you didn't even have breakfast. You have to eat something.' In fact, she's been holed up in the room since.

'I'm not hungry,' Cynthia mumbled.

'It's been such a long time since we managed to all eat together, so for my sake, could you please come and join us?'

'Only if you stop nagging me.'

'Fine, I promise. Of course, your dad will want to know how your day went and what you've been up to.'

'Whatever.'

'I'll call you as soon as he arrives.' Anna turned. Mission accomplished. Finally, her daughter would leave her room! She hurried to finish dinner and set the table.

Cynthia came down when her mother called. Without a word, she pulled out a chair and sat down in her usual place. Anna busied herself with dishing food up on plates. She carried them through from the kitchen and set a plate in front of Cynthia, and then, as her husband came down the stairs rubbing his hands, placed his plate on his designated spot.

'Oh, this looks good! So how is my little Angel?' he looked at his daughter, hoping for a smile, but none came.

'Fine, Dad. What have you been doing?'

'Oh, busy, as usual. Everything is fine and looking good. And you, how've you been keeping busy?'

'Oh, just catching up with friends before the new semester begins.'

'Good, as long as you keep out of trouble!' He chuckled, hoping to hide the real reason for asking and his concern.

'Definitely. Just summer activities, Dad. You know swimming in the lake, tennis, the usual, nothing special.'

Dinner passed with small talk, and Anna kept her word. She never mentioned Antonio or the fact that their daughter has been less than communicative. Though, it didn't go unnoticed that she left the table as soon as dinner ended, back to her room. Her husband took the opportunity to ask her the question she really didn't want to answer.

'Tell me that you managed to get her away from Antonio Vicario.'

'As far as I know, she hasn't seen him, but I cannot swear to that.'

'Keep on trying to convince her, it's important.'

'I'll do what I can. Though you know she has her own mind, and if we push her too hard, she'll only rush into his arms.'

'That cannot happen, ever!' With that, he left for his study, firmly closing the door behind him. He listened at the door for a moment. Satisfied that no one followed, he turned to his desk and picked up the phone.

'*Eric, Arthur here. Where have you got to finding out who ordered the shooting and why? Are we out of danger? Was that only a warning?*'

'*The rumours are disturbing.*'

'*What do you mean?*'

'*The shooting was aimed at us. A warning; definitely. But it's bad Arthur.*'

'*For heaven's sake, give it to me. Don't hold me in suspense!*'

'*The target wasn't the young man.*'

'*What do you mean by that?*'

'*The target was ... was your daughter, Cynthia.*'

'*Is that definite?*'

'*Yes, their intelligence was wrong. They were under the impression*'

155

that she was still dating the son of Bescutti, Antonio Vicario, and needed to eliminate her.'

'What? Why? Is this because we are taking over their market?'

'That's the main impression amongst the informants.'

'But why shoot my daughter?'

'The consensus is that your grief would be so profound that you would withdraw from the business and leave the country.'

'Who gave the order?'

'That's not very clear. All they knew was that the order came from a powerful player.'

'Which powerful player? Didn't it come from the Bescutti family?

'Not clear. If not from them, someone as influential and powerful.'

'We do have various competitors, but not many as powerful as the Bescutti family.'

'True. If it came from them, it would've come from the Patron personally.'

'Not from Georgio Bescutti himself?'

'Not clear, but one said if he was involved, it's not his style and he would've been against it. The question is would he have been forced to carry through the order.'

'Do you believe them?'

'Not sure, he's a shrewd businessman, and he would carry out the family's orders if it's legal, and in the interest of business. Killing innocents is not his way of doing things. Sure, he gets rid of those who put him or the family in danger. Though, normally by putting them out of business, e.g.: bankrupting them etc.'

'You're not defending him, are you?'

'No not at all. Just telling you what it is. We still don't have confirmation of the family's involvement.'

'So, you're telling me you don't think this was his idea.'

'Firstly, I doubt if he would put his son so near to a crime. You can say what you want about him, but he has shielded his son from the family's business all his life, so why lay a shooting at his feet, so to speak.'

'Yes, I see what you mean. If I was in his position, I would've done something else to warn us off.'

'However, the family, on the other hand, is a completely different story. Assassinations, or killings, are second nature to them. They are not aware

of the fact that he has offspring.'

'You sure? If we found out, they most probably know as well.'

'It would depend on who knows, I should imagine – as he married in secret. But – and this would be the kicker – the grandmother would as easily cut her son's throat, as she would a servant. She is ruthless and coldblooded.'

'What a family!'

'Loyalty to the family is everything to her and if you betray her, it'll be curtains not only for you, but everyone you love.'

'Is that the reason he actually joined the family business?'

'The general opinion is it was either that or the possibility his life would've been destroyed. So, I gather if they knew he was married, his wife — and son would've been killed.'

'Does our informant know that Bescutti has this secret life?'

'No, none of them had any information concerning a wife and child. I just put it in play for us to understand what exactly happened.'

'Okay. So, far as they know, my daughter was a target because of me and not because she frequented Bescutti's son?'

'Yes. That's about it. And in my opinion, that is why their intelligence was off the mark. They had no idea who she dated, only that she had to be eliminated while on a date.'

'Do we have any idea who the young man was?'

'You mean the one shot?'

'Yes, that one. Who else are we talking about?'

'Sorry, I know this news is upsetting, knowing your daughter was in fact, the target. But, well, the young man was an excellent hockey player, well brought up; the only child of a good family from Vandoeuvres – a terrible loss for the parents.'

'I can imagine. Now what do we do? I mean, in response to that attempt to scare us out of business. We must retaliate in some way.' Arthur's anger slowly got the better of him. he needed to squash these Bescuttis and not only in business.

'We are not exactly sure that it was the family.'

'Well, we have to warn someone, and it could just as well be them – you know, as an example to anyone who might have been responsible.'

'How far do you want to go, and how hard do you want to hit them?'

'Good question. Bring me some ideas. We'll make the Bescutti family

the example. We'll attack their business with a vengeance. The family might be a problem as they are overly protected on all fronts. On our side, we should double up on our own security, especially in respect to our family members. Don't forget we can call on our associates in Colombia for their expertise if needed. I'll tell you one thing though, if – whoever they are – they attempt another attack in any way against a family member – yours or mine – there will be all-out war and that's a promise.'

'We should be careful. If we declare war, we'll show our hand and be an even greater target. We don't want the opposition to know that we're on to them, is all I'm trying to say.'

'I get it, and you're right. We'll make sure that we do everything under the radar. In the meantime, we should definitely double up on security.'

'Good, I'll get the security in place and see what can be done to surprise them, and I'll let you know. And thank you for thinking of extra security for everyone.'

'No thanks needed. We need to be strong within our ranks; otherwise, we will lose the battle on both fronts against the Bescuttis. Or whoever's attacking us.'

*

The Boss picked up the phone and glanced to the left, making sure that the door was firmly closed. Satisfied no eavesdroppers were near, the Boss dialled Alpha.

'How far have you got? ...You call that progress? ....' The right hand tapped a rhythmic pattern on the desktop.

'Good, I'll take your word for it. ... You have your next step planned? ....' A resigned sigh escaped.

'What about witnesses? ... You know what I need. The next time we speak, I want to hear that everything has been finalised. ...' The rhythmic tapping stopped.

'Yes, I need no problems or failure. I presume you understand the phrase: not acceptable. ... Is that clear?' Without a further word, the Boss replaced the receiver.

*

Maria held her arms out in welcome to Paul. He walked into her hug with the usual reassuring words. He hated the antiseptic hospital smell, and the night he spent next to his partner's bed, heightened the chemical's attack on his sense of smell. It only added to his aversion to healing institutions. He wanted news of José's progress and get out as fast as possible.

Visiting hours were nearly over, and the CAPITAL-speaking nurse appeared, giving him a warning look. He nodded in her direction – message received.

'I only came to check up on him and see if you arrived safely. How are you, Maria? And Phillippe? Does he now understand the importance of staying put?'

'Yes, we're all fine under the circumstances, thank you. I sat him down and explained the situation. He was angry and disappointed that I didn't trust him enough to confide in him from the beginning. He felt I treated him like a child, which he assured me in no uncertain terms that he wasn't. But finally, he understood I wanted to protect him and the younger ones.'

'Good. It's best he knows, he's old enough to handle it and look out for danger signs.'

'That's what I decided as well.'

'Look, I'll have to go. Only family members can stay, and the nurse already gave me the evil eye. How is he doing? What did the doctor say?'

'The prognosis is cautiously optimistic.'

'What does that mean in real terms?'

'Well, he said that they'd slowly bring him out of the coma today and see how he reacts. So far, he has stabilised at the rate expected. So, I suppose that's what they call optimistic. Don't worry. I'll keep you informed and let you know immediately when a change occurs. I'm not leaving his side.'

'Good, let me know if I could help in any way. Your brother and sister-in-law are okay with having the children there?'

'Thank you. Yes, and the kids are happy there. She lets them play video games whenever they like. I suppose for the time being I could lift the restrictions. I don't allow them to play the whole day long, they only have an hour each day for video games.'

'Well, it's like a holiday for them. Anyway, I must be on my way. Keep well, and as soon as he opens his eyes, let him know that I'm waiting for him to get back to his desk.'

'Great, thank you, and have a good day.' Maria gave Paul another hug, watched him leave before turning back. She entered her husband's room, her concern clear. Her husband looked so vulnerable with all the tubes and machines around him. She had never thought of him as fragile but seeing him like that she realised even her rock, her mainstay, could break. She put on a brave smile, as if he could see her.

*

Instead of going home, Paul chose to re-examine some of the information they had. The traffic had eased a lot on the way to the station. He sailed through Plainpalais and couldn't wait to get back into the files. He needed to make sure he hadn't missed the obvious. As law enforcement officers, they always try to see what lies behind details, the subterfuge, and the obfuscation. They look for the various scenarios or escape routes the criminal might have taken missing the obvious – something right in front of them, often overlooked.

Paul realised that's exactly what he had done with Alexandra Labelle. He missed the obvious distress an event in her past had caused her, and he had pushed for information. All the different possibilities it could be ran through his mind. It could be anything, emotional, a scandal, even criminal, but the basics were right in front of him. He just didn't see. Something serious deeply scarred her, and for the truth to come out, would need finesse. And for that, he'd have to dig deep. He had forgotten how to tread lightly. Though, that had to wait for now - put Miss Labelle and her secret aside.

The interrogation with the two lookout men in the presence of their lawyer didn't reveal any more than what they had before, but at least they now had a better idea of who supplied the legal assistance. Though the lawyer didn't reveal his clients' benefactor, he gave a couple of names of others he represented. This put him in a specific category - more on the shady side of the law.

Paul fired up his computer as soon as he got to his desk and pulled out the report on the interrogation while waiting for the Cantonal Police Logo to light up the screen. He clicked on the Serious Crime Unit icon. At the sound of the computer's readiness, he typed in his password and searched for Legal Records.

Consulting the file in front of him, he entered the name of the lawyer and one of the names they got from the legal representative. The first name came up *sub judice*. Paul clicked onto a new tab, called up the local newspaper with the name of the accused in the search engine. From there, he found an article on a drug bust at the home of the accused. He closed the tab, returned to the first site, typed in the next name connected with the lawyer. This litigation resulted in a clearer picture, as the record of the trial was in the public domain. Again, it involved the drug trade.

Paul slapped the desktop – this got more interesting with each bit of information they received. In his mind, that the shooting involved the drug trade became clearer, and José's first impression correct. At least now they have a direction to follow. But why the young man, Marcus Stephens? He had no connection to any drug dealer, and his tox screen was clean. His parents didn't look like people who could be involved with illicit dealings.

Well, there was a place to start – he'd check them out, though he was sure that they would be eliminated as a possible connection. Then, the next logical step would be to check out the family of the girl, Cynthia Gonzales. He quickly looked up her interview. Her nationality, Colombian – well, that explained her temperament. Besides her origin, her fiery disposition could be the trademark of constant pretence and masking.

Information about the Vicario and Bescutti connection they already had. As far as the Vicario family goes, they didn't find anything untoward, unless you call the mother's dubious registration of birth in Valais suspect.

On the other hand, the Bescutti family have all kinds of illegal dealings known to the CP and even the FP, but never proven. They could even be known to Europol and Interpol. From what the SCU had, there was no evidence of association between the two families. Paul and José couldn't find an alliance on a business level, only then there was the father-son connection. Though, Antonio Vicario told them that his father had died. Obviously, they kept the secret of his parentage from him just as it was buried deep from common knowledge.

If this case concerned a drug crime, a drive-by shooting could be feasible, but then from what Mrs Marx gave them, the shooter was not in the vehicle but calmly walked away. Could there be a connection between the shooter and the departing vehicle? Did the car drop him off? If so, would they be able to prove it? So many aspects seemed to contradict. This made the motive for the killing obscure, in fact, now completely absent. There could be various possibilities. One fact Paul couldn't escape would be that the death of Marcus had no reason. They would have to look elsewhere to find a motive.

For the first time in many years, he wished he had someone at home to be his sounding board. Not for the gory bits, but for the puzzle in each case which needed to be unravelled. The pieces which don't fit needed a place to slot into. Those were the ones he needed help with, as he supposed every other detective desired. Alex Labelle sprang to mind. A vision to be treasured, he shook his head. At present, she did not want anything to do with him. Though, he would love to see and speak to her again – perhaps it would be possible. He left it there, now isn't the time.

He looked at the timeline on the crime board. With the information from Mrs Marx and subsequent identification of the shooter, it looked more complete, but not yet there. He wanted to look at everything with fresh eyes. He realised that his watch showed nearly ten o'clock and getting dark outside. It'll have to wait till tomorrow. He closed the files and the tab on the computer. It only took a minute to sign out of the CP SCU site. He rolled his chair back, got up and lifted his jacket from the back of the chair in one movement, more than ready to go home.

*

Leonard called Favre over to Garcia's desk as soon as Paul walked into the station. He had various fax pages in his hand.

'We've received the report from the Terrorism Unit on the blast.'

'*Bonjour, chef*'.

'Yes, well, all that.'

'Good, what does it say?'

'They found the detonator and believe they've seen the signature of the bomber before. They have requested confirmation from Interpol.'

'Why not Europol?'

'Apparently, this man is not directly known by Europol. He worked mainly on other continents and not in Europe. So, they suggested we deal directly with Interpol. They handed the case over to them.'

'Why don't they just give us the information? We could follow up, find the man.'

'They want to be doubly sure they have the right person. Also, they

162

have insisted that we do not interfere. Our job involves only support to whatever they need – nothing else. They made that clear.' Leonard turned away from Favre, not wanting to see the disgust in his eyes.

'But what if their man and our man are one and the same?'

'Well, then we'll have to wrest him away from them.'

'That's not going to be easy. If only we could have a look at their file now – it would save a lot of time.'

'I agree. If we can prove that it had nothing to do with terrorism, we'll have our chance. Then, if the evidence proves that the bombing and the shooting were connected, we will be able to arrest him, lock him up and throw away the key.'

'How tempting. Do you know which way they are leaning?'

'By the sound of things, they are beginning to doubt it is terrorism, as his previous crimes have never involved anything like that. He prefers the clean-up jobs, such as assassinations, scare tactics and torture. From what I've seen, he deals not only with the drug trade, but also human trafficking and high-end jewellery, precious stones. But we'll get more information when the detailed file gets handed over to us.'

'Can't wait! I must say, it's beginning to look like the same person.' Paul rubbed his hands together and turned to the crime board.

Leonard and Favre studied the timeline together. The information they requested concerning the suspected shooter came in during the next couple of hours from Interpol. Nothing which made him look better. They gave further aliases and further crimes for which warrants were out against him, as well as confirmation that no fixed address could be found. The SCU of the CP's progress remained slow because they had to report everything they found to Interpol and, therefore, were double-checking everything.

By eleven, Maria phoned. José would be brought out of the coma at noon and asked if Paul could be there with her. Without hesitation, he told Leonard that he would leave within half an hour. Favre and Leonard continued to put pieces together, expanding the timeline until Paul grabbed his jacket and headed for the hospital.

As the evening before, Maria hugged Paul as soon as he arrived at the door of José's hospital room. They saw the doctor administering to the patient with the nurse standing by. Within a couple of minutes, she came out.

'As soon as doctor finishes, you can go in, Mrs Garcia. BUT ONLY

FAMILY – ARE YOU FAMILY?' Her eyes bore into Paul. He shook his head and nodded meekly. He kept on crossing paths with the CAPITAL-speaking nurse and wished he didn't, as she terrified him,

'Maria, I'll wait out here for news.' At that instant, the doctor pushed the door to José's room open halfway and beckoned Maria in. Paul's eyes followed her until the door closed. Too anxious for his own good, he didn't go to the waiting room and stayed just outside.

Paul watched through the small glass panel as Garcia began moving his head from side to side. Maria took a place on his left, taking his bandaged hand as she spoke to him. The movement of his head slowed. He calmed down and fixed his eyes on his wife. Paul could see confusion in his face, but also relief to see her next to him. She leaned over and kissed him on the forehead. He tried to lift his right arm to enfold her in an embrace, but his injuries prevented him from moving freely, and his arm fell back on the bed. Paul saw him wince.

Maria kept on talking to him and from where Favre stood, it was clear that he asked for information. Dr. Stein then spoke, probably asking Garcia if he could tell him his name, if he knew where he was, what year it was, if he knew the person standing next to him, and, if he remembered anything. Confusion still clouded José's face, though he obviously could reply to all the questions, as the doctor nodded with satisfaction, gently patted José's knee. He evidently said something comforting to Maria because she smiled and again leaned over to bury her head in her husband's neck. The doctor made a note on the file and replaced it, hanging at the end of the bed, leaving the couple to catch up.

'Doctor, how is he?'

'You're his partner, not so?'

'Yes, Favre, Paul Favre.'

'Well Detective Favre, he's a lucky man. I gather he was in a car which exploded.'

'Yes, actually he just got in to drive over to his wife.'

'Well, if he had sat directly on the explosive device, we would have picked up the pieces and not patched him up as we did. The severity of his internal injuries gave us cause for concern, but he seems to have come out of that well. Luckily, he didn't break any bones except for a couple of ribs from the blast's pressure. The concussion was our other worry, but he seems to have handled that well and is healing.'

'That's so good to hear. I cannot tell you how relieved I am.'

'Well, you can go in to see him, but please keep it short and don't try to ask too many questions. Give it a day or two before you ask for information.'

'Thank you; will do. We want to clear this up as soon as possible of course, except not to the detriment of his health. We want him in top shape as soon as possible.'

'Good. For that, you'll have to have patience and tread carefully. Besides the shock of the blast, he suffered the trauma of the event.' With that, Doctor Stein turned on his heel and left.

Paul looked through the glass pane, then left and right, in case the nurse prowled the corridor. Satisfied, he slowly pushed open the door and stepped to the foot of José's bed. His partner saw him, and Maria looked over her shoulder at him, indicating for him to come closer. He took place next to the bed opposite Maria.

'Hi, Partner. What have you been up to?'

'Hi, Favre, just hanging. What have you been up to?' With a raspy voice, he responded with their usual greeting.

'Look, I won't stay long. Just wanted to make sure you're on the mend and report back to the station. Don't you worry about a thing, everything is in hand.'

'What happened? I need to know because I can't remember a thing.'

'That's why we're not going to do anything today. I'll come back tomorrow and see if you remember something. In the meantime, enjoy your wife's company.'

'Thanks, isn't she a sight for sore eyes? She's an angel.'

'See you tomorrow, Partner.' Paul gave José's shoulder a soft touch and moved over to Maria to hug her goodbye.

'I'll be in touch. Look after him.' Paul left the couple to their whispers.

The doctor's words ran through his mind. The bomb didn't go off directly beneath Garcia. He didn't sit on the bomb. How could that be? The Bomb Squad reported that the destruction caused, showed the device was placed under the driver's seat. How did Garcia escape that kind of damage? He'd have to speak to his partner as soon as possible. The sooner they clarified exactly what had happened, the better. But, for now, he thanked Heaven that José escaped fatal injuries.

CHAPTER NINE

Alex pulled out the chair in her bedroom and placed it in front of her wardrobe. She made sure it was stable before climbing onto it to reach for a box, which she had placed on top many years before. She pulled the box towards the edge, balancing it carefully, then clasped the sides with both hands. The weight of the box, heavier than she remembered, caused her to sway slightly backwards. She steadied herself and brought the box down to chest level. Carefully, she stepped down from the chair and placed the box on the dressing table. With a soft breath, she blew some of the dust off, and the rest she wiped away with the ridge of her right hand, which she then rubbed down the side of her slacks. It left a brownish-grey mark on the pale green material.

Alex took a deep breath and exhaled slowly – repeating it, trying to relax. With trepidation, she lifted the lid off the box. It took her a full minute before she could lift the various folders out, selecting one which she set aside. She stared at the file for a long time. Straightened her shoulders and meticulously replaced all the other folders and put the box on the floor next to the dressing table.

Promptly, she turned and left the bedroom. She needed time, couldn't face it all over again. She had told herself long ago that she'll never go through that file ever again – that it was dead and buried. But things had changed – knew she had to. But couldn't it wait?

After a fitful night, she had woken up early, convinced that there was no other way. She had to face her demons – head on – not try to mitigate the impact. She decided to go through her usual routine and get ready for the day. Once done, with her day ahead of her, she would fetch the file which held her past captive.

At last, she was ready. But she didn't exactly feel ready. She needed a cup of tea before tackling the past.

When she reached the kitchen, she stood for a long time in front of the sink, looking out the window. With automatic movements, she lifted the kettle from its base, filled it with water from the Brita, replaced it, and pushed the switch down. With the same mechanical motion, she set out a mug, pulled out a teabag to place in the beaker. By the time the water boiled, Alex felt the time had come to deal with the past. She entered the present, taking her tea to the living room, where she set it down on the table next to the sofa.

With determined steps, she fetched the file from the bedroom and, with the mug of tea, curled up on the couch. Time for the final step in decision-making – how much to tell Favre about her life, which she had left behind so many years ago. All she could do was to go through each piece of paper in the folder.

And there it was. All laid out in front of her. The vestiges of that event's terror threatened to overtake her. It waited for her to relive each horrifying minute, each terrifying second, every humiliating day thereafter. As if it were yesterday, she tasted the air, heard the sounds, and felt the sensations of each moment of the ordeal. Cordite and rust. Gunshots and blood. Fear and shock.

*

A week before Christmas, and they were ready to party! All five of them had decided that this holiday season would be the greatest ever, because it would be the last of their time together at Uni. No one could ever tell if they would end up in the same city, or even the same country after graduation. Come end of the academic year and summer, they would all go their different ways.

They looked at their group as the extended Musketeers. Five is only two more than three and wasn't there a fourth in the old story? So what was one more, right? As a group, Alex, Joyce, Stephanie, Jos, and Hendrik decided to travel from The Hague to Amsterdam for some revelling. Amsterdam was so much hipper than The Hague, and the further from their seat of learning, the better. They all had Friday free and decided to make a long weekend of it. The high-speed train connection was direct, frequent, and perfect for them to spend as much time in their chosen destination over the weekend, especially if they took the early train out. They met up at The Hague railway station at six o'clock in the morning.

Alex loved every train journey in Holland. Over the flat lands of the country, where cold winds cut to the bone; the homes always looked warm and inviting. The lights from within changed the landscape. In some, you could see the bluish tint of a TV screen, as the Dutch habit of limited curtains gave a clear view of the interior. Yes, no matter how cold it was outside, the homes always looked cosy, beckoning any traveller.

In a jovial mood, the five of them got into the second-class wagon, one next to the first-class car. Few other passengers were in the wagon at that time. Just after the conductor had passed, checking tickets, the Five Musketeers became boisterous. They quickly made friends with the other three passengers.

Twenty minutes before the train pulled into Amsterdam Station, four burly men dressed all in black with bandanas covering their features, entered their wagon. Immediately, they ordered the Musketeers and the three others to take their seats, calm down, and keep quiet. One jammed an object in the door joining the buffet car. At first, a couple retaliated with smart quips. They very quickly changed their attitude when the butt of a revolver connected with Jos's head. Another member of the black-clad group passed to the end of their wagon and jammed the other door. The wagon they occupied was now sealed off from the rest of the train. Everyone fell back into their seats in silence. In shock, Alex tried to minister to Jos, blood flowing into his collar, but the leader of the group stepped forward and slapped her across the face. The four men had taken the rail wagon and its passengers, hostage.

'The next time you try that, you'll also get the butt and not my hand. Do you understand what I'm saying?' he looked directly at Alex, then to each of the group. She could only nod, the others mumbled agreement.

'If you lot know what's good for you, you'll do exactly what I say and not attract any attention.' After herding all the passengers to the same spot, his three companions pulled out their guns, taking position in various corners of the wagon. Hendrik moved closer to Stephanie and Joyce. Alexandra stayed next to Jos.

'Here's the plan. All of you are now part of my team. And today we are going to rob the ABN Amro Bank at 29 Leidseplein.' A murmur built up amongst the group of eight hostages with, 'No' and 'No, we cannot' the most common comments.

'Silence, I don't think you realise you do not have any say in this. If you do not cooperate you will be shot. Let me be clear: you will not be hurt; you will be shot.' The leader's voice was calm, quiet, even charming. And blood-curdling in its lack of emotion. The group looked at each other and huddled closer.

'This works out perfectly as you are eight, and we are four. Each one of us will have two of you. That means; one with a gun and two doing the job at hand.' He waved the gun around the group. 'I'm sure you have by now guessed who will be doing the bank job, which means of course, that you will be committing the crime and not us.

'Don't worry' he continued. 'As you will all be guilty, none of you will be singled out. Therefore, your punishment less if any of you did it alone.'

'But…' Hendrik began. Beads of perspiration showed on his forehead. The colour had drained from each face. Joyce trembled uncontrollably and Stephanie bit her nails. Everyone glued to their seats in fear.

'No "buts," you will now listen carefully. The train will be pulling into Amsterdam Main Station in ten minutes. At that time, we will all get out in an orderly fashion and get into the Toyota minivan which will be waiting for us. From there, we will travel to Leidseplein where the bank is situated.

'Three of you will go to the back entrance, and the rest of you will come into the front with me. As we'll be there when the bank opens, we should be the only "customers." We will move to the counters as a group. Six will demand that the Tellers hand over the cash in the drawers, insisting that the batch with the tracker and explosive ink bomb be left behind. The rest of us three will get hold of the Manager and Assistant Manager for the vault.' He looked at each one in turn.

'I assume all is clear so far.' He didn't wait for a reply before he continued. 'If at any time one of you try to warn or give a signal to the bank staff, that member of the bank will be shot in front of you. The culprit will be given a reprieve for the period of the robbery. Upon its completion, a bullet will be his or her reward. Is that clear?'

'Obviously, there would be a Security Guard. What if he wants to intervene?' Hendrik braved the question.

'Well, that will be his last act of heroism, as we will not hesitate to take him out. And for the sake of your own survival, you will stay out of their way unless, of course, you would like to join him in Nirvana.'

A tight-knit group descended the second-class wagon next to the first-class car. They moved as one to the exit and climbed into a white Toyota minivan parked in the pick-up area in front of the main Railway Station. A traffic controller made his way to the vehicle. Without hesitation, the vehicle moved smoothly off into the traffic. The official stopped, no action necessary, the minivan didn't overstay in the pick-up area.

Flow of traffic slowed the progress of the Toyota, but they were still on schedule. During the drive, the leader paired them off. Alex and Jos with one of the gunmen; Joyce and Hendrik with another. The four of them would go directly to the tellers. Stephanie was paired with one of the other passengers and told that they needed to take the back entrance of the bank and await his call, upon which they should return to the Toyota. The two other unlucky passengers had to accompany the leader to the vault. The vehicle stopped at no. 29 Leidseplein, the group spilled out. The allocated three moved off to the side, and as one, the rest entered the bank. As expected, the bank was void of other clients.

The security guard had not yet begun his shift; they saw him through the door finishing his coffee. He threw the empty paper cup in the trash as he entered the main foyer to take up his post. According to plan, they didn't attract any attention until the security guard decided that they crowded the person in front of them, invading their privacy. He moved over to suggest giving each other space. As he came up to the man closest, he reached out, putting a hand on his shoulder.

'Would you kindly take your hand off my shoulder and step back before you say goodbye to this world.' Again, the quiet, calm voice cut through and shattered the previous unthreatening ambiance of the building. The security guard reached for his sidearm, then crumpled into a heap on the floor. The leader had struck the guard with the butt of his gun. None of the tellers noticed. The group's frontline reached the counters. They explained their demands, and the thugs with each of the two hostages, brought up their guns to clarify the point.

The leader, with his two hostages, demanded to see the management team and immediately filed off to pursue their quarry. Each thug from the rest of the group handed over the duffle bag they had brought, with orders to begin filling. With trembling hands, the various hostages packed stacks of notes as fast as the tellers could hand them over.

The Manager and the female Assistant Manager were herded to the vault with their keys, which had to be used simultaneously. Punched and shoved unceremoniously, they descended the stairs and opened the vault under duress. A bit too slow for the leader's liking, he grabbed the Assistant Manager by the hair, throwing her hard against the vault. Her body bounced off the hard steel. The warning that her death would be on the Manager's conscience if orders were not followed without delay numbed the Manager's fingers. He fumbled to get the right key. One of the hostages helped the woman up who had to be steadied and supported so that she could insert her key at the same time. It would have been easier just to take the key from her, but the leader absolutely refused – she had her part to play, and that she would do if he had his way.

Once in the vault, the leader threw down a duffel bag which held two more and ordered the hostages and the management team to fill the bags as fast as possible. Whenever one slacked, he forcefully prodded them with the gun to increase their enthusiasm for the job given. When satisfied, he locked the management team in the vault and gave each hostage a bag to carry upstairs where the rest of his group finished up gathering money. The leader made a phone call.

One of the gunmen overseeing the loading of money at the counter took a call. At that moment, the security guard came to and aimed at the one on the phone, shouting for him to 'freeze'. Instead of freezing, one of the gunmen turned and in one motion shot the guard in the heart. The air froze. Joyce fainted. Alex's knees gave out. The red stain of blood on the guard's shirt burnt into Alexandra's memory. The smell in the air scarred her nasal membranes. Both women were helped by their friends, fearful that another would be shot if they did not do exactly as instructed.

Without another thought, the gunman and his partner roughly pushed the bank staff into the manager's office, locking them in. The leader and his two 'helpers' joined the group at the tellers. He demanded who shot, and why it couldn't be avoided. Though, he made it clear that, with no time to waste, the guilty gunman will have to explain later. He gestured time had run out. He pushed them to leave. Heavily laden, everyone in the heist moved to the bank's main doors and into the waiting minivan.

Alex couldn't remember exactly what had happened next. The only thing she consciously recalled at that moment was they were surrounded by uniformed officers and told to get out and down on the ground with their hands above their heads. They were pushed, pinned down, their hands pulled back. Handcuffs clicked firmly around their wrists. She felt the hard pavement cold against her skin, small gravel scraped her cheek. She could see her friends also restrained. Joyce and Stephanie had tears streaming down their faces. Blood had dried on Jos's head, caking his hair. Hendrik had a terrified look. Their fellow train passengers were in the same state of fear. But the worst was still to come.

The Dutch police took them to their Rail Station site. They separated them, preventing each member of the group from even glancing at the other. Alex and her friends tried to tell the police that they were forced into the situation. No matter how hard they tried to convince the authorities what had happened, no one listened; no one gave them an opportunity to explain. Without ceremony, their passports and whatever else they had on them were confiscated. The leader of the heist had made sure that each of his hostage team would be identified and complicit.

The interrogations began after they were left alone without information for over an hour, obviously to check the authenticity of their identities. Alex knew that, besides the eight passengers, the four gunmen most probably had either false IDs or none, confirming the leader's intention to implicate the innocent eight.

For three days, the interrogations continued. In solitary, they despaired and yearned for contact. Alex asked if she could contact her parents and was told that could be arranged as soon as the interrogating officer gave his permission. She insisted their legal right to contact their families or a lawyer was ignored. This only brought the detective in charge back with the same questions she had replied to on all the previous occasions. Apparently, the mere fact that she asked to contact a lawyer meant she was guilty – the heist her idea. She tried her best to convince them, but they pushed, cajoled, threatened, tried their best to trip her up, make her plead guilty to the crime. She explained exactly what had happened, how they came to be there. But the police didn't believe her.

Each day that passed made Alexandra more and more fearful. The cold in the cell at night reached her bones. With only a thin blanket and inadequate mattress covered in plastic, the nights were difficult. Early each morning, they took her to an interview room, and again forced her to sit in a chair with only one bottle of water for the day on the table. The limited food and hours of questioning made her feel dizzy and weak. They refused her a shower. She felt dirty, not only because the days passed, but because of the nervous perspiration which clung to her. Terror replaced her fear. Being treated like criminals and withholding warm drinks, did nothing for her wellbeing. How could she ever get out of this? No matter how she tried to explain what had happened, nothing helped. One day flowed into the next ceaselessly.

None of the officers believed any of them, even though their account of the events never changed. They were accused of contriving the same story prior to the heist; as well as knowing the three other passengers beforehand and hatching the plan of the theft together. When she asked if they treated the gunmen the same, the detective just said he could not divulge what occurred with any of the other accused.

The bank theft made front-page news with their names listed as accomplices. This caused Alex's parents to immediately contact the police. However, they didn't take steps to support or prove her and her friends' innocence. They felt she had brought shame on her family. Not knowing exactly what she did while at university, or who she cavorted with, they felt that, for the sake of her siblings, they should distance themselves. Her parents thought it prudent to await the outcome. This unfortunately didn't help her case. Why should the authorities believe the word of someone in whom the parents had doubts?

Luckily for Alex, her friends' parents had the best interests of their children at heart and took action. With their help and Jos's father, an attorney, they were allowed out on bail, and the threat of incarceration avoided for the time being.

Through Jos's father, she heard that the four criminals immediately lawyered up, refusing to say a word. This threw suspicion on them, but not sufficient for the authorities to lighten up on the hostages. They still had to prove they had nothing to do with the heist. Because of this, the authorities leaned heavily on the young people.

With Jos's father's help and the consistent accounts of the events by all eight hostages, they were finally released on bail, though not vindicated. Their movements were restricted to the University grounds and their respective places of residence. The three other passengers could only travel between their place of employment and home. None of them could leave the country as they were – if not accused and to be charged – at least witnesses due to appear in court later in the New Year.

The court case dragged on. Her neighbours and her parents' friends looked at her with distrust. Alex had to leave home as her family regarded her as a criminal. She found a room in the students' hostel. At least her parents paid for the room and the rest of the University year's expenses. Alex and her friends' studies suffered, yet they made it through to graduation. After the ceremony she found a room in a house as far as possible from her family home. From there, she set out to find employment.

Where the five friends thought their paths may not cross after finishing their studies, it took two years for the case to be finalised, and the eight hostages vindicated completely. They were finally free to lead their lives – broken as it might be.

Alex never saw any of her friends again. Her parents accused her of betraying the family and never completely accepted her as a member of their unit again.

*

Alex closed the file. Sure, the incessant interrogation in Amsterdam made her wary and fearful of police and authority. Strangely, the fear and terror of that experience seemed not as heavy or real as before. The anxiety of being regarded as a possible suspect in whatever crime had been committed, even if she found herself far away, has lifted. The shame she had carried with her all those years, seemed unimportant now. The feeling that everything she said people doubted the truth of, and looked at her with suspicion, appeared childish now. She still continuously asked herself if she spoke the truth, exhausted her, and now she had a reprieve.

Perhaps she should've done this long ago. Revisiting the whole file, reliving each moment as written on paper, now gave her a different perspective. The severity of the past, and the changes it forced onto her, made her who she was today. She should accept that and build on it, not destroy what she had, or could have, by letting these events be the master of her.

Yes, time to let go. Share her past and let it go. She should give Paul the opportunity to make up his own mind. Either accept her for who she was or leave her be, as her family has. She picked up the phone, hesitated. Would he be ready, would she? She replaced the phone, hesitated a moment, then picked it up again. No, this has gone on long enough – she must face up to her past. So, here goes, she dialled Paul Favre's private number.

*

Paul saw the caller ID on his phone, pleased, but hesitated a moment, then swiped the screen and greeted the caller.

'Good to hear from you, Alex. Am I still allowed to call you Alex?'

'Of course. I apologise for my behaviour yesterday.' A nervous chuckle escaped her.

'No apology necessary. We all have our trigger points.'

'I would like to explain.'

'Not necessary.'

'Well, I think I owe you that. I would like to tell you a story, and then you can make up your own mind about my behaviour. Though, I wouldn't want you to hold it against me.'

'What? I'm a nice guy. Why would I do that?'

'Okay, I'm trying to be nice here!' Despite herself, she had to smile – he had a way to make her feel completely relaxed.

'I'd like to hear your story. Whenever you're ready I'll be there to listen, but now I'm in the midst of this investigation. It's at a crucial stage.'

'Okay, I understand. Give me a call when you have time to get together.'

'Definitely. I'm hoping to wrap this up soon, for everyone sake.'

'Good luck then.' He could hear Alex's breathing change as if on the verge of saying goodbye when she interrupted her flow. 'Oh, I forgot to ask, how is Detective Garcia?'

'He's out of the coma and responding. I haven't spoken to him about the case or the explosion. At least he could name everyone around the bed.'

'That's good news. Well, I'll leave you then. Goodbye.'

'Goodbye, have a nice day. I'll definitely phone you… and soon.'

Favre's smile made Leonard look up with a quizzical look, wanting to know if Favre stumbled onto something which could break the case. In response, Paul shook his head.

'Interpol said we'll have their full report first thing in the morning.'

'Good news! I have a feeling that we'll prove the connection between our case and the blast. We'll be able to get our investigation back and solve the riddle.' Favre couldn't hide his enthusiasm.

'You sound so sure that we'll close the case?'

'Yes, it might take a couple of days to clarify the motive and pinpoint the person behind the shooting, but we'll get to the bottom of it. Of that, I'm sure.'

'That's a great attitude to have. I agree we'll have the shooter. The question though; will he talk? Will he give up his boss?'

'Anything's possible. For the sake of the parents of the young man, I'll do my best to get the shooter to give us everything. They're good people, *chef,* the Stephens. You should have seen them – absolutely broken by the loss.'

'I understand, but Favre, we cannot get emotional about a crime – it clouds our judgement and we tend to jump to conclusions.'

'Yes, you're right. If we can arrest him for the shooting, at least the parents will know who killed their son. The reason for the crime, they might not want to know but eventually will.'

'I understand. At this moment the motive is really eluding us. There's just no obvious reason why the young man was killed.'

'Yes, it's so frustrating.'

'If it was a gang shooting; he was either accidentally hit or an initiation of a new member,' Leonard said, flipping through the papers in front of him.

'Except, from what we know, the victim had no gang connections. Therefore, based on that, we can eliminate a gang shooting – unless, as you said, it was an initiation.'

'So, the threats to Garcia and you could be red herrings to throw us off the scent.'

'The threats are real, make no mistake. But I agree, that on saying it's a "drive-by" was a ruse,' Favre couldn't forget the sight of a vulnerable Garcia in hospital.

'There's something much more serious behind those threats.'

'Oh, that reminds me, I haven't received any information from the Tech Department about the origin of the threats. Did you get anywhere with the Federal Police regarding where the calls came from?'

'No success from there either; a scrambler caused the call to jump all over the world making it impossible to specify.' Leonard sounded disappointed.

'Whoever's behind this crime definitely has a vast organisation to fall back on.'

'Yes, and that's who we should find.'

'I look forward to that, but first things first. Get this killer behind bars for Garcia's and the young Marcus's sake.' Leonard only nodded in agreement

Favre looked with satisfaction at the crime board. They had set out every piece of information and event clearly with times clocked. On one hand, they've made progress, but on the other, they still needed to achieve so much more.

Something nagged at him. He had missed something. In the back of his mind, it didn't add up. The breakthrough they had made by identifying the shooter gave them a starting point. Except which direction it would take, remains a puzzle. Also, what the crime related to, and the motive, remained a mystery. The answer lay in front of them, of that, he was sure. What kind of crime was this?

Favre's eye caught the clock above the crime board. Surprised that six o'clock had come and gone, he picked up the phone and called Maria.

'Hello Maria, how's our boy doing?' ... *'Okay, I'll hang on.'* He played with his pen while he spoke to her.

To Leonard he said, 'She had to step out – no mobiles allowed except in the allocated areas.'

'Good, you're back.' ... *That's good to hear. ... So, the doctor is happy?'* He looked at Leonard and nodded, holding up his thumb.

'Has he said anything about what happened ... Does he remember anything? ... What? Is that normal?' A concerned look crossed his face.

'Oh, I see, so it happens sometimes? ... I mean that he would be confused, or hallucinate? ... And he goes in and out of consciousness? ... You sure he's not just sleeping? I'm sure he must be tired.' Paul looked slightly relieved. *'Oh good, so it is normal. Well, I'll leave you to get back to his side. Give him our best wishes and I'll pop in tomorrow to speak to him. Goodbye until then.'* Favre replaced the receiver and got up to leave.

'So far, so good. Maria says he is in and out of consciousness. The doctor is satisfied that Garcia's making the progress expected and is optimistic for a full recovery.'

'That's excellent news. So, I gather you'll be speaking to him as soon as possible?'

'Yes, I'll see how much he can remember and if he saw anything untoward.'

'Good, I assume you are off home then?'

'I'm off to get a good dinner – the first in a long time. In fact, the last time I ate something nutritious was an omelette yesterday for lunch.'

'In that case, I won't keep you. I need my detectives strong, rested, and healthy.'

'*Bonne soirée, chef,* see you in the morning.' Favre shrugged into his jacket. A grunt from Leonard sent him on his way.

He stopped at the La Primavera Restaurant on the Route de Meyrin, just before reaching Servette. At a quarter to seven, he was one of the first customers and pleased about it. He wanted to eat in peace, take his time, with as little noise around him as possible. He liked the ambiance there - family-friendly, and good food. That's what they were known for. Furthermore, he liked the relaxed feel of the place. As usual, the friendly proprietor came over, greeting him personally. Their specials of the day always sounded tempting and difficult to choose from.

In the mood for some good seafood, he ordered a *Fritto Misto* and a glass of *Pino Grigio* while he waited for the food to arrive. He let his mind wander.

He enjoyed living in Geneva. A native of Neuchâtel, he came to Geneva over twenty years ago and had felt part of the community ever since. The cosmopolitan atmosphere of the city made it an interesting place in which to live, but also a difficult one for his line of work. He appreciated the village atmosphere this international financial hub offers.

With all the events and festivals, citizens or tourists would never have a dull moment here in the City of Calvin if they chose to participate. With the lake lapping the edge of the city, the summers always bring a different feel completely. Just thinking of the sailboat race, the *Bol d'Or,* and the various beaches where swimming is allowed, made him smile. Who would believe Switzerland had such an active outdoor living during the whole summer season? Unfortunately, his duties kept him too busy to enjoy most of what goes on in this city.

The waitress came over with his food, a feast for the eyes. He ordered another glass of wine. He knew he was hungry, but he didn't realise to what extent. His mouth watered when he saw the sumptuous plate of selected seafood. He savoured the aroma rising from the plate. With each bite, he enjoyed the tastes of the various fruits of the ocean. He took his time.

Just before eight o'clock, he wrapped up his meal with an excellent espresso. His mobile rang. Still in a relaxed and satisfied state, he answered the phone. The hint of a smile on his face disappeared in a flash. He threw his napkin down and jumped up, grabbing his jacket at the same time. He went over to the cash register giving them a fifty-franc note, told them to keep the change as he rushed out.

A cold sweat broke out over his whole body. He ran back to the station to get his car, swearing under his breath that he hadn't brought it nearer. Ten metres from his car, he beeped it open. He yanked open the door, inserting the key in the ignition. On the second try to start the vehicle, he hesitated, wondering if an explosion would follow. The engine turned over with no blast. Breathing deeply, he put his foot down and screeched into the road. With sirens blaring, he raced to his apartment block.

Fire engines and police cars blocked the road when he arrived. He stopped, leaving the car as near as possible to his home. He rushed toward a chaotic scene and broke through the cordon of police tape. Like pythons, bulging hoses, and puddles of water, lay as obstacles in his path. He pushed through the crowd demanding what had happened from anyone and everyone, receiving only mumbled replies. A uniformed officer waved him back. He pushed the officer away, showing his Detective ID card. Nearer the building, he found a fireman and told him that he lived in this block and would like to know what had happened.

The fireman directed him to his chief, who explained that a fire had destroyed an apartment on the second floor. He explained that all they could do now, was to battle the fire before it gutted the whole building. As for the cause of the blaze, they didn't yet know, except they weren't ruling out arson.

'Why is that?' Paul asked.

'Because the fire started quickly in the apartment and didn't spread until the place was virtually destroyed. At that moment, the fire jumped to the apartment above and the one next to it. From there, it took on a life of its own.'

'In which apartment did it start?'

'In apartment twenty-two.'

'But that's mine! How on earth did it start? When did it start?'

'As I said, how, we're not sure yet. We'll definitely get to the bottom of it, though I doubt the Fire Inspectors will disagree with me. A neighbour phoned it in at five this afternoon, but when we got here, it was already well advanced. We estimate it started around four, four-thirty. The whole situation is strange, the fire engulfed the apartment far too quickly to have been an electrical fault, or a cigarette, or candle causing the blaze.'

'So, nothing could be saved from my apartment?'

'No, unfortunately I doubt it very much, the place was consumed by the fire. As you can see, we couldn't even get near to that part of the building.'

'Excuse me. I must contact my superior.' Paul turned away and phoned Leonard. He explained the situation and mentioned he feared the next step of the threats issued had been carried out. Despite the disaster, he felt it corroborated his initial impression. This confirmed the explosion which injured Garcia, was aimed at him and was not an act of terrorism. They'd now be able to seriously investigate their case without outside interference. That is, unless the shooter turned out to be an internationally wanted criminal. Then again, from what they knew so far, it could well be the case.

He itched to join the uniformed police taking names and possible witness statements from the residents of the building and those standing around gaping at the disaster. There were many questions he would like to ask, but he would have to leave that up to the officers present to collect as much information as possible. They'll have to go from there to get to the root of the fire. Who besides the suspect would target his apartment? He was convinced that the cause of the blaze didn't come from an electrical fault, or something left on the stove. As he did not smoke, neither had he cooked during the last three days, the only alternative was suspicious circumstances.

As soon as his mind jumped back from the case to the present, he realised his predicament. He rubbed his face with his hands, hoping to wake from a nightmare. He had lost everything. Where to begin? He realised he needed to find accommodation for the time being. First thing in the morning, he could get some clothes at the commercial centre. But now, at Cornavin, he needed to pick up some toiletries. It struck him that he would need a bit more than just toiletries; he would need underwear and a clean shirt before tomorrow morning. A good thing that the shops at the railway station stay open until midnight, it solved his immediate problem.

*

The flames billowing out from the second-floor windows reflected brightly in the car windows below. Alpha stood behind a lamppost, a hundred metres further. His reflective dark glasses danced in tune with the scene. The air

180

was thick with smoke, and the smell of burnt plastic, rubber, and cloth. His mouth curled into a smile.

Two fire trucks were already on the scene, but they had lost the battle. He chuckled. It created such an amusing sight. Those guys with their helmets, heavy boots, and restrictive jackets and pants ran back and forth, moving around like ants trying to cope. They created this comedy of passing on a hose, pulling it against unseen tension. Others struggled with a ladder, to put where? He couldn't see their reasoning as now other windows also billowed flames. They created organised chaos. He enjoyed the entertainment.

How they could ever do their jobs wearing clothing like that, escaped him. It hindered natural movement. No wonder they had to practice day in, day out, while wearing full gear - an oxygen bottle, an axe, and heaven knows what else. In a way, he admired them. They must have that thrill running into a fire. He could only imagine the adrenaline rush when facing danger like that. Gosh, they must be fit and have such fun. And imagine, having fun while working. Definitely his kind of job! Perhaps he should apply to be a fireman. He could have that rush every day when a job comes his way, not just now and then. But on second thoughts, he would have to wear that gear and not his own cool clothes.

Police arrived at the scene, making the whole spectacle even more interesting. They tried to get the attention of the firemen, but none of them had time to talk. The fire spread. More people ran out of the building, carrying children, bags, dogs, or cats. Everyone shouted. No one could understand the shouts. It didn't matter. They kept on shouting. The police tried to ask questions. No one took notice. They only shouted, pointed back at the building.

Two ambulances arrived. The medics treated a couple of burn victims. They gave both oxygen, put one on a gurney, and pushed it into the back of a waiting ambulance. A fireman helped the other in. They closed the doors and sent them off to hospital. Various medics began treating some who had smoke streaks on their face and hair. Others had an oxygen mask placed over their nose and mouth. Two other ambulances pulled up.

Police arrived in numbers. In total, he counted four police vehicles. They blocked the access to the area from all sides and, with their yellow crime scene tape, cordoned off fifty to a hundred metres in all directions from the building in flames. They began evacuating the adjacent buildings.

Another thing he found amusing – how the police always loved their crime tape – most of the time overdoing the taping-off.

The pavement milled with inhabitants. Residents from the opposite side of the road came out with blankets, bottles of water, and thermos flasks. They moved amongst the building's evacuees, giving water, or paper cups of coffee, to the smoke victims. They handed out blankets to those shivering from shock. Ash thickened the air.

Alpha loved every minute of the show. It looked like a jolly block party. He moved amongst the bystanders, listening to the "oohs" … "what a terrible experience" … "wonder how it started?" … "where will they go now?" and many other comments. The ones he liked most were the two young men making fun of the victims – "look at that woman with the curlers in her hair … what a riot" … "that one's in her pyjamas – at this time of day!" … "look he's clutching the birdcage with his budgie as if the cage will fly away!". Alpha saw the old man with the cage and agreed – he looked so desperate, his hair all awry, the fly of his pants half undone. He gave the young men a thumbs-up.

You've got to love people! So many feed off misery, you can get such a high from people's predictability. Alpha did not want to leave but realised that sooner or later they would be dispersed by the police, and he didn't want to give his latest name again. As he walked away, he looked over his shoulder, just in time to see Detective Favre arrive. He hesitated. No, he had to see this – far too good to miss.

His inner self jumped up and down with glee when he saw Favre put his face in his hands. How great is this? It couldn't get any better! And he had a front-row seat! He patted himself on the back. His second warning had hit home. He could not believe how easy it was to get entry to the building – and that where a police officer lived! The old lady actually held the door open for him! How crazy can it get? Pity the pig wasn't home when he threw that Molotov cocktail through the small bathroom window. That would've been the greatest. Get rid of him forever. On the other hand, Garcia was still around. He didn't die as he had planned. Perhaps that's for the best as he now had both to play with for a bit longer. He looked forward in thinking up another playdate with these two.

He hung around for another twenty minutes. The spectacle continued. Dusk descended on the area. The ambulances had all left. The Fire Department had the fire under control; they began their cleanup. Some onlookers still stood around, taking in as much as possible of the disaster. He felt bored. Enough of this, he needed something else to give him an outlet to this pent-up energy the event had caused. He needed a woman. He turned and left to satisfy his need.

*

Arthur Gonzales called his partner, Eric into his office. Their offices overlooked the lake, a suite in the Beau Rivage Hotel - central enough. Out of the financial district, but within walking distance, and well-placed for anonymous meetings at any one of the luxury hotels. The sight of the sun on the water always calmed him, and on this day, he needed to be calm.

'Have you heard about the blast at the police station in Servette?'

'Oh, yes. I heard a detective got badly injured. Apparently, one of the two investigating the shooting of the young man who was with your daughter.'

'That's right. I heard that as well. Did we have something to do with that?'

'No way! I think it must have been the ones responsible for the shooting.'

'Any nearer to finding out exactly who that was?' Arthur really wanted to know who they should target in revenge.

'No, not so far. And that means I really don't know who we should give a warning shot to. But I'm still working on it.'

'I also heard that a fire broke out last night. The blaze virtually destroyed the whole building. Did you know about it?'

'Also, not us. Yes, I did hear about it. I also heard that the apartment where the fire started belonged to the other detective on the case.'

'So, you think these two events were warnings directed at the investigating detectives?'

'Arthur, have you managed to convince your daughter to avoid the Vicario kid?'

'Besides prohibiting her out right, there is not much I can do.'

'You don't think it would be better to explain to her that he is connected to a dangerous family?'

'My wife already mentioned that to her. Apparently, the son, Antonio, said something to her about his family. He doesn't know them at all, never

183

even met, but seem genuinely wary of them. He seems to think they may be Mafia or connected to the Mafia.'

'Well, he's not far wrong there, is he?'

'Okay, now tell me, how far did you get in thinking up a retaliation? I mean, if that shooting was meant as a warning to us to get out of the business. We need confirmation.'

'I've got a few ideas, but as you said, we shouldn't move until we have confirmation on who to target.'

'We'll be patient. Something else: have you arranged for the courier to be met by one of our secretaries?'

'Yes, when the courier passes through customs, our girl will meet her.'

'The courier has the correct paperwork to pass through unhindered?'

'She has a manifest for a sample of what she is carrying.'

'Does she know she's carrying more?'

'No, completely ignorant of the fact. All she knows is that she's bringing a sample through on her way to Spain to vacation with an aunt.'

'So, she'll be here overnight? Make sure she is put up in a decent hotel, not too fancy, but where she could go downstairs for dinner. We'll then go into her room to retrieve the merchandise.'

'She believes the all-inclusive overnight stay is payment for bringing the samples.'

'Good, let's leave it at that. Then let's keep an ear to the ground regarding the shooting and what it relates to.'

CHAPTER TEN

In the WTC building opposite the airport, Georgio Bescutti tried to contact the lawyer he hired to arrange bail for two of his foot soldiers. He had no news from that quarter. No news normally means good news. Though, in this case, he would prefer to know exactly what the status was. If the lawyer says they wouldn't disclose their employer, he accepted his opinion. However, the niggling feeling that he shouldn't trust the situation completely wouldn't go away, as their allegiance lay with the family and not him.

Emilio came in after knocking briefly. He approached until Georgio could see both their reflections in the window. Without turning, Georgio spoke to his second-in-command.

'Emilio, I'm worried about that shooting. Too many eyes are turned our way. I do not know how to steer them away. I didn't order that hit and don't know who did. Do you know anything about it?'

'No, I was under the impression you did and ordered a clean-up.'

'Definitely not. I repeat, I did not order that hit and have no knowledge of it. You should know me better by now! I sent two of our foot soldiers to keep watch where it happened, in the hope they could find out who was involved and why.' Georgio knew Emilio didn't trust him to tell him the whole truth. From the way he looked at Georgio at that moment, he didn't change his opinion. 'They got picked up by the police. I sent a lawyer to make sure they don't talk.'

'I didn't know you sent someone out there. Why didn't you tell me?'

'No, I didn't tell you. I waited until I knew more about the shooting.'

'And now? Oh, I see, you thought I had something to do with it, didn't you? I would never do something like that unless YOU ordered me to. And even then, I would carry out the order under protest. And to clarify that: unless you order it. I work for you and not for the family.'

'That's good to know. Too often the family acts against my wishes. They also try to order my employees to do their bidding.'

'I would never betray you. I try to stay away from the family and their dealings. But the problem, I've always faced, would be what would I do if the family ordered something, which would be against your interest or my own. They would have to seriously threaten my relatives, if they want me to go against you. I only hope I would never be put in that position. People who do not please them get a taste of their cruelty and brutality.'

'You don't have to tell me. Though, if we stand together, we'll win. Why do you think I'm in this business. It's safer for all around. That became clear again when I saw my wife. An impossible situation.'

'That couldn't have been easy. I mean seeing her for the first time after all these years.'

'It wasn't. It brought home what I gave up. Many old memories resurfaced, and it rekindled old feelings. It all came rushing to the fore on both sides – I could feel it. I found it very difficult to let go – again.'

'I understand. I cannot imagine how you did it.'

'Well, let's not talk about it. Please forget I ever brought it up. It is old news and needs to stay in the past. Let's agree that we'll never speak about it again.'

'Agreed.'

'Good, now tell me what else you know.'

'I tried to find out if there were any murmurs or rumours going round about a vendetta or an outright war, but so far not much. It seems as if everyone's trying to find out who was behind the shooting.'

'Okay. I only hope my son will be safe.'

'Do you want to send a detail to cover him?'

'I don't want him to know that he's being watched. But he must be kept safe.'

'It'll be difficult, but we should get our own people to keep an eye on him and not a private security firm.'

'I agree. There are too many mercenaries employed by private companies. You never know who you let into your domain.'

*

Antonio noticed how quiet his mother had been the last couple of days. When he asked her about it, she blew him off. He found it difficult to keep up. One minute she couldn't shut up about him getting more information out of Cynthia and then a 360-degree turn, telling him not to mix with her.

What's all that? He wished she could make up her mind. More irritating: she's not telling him anything about his father or the 'family' as she calls it.

He decided to phone Cynthia. At least speaking to her would brighten his day. It also gave him the opportunity to hear what she has to say. Perhaps she found out something which could throw light on this mystery. It got more complicated as the days passed. Not only the shooting, but all the questions around it. And his father and 'family' have become, like, too much. Yes, he'd phone her, maybe they could meet. He'd ask if she had heard something.

On second thought, he should rather text. His mother might hear him talking to Cynthia if he phoned. So, he pulled out his smart phone and wrote: "Hi Babe, meet Stbcks PP @ 14:30?" He did not have to wait long before the reply came. "OK cu".

He checked his phone for other messages, replied to a couple, and decided to get to Starbucks ahead of Cynthia. With a very quick 'Bye Mom,' he rushed out before she could react, he didn't need an interrogation. More importantly, he wanted to watch Cynthia walk in. It always lifted his spirits to see her arrive for a meet.

He chose the same table as the last time, and didn't have to wait long when she walked in. She wore white shorts and a white t-shirt, which she had tied in a knot over her left hip. Around her neck, she had tied a yellow bandana. Her olive skin popped against the white. She sashayed towards him. Boy, she looked hot – a real knockout! Confidence radiated from her. That in itself turned him on. His light-headedness came from the effect she had on him.

'You want a smoothie like last time?' He asked as she slid onto the chair opposite him.

'Yeah, why not. What're you having?'

'I'm also taking a smoothie, with crushed ice. I need something cold. You want something with it?'

'No, I'm fine, but the crushed ice sounds good, make mine the same.'

He got up and hobbled to the counter to place the order. The brace still had to be on for another week. Despite his self-consciousness about the lack of fluidity in his walk, he couldn't resist glancing over his shoulder to take another look at her. Again, he wondered how on earth he had lost her to Marcus. That guy had nothing on him – no comparison – Goody-goody,

187

taking his girl from him. Sure, he would not want him dead, but he wanted him out of the way. Okay, he told the cops he didn't mind, but hell, who wouldn't mind. She's a girl to keep around.

He returned to the table to wait for their order, caught her eyes going over him. It felt good. It meant she was into him as well. Though, as she looked away, he saw suspicion behind her glance.

'You okay?' He asked as he sat down.

'Yeah, why do you ask?'

'Well, you look nervous – as if you don't trust me.'

'I'm just wondering why you wanted to meet. I hope it's not more of the same.'

'What do you mean, the same?' She rolled her eyes at his question. 'Oh, I see, you mean about the shooting and my so-called family.'

'Yes, that. Is your mother still bugging you?'

'She's been very quiet the last couple of days. I'm not sure why, but anyway she just repeated we shouldn't get involved.'

'You mean you and me?'

'Yeah, and on top of it, I'm still not allowed to go out after seven. Can you imagine staying the whole evening indoors?'

'You must be joking! My parents prohibited me from going out after dinner. I've got to spend the time with them or in my room. You can imagine which I chose. Who on earth would want to spend an evening with their parents?'

'Yes. Funny, my mother said the same. What's with them? Did they get together to mess with our lives? I understand my mother wanting me to keep away from people.'

'What do you mean – keep away from people?' Cynthia wanted an explanation.

'I mean, why can't I go out at night to see my friends?'

'I'm not allowed out either, so that doesn't explain anything.'

'Perhaps it's because of the family. I'm not supposed to meet them and must stay away from you. I can't see any other reason, can you?' Antonio tried to explain but only made matters worse.

'No, but let's talk about something else. It's getting boring, all this "shooting" stuff.'

'No worries. I'm all for talking about other stuff.'

'So, when will the brace come off?'

'In a week, then I'll do more physio.'

'But it is okay, isn't it? I mean you will be playing again, won't you?'

'Oh definitely. The physio will take about a month. I can do it at Uni while training for the season. No permanent damage to the knee, they said.'

'That must be a great relief. I must say I'm very pleased that you'll be back on the field, the end of last season was just not worth watching.'

'Pleased to hear you say that! At least I have one fan left!'

'Of course. But are you going to continue with the same courses as last year?'

'Yes, I am not changing my majors. And you?'

'Same, following the course I set out with. But look, I'll have to leave you. My Mom doesn't know I was meeting you, if she did, she'd freak.'

'Okay, I'll let you know if I hear anything that explains our parents' interest. Take care. I'll text you.'

'Fine. Yes, I think for the time being we need to cool it and only text. But if we meet by accident at the lake for a swim, they won't be able to complain, don't you think?'

'You got it! Okay Cyn, see you when I see you.' Her smile swallowed him, and he had to avert his eyes as she left Starbucks just in case she looked back.

Antonio lingered a while, cursing his injury. In this heat, a swim in the lake would be ideal, but the doctor said no – only walking in the pool. At least that kept him cool. Finally, he made his way home.

As he walked in, his mother stood waiting. 'Where have you been?' He couldn't ignore her or the question.

'Out.' He threw down his backpack and leaned his crutches against the wall.

'That I know. I asked where you have been, and then you can tell me who you met. Or should I guess? With that girl Cynthia. Am I right?'

'I'm going to my room.'

'You're not going anywhere, my boy, until you learn to be civil to your mother and answer the question.'

'Sorry, Mom, but I just wanted to go out for a while.'

'Look, we agreed that you would stay at home and not in the dorm until the business about the shooting is over. That meant you would also not go out too often.'

'But Mom, I can't be cooped up any longer, it's driving me crazy.'

'Until we know that you're safe and not in danger from whoever ordered that boy to be shot, you'll have to do what we ask.'

'Why do you think I would be in danger? For heaven's sake, I didn't even know the guy. And I haven't dated Cynthia for a long time.'

'Five weeks isn't that long. And we don't know what there is between her, or her family, in everything that's happened. Are they involved in the shooting?'

'How could you even think that? Why would they shoot Marcus?'

'I don't know much about these things. But all I can say is that it's best if you stay away for the time being. Your father agrees.'

'What? You saw him? You spoke to him?'

'Yes, I met him a couple of days ago, and we discussed you. He agrees it'll be best to keep a low profile for the time being, and not for you to be exposed to the family.'

'Will I ever meet him?'

'Most probably not, at least not until he's managed to change a lot of things.'

'You mean his family. Are they Mafia?'

'It'll be best if you don't ask that question, and even better if you didn't know.'

'Okay, can I go to my room now, please?'

'Yes, I'll call when dinner is ready.'

'Thanks Mom, sorry if I made you worry.'

'It's better now that we've talked.'

*

Alpha stepped into the Boss's office. Despite the hour, a personal secretary could still be seen around the office. He slunk in assuring himself no one noticed his arrival. He walked up to the desk and waited until noticed.

'You're early. Did someone see you?' The Boss asked without looking up.

'No, I came in the back way. You know that I'm good at being invisible.'

'So, what can you tell me? Have you managed to find the target?'

'Yes, the parents have put a curfew in place. I'll have to execute during daylight hours. Not ideal, but not impossible. I'll just change my method.'

'Have you cleaned up the mess?'

'The witness has disappeared, but warnings have been issued directly to the detectives involved. That'll keep them busy for a while.'

'The witness disappeared, you say, not eliminated?'

'No, not eliminated. The disappearance gives us time, but elimination will happen.'

'Still, you've made no progress. That does not please me at all.'

'Rest assured, the mission will be concluded. You will have a free and clear way in. No one will ever know of your involvement.'

'I depend on that.'

'Don't worry, everything's in hand, Boss.'

'You had better deliver.' The Boss began to study the papers on the desk again.

Alpha took the hint. He was dismissed. Quietly, he moved to the door, opened it a crack and squeezed through. Without a sound, he disappeared down the passage and into the stairwell. A clean getaway, just as he liked it.

In his mind's eye, with the Boss out of the picture, he could see the whole operation under his command. Not long now. The Boss is ruthless, but no match for him, and it'll be easy to usurp the Boss. Laws of the underworld apply: survival of the fittest and leadership to the strongest. He doubted he needed to mention intelligence, because as a strategist, no one could beat him.

Time had come to put his plan into action. He knew the target had gone to Starbucks in Plainpalais earlier, and it had not been the first time since the shooting. He concluded another meeting would not be long in the waiting. With the curfew keeping the target indoors from around seven in the evening to seven in the morning, it limited his available time span. Of course, no young person ever got out of bed before ten – especially not during holidays – shortening the span even more. At least he now had specifics to work with. Excitement built.

He sent a text message to one of his men. 'What news re no. 1&2?' He didn't have long to wait for the reply.

'No.1 out of coma, healing, No.2 @ Station. Orders?' Alpha smiled. After his initial disappointment that Garcia didn't die in the blast, he realised his opportunities to enjoy himself increased. This was good news. Now he'd have such fun when the two become his playthings again. He took his time thinking about what orders to issue. He wanted to drag it out, though at the same time, he wanted it over and done with, and gain control as soon as possible. To do that, the two detectives must be out of the way – a delicious dilemma.

He wrestled with the two completely different choices, an incentive he never knew he had. It fired him up, giving him a high – being torn between two possible actions. To plan his next step was a challenge. It must be interesting and mind-blowing – something that everyone would see and remember.

He sent a text: 'Hang tight. Orders to follow.'

He closed his phone and whistled as he walked towards centre town. He'd stop for a beer and perhaps call that girl from last night. She was good and tough. He could do whatever he wanted with her, and she never really complained. That's how he liked them - not all coy and fragile, moaning whenever he got a bit rough. She only begged for mercy when he wanted her to. Let's face it, that's what they're there for. If he paid for it, they must put out, not refuse. What? Is his money not good enough?

*

Back at the station Paul gathered all the information he had received so far, plus the latest and more complete details on the suspect from Interpol. Another report on his desk came from the Bomb Squad, who determined the signature of the explosive device. The pieces began to fall into place.

His first call this morning had been to the hospital. To his chagrin, the charge nurse controlling the corridors saw him first and descended on him like a determined Rottweiler. Instead of growling, she demanded in her usual controlled but forceful manner.

'WHAT ARE YOU DOING HERE BEFORE VISITING HOURS?'

On route, he had mentally prepared himself for this encounter. Despite his best resolve, he felt his knees tremble. His reply stumbled out. Her glare fixed on him, and with a jerk of her head to the left, indicating he had seconds before she changed her mind. Paul virtually ran to Garcia's room. He only drew his next breath once he reached José's bedside.

The two partners greeted each other with relief and joy. Paul immediately asked what José could remember of the explosion. Apparently, José realised something was amiss when his car wouldn't start on the first try. When he subsequently heard a slight "click'" he dove out of the still-open door. He landed under the neighbouring vehicle, which protected him from the blast's direct hit. He couldn't remember much after his dive, which Paul assured him was best forgotten. Favre updated Garcia with the progress on the case and the fact that Leonard stood fully behind them. Garcia itched to get back to work, though Favre convinced him to take his time. The healing process has been going according to the doctor's prediction, with the possibility of him leaving hospital in four days' time to continue his rehabilitation at home. The prospect cheered up both detectives, but just at that moment, the charge nurse popped her head in demanding.

'WHAT ARE YOU STILL DOING HERE? YOU ARE NOT FAMILY.'

The arrival of Maria and her joyous greeting for Paul saved the situation. Paul stayed for a few minutes longer before taking his leave. After talking to José, he felt confident that the end was in sight, making the drive to the station pleasant.

Paul looked at the Bomb Squad report. The signature of the bomb maker registered on four previous occasions. Next, he spread out the old information laying out the most recent received from Interpol next to it and began to compare and compile. The first surprise he found came with the name of the shooter, the second when the report connected the four previous blasts with the suspect. The first page of the report read:

NAME: Benoit Sebastian Olivier
D.O.B.: 09/28/1984
P.O.B.: Marseille, France
ADDRESS: Unknown
DEPLOYED: 11/01/2004
TERMINATED: 10/15/2014
CURRENT ADDRESS: Unknown

From the second page, a very long comment under 'Remarks' revealed an impulsive and unpredictable person, spilled out. Most of his aliases came from his given name: Benoit Sebastian Olivier. It also didn't come as a surprise that he was a native of Marseille, a city notorious for violent crime and gang wars. For most young men in that area, joining the Foreign Legion at a young age, was common. Most of them became mercenaries after learning skills of survival not available anywhere else. The report stated that during the ten years there, he built up a reputation for psychopathic behaviour, with ruthlessness, torture, and cold bloodedness a regular occurrence. He joined the world of soldiers-for-hire directly thereafter, with his main criterion for choice being the biggest paycheck. The area of his expertise ranged from hand-to-hand combat, strategy, explosives, and he excelled as a sniper. His favourite weapons were knives, but he had proved himself an expert with anything at hand and was a perfect shot. The Interpol report based their description of Olivier on the behavioural analysis given by the Foreign Legion, who rated him as a dangerous individual because he excelled at whatever he tried and never showed mercy.

The report went on to confirm what Favre surmised. In their case, they could rule out a gang-related crime because Olivier worked alone, with only a few foot soldiers who he controlled with threats. The next point they mentioned was that no history existed of him being involved in any drug operations. Apparently, drug operations required a large organisation, and he did not work well with others. Human trafficking, diamonds, and precious stones and metals were mentioned as his preferred products, where he required a minimum number of collaborators. The one point not in the Interpol information was Olivier's current address or where they could find him.

The report unsettled Favre. The only satisfaction he got came from the knowledge they now knew who they dealt with, an extremely dangerous criminal. Paul shivered. He realised that Olivier would not let go and would try to target them again. He picked up the phone and dialled his superior.

'*Bonjour chef, will you be coming into the office? ... Good, see you shortly ... I'm immediately putting extra security on Garcia's family and assigning a second officer at his hospital room... yes, I have the file from Interpol.*' Paul heard the click as the call ended, without changing his habit, Leonard had put the phone down without warning.

Favre replaced the receiver and moved over to the crime board. He added Olivier's full name, date of birth, time served in the Foreign Legion, as well as the four bomb events. He also included the blast at the station and the fire at his home. In his mind, no doubt existed, the connection clear, and Olivier, the person behind the two events. It all made more sense when he looked at it from that angle.

The pieces began to fall into place, Though the motive for the shooting still eluded him. Nevertheless, the progress made showed him which direction to take for the reason behind the crime to emerge.

He pulled out the interview with Cynthia Gonzales as well as the one with Antonio Vicario. He meticulously reviewed both, trying to tie certain facts together. Could their families have been working together which ended in an argument? Did the shooting mean revenge for a deal gone bad?

He needed the two families' histories. Delving deeper into their activities became essential. They warranted another look - perhaps the answer lay in the different types of operation they were involved in.

He pulled up the file for the Bescutti Family on his computer – a mine of information with sub-files and further references to other sub-titles – a spider web of data filled the screen. He printed a hard copy of as much as possible.

No file existed on Gonzales, so he did a Google search for everything on him. He made a hard copy of whatever he found. Gonzales' information stretched over three countries: Colombia, his country of birth, Argentina, and now Switzerland. He also found strong connections to Venezuela. His business interests in agricultural products ranged from sugar, coffee, and bananas. Other ventures included mining metals, minerals, and precious stones. He had offices in all the major cities of the world, dealing with administration and distribution. The financial statements available impressed Favre, though something seemed too squeaky clean, too pat for his taste. What hid behind it all he wondered?

Leonard walked in. 'What have you got?'

'*Salut, chef.* Quite a bit. The Interpol file is very complete and gives us a rundown of what to expect – his psycho personality, or shall we say, his perverted likes. I'm convinced the blast was a direct attack on Garcia, and likewise, the fire at my home by this Olivier.'

'Your instincts have always proved correct. I tend to agree with you here.'

'My problem remains motive. I can't seem to find one.'

'I see you've begun to look deeper into the families possibly connected to the girl. But you haven't taken the Stephens into account.'

'Well, sir, as I explained before, no connection to any kind of crime, shady dealings, or anything suspicious could be found. Therefore, I excluded them from the investigation, except for the fact that their son succumbed.'

'Okay, I'll go with that. So where do you want to begin?'

'Take a look at this.' Favre moved from behind his desk to where Leonard stood next to Garcia's desk. 'I've added all our information on Olivier to our timeline on the crime board. When I consider his penchant to work alone or with an absolute minimum of foot soldiers, we can eliminate gang-related crimes, and I believe drug running. Both of those always involve many factions and groups reporting to their individual areas and not directly to the head of the cartel. Therefore, there are too many cogs in the wheel, so to speak.'

'Fine, so far, I accept your hypothesis. What else do you have?'

'Well, the types of crimes I believe he would be interested in would be human trafficking, precious metals, and stones. We could also consider money laundering.'

'But money laundering is a white-collar crime. Not really an area one would find a psychopathic personality. That's what they described him as, isn't it?'

'Exactly, which is why it is last on my list. I'm leaning towards blood diamonds, emeralds, gold, or silver.' Paul picked up the hard copy of information on Gonzales he had printed out from his desk. 'If you look at this, the father of the young girl – Cynthia Gonzales, who was present at the shooting – has dealings in the same type of items. He mines most of it, I suppose.'

'Fine, but what about the Bescutti family, they've never dealt in ores or any mining explorations. Or do they now also have a finger in that pie?'

'Yes. Besides their many activities, they have been involved in that field. As far as I could gather, it stopped long ago. Georgio Bescutti wasn't involved, but someone higher up in the family was, although I haven't been able to pin down exactly who yet.'

'What else?'

'They both have had international dealings in sugar, soy, and coffee, but these all seemed to be above board. Some cutthroat dealings, but the trades seemed legit. I suppose they all want to have the monopoly to control certain markets. Though, nothing which I can see that would cause a war between the families.'

'Could there be a new player, or a renegade in one of the factions?' Leonard scratched his head, scrutinised the various copies Favre had produced, then looked at the crime board again.

'Could be. Obviously, Olivier works for whoever wants to take over that specific market. Wait! I just had a thought. What if Olivier's running the operation for them or for – as you say – a new player who gave him carte blanche?'

'That would be difficult to find out. So far, we haven't received any information on new players. I'll contact our Organised Crime unit. They must have intelligence on all new players. Give me time till the end of today, I'm sure they'll come up with something useful.'

'Sure, I'll dig deeper into what we've got. Perhaps I'll get a hook and even clarity.' Favre turned back to his desk. He knew finding the motive had become imperative to solve the case and give closure to the Stephens.

Further, he requested whatever the street-cams captured near the station, including those at the two closest tram stops. His second request was for footage from the area around his apartment. Additionally, he asked the Tech Department to collect whatever footage they could find on social media for both the events. If nothing came from this, he decided to canvass the onlookers to hand over whatever video they took while at the different scenes. You never know, one face might pop up at both places, giving them the opportunity to follow him from camera to camera. Now that they know what Olivier looked like, they had the possibility of picking him out in a crowd. That is, if they were lucky and he was there. At least, they would get the general direction in which he went.

Suddenly, another avenue popped into his head. He pulled out interrogations and statements taken from Tweedle Dee and Tweedle Dum. He had to look at this from the beginning, fill in the holes, and match it all up. Something might jump out at him now that he had a wider scope. If only he could figure out who they were working for, Bescutti or Gonzales.

Before he knew it, the clock showed six. He couldn't believe that the day had passed so quickly. He realised again he hadn't had lunch, and his hunger suddenly consumed him. It was time to go home, but first, he wanted to check on his partner. Then he'd call Miss Labelle.

*

Alex put down the phone with a smile, though anticipation crept in, tinged with a touch of panic, colouring the emotion. He'd be here in thirty minutes.

She rushed to the kitchen to check what she had at hand to make a meal. It was after six, and she wouldn't have time to go out for extra provisions before he arrived. She wondered why she had asked if he had eaten.

She thought of issuing an invitation only for coffee, specifically to soothe over their last meeting and assure him that she would tell her story. Perhaps she should have waited, but his enthusiasm had surprised her.

He did ask if she would be prepared to share her past when he came over. Then suddenly the invitation evolved into dinner. She realised that her intention to limit his visit to just coffee would force her to look at him the whole time – whereas, if he came for dinner, she could concentrate on preparing the meal. While she busied herself in the kitchen she could talk, offer him a glass of wine at the counter.

What to serve remained the question. With only salad, pasta, onions, tomatoes, basil, and a few slices of ham at her disposal, she decided that it would have to do. Yes, spaghetti pomodoro with small pieces of ham added to the sauce for variety. He needed his protein.

Secondly, what to wear sprang to mind – nothing too obvious or eager. Slight apprehension accompanied her to the bedroom. She surveyed the contents of her wardrobe. After fifteen minutes of deliberation, she had pulled out various possibilities. A sleeveless pale-blue dress which reached just above the knee won the contest. Her reflection in the mirror pleased her. Quickly, she gathered the pieces she had thrown on the bed which didn't meet her satisfaction, replacing them carelessly and without order back in the wardrobe. In front of her dressing table, she saw her image looking back at her. Something had to be done about that as well. With a fluttering in her stomach, she pulled out the chair, sat down and applied light make-up, smacking her lips together making sure the lipstick showed up evenly. Her nervousness didn't abate as she went through to the lounge to tidy up, and then to the kitchen. He would be arriving within minutes – she had to rush. Thirty minutes would pass in a flash.

She prepared the salad and put water in a pot. The doorbell rang just as she put the pot on the stove. Without turning on the heat, she hurried to open the front door.

'*Salut!*' She saw him hesitate for a second.

'*Salut.* Thank you for the invitation. You look great.'

'Thank you, please come in. Are you hungry?'

'I could eat. Thanks for the invitation. It's always a pleasure to have a home cooked meal, much preferred over takeout and Bistro. You get tired of both very quickly.'

'Well, I hope it'll be okay. It's only a salad and pasta.'

'That will be absolutely perfect. Thank you.'

'Well, come on over, sit yourself down here at the counter and have a glass of wine, while I prepare our meal.'

'That sounds very welcome after the day I've had.'

'Sounds difficult.'

'Well, more tiring than anything else, I had to go through metres and metres of street camera footage and social media videos. My head's still spinning.'

'You can put all that aside and enjoy your wine. Red okay?' When he nodded, she poured him a glass of Gamay.

'Definitely, and while I sip my wine, you can tell me your story.'

'Oh yes, I did promise. Fine, let me get a glass as well. I'm going to need it.'

'Is it that bad?'

'It depends on how you look at it, and I suppose; how you react after hearing the whole complicated saga.' They clinked glasses. 'Well, here goes!'

Alex turned toward the stove, hoping he wouldn't notice the slight tremble in her hands as she turned the heat on under the pot. While she took the spaghetti out of the cupboard, she began recounting the events which had happened so long ago and left deep scars. She put the kettle to boil, took the chopping board and laid a paring knife on it.

Her story took form as she moved to the fridge, from which she retrieved three ripe tomatoes and basil. She bent down to a bottom cupboard, found an onion and garlic from a wire basket next to the potatoes, trying to concentrate on her actions and not on him staring at her. From the roll of paper towels, she pulled off two sheets, setting them beside the chopping board. Periodically, she stole a glance to see Paul's reaction to what she had said, but his eyes followed her movements. He seemed completely captivated with the rhythm of her hands following her words. Neither noticed the time pass.

The sound of the water in the kettle boiling brought her back to the task at hand. She turned, took down a glass bowl above the sink and filled the bowl with the hot water. She noticed the water in the pot was also boiling, grabbed the packet of pasta, shook out half, and placed it in the pot. A slight frown of concentration appeared on her face as she fanned out the spaghetti sticks to cover the whole pot. With her little finger, she tested the temperature of the water in the glass bowl. Satisfied, she placed two of the tomatoes in the hot water. Careful not to cut a finger in front of him, she sliced the third tomato and added it to the green salad.

A slight rattle of pans broke the sudden silence as she brought down a pan from above the stove, placing it on the burner. She poured a small quantity of olive oil in and turned up the heat and continued her tale. Periodically, she pushed the spaghetti sticks deeper down into the boiling water, minimising the fringe. Then she turned back to the cutting board, where she skinned the onion, placing the skins on the paper towels. After rinsing the onion under cold water, she wiped it dry and expertly chopped it, hoping her eyes would not water. Relieved, she added it to the hot oil. While it sizzled, she crushed the garlic to add. Again, throwing him furtive glances, she removed the tomatoes from the hot water and skinned, cut them in half and de-pitted them. Reassured that he didn't seem disgusted with her tale, she cut the tomato into small pieces and added it to the sizzling onions with salt, pepper, and oregano. The basil, rinsed, came last. She chopped the leaves, adding it to the tomato, onion, and garlic mix, turning down the heat under the pan. She left it to simmer. The spaghetti was virtually all covered by boiling water. She wanted another glass of wine to calm her nerves, but it was time to set the table. She paused from telling her story.

'You okay?' Alex asked, avoiding his eyes.

'Oh yes, thank you, I love to watch you cook.' Relieved, she refilled their glasses.

They decided to eat there at the counter. She proceeded to set out salad and dinner plates with utensils and napkins. She continued describing her experience of so long ago between sips of wine and tending to the preparation of the meal. She added the fresh tomato to the salad and tossed it with a light olive oil and vinegar dressing, ready to serve. Her eye caught him looking at her as she reached the point where they were forced into the bank and ordered to approach the tellers. She hesitated, but he asked her to continue. With a deep breath, she took up where she left off.

At last, the pasta was ready. She took it off the heat, and before draining it, added the cut-up ham to the tomato mix. Then she drained the pasta, rinsed it with cold water, slid it back into the pot sprinkling olive oil on it.

She shook the pot. The spaghetti had cooked perfectly – al dente – and slid from side to side, allowing the oil to cover it evenly. Happy to be able to keep her hands busy, she pulled out a large bowl into which she emptied the pot of pasta. She added the simmering pomodoro from the pan and gently mixed the sauce through the strands of pasta with tongs. Satisfied, she covered the bowl and turned to Paul, announcing that dinner was ready.

She took a seat next to him, and side by side, she served the salad, pleased that she didn't have to look at him face to face. He insisted she continue her account. When they finished the salad, she removed the plates and brought over the pasta. He refilled their glasses with wine, and they tucked into the meal. In between bites, she finished off her experience in Amsterdam, explaining her terror of being interrogated, how the days seemed like months. He only nodded, and chewed on not only the spaghetti, but the story she recounted.

A long sigh escaped her as she finished. A lengthy silence crept through the apartment until it felt unsupportable. She couldn't meet his eyes, knew she had to break the silence and under her breath she mumbled,

'Now you know everything.'

'I don't know what to say.'

'I understand. I don't blame you. At least you got a meal out of me.'

'Well, thank you, the meal was just what I needed. It's definitely "moreish" and I'm very tempted to camp out on your doorstep on a permanent basis.'

'Look, I know you're trying to let me off easy, but I'm a big girl, I can take it. I realise that you couldn't and wouldn't care to spend time with me now that you know my history. I'm sure there must be some regulation or something which prevents you from fraternising with criminals.'

'Yes, there's that, but you're not a criminal. You were a victim. You committed a felony under duress. Because it was evident by the exact same accounts given by the other innocents involved, they couldn't charge you with the felony. You were not only constrained but forced by gunpoint to do their bidding. You were in the wrong place at the wrong time.'

'What do you mean? You understand? You're not suspicious of me?'

'Of course not. You didn't do anything wrong.'

'But at home, everyone - all the neighbours and my family - treated me like the criminal I believed myself to be. They still accuse me of being part of a bank robbery.'

'Well, they're wrong. Acting under duress is something completely different in the eyes of the law. For instance, if you had killed someone, it would've pleaded down to manslaughter. But you didn't, and the bank robbery was foiled with the help of you and your friends. Therefore, you all got a pardon.'

'Only, that doesn't clear me from what happened. Also, how could I ever forget?'

'Well, you shouldn't feel guilty at all – you were not responsible. As far as the Dutch Police Force is concerned, you are innocent and as far as I'm concerned, you can put it behind you. Try to forget and move on. I can help you with that.'

'What do you mean?'

'Well, as you know, I'm an expert on how the criminal justice system works. So, I can give you some backup analysis on how they see things and why you should accept that you were – and are – innocent. That whole experience wasn't your doing. Chalk it up to a learning event."

'I'll try, but you know the nightmares still come.'

'When you start to accept your own innocence, the nightmares will begin to fade. And I have other ideas of how to minimise the scarring it caused.'

'Such as?'

'Well, of course, that is if you agree. I suggest we go out for dinner one evening, and from there we could think of other activities.'

'Are you asking me out?'

'I suppose I am. Purely as therapy, you understand?'

'If you think I need therapy, I'm prepared to take my medicine.'

'That's settled then.'

'Let's have some coffee.'

'That'll be great, but then I must take my leave. With my partner out of action, I have another difficult day tomorrow.'

'I understand. How is he doing?'

'He's making progress, and we hope that he'll be back at work soon.'

CHAPTER ELEVEN

Paul whistled as he walked into the station, confident that he would find a break in the case today. Last night's dinner had helped, especially the company. He now completely understood her nervous attitude when he and Garcia asked questions about the shooting.

He shook off thoughts about Alex and began to sort out the various videos he still needed to look at. He also arranged the prints of the frames he had selected at the blast and the fire, with their timestamps. He fired up his computer, opened his account, and saw the Tech Department had left an e-mail. They managed to get some further private video footage, which they attached. This would take time to peruse, he got up and fetched a coffee.

The attachment included five different files, all taken by onlookers at both events. The Tech Department had managed to obtain shots from different angles, thereby creating a complete virtual 360-degree view. The patched footage covered different times, arranged into five files, each a continuous sweep of the area.

Favre opened the first one, which covered the fire, and let the video run through to the end. He checked his earlier prints made from the street cameras and reran the video, stopping at regular intervals. He ticked off the person repeated in both the official and private footage. He repeated this sequence with the next two videos, which also covered the fire, each patched from different times. The first three videos focused on the apartment fire. One man couldn't be seen clearly, his face partly hidden. Like many of the onlookers, this man appeared in all the videos, spanning nearly three hours, but was never clearly captured. Paul marked him down anyhow.

It was long tedious work, so he got up and fetched another coffee. As he sipped from the cup, he walked around the office to stretch his legs. He puzzled over the crime board, shuffling through the various prints. He looked again at Olivier's photo, which they received from Interpol, and the artist's sketch of the shooter, based on Mrs Marx. Feeling sufficiently refreshed, he got a sandwich from the dispenser and another coffee, which he took to his desk to continue his search.

He moved on to the fourth video, taken at the tram stop in front of the station, and did the same as before. From this group, he had all the prints ticked, but so far, no one appeared at both events. He was on the point of closing the fourth file when he noticed a man half obscured. He bookmarked the spot and opened the fifth and final video, also of the tram stop at the station. Again, he meticulously checked the ticked off prints; the man he saw earlier always seemed to move around, always half hidden. Though, no one appeared at both events, unless the half-hidden face belonged to the person who attended the fire and the blast. In this last video, the left side of the man's face was visible, and in the previous video – the video at the fire – part of the right side. Since the height of the man seemed to match, he decided to try another tactic. If he could piece together the two sides to form a full face, he might have an image which could be run through facial recognition. A long shot, he was sure, as the images were not the same size, but then again, the Tech people were wizards. They could also tell him if the two parts belong to the same person. He called them, explained what he wanted, and sent the bookmarked sections, hoping for quick response. He also sent them a photo of Olivier, just in case. If Olivier appeared at both, they'd have concrete confirmation that the shooting, the blast and the fire were all connected – time to move on to the next step.

He called the Duty Officer to bring Tweedle Dee and Tweedle Dum to interrogation room two. When asked if he wanted them separated, he said no. This time, he wanted to ask both questions and see how they reacted to the answer the other one gave. He chose various photos and collected their files in preparation for his discussion with the two.

As he got up, his phone rang. The call came from the two plainclothes policemen watching the comings and goings where the shooting happened. They reported that no suspicious vehicles stopped for longer than the normal time. Nevertheless, other activities were noteworthy, causing them to keep a detailed record of movements. Favre asked them to continue.

They noted two pedestrians – never together – repeatedly walking by, casually checking each building. This activity had happened regularly over the last four days, and the two alternated. They also seemed to have made the local cafe their stopover spot. At seven a.m., they were seen cruising by in a black SUV, and the same vehicle passed again at nine p.m.. During the day, it was parked in the local supermarket underground parking. The four officers made discrete inquiries and stopped at the café where the two individuals were seen.

The proprietor found the attitude of the two strange. He described it as a relay team – they would only bump fists, then one would get up and leave, while the other stayed for about thirty minutes. Then the cycle would repeat throughout the day. "It's bad for business," he kept on repeating. Two strangers hanging around, and not ordering much, drinking three coffees each over the whole day, and having a light lunch. His regulars began to ask questions. He wanted these two gone from his premises.

Favre instructed them, with their relief team, to apprehend both individuals at an opportune moment, check their IDs, and bring them in on a loitering or nuisance charge.

'Tell them the café owner made the complaint,' he added. Further, he asked to be informed as soon as they had been brought to the Servette Station. The officers were to continue their surveillance as instructed until further notice. Favre replaced the receiver, gathered the file, and headed to interrogation room two.

The two Tweedles sat side by side on one side of the table, each with one hand handcuffed to the iron ring attached to the table surface. Favre joined them, nodded to the officer standing in the corner of the room, throwing the file down on the table as he sat down.

'Now, I suppose the two of you know why I brought you up here again.'

'Huh? What? Why did you bring us in here again? We were supposed to leave here this evening. And where is our lawyer, you're not supposed to talk to us without him here.'

'Calm down, you will be leaving here shortly. But before you go, I wanted to show you a couple of photos. As for your lawyer, he'll join us shortly.'

'We're not going to say anything until he gets here.'

'Of course. In the meantime, just look at these pictures.' Paul pulled out the photo of Arthur Gonzales first, carefully placing it on the table in front of them. He watched their reaction closely. Nothing flickered in either of their expressions. The second photo, that of Georgio Bescutti, he placed next to the first. This time, both sat back slightly, and without turning their heads, their gaze shifted towards each other. Silently, Favre shouted 'Bingo!' Then came the third photo, that of Benoit Olivier, which he set down beside the others. Favre couldn't detect any reaction. Still, he knew it didn't rule out an existing connection.

'So, I'll tell you a story. The two of you work for the Bescutti family to find out who witnessed the shooting. Then, when you found them, you had to eliminate them.'

'No! No! We only had to find out why the young man was shot. We don't know anything 'bout elimination! Isn't that so, Xavier?' Both men shook their heads and nodded vigorously.

'Yeah, yeah, we only had to watch and report why, and who shot that boy.'

'I don't believe you. I still think you had to bring them to the family so that they could deal with them.'

'No, we assure you, we don't know anything. The boss only said we had to watch and report what's said on the street.' Xavier voice hinted at panic.

'So, Mr. Bescutti ordered this third man, Benoit Olivier, to shoot the young man?'

'We don't know no Benoit Olivier. We've never seen him before. We don't know anything about orders to shoot. Do we, Xavier?'

'Where's our lawyer? He'll tell you. We're not saying anything else.'

Paul knew they were through talking to him. He decided to let them wait in room two until their lawyer and transport arrived.

Nevertheless, from the session, he found out whom they worked for, and most probably, were either not privy to the orders to shoot, or Georgio Bescutti was not involved. That, of course, doesn't exclude the rest of the family. His disappointment at the lack of recognition in either man when they saw Olivier's photo was evident in the frown on his face as he headed back to his desk. He heard his desk phone ring even before he reached the bullpen.

'Favre.' He lifted the receiver before sitting down. As he listened, he pulled out his notebook, sat down, and scribbled a couple of lines.

'Good, how soon can you get them here? ... No, I'll be here, I'm not going home soon. ... Good, book them in at the desk, The Duty Officer will handle the rest, but please let me have your report directly, I'll be at my desk. Just come through. ... Yes, you can sit in, no problem. We think there might be a connection with the shooting that we are investigating.' Paul ended the call and immediately called Leonard asking him to come in

without delay.

*

Half an hour later, Paul Favre received a call that the two men he expected had been brought in and taken through to be processed. The plainclothes officers who accompanied them were directed to his desk. When Favre looked up, he saw Pichon and Borel walking towards him.

'*Salut!*' He held out his hand in greeting. 'Did you have any problems with the two?'

'Good afternoon, no, no problems. They argued and resisted at first but then realised there was no point, and they were better off just playing along,' Borel spoke first.

'What reason did you give them for bringing them in?'

'We told them the café owner had lodged a nuisance complaint, and they were upsetting his regulars by their presence. They argued it only merited a warning and we should let them go home. In any event, here is the file on their movements,' Pichon explained.

'We retaliated with the fact that we have to keep the local businessmen happy and needed to bring them in for identification purposes, etc.' Borel sounded apologetic.

'Good, you did well.'

'Here's our report of their movements,' Pichon handed over their file.

'Why don't the two of you get a coffee while I look at this?' Paul reviewed the file quickly, noting the routine the two men had set in place.

'Thank you, coffee would be welcome.' They got their drinks and came back to Favre's desk.

'Are we charging them officially – if so, with what?' Borel still sounded unsure under which misdemeanour they should've been brought in.

'They are now being officially booked but not charged. Let's chat to them and see how it develops. We can always think of something to keep them here a little longer.' Favre's phone rang. As he answered, he nodded, said thanks, and replaced the receiver. 'Let's go, they're in interrogation room one.'

'You're going to talk to them together? Don't you want to separate them? Talk to them individually?' Borel asked.

'At first, I want to put them at ease. Together, they'll let their guard down and then, using the pretext of wanting their statements, we'll get one out to IR two keeping the other one in IR one. That's when we'll turn up the heat.'

'I agree, it's a good tactic. I'm ready, shall we go?' Pichon wanted to know.

'Yes, let's go.' Favre grabbed the file of their previous warrants and the photos, along with a fresh notepad, and led the way.

The three of them entered the room where the two men sat side by side, watching the door. Favre pulled out a chair, and Pichon did the same, while Borel stood behind them. The officer who stood guard before, left the room. Paul deliberately placed the notepad on top of the files in front of him. He introduced each of them and waited for a response from the two. He pulled out a pen from his inside jacket pocket, continued when they remained silent.

'Let us begin. Please give us your names.'

'We've already given you all our details.'

'We know. This is just for quick reference. The quicker you reply, the sooner you can get out of here. You know we have a job to do and follow up on all complaints.'

'Okay then. I'm Peters and he is Schmidt.'

'And your respective residential addresses?'

'You got all that when we were booked. We still don't know why it's so urgent that we must be here. Why couldn't we just get a warning? We promise we'll stay away from that café in future.' Peters seemed to be the spokesman of the two.

'As we said, we must follow up on all complaints. Now, tell us, why were you in that area for the last four days playing tag?'

'We were checking out real estate.'

'Now, come on, don't kid a kidder! What would you really want in that area?'

'As I said, just checking out the neighbourhood. Before renting a place, you need to know exactly who lives next door.'

'Okay, so where did you think of renting a place? Which building did you prefer?'

'There were two. Both allowed pets, and that's important to us.'

'So, you have an animal? What do you have – a cat, dog, or bird? Or perhaps a goldfish?'

'We have a dog.'

'So, you're partners, is that it? Wanting to make a home for your little family?'

'No! We're not partners!' Schmidt virtually shouted.

'You mean you're not a family, you're not married?'

'Of course not! I told you, we're not partners, we only work together.' Schmidt was losing his quiet demeanour. Peters only shook his head in disbelief.

'But you gave the same address as your residence and are looking for a place together. What are we to think?'

'It's only for convenience. Since we work for the same people and usually the same hours, it's only logical that we try to cut costs by sharing accommodation.' Peters smoothed over Schmidt's outburst.

'Okay then. We would like you to write down your statements, laying out exactly what you were doing there and why. So, Officer Pichon will take your partner Mr Schmidt to the next room where he could write his statement in comfort. And you could do yours here.' With that, Pichon got up and gestured for Schmidt to follow him.

Once they'd left, Favre pushed the notepad over to Peters. 'Now I want you to write a very complete account of the four days you spent in that area.'

'Okay.'

'Good. Start writing,' Favre watched him carefully. Borel took the chair vacated by Pichon. Paul knew Pichon would follow the strategy. Peters continued to write.

'Don't forget to put down everything.'

'I'm doing that.'

'I mean the routine you worked out with your partner, why you did it, and for how long. Also, why did you pick that area specifically?'

'For heaven's sake, you keep adding things. It's quite simple, we were there to look at a possible place to live.'

'Well, keep writing – as complete as possible.'

Peters just shook his head but kept writing with frequent hesitations. It seemed like he was trying to come up whatever would please Favre. Finally, he finished and pushed the notepad back to Favre, who pulled it towards him and quickly looked over the page. Everything written looked reasonable but lacked substance. Calmly, Paul set aside the statement and lifted the corner of the file with the photos. Without showing his hand, he pulled out the photo of Arthur Gonzales and placed it face up in front of Peters.

'Do you know this man?'

'No, never seen him before.' Peters showed no reaction or recognition.

'You sure?' Paul carefully took out the next photo, that of Georgio Bescutti, and placed it next to the one of Gonzales. 'Have you seen this man before?'

'No, what's this all about? I don't know this man either.'

'Are you absolutely sure?'

'Yes, I told you, you want me to swear on the Bible?'

'No, that won't be necessary. Although, there's something else, we would like to know. We need your help, and you might be able to provide it. Are you in agreement?' Paul waited for a reply.

'Always prepared to help the fuzz.'

Paul Favre put the third photo face down next to the other two. His hand hovered over the corner before turning it over. He hoped his effort for dramatic effect would unnerve Peters. Slowly, Paul turned it over, watching Peters' eyes for any flicker of change in his glance. No movement betrayed his reaction, except Paul was rewarded by the pupils of Peters' eyes dilating. The obvious change in his blood pressure clearly registered. Peters remained completely still, but the increased pulse in his neck visible. Then he raised his eyes to look up at Favre, shifting his gaze to Borel and back to Favre.

'So, you know this man.'

'No, I don't know him, never seen him before, like these other two.'

'His name is Benoit Sebastian Olivier.'

'No, that is Jean Baptiste.' Peters slipped, caught off guard.

'Oh, so you do know him. Where did you meet him?'

'No, no, I made a mistake, I don't know him. He looks like a friend of mine.'

'You work for him, don't you?'

'No, told you, I don't know him.'

'Come on now, we know that's not true. We saw your reaction. What were your orders?' This was going too slow. Paul needed to speed up the interrogation. He got up, with one hand on his hip, the other rubbing his forehead, and took a couple of impatient paces. Suddenly, he turned back, bent down to face Peters, and slammed both fists on the table.

'This is enough! We know you report to him. Don't forget, we have your phones and can pull all your communications with him. What kind of work do you do for him?'

'We don't work for him.'

'Your reaction tells us otherwise, so spill. What kind of work does he do?'

'How should I know; I told you I don't know him.'

'Not true. As I said, we're going to dump your phones, and then we'll have proof.'

'Go ahead. I'm not saying another word. I want my lawyer.'

'Not necessary, you just answered my question.'

'What? What do you mean? I didn't say anything. You cannot do this! Hey, where are you going? You cannot leave me here!'

'Borel, please read him his rights and arrange for him to contact his lawyer. Then I would like you to come with me. We can leave him here. He's not going anywhere.'

With a smile, Borel read Peters his rights. As Favre walked out, the duty officer came in with a phone. He asked for the lawyer's number to be dialled, and once done, handed it over. He waited while the call was made. The guard took up position opposite Peters when Borel left to join Favre and Pichon.

Favre nodded to Pichon as he and Borel entered IR two. He picked up Schmidt's written statement, speedread through it. He pulled out a chair and sat down.

'This is good, very detailed. I'm pleased to see that you made such a great effort to be precise. Except what's missing here is, who gave you the order to do your routine surveillance.'

'What do you mean? We told you we were looking for an apartment.'

'Well, no, your partner just told us that you worked for Benoit Sebastian Olivier, also known as Jean Baptiste. So, you can now tell us why he wanted you to spy on the neighbourhood. Don't forget, we already know, so if you don't tell us the same as your partner did, you're going to be in real trouble.' Favre spoke calmly and waited. Schmidt looked from one to the other, covering all three faces in the room. He seemed unsure what to believe or how to react.

'What? What did he say? We didn't spy. We were looking for an

211

apartment.'

'No, that's not what he said. Now it's your turn to tell us your version.' When Schmidt didn't reply, Favre continued.

'Okay, this is how it's going to go. I'm going to show you some pictures, and then you are going to tell me who they are. Now, again I must warn you that your partner already identified them. So, all we need from you is confirmation. You understand, don't you?'

'Yes, I understand.'

'Right, here is the first one.' Favre put Arthur Gonzales' photo in front of Schmidt, who looked up, his expression blank.

'Who's he?'

'That's what we are asking you. You must tell us all about him.'

'But I don't know him. Perhaps Peters knows him. I don't, never saw him before.'

'Okay, so here's the next one.'

'I don't know him either. Is he this one's partner?' Peters pointed from Georgio Bescutti's photo to that of Gonzales.

'Now, this is another photo we wish you to identify.' Calmly, Favre placed the third print next to the other two. It was clear that Schmidt was the weaker of the two—his reaction to Olivier's photo was obvious. He sat back, raising his hand to cover his mouth, and nervously looked from one person to the other.

'Good, I see you also know him. Now this man you can tell us about, can't you?'

'Huh, … what? No, I can't tell you anything about him.' Favre gave him Olivier's full given name and the name under which Schmidt and Peters knew him. Schmidt vehemently shook his head. 'I don't know anything about him! Can't tell you!' The way he cringed confirmed that Olivier was indeed a dangerous man.

'We can see he scares you. He is a very dangerous man and is wanted all over the world. I understand that you are worried what he'll do to you. But you don't have to worry, we will protect you completely.'

'Why? What do you want?'

'Where did you meet him?'

'I only know him through Peters.'

'And how does Peters know him?'

'From Marseilles, he comes from there too. I don't know what you want.'

'Nothing much, we only want you to tell us what you know about him and where we could find him.'

'Oh no, can't do that. He'll kill me.'

'Not if you are under our protection. We are the only ones who could keep you safe. As I said, we would be prepared to do that and forget about this charge you are facing, if you tell us all about this man.'

'But there is no charge against me.'

'Well, we have given you time to help us. Except if you don't, you will be charged with spying because that's what you were doing: spying on neighbours and businesses. We could make it more serious as well and bring in suspicion of terrorist activities.'

'What, you can't do that! I'm not a terrorist! We were only supposed to look out for an old woman with a dog and find out where she lived. Nothing else. We never did any spying or anything like that what you said!'

'And did you find her?'

'No, we never saw any old woman with a dog. There were other people with dogs, but not an old woman.'

'Did you tell him this?'

'Yes.'

'So, what did he want you to do next?'

'He told us to keep on looking, that it was important to find her, but not to be stupid and be caught.'

'So, what will he say now seeing you've been caught? I bet he won't be pleased.'

'He'll be very angry and punish us. I'm telling you that's all, we weren't spying, just looking for the old lady. You must give us protection.'

'Okay, we'll start easy. What other work does he ask you to do?'

'I don't know, we only have to be lookouts.'

'What does he do for a living?'

'What do you mean? You mean like work? I don't know, he's one scary dude.'

'I believe you, but you haven't told us where we could find him.'

'I don't know. He always met us in a carpark or behind a warehouse near the airport – never the same place.'

'You must know where he lives. Don't hold out on us now. It won't be to your advantage,' Favre sensed that they wouldn't get much more out of

Schmidt, who was sweating profusely from fear. Clearly, Peters was the hardier and more experienced of the two. Favre could only imagine what awaited these two if Olivier got his hands on them knowing that they gave him up – at least to a certain extent.

'Honestly, I don't know where he lives, perhaps Peters does.'

'So, how do you know when and where he wants to see you?'

'He sends us a SMS. You know a text message with the time and place.'

'I know what a SMS is. What's his phone number?'

'He changes his phone often. You know he uses those throw-away phones. So, we don't have a number for him. He contacts us, we don't contact him, it's not allowed.'

'Okay, make a list of all the places you've had to meet him.'

'What? I don't remember all of them.'

'Well, try. It's important if you want us to give you protection.' Favre pushed the notepad back across the table with a pen. 'We'll be back soon. It'll give you time to remember every meeting spot.'

Defeated, Schmidt pulled the pad over. The guard came into IR two as Favre and his colleagues left to confer. At Paul's desk, they met Leonard, who, without preamble, wanted an update of everything they had learned.

'It would be impossible to pinpoint where Olivier phoned from if he used throw-away or burner phones. The Tech Department could try, but they'll tell you the same thing. That's why these guys always use them,' Pichon explained before Leonard could pose the question.

'Okay, so how do we pin this man down?'

'We're going to try and connect the various meeting places to see if a section of the city shows a preference. That's all we'll be able to do from the information we have,' Favre said, frustrated and desperate for a way to find Olivier.

'At least now we know that he was looking for Mrs Marx, confirming that he was the shooter. But why? Have you found a motive yet, Favre?'

'No, *chef,* still a mystery to be solved, but I am working on it.'

'Well, find that, and we'll be on our way to solving this crime. I'll leave the three of you now. Let me know how you progress.' Together, Favre, Pichon and Borel mumbled consent and goodbyes.

'I just had a thought, it's rather stupid, I know, but I want to throw it out there in case it makes us think of something else,' Borel spoke for the first time.

'I'm open to anything and everything. Let's hear it.'

'Favre, look I know you've been on this from the beginning, but what if the young man wasn't the target, and it was the girl? What if Olivier missed? You know, she could've been in his sights, and just at the right, or wrong – if you want to look at it like that – moment, she turned her head or bent down or something? And bang, the bullet hits Marcus.'

'You're right, it sounds stupid, but Garcia had a similar notion. We'll investigate that angle. It might bring us closer to the motive, as the young man and his family are all completely clean. They have absolutely no connections to the underworld of crime – not even unpaid parking tickets or outstanding debts.'

'So, what do you think? Should we look at it from that angle?'

'Why not, give us something to get our teeth into.' Favre walked over to the crime board and looked at every person listed. 'From what we have, the Bescutti family and Olivier seem to be the most dangerous, Gonzales is dubious, but we have nothing on him yet. His organisation is still new here, but the Americas might have something on him.'

'I'll get on to Interpol and the FBI immediately,' Borel offered.

'That would help, thank you. I need to speak to Georgio Bescutti, but I shouldn't go alone. Pichon, do you think you could accompany me? I'll clear it with your supervisor. I'll get him to release the two of you from guard duty and get permission for you both to be seconded to me for the time being.'

'Sure, no worries, I would like to meet Bescutti. I've always been interested in that family, and it'll open doors to the Organised Crime Unit for me,' Pichon said.

'Thank you, Detective. I am sure there wouldn't be a problem as this case concerns one of our own now. He wouldn't object to us helping you,' Borel agreed.

'Good, let's do it then. You're okay with finding background on Gonzales?' Borel nodded. 'You can use Garcia's desk. I really appreciate your help, both of you.' A thunderclap made all look up.

'Well, we have our storm at last. Hope it breaks the heat. It's late, let's all get home and start fresh in the morning.' Favre tidied his desk.

'I'll stay a little longer, make a couple of calls – the FBI should be at their desks now.'

'Goodnight then, Borel. See you in the morning.' Favre picked up his jacket; Pichon said goodnight as well and they walked out together.

CHAPTER TWELVE

The violent storm the evening before, brought down some trees, blocking the road into town in the Conche area. Arthur Gonzales had to take a detour, because he didn't want to wait around for another hour until the road was cleared. He arrived at his office forty-five minutes later than planned. The courier, due to arrive first thing, was expected at the hotel soon.

Eric should be at the office by now. He called through to his secretary, asking if Eric had checked in. Her negative reply unnerved him. He couldn't understand what could've gone wrong. Everything was planned to the finest detail.

'He's here!' The secretary called out a minute later.

Without knocking, Eric hurried into Arthur's office and, without preamble, brought him up to date.

'Our courier has been intercepted.'

'What? By whom?'

'That still has to be determined.'

'How did that happen?'

'Our girl waited at the Arrivals and saw her coming out. Our girl held up the name board taking her place right in front, impossible to miss. Immediately, a man stepped forward, took the courier by the arm, smiling and joking, leading her away. There was nothing our girl could do, except try to attract her attention, but the man prevented that. He kept her occupied and out of our girl's eye line.'

'Sounds like a real professional move.'

'From how she described it – definitely. Then, the man jumped the queue for a taxi, hustling the girl into the first one and drove away. Our girl only got one number of the three-digit registration – six – but the company she got: Taxiphone.'

'Could we get them to give us the destination of the ride?'

'I should think so. We have the exact time the man commandeered the taxi.'

'Do you think our girl could give us a description of the man who

217

intercepted the courier?'

'Actually, she managed to take a photo with her cell. Unfortunately, she only captured his back. She described him in general and tried to remember specifics about his face, as well as his walk and attitude.'

'Good, she's clever by sound of things.'

'Well, that's why I chose her. She's very observant and quick-thinking.'

'Are you going to get on to Taxiphone, or is she doing it?'

'I want her to give it a go. If she doesn't succeed, then I'll take over the call. A female might sound more convincing, we'll give a story that we're very worried the passenger might have come to some harm by the hand of this man.'

'Good thinking. Get on with it, then, and hopefully the issue would resolve itself.'

'I've placated our buyers. They're giving us a bit of leeway, but not much. I'll see if I can change their minds.' Eric Pichat tapped the top of the desk before turning to leave.

'We really need this deal to go through. First impressions count, and we want repeat business from this buyer. It'll open doors for us.'

'I agree,' Eric said over his shoulder.

Arthur Gonzales tried to control his anguish. On top of this loss, they still have not found further information on the shooting. If it was a warning, retaliation, or a random act has still not been established. He didn't want war, but he needed to be prepared for whatever came their way and do what was necessary. The thought that his daughter might still be in danger, and even killed by unknown forces, terrified him. This shooting could have been disastrous. Only by the grace of God... He put the piece of paper he had been holding down and went through to his partner's office.

'Eric, sorry, I can't wait. This situation with the courier is priority, only I'm terrified for my daughter's safety. Have you heard anything further?'

'Nothing specific. Only that other people are also trying to get to the bottom of it.'

'You mean our competition, the Bescuttis, are also poking around?'

'I've only heard of Georgio Bescutti asking questions. The rest of the family seems to be keeping mum. I suppose Georgio would be the representative of the whole lot, don't you agree?'

'With that family, I wouldn't like to venture a guess. They have so many different areas of interest and levels of dealings, it'll be impossible to rule them out completely. Their cruelty also varies in degrees, depending on who in the family, or which arm of the group, is involved.'

'That really is not what I want to hear. You are not putting my mind at rest.'

'I'm sorry, but that's the situation at this moment.'

'Well, I'll have to live with that for the time being. Okay, so have you managed to find out anything more from our young woman?'

'What worries me about her description of the abductor – I believe we can call him that – is that he looked dangerous. Tall, strong, and athletic, what she saw of his face that struck her, were his eyes – icy blue, she described them as.'

'Did he see her? Do you think she could be in danger?'

'I hope not. She didn't mention that he saw her, but she did have the board with the courier's name. Still, you can never be too careful, can you? I'd better warn her to be on the lookout for anyone following or watching her.'

'Definitely. Better safe than sorry. She could lead this man right to our doorstep.' Concerned for protecting their operation eclipsed Gonzales' concern for his young employee.

'Yeah, I understand, still I want her to be safe as well.' Contrary to his partner, Eric saw the dangers to life in a slightly different manner, clearly not in equal measure. He had a soft spot for the young lady.

'You're right. Place a guard at our entrance. Then, let's see if we can placate our buyer and salvage our reputation. As I said before, first impressions are the most important.'

*

A tentative knock on Georgio Bescutti's office door made him glance up. Emilio never knocked tentatively. And as far as he knew, he had left earlier on an errand. The secretary, a middle-aged woman of nondescript height, weight and looks, carefully opened the door when he called out, 'Enter.'

'Sir, I'm sorry to trouble you. There are two men here to see you.'

'I don't have time. Tell them to make an appointment.'

'Sir, I'm sorry, but they insist.'

'No, I cannot see any one this morning. Tell them to come back this afternoon at one.'

'Sir, they're from the police. They insist on seeing you now.'

'What? The police, what do they want?'

'They didn't say, just that they have to speak to you immediately.'

'Okay, give me five minutes and bring them in.'

'Yes, sir.' She slunk out of the office. He could hear her talking to the men and their disgruntled reply. She obviously got through to them, as he had five minutes to clear his desk and mentally prepare himself to receive the police.

The door opened, and the secretary glanced from him to somewhere over her shoulder, then back at him. He nodded and gestured for the police officers to enter. The first through the door, fair, tall, and lanky, nodded to the woman. He walked over to Bescutti with hand outstretched, introducing himself as "Detective Favre" and his colleague, "Officer Pichon." The second man, of medium complexion and height, also shook Bescutti's hand in greeting. The woman pulled the door closed behind her as she left. Georgio Bescutti invited them to take a seat. They glanced around the room before settling into the two easy chairs facing the businessman.

'So, to what do I owe this visit?'

'Well Sir, no doubt you have heard about the shooting of a young man in Paquis about a week ago? We thought it prudent to talk to people across the board to try and find possible witnesses or information.'

'And you thought of me, and may I ask; why would that be?'

'Incidentally the young woman with the victim is the ex-girlfriend of your son.'

'How do you know about my son? It's not public knowledge.'

'We have our sources. It's not important at this time how we know. Please, we need information.'

'Fine, what do you want to know?'

'We had two of your men at the station. They've now been transferred, and their lawyer has arranged for their arraignment soon.'

'Yes, did they tell you they work for me?'

'Actually, no. They didn't, but we gathered it from a few other things.'

'I asked them to see if they could find out anything about the shooting – such as who did the shooting and who was the target. I had no information, and I wanted to know if it posed a problem for my son.'

'Fair enough, that's understandable.'

'I don't want him to be in danger.'

'Well, Mr Bescutti, we know you deal with many people in the city and the Canton; therefore, you have a wide reach. You have sources of intelligence which we don't have.' Favre said. 'All we ask is that you tell us if you hear anything. In the meantime, I'd like to show you a couple of photos. Is that okay?'

'I suppose so, not sure that I'll be able to help, but let's have a look.'

Pichon handed the file to Favre, who opened it and pulled out the first print.

'Do you know this man?' The face of Arthur Gonzales looked back at Georgio. For the sake of clarity, Paul gave the full name.

'Not personally. Never met him face to face, but I know who he is. He's a trader from Colombia, isn't he? He and his family only recently took up residence here.'

'Yes, that's correct. So, you say you don't have any dealings with him or his company?'

'Exactly, I haven't dealt with him. He could be in competition with another part of my family. As you know, I don't have much to do with the family business. I have my area of activities, and they have theirs. We hardly ever overlap.'

'And your activities are?

'Well, a wide range actually, but the main areas would be sugar, maize, and oil. As you know, that's a very fragile and volatile market. I think Mr. Gonzales deals in coffee and precious metals. Am I correct?'

'You are, sir. Apparently, he also deals in gemstones. Doesn't your family trade in these items?'

'Some of them do, I'm not sure to what extent anymore. It used to be my mother's field. Unfortunately, I cannot help you – not my area of expertise.'

'Okay, now could you tell me if you've ever come across this person before?' Paul set the photo of Olivier down on the desk in front of Georgio.

'Now, that is a dangerous man.'

'You know him?'

'Not really. He came to me last year, offering his services. I sent him on his way – I didn't like the look he had in his eyes. Killer's eyes, I call it. And I don't have any use for someone like that. What could he do for me? Guard every grain of sugar or protect every drop of oil? No, he's an enforcer

– I don't need one.'

'How did he react to rejection?'

'That was the strange thing, which convinced me even more that he was not a person to mess with. He had this smile that sort of said, "You'll remember the day you refused my offer." Needless to say, I didn't like him. So that's the extent of me knowing him. I can't even remember his name, to be honest.'

'One last question. As I said, the young man killed in the shooting was with your son's ex-girlfriend. Did you know that?'

'My son has never met me. I've kept that completely secret – I don't want him anywhere near the family business. Incidentally, I apologise for my earlier reaction regarding my son.'

'Well, we understand why, and it's your choice. Did you know that the girl broke up with your son?'

'Actually, no. But then I'm not privy to his dating life, and it doesn't concern me, only his wellbeing is of interest.'

'Did you know that the girl is the daughter of Arthur Gonzales?'

'No, I didn't. I knew there was a child. I really didn't know if it was a boy or girl. So, she's his daughter?'

'Does that make a difference to the way you look at the shooting?'

'Well, no, it doesn't. Of course, this raises other questions.'

'Like what exactly?' Favre asked, pen hovering over notebook.

'I would have thought that her being my son's ex, and him being a possible opponent or competitor – whichever way you would like to put it – or part of my family's business, would make you wonder if one of us organised the shooting.'

'What are your thoughts about the shooting, if I may ask? Do you believe it was retaliation, a warning, or personal?'

'Well, I really wouldn't be able to tell you. Sure, I wanted information, but only to the extent that it put my son in danger. It never crossed my mind to find out why it happened. I suppose it could be anything.'

'And as you say, her father being a possible competitor.'

'But why shoot the young man who had nothing to do with either her or my family?'

'That's our question – the "why". Unless they thought she was still dating Antonio.'

'Surely her parents would know who she dates. I don't think that holds

222

water.'

'We've identified the shooter, but the motive still escapes us.'

'So, who is the shooter?'

Favre tapped his finger on the photo in front of Georgio. 'This man.'

'What? This is serious. My impression of him was that he'd do anything for anyone who paid him enough – whether there was a reason or not.'

'Well, Mr Bescutti, we think you understand why we're going around asking for help to find witnesses and information.'

'Yes, look I understand. I've insisted my wife put a curfew in place for my son, as well as staying away from the girl. Nevertheless, I'll definitely ask around.'

'Thank you. We'll be speaking to Mr Gonzales, the girl's father, as well. Please keep us informed if you become aware of anything. Goodbye, Mr Bescutti.'

Favre and Pichon left for the station to learn what Borel found out about Gonzales before paying him a visit.

When they reached fresh air, Favre said that, even though Georgio Bescutti had never been caught crossing the line, his dealings to undercut his competitors had raised eyebrows. However, he had employed dubious tactics on occasion, he didn't do anything illegal.

*

The full report from the FBI on Gonzales did not match the same detail as the Interpol report on Olivier. However, it gave sufficient information to establish that Gonzales had been active in various activities which bordered on the illegal. Also, some transactions would be classified as criminal in certain countries.

Favre conferred with Borel, and they decided as he had gathered the information from the FBI, he would accompany Paul to talk to Gonzales. Pichon didn't object; he wanted to try and track down the image of Olivier on the CCTV cameras and other footage.

They took the lift to the penthouse suite of the Beau Rivage, where Gonzales had his offices. His secretary announced them, and when Gonzales gave the go-ahead, she escorted the two through. He stood up from behind his desk, guided them to the seating area of the room he used as his office.

'Good morning, gentlemen. Does my partner need to be here as well?'

'That's your call. Our visit concerns the shooting of about a week ago.'

'It might be an idea, he knows as much as I do, and perhaps he's heard something more. Hold on, I'll call him.' Gonzales buzzed his secretary, asking for Eric to join them and bring coffee. Favre held off with the introductions until the partner came in, closing the door behind him.

'Good morning, I'm Detective Favre, and this is Officer Borel.'

'Good morning again, this is my partner Eric Pichat, and I'm Arthur Gonzales. How may we help you today?'

'As mentioned to Mr Gonzales we are here in connection with the shooting in Paquis about a week ago.'

'Yes, we know about that.' Eric seemed ready to say more but paused as the secretary brought in a tray with the coffee.

'That's the beauty of having our offices here – instant service,' Gonzales said.

'Yes, I can see the benefits. Now, to get back to the shooting. Your daughter was present when it went down, not so?'

'Yes, it was a traumatic experience for her, and I've forbidden her to go out after seven in the evening until we know there is no more danger. You can't be too careful.'

'We agree. We are also aware that she used to date a certain Antonio Vicario.'

'Again, yes, her mother and I have both urged her to stay away from the young man.'

'Have you succeeded?'

'Not completely, but we are trying. It seems as he's one of the few friends around during the holidays. So, besides locking her up in her room, there's not much we can do except trust her to do what we ask.'

'Why is that? You want her to stay away from Antonio?'

'Well, it's not a widely known fact – only a select few are aware – but we have it on good authority that he's the son of a member of the Bescutti Family.'

'And you know which one?'

'No, but does it matter?'

'And this poses a problem for you?'

'Well, of course. Firstly, it's rumoured that this Family is connected to the Mafia, and secondly, we're business competitors. That, as you well know, never bodes well in any relationship the children enter into.'

'So, that family's possible connection to the Mafia worries you? Even though you're known to have had dealings with some of the South American Drug Cartels. Doesn't that make it "birds of a feather," as they say?'

'Who told you we've had dealings with the Cartels?'

'You forget, we're the police and work closely with Europol, Interpol, and the FBI. So, take your pick – anyone of those could've given us a heads-up.'

'Well, that's in the past. We avoid dealing with anyone who have dubious backgrounds.'

'That would cut down your market tremendously, wouldn't it?'

'Sure, but we have to be clever about doing business here in Europe. We want to survive and stay on the right side of the law.'

'That is why our importation of precious stones, and all other trades are well documented and completely legitimate. We have the manifests and Letters of Credit to prove it.' Eric spoke for the first time since their introduction.

'We don't doubt that; however, we look at the big picture. Now, getting back to the shooting, we'd like, if possible, to ask your opinion.'

'What do you mean, "ask our opinion"?'

'Well, do you think the shooting could've been a warning, retaliation or because of something personal?'

'We have no idea; we tried to put out feelers to find out who did the shooting and why. So far none of our contacts have heard anything.'

'Okay, well, if you do hear something, please let us know immediately. In the meantime, we'd like to show you a couple of photos.' Favre handed the first photo to them. 'Do either of you know this person?'

'We know him, never met personally, but he is well known in the business world. That is Georgio Bescutti. Why are you showing us his photo?'

'We're just making sure we cover every aspect of the crime. He is also the father of your daughter's ex-boyfriend.'

'Oh, so he is the father. Interesting.'

'This, of course, is not information to be broadcast – not only for privacy, but also for safety reasons. We would like to avoid putting a target on the boy's back.'

'Okay, we understand.' Gonzales looked at Pichat, and both nodded in agreement.'

'But why would he become a target, and by whom?' Eric wanted to know.

'Well, besides the father, the rest of the Bescutti family doesn't know that he exists and if they do, it might cause problems for the young man.'

'Are you sure about that? We managed to find out from a source within the family.'

'Who is this source close to?'

'The mother, or grandmother – you could call her the "Godmother" - she's ruthless. Our source overheard her talking to someone on the phone, also telling them to keep it quiet as it is a family secret,' Pichat replied again.

'Okay, let's leave the Bescuttis aside. Please tell us if you know this person?' The second photo was handed over.

'Who is this?' Arthur handed the photo over to his partner. 'Eric, have you seen this man before?'

'No, he doesn't look a nice guy, does he?'

'Are you sure, neither of you ever saw him before? He didn't come to offer his services?'

'Not to me. Eric, did he contact you?'

'No. Perhaps he only spoke to the secretary. You know we've been travelling a lot, and when we're out of town, she handles everything.'

'Could you call her and ask, please?'

Eric got up immediately, opened the door, and called the secretary in. She came in, wanting to know if they would like more coffee, but Eric asked her over to look at the photo the police brought. Unsure, she came over, standing just behind Gonzales, he half-turned and showed her Olivier's photo.

'Do you know this man?'

'Oh, yes.' She took the print and studied it. 'He came in last year wanting to speak to you. You were on that two-week business trip to Colombia. I told him to come back the next month or so, but he never did.'

'Did he say anything or give his name?'

'He flirted with me, wanted me to go to dinner. Only I had plans, so I declined. He was quite charming. He introduced himself as Jean Baptiste. I remember that because it's the same name as a school friend. Is anything wrong, did he do something?'

'Well, nothing for you to worry about, but if you hear from him again, please let us know.' Favre and Borel gave her their cards. 'Either one of us.'

'Is that all? Can I get you some more coffee?'

Gonzales looked at his two guests, who both shook their heads. Without another word, she left, closing the door behind her.

'Okay, could you now tell us who this man is and why are you interested in him?' Arthur wanted to know.

'He's the shooter. He also sent two of his men to find the only witness. Luckily, we managed to pick them up before the witness was found.'

'Wait a minute,' Eric interrupted. 'Let's just look at something.' He got up and fetched his laptop and brought over notes made by their young employee who was supposed to meet the courier. He brought everything over to where they were sitting.

'Do you think this could be the same man? We have not reported it yet, as we thought it might have been a misunderstanding. This morning, a courier arrived from Colombia with sample gemstones. I'll give you the manifest. However, to make a long story short, our girl waited to collect her from the arrivals gate when a man intercepted and hustled her into a taxi. We've not heard from her at all since her arrival.'

'Well, it's difficult to compare from the photo your employee took with her phone, but physically it seems to be right. Her description of the man could fit. Is she here now?'

'Yes, just one floor down. We have another, smaller suite from where our other employees work. I'll call her to come up.' Eric pulled out his mobile phone and punched in a number. After a few words, he turned back to them. 'She's on her way.'

'This man, current name Jean Baptiste, has various aliases, but his real name is Benoit Sebastian Olivier, and he is one of the most dangerous men we have come across. We'll continue discussing him once your girl has left – we don't want to scare her unnecessarily.'

'Fine. Oh, here she is now.' A soft knock announced her. Eric opened the door for her. Her eyes widened when she saw the gathering.

'What's wrong? Did I do something? Is it about the courier who disappeared?'

'Well, yes. These two gentlemen are from the police, and they'd like to know if you can identify the man you saw at the airport. But we'll let them show you the photo and ask you questions.'

'Okay, I suppose that'll be fine.' She nervously looked from one to the other. Finally, her glance settled on Favre who handed over the photo of Olivier.

'Is this the same man?'

'I think so.' She looked from Gonzales to Pichat. 'Yes, I'm sure it's him, his eyes were really cold, gave me the shivers.'

'Okay, do you think he saw you?'

'No, I doubt it. Maybe when I followed them to the taxi rank, but they sped away so fast that I couldn't even see the registration plate.'

'I've tried to get Taxiphone to give us some information. They weren't forthcoming. Perhaps it would be easier for the police to do so, what do you think, Arthur?'

'Okay, let us take a formal statement on the loss of your samples. That way, we can officially make enquiries. We'll need documentation and to lodge an official complaint and open a case docket. If you could get your secretary to gather all the documents and get that young woman to type out her account of what happened at the airport, that'll give us a starting point. You all need to come into the station to sign statements, etc. but for now, let's concentrate on the shooting by this Olivier.'

'How solid is the witnesses' description?'

'Actually, very good. From street cams, CCTV, and other footage, we were able to confirm the description.'

'That sound pretty solid.'

'Now, we didn't finish our previous question. Now that you know a bit more about the players, tell us what your opinion is on the shooting? Retaliation, a warning or personal?' Favre watched them closely. He couldn't read them. Gonzales shrugged, Pichat shook his head with pursed lips.

'As we said, we tried to find out and still feel it might be a warning, as there's no reason for retaliation. Personally, besides the fact that my daughter was present, I cannot think of any other personal reason. Perhaps it's a warning on a business deal.'

'It depends on which product or trades we are referring to. We deal in oil, sugar, maize, precious metals, and gems,' Eric added.

'If we take this morning's interception of the courier into account, it could be a warning or an attempt to take over our business,' Arthur took a stab at the motive.

'That's a possibility. But he must've had orders from someone. He approached both Bescutti and you – via your secretary – to offer his services. Georgio Bescutti turned him down and you were out of town. He could have gone to someone else. Do you know who that might have been?' Paul looked at Borel.

'Who else deals in precious stones? What do you think about a competitor in gemstones? If we consider this morning's interception, it's probable that the shooting could've been a warning directed at you to get out of that side of the business.' Borel opened his notebook.

'Could be, but as you said, he must be taking orders from someone. Besides Olivier, that's the person I'd like to find,' Paul Favre stated.

Favre conferred quietly with Borel, nodding in approval as the others looked on.

'According to the FBI, you've made various enemies in South America. Could anyone of them be a threat?' Borel asked as he paged back into his notebook. 'I have a couple of names here, which might jog your memory.' He mentioned four names and looked up for any reaction. Gonzales got up and walked around the room.

'No, I don't think so. But I suppose anything is possible.'

'Which one on the list would have the reach to retaliate by wanting to destroy your business you have only recently established in Europe? You must have an idea or suspect one of these. Or do you believe it could be a new player?' Borel pushed.

'To be honest, I just don't know. Sure, I've made enemies, but business is business and most – not all – of my business partners accept that principle. They'd do the same to me, though none would kill an innocent man just to teach me a lesson.' Arthur rubbed his face as if to wake himself. then sat back down. 'Undercutting, diverting a shipment, stealing, and lying could happen, but not the assassination of a relative or friend who had nothing to do with the transaction. That just wouldn't happen.'

'So, any other ideas?' Favre asked.

'None. Yes, none for the time being. I will have to think about this.' Arthur looked at Eric, who agreed that they'd need time to come up with other possibilities.

229

'Good. Well, before we leave, have you heard about the explosion at the Servette Police Station and the fire in Eaux-Vives?'

'Yes, why?'

'We think he was involved in that, as well as targeting the detectives investigating. Detective Garcia was critically injured in the blast, and the fire was at my home.'

'Is Detective Garcia okay?'

'He'll recover, but it's a long road ahead. I presume you understand why we feel everyone should be warned about this extremely dangerous man.'

'Thank you, we'll definitely be on the lookout and let you know if we hear anything.'

'Good, we'll take our leave. We need you to come in to make formal statements. All of you that is, your secretary, the young woman who were supposed to meet the courier, and the two of you in connection with the loss of the shipment.' Favre and Borel got up, shook hands, and left.

Arthur moved back behind his desk, sat down. He swivelled his chair to look out over the lake. Eric took a seat in the visitor's chair in front of the desk, crossed his legs. With his right elbow on the chair's armrest, he rested his head on his fist. Both men's concern went deeper than they wished to admit.

'Have you found out anything further which you didn't mention when the police were here? Surely there must be some murmurings?' Gonzales spun round in his chair to face Eric.

'The only thing we have heard came from a disgruntled employee who said that the young man wasn't the target.'

'What? Are you saying that my daughter was the target?'

'Not sure. Apparently, their intelligence was wrong. They thought your daughter was still dating Antonio.'

'So, this Antonio, the son of Georgio Bescutti, was the target?'

'No, the rumour was that the girl was the target.'

'I cannot believe you held that back from me! My daughter is in more danger than I thought. You should have told me.'

'I only found out minutes before the police arrived.'

'You should've told me. Okay, okay, what do you make of the information?'

'From what I can figure out, they wanted to get her out of Antonio's life to clear the way. Only, what I can't piece together is why? Clear the way for what?'

'Who do you think is pulling this Olivier's strings?'

'No idea. Though, the murmurings come from the Bescutti camp.'

'Perhaps that's where we should begin our enquiries.' Arthur continued. 'Another thing, when was the courier supposed take her flight to Madrid?'

'This evening at eight.'

'We should get our girl to go to the airport and wait for the courier. When she checks in, our girl could approach and find out what happened and what she knows. Our girl should also suggest that the courier spend another night so that we can recuperate the product hidden in her carry-on. We can't lose that shipment, it's too important.' Arthur ended the discussion.

'Good idea. We'll tell her we want to make up for her inconvenience and really give her a night on the town.'

'Anything that'll keep her here for longer to get access to her luggage and give us the information we need.'

'Okay. We'll see where digging for further rumours in the Bescutti camp will lead us.' Eric got ready to leave but turned back. 'When do you want to go to the station?'

'In about an hour, get everyone concerned together and we'll go at the same time.'

*

Leonard, in his usual stoic manner, was waiting for Favre and Borel when they arrived at the station. Pichon, on the other hand, quivered with excitement. He rushed to join the group.

'Those Tech guys are awesome! Those two half-faces we sent them; they matched completely, don't know how they do this stuff, but they did!'

'Fantastic, did they give us what we wanted?' Favre couldn't supress a smile.

'They managed to put together an ID from it, and it's incredible. It's him at the different scenes. I can follow him from various cameras and got the general directions he preferred.'

'That's great! Now we know that he is the person we need to find. Let us give you what we found out before we go any further.'

They went over all the information and impressions they gathered from the two meetings. The fact that Olivier had looked for a position as enforcer in both the Bescutti and Gonzales camps had to mean something. The comparison between the meetings was less substantial than they'd hoped, but the fact that the outcome brought them closer to Olivier, and more eyes on the road by courtesy of Bescutti and Gonzales, satisfied them all, even if only slightly.

'So, what's our next move?' Leonard wanted to know.

'Firstly, we need to find this man. Get him off the streets and in here to answer some questions. We cannot take the chance of him being on the loose and planning another attack on either Garcia or me.'

'But we have no leads. We have no idea where he could be hiding out,' Leonard said.

'Well, as Pichon said, he's been trying to follow Olivier on CCTV, street cams, and the video footage we've received from all the different scenes. The shooting, the blast, and the fire at my apartment, I know, tedious work, but it's probably our only chance.' Favre looked at Pichon.

'Did you find something?' Leonard asked.

'I think I've found three general directions which he took more often than any others.' Pichon replied, looking at Favre for guidance.

'Okay, could you insert those dates and times on the timeline to give us an overview please? We can now petition the street cams' CCTV footage and other sources from those *quartiers* in which direction he went. It would put us in the position to track him further and perhaps pinpoint his lair.' Favre felt more positive than he showed.

They gathered in front of the crime board, watching as Pichon took his notes and a marker to insert various places and times that fit the dates already on the board. A pattern emerged. One seemed to lead to the red-light district in Paquis, and the other led to Acacias. Both seemed equally preferred. Leonard gave the order to requisition the camera and video footage from the different suburbs to enable them to follow Olivier's movements. They estimated it would take a day to be able to go further.

Finally, with everyone showing signs of mental exhaustion from all the information spinning around in their heads, Leonard gave permission to wrap up and tackle the investigation again the next day.

Relieved, Favre took the opportunity to visit and check up on Garcia's progress.

CHAPTER THIRTEEN

Alpha rolled a few of the gemstones in the palm of his hand. He loved the feel of them - like satin with an inner warmth. It was difficult to express in words, but it made his heart beat faster, and a mellow feeling settled in his stomach. The dark green, with a blue shadow, gave a depth which made him feel as if he was falling into a pool of the most delicious comfort. He felt surrounded by a sense of homecoming. How could emeralds give out such a great sensation? They were only stones, but they had the ability to move him and push his mind in directions which offered possibilities he never dreamed of. Nothing in the world compared to Colombian emeralds and what they represented.

One by one, he placed the gemstones on a piece of black velvet next to the other five, which made up the sample he retrieved from the courier. He had to tear himself away from these beauties, but there was work to do.

The courier still whimpered in the broom cupboard. He could shut her up, but then she had information he needed. All she cried about was her aunt in Spain and her flight leaving tonight. Well, there would be one passenger who wouldn't be checking in. It was time to get back to business. Now, how should he go about it? He relished the idea of making it last. Young girls squirm in such an exquisite way, and when they start screaming it makes them so much more enchanting. He'll give himself an hour with her, but then he'd have to get back to his mission.

Disappointed that he'd have to set her aside for the time being, he left her slumped in the cupboard. Aside from the person who had given her the sample and the fact that she was supposed to be met by a woman, he was none the wiser. Her carry-on also held nothing of interest. The address of the aunt on a letter was the only thing except clothes for a short stay. She was of no use to him. He would have to get rid of her permanently or dump her somewhere. She only spoke Spanish so he could unload her anywhere and save him cleaning up after. It'd take a while before someone made head or tail of what she said, and even longer for her to make them believe her. Another red herring for our "finest" to unravel, giving him more time to come up with a tactic.

Alpha scratched his head. The conundrum of what his next attack should look like drove him to distraction. Should he wait until both detectives were together, take over the vehicle's computer system, and control the car as he wished? If they lost control, it would drive them nuts. He could send them off to Le Bout du Monde with a chance to force them off the cliff there. Or he could cut the brake lines and see where it takes them. But that's lame, nothing special. It would have to be impressive, big, and unforgettable. He was leaning more towards creating an explosion of acid, a dirty bomb, or something that made a lot of noise and would ensure suffering with ultimate death, but not immediate. It was a real predicament.

He stood back from his wall, where he had stuck various photos – his own special crime board. He called it his wall of fame, but it was more like his target board. He had the two detectives, side-by-side, with a photo of the fire taken from street level linked to Favre with a red string. A photo of a partly obstructed view of the blast site at the station also connected with red string, except this one linked to Garcia's photo. Also on the wall, was a photo of the scene of the shooting, linked to a newspaper clipping of the event. The only photo of the victim, along with the date, came from the article. The wall began to look like a GPS tracking system for various possible routes - not neat, but he loved it. His eyes shone with excitement.

He swiped the screen of his mobile phone and punched in a number. He touched the green dot, sliding it to the right, and waited. The call went through, rang twice and then went to voicemail.

'Where are you? Why aren't you picking up?' This was getting frustrating, they hadn't been available to report yesterday evening or this morning. He demanded a twice-daily report, and they'd failed. That was it! They were finished. He should put their mugshots up on the wall as well. It wouldn't take long for him to find them - they weren't geniuses. Now, he had to decide in which order he would take care of those on the wall. Should he look for his two idiots first or plan the next attack on the detectives? His sense of revenge and pride boiled over in him. Which to appease first, remained a difficult choice.

Tomorrow, he had to report to the Boss about why the actual mission had still not been completed. That was going to be tricky, but he'd get round it. The Boss would want full details - it never paid to keep the Boss waiting or keep quiet about information in hand. Without feedback from his two guys, he'd have to think of something. Not finding a way to get the original target in his sights, remained the problem. The witness of the shooting was only the second objective. The only person crueller than himself was the Boss, perhaps because it would be unexpected. Therefore, the original target should be addressed without delay.

That the Boss had taken him up on his offer surprised him. In fact, he'd never expected employment from that quarter. In the end, he understood – working behind the scenes was quite often more effective. He wondered how many years this had been going on. No one else seemed to know what was happening under their noses. Interesting. It showed that every organisation had its shadow side, and to make money, there was always a way in. Well, it wouldn't be long before he'd be able to take over completely. The Boss didn't even know how helpful all this was - an opportunity not to be missed. Well, using people was the way of business, and trampling them into the ground meant success. Very soon, the Boss would learn this essential fact was open to everyone.

*

The authorisation to obtain video from the street cameras had come through when Favre arrived at the station at the start of the day. He immediately got Pichon to request the footage; Borel was asked to contact the banks on the suspected routes, to get video from their ATMs.

Favre studied the timeline on the crime board. Now that they knew the rough movements of Olivier, he hoped they would be able to pinpoint who he worked for. Olivier obviously had to visit the person who commissioned him at various times.

Favre knew nothing further would be gained by interviewing Olivier's two lookouts again. They've revealed everything they knew, at least Schmidt had, Peters remained as mute as before – only demanding a lawyer.

Suddenly, Favre realised he needed to change his train of thought – an essential element to see the case from a different angle. A breath of fresh air while waiting for the camera footage to clear the cobwebs away was called for. He picked up the phone and called Alexandra, inviting her for a quick coffee.

Fifteen minutes later, he slipped into a booth at the Paradiso near Cornavin, the railway station. Both Martel and Starbucks next to Manor were too noisy for a quiet discussion. Total silence surrounded him two minutes later when Alex arrived. Unable to take his eyes off her, he automatically got up as she sat down opposite him, then lowered himself back onto the bench.

'Hello, it's good to see you,' Favre greeted her first.

'Hello, I was surprised to hear from you so soon.'

'Well, spur of the moment and all that! Do you mind?'

'No, not at all, it's a pleasant interlude during an otherwise quiet morning.'

'How have you been keeping?'

'Well, can't complain. First, tell me, how is your partner, Detective Garcia?'

'I saw him last night, spent quite a bit of time with him, and I can tell you he's itching to get out of hospital.'

'That's a good sign, isn't it?'

'Yes, but he'll have to wait a couple more days - unless the medical staff get so fed up with him that they kick him out.'

'I bet he's trying his best for that to happen.'

'You've said it. It's as if you really know him. Have you met in a previous life?'

'Aren't all men like that?' Alex laughed. 'So, why did you want to have coffee during working hours? It couldn't be just because you felt like it. And it certainly couldn't be to break the monotony of your day because I doubt that exists.'

'Well, no. We're getting close to a break in the case. We know who the shooter is but not where to find him or who he works for - at least, not yet. So, we still have a way to go.' Favre did not want to say too much. At the same time, he wanted to put her mind at ease.

'Are we still in danger? Mrs Ginet's already paranoid, and she'll be unbearable if she finds this out.'

'Better not tell her then, except that you are safe. We've pulled two other men off the street.'

'Were they watching us?'

'No, in fact, they were looking for Mrs Marx. We intercepted them, but they had no information. By the way, they are safely locked away as well.'

'That's good to know.'

'Again, I suggest you don't tell Mrs Ginet any of this. She can get a bit curious.'

'I agree, I won't say a word.'

'So, to answer your question - why coffee during working hours? Well, I needed a complete change of scenery. You know, to clear my head. With everything that's happened, I needed a moment away from it all.'

'I understand that, pleased that I could help.'

'I suppose you heard about the fire two nights ago?'

'Yes, do you know the apartment block?'

'I do, very well. It was my home they set fire to.'

'What, someone set fire to it? Who?'

'Well, the suspect appears to be the same man who did the shooting, as well as the one who planted the bomb at the station.'

'Good grief, he's targeting you!'

'Seems like it.'

'But you're in danger.'

'Not if we catch him first - and make no mistake, that is our intention. Enough of this, I didn't come here to discuss the case. I wanted a ray of sunshine and optimism. And I wanted to tell you something about myself, seeing you opened up to me.'

'Oh, I'm sorry. What would you like to tell me? You are not married or in a relationship, are you?'

'No, nothing of the sort.'

'Well, what is it?'

'I'm divorced and have a daughter. She's twelve now and lives with her mother. I only see her once a month for a weekend.'

'Oh, that's not much. What's her name?'

'Lilly.'

'Nice name. You must miss her if you see her only once a month.'

'Yes, very much. My ex got custody because she said my job was dangerous.'

'I'm sorry. We'll talk about something else. Which movie did you see, or book did you read that really made you laugh?'

'Well, now that is really changing the subject.' A genuine smile crossed Favre's face. He had done the right thing in taking a breather with Alex.

They spent another half hour together before Favre said goodbye to get back to the investigation with a fresh eye.

When Favre arrived at the station, Arthur Gonzales, his partner, and their staff were there giving written statements. Some of the video and street cam footage had been delivered as well, and he found Pichon and Borel going through them frame by frame. They could track Olivier's movements during the last couple of weeks and had marked out three routes which seemed promising.

The three points Olivier favoured turned out to be a room in Paquis, which they decided must be when he hired prostitutes. The second, an apartment block in Acacias where apparently, he lived and thirdly, a building near Rive, Centre Town. The latter they assumed would be where he met his present employer. Pichon found possible addresses for the various points; only to pinpoint the exact destination, the floor and number of apartment or office, was impossible. They would have to stake out all three places.

*

After Paul issued the various orders, he phoned Maria for an update on José. He missed discussing the investigation with his partner. Their back-and-forth tossing of facts always allowed him to see a case from a different angle. José's instinct – no, more like intuition – was sorely needed at this moment. Their rapport made them a unit which could not be surpassed. Oh, boy, how he needed his partner's help to find the motive for this crime! The mystery tormented him. The ringing stopped and Paul moved the phone to his other ear.

'*Bonjour, Maria, how is our boy?*' ... Paul chuckled at her reply. '*I can believe that: antsy is his middle name when there's a case to be solved.*' ... relief flooded Paul's face. '*Good, I'll be there in thirty minutes, can't wait to see him.*' He put the phone down and grabbed his jacket off the back of his chair.

'I'm off to the hospital, see you later,' he said over his shoulder as he walked out, his mind already in overdrive on how he could get José's help without overtiring him or delaying his recovery. Preoccupied, Paul joined the heavy traffic while driving through Plainpalais. Still mentally working through the available facts, he pulled into the parking area at the hospital and stood in front of José's room before he managed to shut off the stream of thought. He pushed open the door.

'Hi Partner, what've you been up to?' Favre moved over to the bed, and as Maria got up, he gave her a hug.

'Hi Partner, what've you been up to?' José lay in a half-sitting position on the bed.

'Same-o-same-o. You know what they say, no rest for the wicked.'

'You trying to tell me that you've been doing a full day's work without me there to make sure you don't lag off?'

'Well, you know how it goes - without you, no one works at their full potential. That's why we need you there.'

'I'll leave you boys to enjoy yourselves,' Maria said. She bent to give her husband a kiss and blew one in Paul's direction as she left.

'Thank you, Maria. Hope to see you soon.' Paul said, turning back to José.

'Good, now that we're alone, tell me what you've got and let me show you how it's done. I sure did miss this.'

'Thought you'd say that, here goes.' Paul ran through all the information they've gathered. He also gave his impression of Olivier and his two-foot soldiers. Though, José found the interviews with Bescutti, Gonzales, and the latter's staff, more interesting.

'So, who do you think is behind this, and what could the motive be?' Paul asked.

'Well, those are the two conundrums which face us. There seems to be underlying facts from the discussions you had with Bescutti and Gonzales.' José smoothed the sheet over his midriff before looking up at Paul. 'You remember what I said right in the beginning of this case?'

'You said so many things, how am I supposed to remember.'

'I said I was convinced that the shooting revolved around the girl. To me she was the key to the whole case. I'm still sure of that. Find what connects her, and we'll find the motive.'

'Okay, but what about who's behind it?' Favre asked.

'Well, I haven't worked that out yet, but the connection remains. There must be something which links it all together.'

'I agree, let's run down the suppositions. Oh sorry, that's if you're up to it.'

'You're joking, I presume. Of course, anything to alleviate the boredom of being stuck to this bed.'

'But I don't want to tire you out.'

'You'll see pretty quickly when I'm tired, I'll fall asleep on you.'

'Okay, I'll watch out for that.'

'Let's begin. You said Bescutti claimed he knew nothing about the shooting. And he wasn't aware that his son, Antonio had broken off with the girl, Cynthia. Also, he didn't have any interest in her, knew of her father, but never had business or came across him before.'

'Yes, that's about it.'

'Then you said, our other selected malefactor, Gonzales - who just happens to be the father of our young seductress - was worried.'

'They were putting out feelers to find out if the shooting was aimed at their business, a jealous act from her ex-boyfriend, meaning the Bescuttis, or gang graduation.'

'What impression did you get when you spoke to him? Were they worried? I find it interesting that they tried to investigate the motive on their own, before we even approached them. Does this indicate guilt?'

'Well, he seemed cooperative enough. I do feel they held something back. Then, I suppose they detected our disbelief, they came up with the story that a stranger intercepted their courier carrying samples from Colombia.'

'Where did this happen?' Garcia asked.

'Apparently, one of their employees waited at the Airport arrivals to meet the courier and saw a strange man approach her and lead her away. Gonzales's employee took a photo of the man, and it matches Olivier's mug.'

'Wait a minute, Olivier abducted their courier who came from Colombia? Don't you think that confirms the suspicion that he was employed by Gonzales's competition?'

'We're not using the word 'abducted' at the moment, but intercepted. Until we find her and hear her side of the event, we cannot say for sure one way or the other. On the Gonzales competition angle, I agree; that has been at the top of my list.'

'Well, there you have it, a possible motive.'

'Yes, a possible motive – not a definite one. That leaves the identity of the chief operator behind the operation.'

'I like that "the chief operator behind the operation" – it has a ring to it – not the usual "brains behind the crime".'

'Oh, get serious. We need to solve this, no time for jokes.'

'A little bit of joviality brings clarity. It expands the mind.'

'Okay Dr. Phil. But let's get back to our assumptions.' Favre's eagerness to close the case pushed his impatience.

'Fine. I need a bit of joviality in here, far too depressing otherwise. But you're right, we shouldn't waste time. My instinct tells me that we need to look at who deals in precious gems. I ask myself, why did this Olivier abduct, sorry intercept, Gonzales' courier? If this concerned competition, then we need to look at who could be the competition.'

'Well, then we get back to Gonzales, that would be a direct attack and warning. The other traders in that product fall in three categories. One: legally registered, two: the not-so-legal, registered but dealing under the table in greater quantities, and finally three: dealing completely under the radar in quantities we could only dream of.'

'We'll rule out the first category. Gonzales, I would suspect, falls under the second, and whoever employed Olivier, would likely be from the third group. Much more difficult to find, except I still feel we should look deeper into the Bescutti family.'

'Well, José, you've been right before, only here I have to differ. Georgio Bescutti gave absolutely no indication that he dabbled in that field.'

'You might be right. Still, don't forget Georgio is not the whole family. He most probably doesn't even know about what the rest of them get up to.'

'That's probably true. What about the other "families"? Don't forget we have various groups acting in that shadowy world. We have quite a few East European groups like the Russians, the Ukrainians, those from the Balkans and don't forget we have the Arab world's method of doing business.'

'True, the Russians and Serbians are strong in gemstones, and of course, the Saudis deal constantly in precious stones. And the latter would also be interested in Gonzales's other trades. So, giving him a warning would be obvious,' Garcia added.

'According to Special Branch, there is a new group at play from Hong Kong. Very much under the radar, SB only picked up rumours about them last week. Maybe we should put them on the list. They could be strong contenders as suspects.'

'Why don't I know about this lot?'

'If you remember, you've been snoozing on the job, hiding away here.'

'That's not fair, you gave me no choice.'

'My bad. Anyway, now you know. We should throw them into the mix. But look, I've overstayed my welcome. I am going to leave you to chew on what I've told you and we'll pick up the conversation again tomorrow. What do you say?'

'Okay, no matter how much I would like us to carry on, I'm beginning to tire. Thanks, mate, looking forward to your visit tomorrow – about the same time?'

'That works. See you then, have a good sleep and get better soon, we miss having you around the bullpen.'

'Can't wait to get back, it'll be a while yet, am going as fast as I can. Bye for now.'

Garcia didn't want Maria to know about the fire at Paul's apartment, so, between them, they arranged that on Garcia's discharge from the hospital, he would book into the Hotel room next to Favre. Both decided it was the best decision with Maria leaving to be with the children, as they could review the case constantly. Paul could also make sure he goes to physio.

*

At the Gonzales home, Arthur pulled his wife aside. Their concern for their daughter, Cynthia, consumed both.

'Police came to the office today.'

'What for? Because Cynthia was present when the shooting happened?'

'Yes, and to find out if we knew anything about it.'

'What do you mean? What would you know about it?'

'It's complicated.'

'What do you mean, complicated? Arthur did you do something that could get us in trouble? I don't want to move and uproot Cynthia at this time of her education.'

'No, definitely not. I agree, I prefer us to stay here, it's safe and secure. But they came to ask if we knew the man they've identified as the shooter.'

'Why you?'

'Because, as you said, Cynthia was at the scene and could possibly

242

have been the target and not the young man who died.'

'What? Are you telling me they wanted to kill my daughter?'

'No, no, calm down. They were just being careful, covering all the possibilities to find the criminal. Don't forget we do business with people all over the world, and obviously, they would ask for our help.'

'Arthur, tell me. Do you know the shooter?'

'No, of course not – why would I know him. Why do you ask a question like that?'

'Well, because the police asked for your help. That's a first!'

'They wanted to know if we heard something or if we've had threats or warnings.'

'Have you had a threat that I don't know about?'

'No, nothing of the sort – don't forget it's their job to cover all bases.'

'Couldn't you deal with them? The police, I mean?'

'We're not in Colombia now. They do not take payoffs. With your Swiss upbringing you should know that. To tell the truth, we had an incident at the airport yesterday and we thought it might be connected.'

'Well, was it?'

'It looks as if the man involved at the airport came to our offices two or three months ago asking for a job. That's why we had to make statements at the station.'

'Oh, I see, so that's why they think there might be a connection.'

'Yes, and of course, they wanted to make sure we realise the danger involved. They agreed with our decision to put a curfew in place for Cynthia. Apparently, that boy, Antonio, is also under curfew for the same reason. They're not taking any chances, so rest assured they have our security in mind.'

'What does that mean? Are they watching us?'

'No, not exactly, they are keeping an eye on whoever this man is.'

'Should we say something to Cynthia?'

'We shouldn't scare her. Only make sure she understands the importance of doing what we say. Now is not the time to rebel.' He turned to go to his office, hesitated, turned back. 'And she should stay away from that Antonio.'

*

Anna watched her husband leave, closing the door behind him. She knew once he ensconced himself in his office, no more conversation or information would be forthcoming. Well, that meant she had to deal with their daughter. With a sigh, she mounted the stairs to Cynthia's bedroom, where she knew she would find her daughter on the bed, earphones in, texting to who knows whom, and impossible to reach. Her world wasn't the world Anna and Arthur lived in, and every day that world seemed across a greater divide. For Anna, it felt as if they were outsiders looking on, completely helpless to keep the monsters away.

Her tentative knock on the door received no response, so she knocked again, a little more determined. In a way, she felt reticent in confronting her daughter. Or was it fear? Nowadays, she couldn't be sure what to expect whenever Cynthia came downstairs. They didn't seem to exchange any meaningful conversation. It's more like one-syllable replies to a question, and Anna began to feel that resentment had built up because of the restrictions they have laid on her. Would she never understand that it was for her safety, her protection? That was the job of parents, which never ends, no matter what the age of the child. With her ear to the door, she waited for Cynthia's answer.

'What?'

'May I come in?'

'If you have to.'

'*Ma chérie,* I just want to see how you're doing, and let you know what's happening on our side.' Anna ignored the rebellious and negative attitude of her daughter. She realised she would have to push through the personal hurt if she wanted to get Cynthia to listen. With the doorknob in her hand, she carefully turned and opened the door enough to put her head around. Cynthia didn't even look up.

'Okay, whatever.' Reluctantly, Cynthia pulled the earphones out and looked up. Anna moved towards the bed and tentatively sat down on the edge.

'How was your day?'

'How do you think, Mom? I'm not allowed to go and see my friends, so I'm stuck here. I feel like a prisoner.'

'No, *chérie,* we don't want you to feel like a prisoner in your own home. We just want you to be safe.'

'But it's been weeks since the shooting, so why must I still have a curfew?'

'Your father told me that the police came to his office to talk to him and his staff. They were wondering if the shooting could have been a warning to us or his business.'

'So, is it?'

'Well, we don't think so. That is why we've been so worried about your safety. We don't want to scare you, but we also don't want to keep things from you. It's difficult to be a parent sometimes, and this is one of those times. We really would like you to understand and accept our request to stay indoors after six. The police also think the curfew is a good idea.'

'Great. So, everyone is ganging up against me.'

'Apparently, they spoke to Antonio's father as well and ...' Anna couldn't finish.

'What? How? Antonio doesn't even know his father, so how could they speak to him?'

'Well, it looks they found him and thought he might know something or even be involved.'

'No wonder they call the police "pigs"; they suspect everyone. Perhaps they even think that I had arranged it all.'

'*Ma chérie, calmes-toi.* No, they don't. Though, they do think the motive for the shooting might have something to do with you dating Antonio. That's why we asked you to please stay away from him for the time being. Do you think you could do that for us, please? Just for the time being, as I said.'

'I don't believe it! I'm not a child anymore, and I wish you and Dad would accept that and treat me accordingly! All you had to do was to tell me the truth from the beginning. I would've understood.'

'We only wanted to protect you from all the bad in the world.'

'The monsters, you mean. Well, there aren't any monsters except those which parents create for their children.'

'Be serious, please tell me you understand. It would put both of our minds at rest.'

'Okay Mom, I'll be careful.'

'And do what we say?'

'Yes, I won't see Antonio. And I won't go out after six. And I won't go out alone. Are you happy now?'

'*Merci, ma chérie* that's all we ask. I'll leave you. Good night *ma belle, je t'aime.'*

'Good night, Mom, love you too.'

Anna got up, stroked her daughter's hair, and gave her a light kiss on her forehead. She turned towards the door to leave, looked back at Cynthia. The earphones were already back in her daughter's ears with fingers dancing over her mobile phone before Anna even closed the door behind her.

*

The sun began to set, and the Jet d'Eau spouted white against the fast-greying sky. Even so, Paul decided to go back to the station. Despite the heat not having dissipated, and looking forward to a shower, he couldn't wait to get back to his desk. After his discussion with José, his eagerness to find out how far Borel and Pichon came with locating Olivier, as well as looking deeper into the possible other organised crime groups, took over.

Slight disappointment awaited him as he reached his desk. The first thing that caught his eye was an urgent notice that all officers not on active duty, were called to be on standby. That meant Borel and Pichon, who were on loan to their Special Crime Unit, might be called away at a moment's notice.

The reason: a demonstration with a march from the UN to Place Neuve, crossing the city to protest climate change, was scheduled for the next day. The demonstrators targeted big businesses and governments, to immediately change their attitudes and methods to limit carbon emissions; after that 16-year-old Swedish girl, Greta Thunberg, accused governments of being the cause of the disastrous state of the environment. Her protest sparked a global movement which took on a life of its own. Students and concerned citizens took to the streets, leading to strikes and demonstrations. Some of these became violent, resulting in people being injured, and property damage. Therefore, all cities called for extra police presence at each event. Even though, in Paul's opinion, any attempt to rectify the damage already done was, in fact, too late. The environmentalists believed that constructive change could reverse the damage – wishful thinking. It seemed as if everything had become a wilderness where everyone waded through aimlessly, with no one realising the impact all types of crime had on humanity.

Again, his mind listed various types of crime. He deplored the fact that, at present, only crime against the environment came under the spotlight. What did people regard as real crime? The lines were becoming blurred, leaving everyone confused. The scene of the young Marcus lying in a pool of blood, flashed. To Paul, that was real crime, but he felt as if he was fighting a losing battle. Worse, he seemed to be a lone voice in this chaotic wilderness. Anyway, enough of this, he needed to put these mental discussions aside and get back to what mattered, the present case and its players.

He always had the East Europeans and Russians high on his list of possible contenders as the brains behind the shooting. Only now, he had to bring in the Yakuza. He honestly hoped that they could be ruled out. From what he knew of that group, he wouldn't want them to get a foothold in the country.

A thought popped up – from the information they had received on Olivier, Japanese was not mentioned as a language he spoke, and Cantonese and Mandarin seemed too far removed. Could the Yakuza be Olivier's handler? They would speak English. He fired up his computer, and when he could access his account, he sent a message to Special Branch for more information on the Yakuza, and specifically, if they noticed a new contact the group acquired. Each of these groups had complicated networks, and he wondered if he would ever get to the bottom of it. Nevertheless, he had to push forward. He included a photo of Olivier and requested a list of any other criminal organisations working in Switzerland.

On the personal level he was getting worried about Olivier. Psychopaths become bored easily and a few days have passed since the fire. Favre asked himself what Olivier had planned for them next. He'll have to be extra vigilant and warn Garcia. After the scare with Phillippe, Garcia's son, he thought it prudent to make sure that Maria leaves Geneva again.

*

'It's late, and I haven't received an update from you,' the Boss spoke into the receiver in a level voice. It carried a deadly threat which belied the outer calm. *'You assured me that things were in hand and near completion. ... What have you been doing? ... That's not enough, and you know it. Get it done within the next twenty-four hours. Is that understood? ... 'Yes, now*

you have a timeline. Get it done, or else.' Without another word the Boss put the phone down.

Irritated by the lack of progress, the Boss paced the floor. At present, everything seemed stagnant. Suspicion and mistrust of the intentions had increased of those entrusted with this mission. Perhaps it was time to personally take things in hand. What do they say? If you want something done efficiently, do it yourself. Yes, that was about where they were now. This Olivier came highly recommended though, obviously the actual project was not revealed. But he's supposed to be an all-rounder and very effective in all circumstances – not at all squeamish if drastic action was needed.

Well, until tomorrow evening then. Nothing else to be done, though patience was thinning drastically. That's all for now, better call it a night.

CHAPTER FOURTEEN

Ignorant of the arson attack on Favre's apartment which engulfed the whole building, Maria agreed without reserve that her husband stay with Paul while she left to join their children at an undisclosed destination. The news that Garcia would be released from hospital later in the day to recuperate further at home with regular visits to the physiotherapist, delighted Favre.

Of course, Paul knew if left to his partner, the recuperation will not be done at the Hotel where he booked the adjoining room for José, but at Servette Station. No way would José stay away from his office desk. Even if Maria didn't leave, and José could go home, he would insist on going to work. Paul assured Maria that he would personally take José to his physiotherapy sessions. That was the only way Maria would agree to leave Geneva.

With the prospect of his partner's release from hospital, Paul felt elated. He realised a weight had lifted off his shoulders, because his partner would be at hand to chew over the case's facts. Now that they reached the presumed three-quarter mark of the investigation, a springboard for his musings was essential. He doubted Olivier would give up the person who hired him. Still, there might be an indication if they read between the lines.

This was where José came in. He always saw the obscure behind the obvious, often breaking a case wide open. So far, his intuition that they had to look deeper into the girl, Cynthia's life, had been correct. That her family was involved, unknowingly or knowingly, gave them a direction in which to look for the motive behind the shooting. The disappearance of the courier, and with it the loss of the sample emeralds, linked Gonzales indirectly to the motive.

So, who wanted to take over the gemstone market, Paul asked himself. He looked at the crime board again. He decided to phone the Organised Crime Unit before trying to fit each fact displayed into its right place. The OCU might by now have the information about all the other groups who may be involved, which he had asked for. He could also get Borel to research these gangs independently. A different way of looking at things might come in handy.

Where was Borel? He looked around the room, silence overpowered the space. At first, he could not understand why it was so quiet. On his arrival at the station, he had only seen the Duty Officer at reception. Then he remembered – the Climate Change Demonstration, where all available hands were called to duty. He virtually jumped when the phone he had brought to his ear rang.

Out of six, line one blinked on the telephone console, he pressed the button and responded *'Favre'*. The call came from the OCU, advising him that they had sent through information on organisations currently active in the country, and especially, the Geneva Canton. Paul didn't waste time and fired up his computer. Impatiently, he waited for the Cantonal Police emblem to fill the screen. When the desktop icons appeared, he navigated the cursor to his e-mail account, clicked to open it. It took only a moment for the list of his recent mails to be displayed. The first on the list, and therefore the latest to be received, came from the OCU. He opened it without delay, reading the body of the mail, which advised that if further information was required, he should contact the undersigned. He saw four attachments, which he opened one after the other, quickly scanning each. He gave the computer another command and sent everything he received in that OCU e-mail to the printer. While waiting for the printing to be done, he got a coffee and prepared to sit down for the duration, studying the documents.

Even though the reports were only a summary, the concise detail gave Paul sufficient information to form an opinion on the different players. One of the points which became very clear was the concern the OCU had about the rapid growth in activity of the Yakuza. Never before a real presence in Switzerland, they had popped up five years ago and since then showed a steady increase in reported events, though, never noteworthy until this past year when it escalated. The Unit thought that the strategy of the Yakuza was not to draw attention until they were ready for the complete takeover. According to the OCU, that time has now come.

Paul knew the danger these groups held. However, going through the reports made his blood turn cold. The Russian gangs and their cruelty were well known, their expansion in the country, were frightening. It made the old-style Mafia look lame, except that didn't absolve the Mafia. Their new methods were more intelligent, and also cruel, only in a different noncorporeal way. Where would it end if the country couldn't stem the problem? More to the point: which group controlled Olivier and exploited the situation? Looking at these reports, Paul found four possible organisations: the Russians, the Colombian Cartel (recently branched out into precious metals and stones) the Yakuza, and the Serbians. Any one of them could be the puppet master. Though, what surprised Paul was that the Mafia didn't feature on the shortlist. His previous feelings that the Bescutti family could've been involved had now been reduced even further. Firstly, after they spoke to Georgio, and now according to the OCU's report, that family appeared last on the OCU list. Oh, how he needed José's input now – well, it won't be long before they would be able to discuss everything in detail.

Paul realised that he felt stiff from sitting. The wall clock showed one-thirty. He couldn't believe that he had been bent over these reports for more than four hours. He phoned Maria. It would soon be time to pick up José. He arranged a time with her and got back to the files in front of him.

Olivier's arrogance was the key to finding him and getting to the bottom of the whole story. His penchant for watching his handiwork, and how it played out overpowered his common sense. That was the key to catching him. Nevertheless, Paul decided not to underestimate Olivier – they needed to keep their eyes open for his next move. He phoned Leonard and brought him up to date before he packed up to collect José from the hospital.

*

A hospital employee pushed a protesting Garcia out in a wheelchair, Maria, a step behind carrying José's bag, ineffectively tried to calm him down. That it was hospital policy for a patient to be taken off the premises by wheelchair made no difference to Garcia. He wasn't impressed in the slightest, and verbally let everyone in the vicinity know how he felt.

Favre watched the scene play out as he pulled up onto the concourse outside the hospital's entrance. To minimise the torture Maria had to endure, he jumped out and opened the passenger door. He greeted everyone, helping his partner out of the chair and into the car. Maria handed him the bag, and he gave her a hug, wishing her *bonne route*. He wasn't sure when he would see her again, but he hoped that it would be soon. Further, he assured her that José would be in good hands, and his physiotherapy followed exactly as recommended.

'*Tout va bien mon, ami ?*' Paul glanced at José as he turned the key in the ignition, gently pulling away from the hospital entrance.

'Yes, everything's fine, just infuriating and humiliating being pushed out in a wheelchair. They make you feel like an invalid.'

'I understand, though don't forget, you were one for a while there. No way could we avoid that. So, let's concentrate on the good things.'

'Such as?'

'Well, for one, you're out of the hospital, and for another, you're going to live in a hotel with me as your next-door neighbour! Isn't that good enough to feel better?'

'If you put it that way, oh definitely – life is looking up!'

'Good, Maria agreed to no contact from her side, and that you'll update her on a regular basis.'

'Yes, no problem there. She's just worried about keeping the children safe. And of course, that I follow the doctor's orders. For the rest, she's not concerned. She says I'm able to look after myself, as long as I come home every evening.'

'That's good news. So, she trusts me to keep you on the straight and narrow. Just think, we'll have time to go over the investigation in detail without interruption from outside sources.'

'You mean like me having to go home to my wife and children?'

'Well, yes. There wouldn't be a clock that we must work to. Of course, rest is your primary concern to regain your usual hundred percent. So, you'll have to promise that as soon as you begin to feel tired, you'll tell me, and we'll take a break.'

'No worries there. Although first, I need something good to eat.'

'Those words confirm that you are well on the way to recovery. You really worried me while in hospital when I couldn't even tempt you with a little extra nutrition from your favourite resto! Give me fifteen minutes to get to the hotel, and we can have some take-away brought in.'

It took nearly twenty minutes before they pulled up in the Hotel's parking garage. However, as all had been arranged beforehand, José's check-in took only five. Paul carried José's bag and opened the room for him. It took even less time to get José settled in, where Paul left him to return to the station. They arranged to meet in an hour to go over the files and plan a possible strategy on how to go forward.

*

José stretched out on the bed. He couldn't wait for Paul to leave. He ached all over, and that was the last thing he wanted Paul to know. He had an hour to recuperate and get the pain under control. He had taken a pain killer just as his partner closed the door behind him and flopped onto the bed without even taking off his shoes. He wouldn't dare do that at home - Maria would have a fit. Now, the pill just had to do its work.

The room's only colour came from the pale green curtains and bedspread. The light wood of the bed, desk, coffee table, and easy chairs gave it a clean, fresh feel. He lay on his back, staring at the ceiling. The Hôtel NH Geneva City's ceilings were like any other modern hotel he's ever been in. Blank walls and ceiling, eggshell white, only broken by a few spider-web fine cracks that followed no pattern. No matter how hard he tried, he couldn't see a face or a map in them. The comfortable, practical decor made his eyes glaze over, and he drifted into a harmonious floating. Waves of pastel colours carried him further into nothingness making his body sink into the bed until he felt part of it. It was impossible to distinguish where his body ended, and where the bed began, or vice versa. Nothing mattered, the bed gave support where needed and comfort as required. The pain had subsided, and before he knew it, he vaguely heard the door open, and Paul stood over him.

'Hi man. What're you doing here so soon? I thought you said you'd be back in an hour. Did you bring something to eat?'

'Hi. Actually, I've been held up a bit. It's an hour and a half since I left you. And to answer your question, yes, I brought some good *osso bucco* from the Italian. Will that do?' Paul held up the bag with the food which he placed on the coffee table.

'Great, that's exactly what I need. Was it their special for the day?'

'Yes. I was worried that you would've wanted something else, but this'll have to do. Anyway, Leonard was in the office, and sends his regards, wants us to keep him informed.'

'Goes without saying. You've got all the files?'

'Yes, are you up for it?'

'Can we eat first?' José slowly swung his legs off the bed, got up

253

tentatively, and took a seat in one of the chairs at the coffee table.

'Of course.' Paul unpacked the thermal cartons, serviettes, plastic utensils, placing one set in front of Garcia. He brought two glasses filled with water, from the bathroom.

José watched his partner arrange everything and wondered how, after the injury, he could be of any use. On one hand, he couldn't wait to get his teeth into the case again, and on the other, he felt afraid.

He asked himself: afraid of what? Afraid of letting Favre and the rest of the team down, of being overlooked, afraid of losing his family, or was he afraid of being injured again? He didn't know the exact cause of these unnerving feelings. Except, they were there, and they were governing his thoughts and emotions. He used his willpower to avoid the fears overpowering him and turned his attention to Favre. Concentration on his partner and the case will carry him through. That he was sure of.

'Good, let's eat. The aroma is already a hundred times better than the hospital food, and I can just imagine how much better the taste will be!' Garcia smiled and picked up the plastic knife and fork.

'I've looked forward sharing a meal with you again, my friend. I really couldn't wait for you to get out of that hospital. Enjoy.'

'*Bon appétit.*' Favre lifted his glass of water, gesturing a toast. Garcia responded with the same gesture, before their eyes fell on the food. For the next fifteen minutes, all that you could be heard were smacking lips, "uhumm", "ahh" and "this is good!" until Favre pushed the food receptacle and utensils toward the middle of the small table. He leaned back rubbed his stomach, belched. José looked with pleasure at his partner. Gosh, how he missed this camaraderie. He relaxed – things were going to be all right. He finished off his meal and placed his empty container on top of the other.

'So, tell me what you haven't laid out to me yet.'

José listened with interest as Paul explained the work Borel and Pichon had done on tracking Olivier, and the invaluable information they got from the different cameras and social media. Paul praised the two young officers, admitting that they would not be where they were if not for the diligence and hard work of these two.

The enthusiasm showing on Paul's face made José feel inadequate. With his present condition, he was very conscious that he could not give his full attention or strength to the case. His forced medical leave might not be lifted if he cannot improve his general wellbeing. Aware of what the job demanded, though they seldom chased and tackled suspects, he knew his body would let him down if required to move fast. He could not meet the required status.

His fear of being left behind or losing his job emasculated him. He felt worthless. How could these two young bucks take his place? With years of experience behind him, and a nose for the job, he tried to convince himself they would never be able to develop the same. Except, his doubts remained. What if that wasn't enough? Favre depended on his feeling for a situation. Or has Favre's confidence in him waned, shifted? Perhaps he had found someone else to rely on. He'd have to prove his worth anew and to do that he would have to clear his head immediately. Losing confidence in his ability was suicide. He had to pull his weight no matter how – and now!

'So, tell me where I can jump in to maximise the effort.'

'You have to recuperate, don't jump the gun.'

'I cannot sit on the side lines where I've been since the blast. You cannot keep me from doing my job!'

'Oh, don't worry about that – I'm putting you to work.'

'You know I'm not a desk-job person. Please don't tell me you're delegating me to looking at videos while you have the pleasure of running around interviewing people?'

'No, that is the job of Borel and Pichon, they're very good at it. You know young people live on social media and such; they never take their eyes off screens. What I have in mind for you is a little more involved and only you can do it.'

'And what's that?'

'I need your insight – you know; that thing you do, when you always throw a spanner in the works and catch me off guard.'

'What do you mean? I never disrupt an investigation.'

'No, that's not what I'm saying. You see things that I miss, a sort of behind-the-scenes detail you pick up that at first sounds so out of context but proves to be on target.'

'Oh, good. So, that means you did miss me and need me!'

'Of course, you oaf! This investigation would've moved much faster if you weren't incapacitated. You were sorely missed, but now you're back, and we can move on. The only thing is, you need to tell me when you get tired. I might not notice and push you beyond your present stamina level. Don't forget, I want you to be well-rested in two days' time for your first physio.'

'No problem I'll be able to take it.'

'Old friend, you forget I must answer to Maria. Therefore, there's no way you are going to step over the line and avoid your rest or physio.'

'Okay then, let's get to it. I'm fine for the moment. What would you like me to look at first?' José shifted and settled in for the day.

'Have you had time to look at the transcripts of the interviews with Bescutti and Gonzales in more detail? Also, I would like your input on the OCU's list of operators in the field. I found it interesting that Bescutti was not on the short list for those trading actively in gemstones.'

'Yes, that's surprising. Though, I would like to look at everything again. My head is much clearer now.'

'Good, take your time. I'll leave you to get on with it and come back later, say around five? That'll give you time to take a quick rest as well.'

'Sounds good – see you later, Mate.' José took the file Paul held out.

'Later.' Paul said and left.

As soon as Paul closed the door, José got up. The pain was constant, but at least it would be under control for at least another hour. He moved slowly, any sudden muscle usage burnt and tore at his body. At the desk, he lowered himself carefully onto the chair, opened the file, and took up notepaper and pen. Something worried him – certain things didn't add up. He couldn't wait to re-examine the transcripts. Perhaps he might just see something everyone else had missed. Suddenly, he thought of something and pulled out his mobile phone.

'Hey, Favre ... Yes, I know, I miss you already ... No everything's fine, something else I just thought of. ... Could you take a photo with your mobile of the crime board as it is at this moment, and send that photo to me, please? ... Well, I know it sounds strange, but if I could see how you've compiled it, it'll help me to picture the case. ... Yes, send it to me by e-mail, I can then look at it on a bigger screen ... okay, thanks, see you this afternoon.'

He exhaled, he knew it sounded strange, but his excitement grew as he thought of matching the board with what he would be reading. He couldn't wait and rubbed his hands together. Now he would have the tools necessary to do his best and prove his worth.

CHAPTER FIFTEEN

Alpha tracked Cynthia. He was getting tired of this girl who had messed up his life. Why couldn't she just do the same things every day? Why did she have to jump all over Geneva? By the time he managed to put a bullet between her eyes, he would know the city even better than before. Student hangouts did not hold much attraction for him, except that some of the young flesh was very tempting. Though he had always avoided these spots because of the rowdy young adults, perhaps he should reconsider that. He could find free satisfaction, and lots of it – why pay if it's freely available and offered? Girls seemed to fall for the seduction of an experienced man; he would score without even trying. And the plus point: it seemed to be the only place this brat went. Maybe he could get her to put out before he ends her. He would enjoy amusing himself with her for a while. Well, there's a thought.

Another thing, he had never realised there were so many Starbucks in Geneva – it felt as if the company had swamped the city.

Cynthia's taking up far too much of his time – he wanted to get to those two pigs. It'll be much more interesting to off them than the girl. But then he gets paid for the girl, and the two flatfoots are for his own entertainment. He would enjoy that job immensely. Later. He now had to concentrate on the brat.

In his pocket, his hand closed around the switchblade, its stiletto blade neatly tucked away in the handle. With a click of a button, the blade would dart out, ready to do the necessary damage – deadly and silently. Then he thought of the mouth-watering possibilities if he forced her to go with him, instead of finishing her off. His earlier reverie came back, tempting him again, but he shook it off. He moved nearer. Some friends had joined her, forced him to sidestep, losing his momentum. Where did they come from? These pests were everywhere. He couldn't do much while they were around. Another opportunity lost. When would she be alone? He'd have to follow at a distance – see what happens. As usual, Rive was a hub of activity, cars, buses, trams, people getting on or off public transport. It was a challenge, though not impossible.

His phone buzzed, indicating a message had been left. Annoyed, he pulled his mobile out, swiped the screen. It was a text message from the Boss. Now, more irritated than annoyed, he opened messages. He had a strong suspicion of what it was about. He was right, it read: *'What have you done to resolve the matter.'* He texted back: *'In hand,'* throwing the phone against the nearest wall in frustration.

Pedestrians turned, stared at him. He saw Cynthia look over her shoulder, curious. Her friends giggled, pulling her attention back to them. Alpha swore under his breath and bent down to retrieve the instrument and the back cover, which had come off as it hit the hard surface, hoping she didn't notice him. A corner of the cover had chipped. Nevertheless, he pushed it back in until it clicked into place. To check if the phone still worked, he slid his finger across the screen. It lit up and he checked his messages. Yes, the phone responded. Relieved he closed the app and slipped it in his pocket. His hand closed around the knife. Reassured, he moved along the pavement.

Three paces away from the girl, he watched her group from the corner of his eye. None of them took any notice of him as he overheard their plan to go to Balexert for the latest movie. Cynthia's voice carried as she argued against it, saying it would take her beyond her curfew. The other girls groaned, begged her to just once ignore parental restrictions, and go with them. Their pitiful performance finally convinced her, on condition she chose the movie.

Alpha smiled, today was the day. He'd get her after the movie as she left the centre, much easier. Their plans gave him two hours to plan his other exploit, which meant he had to check up on his informant. So far, everything he had given him was spot on. Insiders are hard to come by and expensive, except this one was worth it. And Alpha could afford it, with his big payday coming up. On top of that, his plans would give him the opportunity to make a killing.

At that precise moment, his plans changed. He saw her signalling that she needed a moment. He watched her turn back, re-entering the coffee shop. Cynthia's friends chatted amongst themselves, and began to slowly move off towards the number ten bus stop. Obviously, they expected her to catch up.

She was on her own. He moved quickly. He saw her pull out money to pay for her drink, handing it over at the till, waiting for the change and her drink. He took two further steps. When she turned to leave, he was in the entrance, half blocking her way.

With his hand on the flick knife and a mumbled *'pardon,'* he brushed against her. At a speed unnoticeable to anybody nearby, he pulled out the knife. He pressed the button. The blade sprang out from its hidden cavity in the handle. The stiletto plunged deep into Cynthia's side. Alpha twisted the blade before withdrawing it. Without a further gesture, he moved to the counter. He locked eyes with the young man who asked what he would like, and he ordered a black coffee. He never looked back.

The slight commotion which ensued at the entrance drew the attention of the young man. However, Alpha brought him back by striking up a conversation. Everything settled down for a minute or two. Then a scream came from just outside the Starbucks. People began running towards a point outside. The young man dropped what he was doing and rushed from behind the counter.

Alpha outwardly looked confused, concerned, and followed the young man to see what had happened. Inwardly, he felt extremely gratified and had difficulty supressing a smile. Though – with slight regret – it was over far too quickly. He should have caught her later and taken her to his place to play. Nevertheless, what a great sight. He enjoyed seeing all that blood seeping through her clothes.

People were crowding around the crumpled form on the pavement. Someone called for something to stem the bleeding. A woman pulled off her scarf. The young employee gave a dishcloth before dashing indoors for more towels. Another person advised putting pressure on the wound, adding that someone should phone for an ambulance. The chattering girls came back to see what the commotion was all about. One pushed through and began screaming uncontrollably. Her friends crowded in as well. When they saw Cynthia lying there, they joined their friend in screaming, yelling for help, for an ambulance, and for someone to do something. Traffic stopped. Mayhem broke loose.

Various onlookers took photos of the scene with their mobiles. Alpha watched with great satisfaction, wondering how long it would be before the spectacle swamped social media. He made a big show of pulling out his phone, punching in numbers. When a middle-aged woman called out that help was on its way, Alpha snapped his phone shut and, with feigned thankfulness, patted her on the shoulder. Stealthily, he moved to the edge of the group surrounding the inert girl. Now he'll have time to concentrate on the pigs. His heart swelled with joy. Wasn't life great!

Elated, he texted the Boss, *'It's done.'*

*

Cynthia's mother's voice echoed in her head. "Where are you going?" "You can't go out." "Go to your room." "You are not to see Antonio." "Who did you meet?" "You have to be back before six." It never stopped. It drove her mad, that continuous loop. Lately, everything was prohibited. It's not fair! All she wanted was to hang out with her girlfriends and go downtown or to the movies.

She didn't do anything wrong. The restrictions her parents placed around her like barbed wire, choked her. Each word her mother had uttered tumbled this way and that in her mind. It felt as if her head was on fire. They were so overreacting! What were they on about? No way could she be in danger, it's all just a ruse to keep her from seeing Antonio. What a relief to be out of that house – she suffocated there. At last, she had escaped. She took a deep breath, threw her head back before exhaling slowly. Yes, it was great to taste the fresh air. A movie would do her the world of good. All she risked would be her mother's chagrin, so why not go to the cinema? And the curfew! Well, she'd only be about thirty minutes late – maximum an hour – no reason for her mother to lose her cool.

Some man in the small group in front of the coffee shop had a temper tantrum. She didn't recognise him, but somehow, he seemed familiar. She heard the expletives and the sound of the person's mobile hitting the ground. Gosh, some people can get so uptight!

She turned back to her friends. Her decision made; she'd go with them, but before leaving, she must get her iced coffee. It would only take a moment. She could catch up with them at the bus stop.

While thinking of the different choices of films to see, she collected her drink and ignored the young man at the counter trying to catch her eye for her mobile number. Dismissively, she threw her head back, turning to the door. Her mind on the possible films available, she knew which one she wanted to see.

There he was again – she was sure it was the same person who had thrown his phone – crowding her in the doorway. The thought that he might be following her, angered her. Obviously, it could only be her parents trying to keep tabs on her. What do they think they were doing? Who do they think she was? Didn't they trust her? Now, more determined than ever to break curfew, she glanced at the man, hoping he'd get the message. He was intrusive and rude. A slimy creep – handsome in a dangerous way. Well, she'd give him a wide berth.

That intention fell away as he pushed against her. The doorframe pressed hard into her back, and suddenly her stomach was on fire. No, it was her chest. No, her lungs hurt. She couldn't make out exactly what was happening. Her knees didn't want to lock. Both legs just gave in, and she felt strangely faint. At the same time, warmth spread over her abdomen. Strange, her hands and feet flooded with a terrible coldness. She tried to call out to her friends, except her voice let her down. Her head swam. She lost her footing, falling into a couple seated at the table next to the entrance, her drink spilling over them. They jumped up annoyed, then tried to avoid her and, at the same time, catch her. Her apology for bumping into them only a whisper – lost in the clatter deafening her. Then all went black.

*

Paul drove to the hotel, wondering if José would be fine alone for the full day. The evenings posed no problem, as the first one proved. They would spend them together; most probably discussing and finally solving the case. Various appointments for physiotherapy were already on the agenda for his partner, and Paul had decided to personally take him. That way, he could follow the progress and know how far he could push José.

His radio crackled to life: "Stabbing downtown. Victim critical and being transported to HUG." These things are happening too often nowadays for his liking. He ignored the incident report. There were enough others on duty to handle a stabbing. He pulled into the hotel's parking lot, tired and hungry, but eager to meet with his partner.

'Hello, Partner, did you get some rest? Don't forget you have your first outpatient physio treatment in the morning.'

'Oh yes, I know. But look at this, I found something strange. Let me show you.'

'Don't you want to eat first?'

'What a good idea – this can wait a minute or two. We can talk while we eat. What did you bring?' José rubbed his hands together, licking his lips.

'Lasagne from La Primavera – your favourite Italian. We'll get something from Burger King tomorrow. For the time being, you have to eat healthier.'

'And lasagne is better? Oh, all right, I love it and feel like eating. I'll get the plates and utensils you brought yesterday. I washed and put it all away to make room for me to spread out the file.' José painfully lifted himself out of the chair, moved over to the small cupboard on which the kettle and cups stood. He pulled the items from the paper carrier bag, setting them on the desk. Without another word, but with a groan, he moved back to the chair, sinking carefully into it.

'Oh, I can see that – where am I to sit?' Paul looked around the room. José had used his time constructively. That he had worked on the case was evident, he waved his hand over the paper carpet. 'Are you sure you're not too tired after doing all this?'

'I admit I'm a little tired, and sure once we've eaten, I'll be fine. I want your opinion on something.'

'You really did find something.'

'Well, more a hunch, or suspicion if you want to know. I asked myself how Olivier always managed to be one step ahead of us. From the info in the file, he seems reasonably computer literate, though not on the level of a hacker. So, if he couldn't get our schedule from hacking our computers, where did he find it?'

'Okay, I'm with you so far. Except, you can get all the information you want from the internet about how to do something, and hacking is one of them. Are you sure he couldn't access our agenda?'

'Not really. The level needed to break into the police systems is much higher than what you could learn online. So, I looked more carefully at all the prints from the CCTV footage Borel and Pichon reviewed, and I found something interesting. Or I think, I did.'

'You sound excited. Come on, spill! Do you think it'll help our case?' Paul sat down, opened the boxes, ready to eat, and anxious to hear what his partner had to say.

'Well, I've been following the suspect on the timestamped prints. I linked them to the crime board.' José put a forkful of lasagne in his mouth, chewed twice before continuing. 'I saw him contacting someone. It might be nothing, or just a chance meeting. Only, something just doesn't smell right.'

'You said you had a hunch, but what are you talking about?'

'As I said, Olivier always seemed to know where the two of us would be. I found that strange. So, when I discarded the hacking angle, I then looked to see if he tracked our phones. That also seemed not that easy to do, even though he had our private home numbers. Our mobile phones are department-issued and therefore, not trackable.'

'Is that true? I thought all phones are traceable if you had the GPS on.'

'Yes, that is true, but ours have an extra feature which blocks outside tracing without a departmental password.'

'So, what are you saying? What other way is there?'

'Well, I scrutinised every face on those prints to see if he received some help from an unknown quarter.' He scraped the last bit of food from the thermal box and looked up at Paul for a reaction.

'Did you find a face which appeared more than once?'

'No, something else. I found a badge which seemed vaguely familiar.'

'A badge? What do you mean a "badge"? Like a shield? Like those security or police officers wear? And how did you match it up with our schedule?'

'I could never see the face who wore the badge, but yes, one worn by an official. I picked it up on two occasions quite near to Olivier. In fact, once next to him, and another time with one body between them. It's not very clear the second time, but it's worth looking at.'

'Fine, you've piqued my interest. What badge? To which department does it belong?'

'Let me show you.' José laboriously rose to retrieve the two prints from the bed. As he lifted them, he continued. 'The first time it appeared is in Navigation Square after the CCTV picked up our man coming from the direction of the shooting. The second time was in Paquis, the day before your apartment burnt down. Here, take a look.' He handed the prints over and sat down again.

'Yeah, I see what you mean, it's not conclusive. Did you run it down for authenticity? It could be a forgery. It closely resembles our Cantonal shield. And the person wearing it, could you figure out who it is?'

'You'll have to do that at the station. I cannot access facial recognition from here. But for authenticity, according to the web, it is our symbol. Though, whether it's authentic, I cannot say. I could only compare – the image is not that crisp. Perhaps our people in Tech could do better.'

'Well, old partner, you've done a great job.'

'Not so much of the "old" please.'

'Just to say, Borel and Pichon went over the footage carefully and never picked it up. No one could ever replace you and your nose! You have just proven it again – as if it needed proving. Can't think how far we would've been on the case if you weren't laid up. Anyway, you are here now. And I'm going to make sure you do your physio so that you can be at full strength as soon as possible. I need you, Partner.'

'Amen to that. I'm sure Maria will be pleased as well. Getting this case solved will enable us to get our lives back. Not that I'm complaining being here with you rather than recuperating at home. It's just that Maria will fuss over every little thing. It'll drive me crazy. I do miss the children, though.'

'Well, at the rate we're going since you left the hospital, I see it all wrapped up sooner than you think. But José, enough for tonight. You need to rest and be ready for your session in the morning. I'll gather everything up exactly as you set it out, in chronological sequence. You can look at it with fresh eyes tomorrow after treatment. What do you say?'

'I do feel wacked. Okay, mate, let's call it a night. Thanks for clearing up.' With that José went to the bathroom and prepared for bed. When he emerged, Paul called out 'Goodnight', closing the door behind him.

CHAPTER SIXTEEN

A new day! Alpha looked at the text message. A smile spread across his face. His informant always came through, what a find! He delivered more than he could ever have wished for. And this time: what great news, nothing else could've made the day brighter! When he woke this morning, he knew it would be a special date on the calendar.

He now had the exact time of the fat pig's physio treatment, and the other one would be taking him. Things couldn't have turned out better. It meant they'd be on the road he had in mind in roughly thirty minutes. He wanted the two together, now it would come to fruition!

He checked his watch – perfect – he could finish his coffee leisurely. He'd have plenty of time to get there way ahead of them. The lying-in wait can sometimes be very exhilarating. It pumps the adrenaline.

The Boss's satisfaction for a job finally done, showed in the congratulatory message he received, with confirmation that the final instalment of the contracted amount had reached his bank account. Fine, it did take some doing with failures along the way; however, it was concluded as requested. Though, he still wondered what it would've been like if they had manged to take some time to play some of his preferred games. Never mind, plunging that stiletto into her felt so good. That little twist at the end virtually brought him to climax. What he experienced at that moment blew his mind. Just think what would've happened if he could've drawn it out. Pity it was over so quickly. Oh well, now he could carry out his own project. With his mind filled with the delicious possibilities, he rinsed his coffee mug at the sink and placed it on the drying board.

On his way out of his studio, he stopped, couldn't resist, he tarried in front of the mirror admiring the reflection. Yes, he was a magnificent specimen of the human-race, and a prime example of the male species! Now he was on his way to complete this cycle and begin his new life at the head of the black-market gem trade. He chuckled as he thought of the look of incredibility that would appear on the Boss' face when the power shift became evident. So far, the Boss had no suspicion of his aspirations and insatiable desire for power. Now he was on his way to having everything – just as planned. He smiled back at his reflection and said: 'Let's go!' With a nod to himself, he opened the door and left.

The traffic flowed at a slow rate, being the start of morning rush-hour, yet it moved. He would be in place as planned. Sure enough, he passed Bout du Monde and crept slowly up to the spot he had selected, parked, and waited for Garcia and Favre to arrive. From here, they would be visible coming up just before the curve. He lowered both his, and the passenger-side window. The heat of the day slipped into the air-conditioned car, causing the temperature to rise to an uncomfortable level. Alpha loved the heat, couldn't understand why the locals thought it a heatwave.

He turned the ignition and revved the engine. How he loved the sound of that horsepower! Timing was everything. He lifted his foot off the brake, revved again. Through the seat, the impatient tremble vibrated through Alpha's body. Oh, how good that power felt. He sensed the restraint underneath him. The handbrake tethered the force. Oh, he was so ready to do this – ramming them with a sidelong hit, towards the front, would push the target car through the curve, crushing the barrier, and sending it over the cliff. He shook his head. No, he had to stick to the plan. It wouldn't do – damaging his own vehicle would cause problems and the source of endless questions.

And there they were! Alpha straightened, craned his neck, his hands gripped the steering wheel. The target was about twenty metres behind a silver BMW, with a clear road behind. A sneer developed and he muttered 'now I've got you, you filthy pigs!' He let go of the steering wheel and closed his right hand over his gun. With patience and cold precision, he lifted his arm, aimed, and fired.

*

'Are you ready?' Favre called out through the connecting door of Garcia's room.

'Hold your horses! I'm coming.'

'Hurry up, we must go. I don't want you to be late for your first appointment.'

'Tell me again why I must see this physio who's to hell and gone across town? I would've preferred someone nearer,' Garcia said, stepping through the door and closing it behind him.

'You heard what the doctor said - this person specialises in violent body trauma. The bomb blast counts as such. There's no other choice unless you want your recovery to take double the time.'

'No way, just let's go.'

During the drive, they wondered when it would finally cool down. A crackling of the police radio interrupted them. A metallic voice advised that Captain Leonard requested Favre return to Servette Station as soon as Garcia finished his physio. Garcia looked at Favre, who only shook his head. No further information came over.

'I suppose he wants an update. I'll tell him your impressions and that you are trying to confirm them.'

'I think we should keep that to ourselves,' Garcia said cautiously.

'We'll have to tell Leonard.'

'Not yet. We need to confirm the suspicion first. Also, we should only discuss it with him and no one else. We have no idea who's supplying the information.'

'You're right. I'll be careful. You never know who's listening. This is terrible. We don't know who we can trust amongst our own!'

'I don't want to sound paranoid, but after what has been happening, may I see things which aren't there. As they say, "Trust no one," and I'll follow that advice until we've found all the answers we're looking for.' Garcia turned towards Favre.

At that precise moment, a load clap sounded. The vehicle swerved, wallowed on its four wheels. Favre battled for control. The car turtled and came to rest on the edge of the cliff. Metal screeched as the now bent barrier tore and scratched the car's roof. The car snagged on the barrier, balancing precariously. Dust and foliage polluted the air. Every particle clouding the area made motion happen as if an age has passed before the next movement. It took a lifetime for everything to settle.

'What just happened?' Favre asked, shaking his head to clear his vision. No reply came. Again, Paul tried to focus. He felt numb. Something was wrong. A slight rocking motion kept on disturbing his equilibrium. Where did it come from? His head was pushed against his chest, and breathing had become virtually impossible. He tried to lift his head to inhale. The movement only increased the rocking. When he tried to touch his head, he realised he couldn't move his arm. Why couldn't he move? He felt impaled. How did he get here? Why was it dark? Not a sliver of light came through. Confusion flooded his entire being. Everything was upside down. He couldn't see his partner. Dust floated in the air. Where were they? Why didn't José answer him? Panic touched the edges of his mind. He forced it down – no time to panic.

Slowly, his vision cleared. With it, a searing pain burnt in his back and chest. His knees pinned the steering. Yes, everything was upside down, his seatbelt held him strapped to the seat. He hung more-or-less upside down, with the back of his neck and head pressed against the roof. His effort to assess the situation only resulted in further agony. He had trouble keeping his head clear. It felt as if he had a hole in the top of his head. Even the movement of his eyes hurt. He forced them to his right. He tried to concentrate. The last thing he remembered was driving. Yes, he was in the car on his way to … where? … He couldn't recall. From beside him, a groan escaped from a crumpled bulk. It must be Garcia! Oh yes, they were chatting about the case they were working on. What on earth had happened? They must get out, but how? Fresh blood dripped from his nose choking him, blurring his vision. He coughed and blinked in a determined effort to clear his eyes. They began to water - strangely, it helped with his sight.

'Garcia! José! *Tu m'entends?* Can you hear me?' He thought he shouted, yet his voice came out hoarse and shaky. 'Come on, stay with me, we must get out of this death trap! The car's going to go over the edge any minute now!' He heard José's raspy breathing and wondered to what extent these new injuries impacted José's recovery. The question more immediate: will his body survive this added abuse? Besides the difficult breathing and groaning, no other sound came from Garcia. Paul tried again to rouse his partner, to no avail. In the meantime, the car had stalled, but he could still hear the soft whirr of the wheels winding down their spin.

He'll have to do this on his own. He tried to move his right arm again. Pain shot through to the shoulder. A scream escaped. He realised that it came from him. He attempted liberating his left arm, which his bodyweight pressed firmly against the door and window. When he moved his fingers, no pain shot anywhere – a good sign. Carefully and very slowly, he managed to free the arm. This time, the car groaned. He reached down to his belt, unclipped his mobile phone, and pressed any key and the speaker. All their phones were programmed to automatically speed dial the emergency services by activating only one key. He heard it ring. It took a few ring tones before a response came. The voice was calm and in charge, asking how he needed help. As he replied, giving his name, rank, their situation, and position, he saw feet approaching. He heard a man ask if they were alive. When he called for help, the man put his foot on the back of the vehicle and began to rock it.

'Hey, what are you doing? Stop! We'll go over the edge! Stop!' Favre panicked; he did not know how to stop the car from falling off the cliff. He could hear the person from the emergency services trying to get his attention. He couldn't react except to shout, 'Please help, we are in danger of going over the cliff. Send help immediately.' From outside, the rocking continued.

'Good. That's the idea, you pigs! You thought you could best me, well you can't!' A sneering laugh told Favre exactly who stood beside the car.

'Olivier! You're not going to win! My colleagues are onto you. It's only a matter of time before you're behind bars!' Paul couldn't think – pain overwhelmed him with every move. He knew he had to free himself and José before going over the edge. The barrier still snagged part of the roof, the only thing preventing their fall.

'Oh, make no mistake, you lot will never find me. And the bitch who gave me the job will wish she'd never met me! Her days are over as Ruler to a Dynasty. I'm at the head of the organisation now! You people are so ignorant, it made it all too easy.'

Paul's vision clouded. He couldn't hold on much longer, but he refused to let Olivier get the upper hand. Also, he needed to be sure that his partner was okay. Taunting Olivier would be the only way to make sure he took his foot off the car – it would give them time. Time they desperately needed for the emergency services to arrive.

'So, it's a woman pulling your strings?'

'You don't know what you are talking about, idiot!'

'But that's what you said.'

'No, she's a means to an end. My goal of total dominance. And I've succeeded!'

'Olivier, why did she want to get rid of us?'

'Oh no, you two are my own project. How could I resist? She only wanted the little bitch eliminated, to ensure the gem trade would be hers and hers alone. But then you had to get involved and mess up my timeline, costing me my bonus.'

'You do know that if you kill an official of the Police Department, no one will rest until you are caught.' Paul heard feet crunch across the gravel to the driver's side. Then it was next to his face. Olivier bent down and they were eye to eye. Paul saw the familiar features. The photos did not show the real coldness of the eyes.

'Oh, and you can call me Alpha! Before the day is over, I will be the top dog in all organised crime, mark my words. I am number ONE!' he sniggered.

'Congratulations! So, you've done it, yet we're still alive. I intend for us to stay that way.' Paul's voice croaked, and he fought the blackness which tried to envelop him.

'Not for long – you've been a thorn in my flesh with your ability to evade every trap I set. However, here you are with nowhere to go but down. Oh yes, and just for your information, when I'm finished here, I'm going to that tart of yours and have a bit of fun.'

'Who are you talking about?' Paul desperately wanted to keep Olivier's attention.

'Oh, now you plead ignorance. Well, I'm not that stupid. You couldn't keep away from her, could you? The delectable Miss Labelle, yes, her name says it all. I can just imagine how she'll taste.' Olivier's face disappeared from Paul's view.

'She has nothing to do with this. We had to dismiss her as a witness because she saw nothing. She gave her statement, and that was it.' Favre felt frantic. Garcia was groaning louder and seemed to be coming round. In the distance, sirens blared. Paul wondered if it came for them or for another crisis. He heard a car slow and stop. The driver shouted through the window, if anyone needed help. Alpha replied that all was in hand, and they should move on because the road should be kept clear for the emergency services. The person drove off.

The sirens grew louder. The car rocked violently as Alpha stepped heavily on to the back before turning quickly towards his own vehicle. With excruciating effort, Favre turned his head and watched Alpha's feet leave the scene. The calves came into view, then the knees, until the bottom half of the body crossed the road. He saw him open a car door and get in – the registration plate clearly visible. Paul hoped, despite his headache, he would be able to memorise the number. He heard the engine start, followed by the screech of tyres. Alpha's car shot out of the spot where he had parked, making his escape. True to form, the psychopath that Olivier was, left the two policemen to their fate, teetering on the edge. The sirens were now ear-splitting, only faded as Paul sank into oblivion.

Favre regained consciousness at the sound of Garcia stirring and trying to speak. Favre managed to whisper reassurance, telling him to hang on - help was on the way. Two police vehicles and a fire truck pulled up, with ambulances behind. Men jumped out, placing orange cones on the road on both sides of the upturned car, effectively closing off that part of the road. Discussions on how to proceed quickly turned into action. Three men pressed down, putting their weight on the back of the vehicle, preventing further rocking or slipping. Others pulled out chains with large pulley hooks, ready to be attached. Two others stood ready with the jaws-of-life to pry open the doors. Frenzied activity on all levels became palpable. Everyone worked as fast as possible to rescue the two trapped men.

They pulled Garcia out first and applied the necessary care before loading him into an ambulance. With sirens blaring, they drove off while the other paramedics dealt with Paul.

The police tried to speak to Favre before he was taken to hospital. He floated in and out of blackness, and no coherent statement could be taken. He mumbled something, referred to the Greek Alpha and Omega, followed by some numbers and the words "la belle". It made no sense, though they noted everything. For further details, they would have to wait until the doctors gave the all-clear.

*

Leonard disguised his concern by complaining that he had to visit the hospital far too often recently. He paced, hands in pockets. The anger he felt towards the suspect needed to be controlled; he should not show his real concern. No doubt existed on who orchestrated the accident. From what the police at the scene reported, it pointed directly to their prime suspect. Further, just before the medical staff took him in to the operating theatre, Favre whispered to him that there was a mole supplying information. Unfortunately, he passed out, and the staff pushed Leonard out of the way. He had to let it go – for now. He trusted his two lead detectives. They must have evidence to that effect. Nevertheless, this was serious.

No opportunity arose for him to give Favre and Garcia the news that the girl, Cynthia, daughter of Gonzales, had suffered a near-fatal stab wound, and was at this moment in ICU, fighting for her life. How would they have taken it? There were so many pieces in this case that didn't fit, giving him sleepless nights. Doubtless, many more would follow until they apprehended Olivier, and the case solved. He could only imagine what his men must have felt as they experienced the psychotic behaviour of this Olivier first-hand.

It was essential that he took someone into his confidence, except the conundrum now was who? He watched the other officers waiting on news at HUG's ER reception. One of them? Could the informant be here, showing concern? Favre's words, "Trust no one, there's a mole," rang in his ears. Could it be true? Could he afford to wait twenty-four hours for Favre to tell him more? How could anyone of his men betray a fellow officer?

He realised that none of them missed the point that this event involved the same two detectives working on a sensitive case. The consensus was that the various misadventures these two detectives experienced during the last few weeks, were more than coincidence – they were targeted. It brought an underlying dread to everyone present. Their work made them vulnerable. However, he could not afford his officers to fear doing their job or feel that their salaries did not deflect from their worth, even while being in the crosshairs of a villain. Fine, this situation brought danger nearer – only they had signed on knowing the risks. Though, he worried about the possible temptation to take a pay-off for information.

The charge nurse approached Leonard. Everyone stood up, moving forward, eager to hear the prognosis. Leonard shifted on his feet, listening carefully, his head dropping to his chin. He looked up, nodding. As she left, he turned towards his men, hesitated, then told them that the doctor would be through soon to give a detailed update of the men's condition. For the moment, all they knew was that both were critical. The next forty-eight hours were crucial in the case of Garcia, and twenty-four hours would tell them how Favre would fare. Tentative sighs of relief spread amongst those present. He watched each man's reaction who stood in front of him.

Then, with a sigh Leonard pulled out his phone and called Maria. He hated the idea of telling her that José was again in intensive care.

*

Arthur and Anna Gonzales flanked their daughter's hospital bed. Tubes and IV drips were attached to the fragile body. Machines beeped, breaking the silence. Each parent held one of her hands, careful not to interfere with electro connections measuring her vitals.

Anna's lips moved in silent prayer. Periodically, she wiped her nose and dabbed her eyes. Her husband's thumb gently stroked the back of Cynthia's hand. They briefly looked at each other, not wanting to take their eyes off their child.

'She looks so small and frail. She's so pale.' A sob escaped Anna.

'She lost so much blood, it's amazing they managed to get her here in time.'

'She's our baby, and look at her now. How could this happen?'

'I don't know how, or why this happened.' He dropped his head into his free hand. 'You're right, she's so vulnerable. I don't know how to protect her, or you. I tried my best.'

'Well, obviously it wasn't good enough. What, or who, did you get involved with?' Anna couldn't hold back her anger, 'Look what you did to her! You insist on dealing with these so-called businesspeople. It's now clear – they are not people we want in our lives. They are criminals!'

'Anna, calm down. We don't know if it's one of my trades which went wrong, or any of the people I dealt with. Please be reasonable.'

'Look at her! And you want me to be reasonable? Forget it. I don't accept your explanation.'

'Please,' he pleaded with his wife, 'You know everything I do; I do for you and our daughter.'

The nurse came in, reprimanding them for being loud.

'We can hear you down the corridor. If you cannot keep it together and quiet down, I'll have to ask you to leave.' Her stern stare silenced both parents. 'Your daughter is fighting for her life, the least you could do is be supportive and loving.'

'Sorry. We understand. Do you think she can hear us?' Anna asked.

'Any arguments you have disturb her. The patient needs quiet and calm. In fact, for the time being, only one of you would be allowed at any one time in the ICU. So, decide – who will be taking a break?'

Arthur sheepishly looked from his wife to the nurse. 'I'll go to the cafeteria and get a coffee. Anna, could I bring you something from there?'

'No thank you. I don't need anything.'

'Incidentally, the police are again asking to speak to you about your daughter's stabbing. They are here on another matter,' the nurse said.

'Fine, I'll speak to them.' With that, Arthur glanced at his wife, hoping to see some forgiveness. He bent down and gently kissed his daughter's forehead, and without a word, left the room.

On the way to the cafeteria, he passed the ER waiting room and noticed all the policemen standing around. He recognised Leonard and went over.

'*Salut,* Captain what is going on? Are all these officers here for my daughter's case?'

'Not exactly. The two detectives investigating the shooting of the young man your daughter was with, have been seriously injured. They are both critical. We should know in a couple of days if they'll pull through.'

'Wasn't one of them involved in a bomb explosion not so long ago?'

'Yes, and today's injuries, on top of those he has been recuperating from, have jeopardized his chances of healing completely. We're keeping our fingers crossed that he's stronger than the doctors think.'

'And the other one, Favre, didn't a fire break out in his apartment?'

'Yes, he is the other detective injured in this accident.'

'So, who is dealing with my daughter's stabbing? Everyone seems to hanging around here and not looking into possible suspects.'

'Make no mistake, it is well in hand, and we do have a suspect for whom we have put out an APB – an All-Points-Bulletin – if you don't know what it means.'

'I know what it means. But I still want to know what you are doing about my daughter's case.'

'We think the two cases might be related.' Leonard looked over to the men, caught the eye of Borel and Pichon, calling them over. 'I think you've met either one of my officers Borel or Pichon. One of them visited your premises with Detective Favre in connection with the ongoing case.' The two shook hands with Mr Gonzales.

'Yes, Officer Borel accompanied the detective. Pleased to meet you, Officer Pichon.'

'They are the ones investigating the stabbing and have interviewed various bystanders already. Luckily, there were people who could help immediately. It gave your daughter a fighting chance to pull through. There are a lot of questions we need to ask you.' Leonard indicated to Borel to take over the conversation.

'Sir, do you think we could go somewhere and talk?' Borel asked.

'Of course, I was on my way to the cafeteria for coffee.'

'Good, it's as good a place as any. Why don't the three of us go and have a chat there?' Pichon joined in.

*

Captain Leonard watched them leave and wondered if his two officers had the wherewithal to break through the guard Gonzales had around him. It obviously came from all the shady dealings he had been involved in. The two were good, only they weren't Favre and Garcia – well, very few of his men came close to those detectives. At least these two had worked together. He hoped they had learnt a thing or two from the more experienced men in the short time.

That the two cases, or shall we now say three, were connected, became clearer with each clue. If you count the bombing and the fire at Favre's apartment, it would be five: the shooting of the young man, the bombing, the fire, the stabbing and now the car accident.

The day before, Favre had telephoned him to report on Garcia's progress. He confirmed that his partner had settled in at the Hotel and had requested all copies and a photo of the crime board. He was studying backgrounds, faces and oddities. That was Garcia's strength – his intuition, which picked up on something out of place – something everyone else would discard as immaterial or irrelevant. Favre only said that Garcia was working a different angle and found something he wanted to show him, immediately after the physio appointment.

The whispered statement Favre had made before he was wheeled into the OR, plus the report of his mumblings at the scene, tied everything together. Though, he would refrain from mentioning any of this to Borel or Pichon until Favre could enlighten him further. Let them carry on with the investigation in their own way. It would be interesting to see what conclusions they drew, and if they would find anything suspicious on their own.

The day seemed to drag on forever, though he knew it was only early afternoon. The waiting for news exhausted him. With every year that passed, he felt it more. Perhaps it was time for him to retire; his wife had been nagging, but he had not yet reached retirement age. For those in the police force, the option to take early retirement came at the age of fifty. He could never do that – being at home would drive him mad. No, he'd carry on at least until he reached sixty. It won't please the wife, but he was convinced that being at home all the time would also not be what she wanted.

Oh well, no time to worry about that now - there were more important and urgent matters to attend to. Maria would be arriving any minute now. Then he wanted to check on that young woman Favre and Garcia interviewed, a Miss Labelle. That name had come up in Favre's delirium. No harm in checking up on her, seeing what she knows, and making sure she doesn't become the next casualty.

*

The curl on Alpha's upper lip said it all as he sped away. He couldn't help but revel in the joy of accomplishment. The sound of approaching sirens preceded the flashing blue lights. It filled the air as they came into the bend. He knew he had avoided capture as he pulled out of view.

He drummed his fingers on the steering. Oh, how glorious! He got those two pigs good and proper. They would feel the pain a while before it'll be lights out! And he had the opportunity to rub it in. The thin one, Favre, had heard him when he said he knew about his *chérie*. He saw comprehension flash behind his eyes – it told such a delicious tale! So, he wasn't the cool and collected dude he tried to project. And yes, seeing the fat one dangling, with only his seatbelt preventing him from landing on his head, completely out – perhaps even dead – was rewarding. Watching the blood dripping into Favre's eyes, made him lick his lips.

A quick glance in the rear-view mirror confirmed that he was clear, no one had followed him. It was surprising how fast the First Responders and Police had arrived – he wondered if they were on the radio when it happened. It didn't matter; they got what they deserved. With distance, the sirens faded, and the flashing lights were no longer visible. For now, he had to play the waiting game where the cops were concerned. Once the two were in hospital, his inside man would let him know how they were doing. It wouldn't be long now. Everything's going according to plan.

He felt like bursting into song. He was in the mood for a visit to Paquis.

That whore from two nights ago could be available. She did run out screaming that he should never call her again. Still, wasn't that an invitation? They say that when a woman says 'no,' she's actually begging for it. Yes, a real celebration was on the menu. Perhaps he should forget about the street walker and call on this Labelle woman, she might prove to be fun.

No, at this instant, he needed to pay for it. Paying for what he wanted confirmed his superiority, his power. It showed he had money to do whatever he wanted. Money was power, no matter how you looked at it. Let's face it, prostitutes had the same attitude – they were in that profession to line their pockets. For a buck, they would do exactly what he asked for. Now, he needed a woman who understood this and wouldn't ask questions. He couldn't wait.

CHAPTER SEVENTEEN

Leonard rubbed his eyes – red and dry – wishing he had his eye spray with him. He checked his wristwatch, it was six a.m. In the ICU, the medical staff had begun their day shift, moving from patient to patient, taking over and reviewing the charts at the end of each bed.

His back ached from trying to sleep curled up in one of the chairs in the hospital waiting room. He refused to go home until he knew his two men were out of danger. His wife understood these situations. The doctor had updated him around ten p.m. last night. Both men survived their respective surgeries. In their critical condition, they were carefully watched and cared for in the Intensive Care Unit.

Leonard had sent all the other officers either home or back to their duty stations when their colleagues left the operating room. He stayed on. He couldn't leave them. Since then, the nurse had come out a couple of times, only to tell him to go home, he would be advised as soon as there was any change. He refused. He wanted to be there when either man regained consciousness. Another pressing point was he wanted to ask Favre what he meant by not trusting anyone. Also, he wanted to know what he could remember. They had to apprehend this Olivier if he was the one responsible.

Maria had not arrived yet, and Favre had no one, therefore, for the moment, he was the nearest thing both had to family. They were his best men, and he couldn't lose them. The department would be lost without their expertise. He worried that the younger officers lacked the same sensibilities for the job and, perhaps more importantly, the enthusiasm. How to inspire the younger men was beyond him. For that, he blamed the Unions. His hopes lay in Favre and Garcia leading by example, with the others picking up the method in which to analyse and look at a case – to learn from them. Was he asking too much? No, he had faith in all his men.

He got up, stretched, and made his way to the cafeteria. He was in urgent need of a cup of coffee to wake up and get rid of the foul taste in his mouth. There might be an apple or banana available – anything to give him a bit of energy to face the day. He found what he wanted. As he returned to the waiting area, the nurse approached him from the ICU.

'Captain Leonard, Detective Favre has woken up. He's very groggy; and is asking for you. You can see him, but only for a couple of minutes.'

'How is he?'

'He is still critical and far from being out of the woods, though we are optimistic. Let's hope he stabilises within the next twelve hours. That would give us a better indication of his recovery. Please follow me, just do not excite him. And do not stay more than five minutes.'

'I won't. I'm just so pleased that he has woken up. I only need to ask him a couple of questions, then I'll leave him in peace.'

'Good. I'll check on the two of you in exactly five minutes.' With that, the nurse pushed the door open, letting Leonard pass through. 'He's in the second bed on the right.'

The room had six beds, and the first bed, directly on Leonard's left, was occupied by none other than Garcia. Leonard glanced in his direction and saw only a still figure attached to many tubes, wires, and breathing apparatus. He hesitated a second before moving further into the room to Favre's side.

Relief flooded the captain as he saw that Favre was not intubated, with only an oxygen mask covering Favre's face. The heart monitor beeped: his pulse and blood pressure registered on the screen. Two IVs entered Paul's arms one was blood, the other a clear liquid which Leonard supposed would be pain medication or antibiotics. Favre's head was bandaged, and one of his legs, in a cast, hung from a pulley. His chest was bare except for the monitors and a rectangular gauze bandage covering his sternum. A cut on his forehead had stitches, and a plaster covered his nose – obviously broken. He tentatively touched Paul's shoulder. It was painful to see the effort his detective had to make to turn his head slightly towards him.

'*Bonjour, mon ami.* I won't tire you out and only stay for a few minutes – nurse's orders, you know. I won't ask you how you are, just know that we are all very concerned. Everyone wishes you a speedy recovery. Let's not waste your energy. I think they explained that you were involved in an accident. We'll go into that later. Firstly, tell me why I shouldn't trust anyone, and what you remember?'

'*Bonjour, chef.* We found a mole in the department.' He swallowed painfully, his voice barely a whisper.

'Do you know who?'

'Garcia picked him out – on the photos. You'll have to scrutinise those in his hotel room. I think he marked them.'

'Fine, I'll go there straight from here. What else?'

'Please protect Miss Labelle – Olivier threatened her.' Paul's breathing was laboured.

'So, Oliver is definitely the person responsible?'

'Yes, without a doubt. He calls himself Alpha. I gave those on the scene a partial of his car's registration. I couldn't see any more.'

'Good for you. I'll follow up personally.'

'Better get someone from outside, like from Intelligence, to help you.' He swallowed hard, turning his head to shift his shoulders and alleviate the pain.

'I'll leave you now. Get some rest and regain your strength. I'll come back this evening, then we'll speak again.'

'Wait, before you go. He said something about usurping the person who paid him for the shooting. It's a woman.' With that, Paul Favre's body sank back as he lost consciousness.

Leonard looked around, unsure on what he should do. Luckily, just then the nurse came in, crossing the floor quickly when she saw the monitor had changed rhythm.

'What happened? Is he okay?' Leonard felt panic take over.

'He passed out from the effort of speaking to you. I'm calling the doctor. You had better go – you can come back later.' The nurse pressed a call button and busied herself with her patient.

Leonard left the room with a glance back at Favre, stopping for a moment at the end of his other detective's bed. He said a silent prayer for both men. He had a lot to think about. First, he should set his men's minds at rest with news that even though both are still in critical condition, things were slightly improving. They would be told when either one of the injured had stabilised. He telephoned his secretary, who had many questions. He cut her short, relaying what he wanted her to write on his behalf in an email and have it sent to all at the station.

At the hotel reception, he reported that as Garcia's superior in the Police Department, he would be entering Garcia's room to collect files. Further, he left strict instructions that no other person be allowed to enter, not even housekeeping. Apparently, Garcia had left similar instructions. That the room be sealed off until further notice drew objections. The same applied to Detective Favre's room, which exacerbated the problem, and the young girl at reception spouted rules and regulations. Finally, she called the manager, and after an authoritative instruction by Leonard, no argument ensued. He was assured that his wishes would be met. It was not a day to argue with the captain!

'You've been busy,' Leonard said to the absent José as he looked around the room, which was strewn with copies of printouts and photos on every available flat area. 'Now where shall I begin – you have a system – I only have to find out what it is.' Without disturbing a single sheet of paper, he stepped from one end of the display to the other. On the surface, it looked haphazard, but the captain found José's method.

He saw the person whom they knew as Olivier, circled in red wherever he appeared. A corresponding red cross appeared on the copy of the crime board, tying the two together. Black, green, and blue markers also appeared. These seemed to represent vehicles, transport routes, and various officials. Leonard realised that careful study of all the materials would be necessary, and for that, he needed time and seclusion. He carefully gathered everything, trying to keep the sequence in which José had laid it out; he filled a cardboard box, which he presumed it came in, to take home.

This whole case began with the shooting of that young man and the girl with him, who now, strangely enough, has been stabbed and is fighting for her life as well. Leonard knew he had to add this latest information to that laid out by his detective. It could not be a coincidence that she was present. It had become crystal clear that a link existed between the suspect and the Gonzales family. How and why, he could not see – yet. He'll have to read the typed-up reports of the various interviews to get a clearer view.

He decided he would work mainly from home with periodic visits to the hospital and the station. He pulled the door to Garcia's hotel room closed. From his car, he contacted the First Responders and Police, first on the scene, for a copy of their report to be hand-delivered to his home address. Further, he instructed them, for the time being, not to forward any copy thereof to any other department or anyone without his prior approval. If they received a request for a copy, the name and coordinates of the person should be taken and passed on to him and only him. He would personally distribute copies to the interested party. It did not surprise him that no one questioned his demand. This was a sensitive, high level, and extremely confidential investigation – there had been an attempt to murder two of their own.

'What are you doing home at this time of day?' Mrs Leonard, coming from the kitchen, wiped her hands on a dishcloth. 'It has been years since you came home for lunch.'

'Yes, well, is there something to eat?' He put the box down on the table.

'Not if you are going to leave that box there.'

'Sorry, I'll take it through to the *bureau*. I'll be working from here for a few days. Though, I'll pop out to the station and then check on the progress at the hospital.'

'No problem. It'll be good to have you here; I could at least make sure you eat. Since you were promoted, you've skipped far too many meals. How are Garcia and Favre? When you phoned last night, I was really worried they might not pull through, but this morning you sounded hopeful.'

'It was touch and go, especially Garcia. That man is as strong as an ox! Surviving the bomb blast and now this – the doctors are amazed. Then again, he is really like a terrier. He won't let go until he's got his quarry completely at his mercy.'

'What are you saying? You think once this case is wrapped up, he'll have a relapse?'

'There's always that risk. No, I don't think so, he has Maria and the children to carry him through.'

'I hope you're right. Now, let's put all that aside and have lunch. You can tackle the job again after you've eaten.'

'Sounds good. What's for lunch?'

'Well, what about escalope of veal?'

'Perfect. I'll get this set up and begin going through the lot. Call me when lunch is ready.' He disappeared into the office with the carton. He set it on the easy chair next to the window while deciding which wall to use.

From the east wall, he lifted three paintings, standing them out of harm's way against the wall behind the desk. He opened a desk-drawer and pulled out a box of thumbtacks. From the carton, he took out the various piles he had collected from the hotel, according to how he perceived José's method. Within an hour, reconsidering a few times, he had the east wall covered, hoping his memory didn't let him down.

He stepped back and looked at the wall as it now represented the case.

What he needed was some string or, better still, yarn from his wife's knitting basket. Red would be best, he decided. He called out to her, and within minutes, he had everything he needed to link various faces, places, and vehicles. The only thing missing: the photos and reports of the girl's stabbing. He would requisition all photos posted on Facebook, Instagram, Twitter and whatever else. He wondered if they had collected all the videos bystanders took of the event. There might be a clue or even a photo of the suspect in it. He was not sure who handled that case; however, he would get that from the station as well as the incident report.

'*A table!*' His wife called from the dining room. During their lunch, they spoke about their children, family, and the neighbourhood. His preoccupation didn't go unnoticed.

'Look, I know you want to get back to what you were doing. I'll clear up and bring you your coffee in the *bureau.*'

'No, I'll have my coffee with you, then check up on Favre and Garcia before going to the station. That way, I'll be clear to work on the case the rest of the day.'

'Have you heard from Maria? When will she get here?'

'She said as soon as she could get the children settled at her brother's.'

'I thought they were with them already.'

'No, because of what happened last time, they went somewhere near Basel. I only had an emergency number to call her on. Not even I knew their exact location.'

'But you are their boss! That's ridiculous.'

'No, the threat was real and very close to home.'

*

At the HUG, the nurse left the ICU just as Leonard arrived. She smiled, Favre was still critical, but lucid. He had shown progress. Garcia, on the other hand, had been placed in an induced coma again, allowing his body to recover and repair without having to fight excruciating pain.

Leonard pushed through the door, hesitated at the foot of Garcia's bed, then moved on to Favre's where he silently watched the patient. The IVs, heart monitor wires, oxygen, and pulley were still in place. The blood was gone, and at least he looked restful. A moment later, Paul turned his head, opened his eyes. He tried to move, but the grimace on his face showed his pain level was still high. He moved the oxygen mask half off his face.

'No don't try to sit, lie back. Do you feel a bit better?' The captain touched Favre's shoulder in greeting.

'*Salut.* Not really, despite the pain medication, I'm beginning to feel aches all over.'

'Well don't forget you were in an extremely serious car accident.'

'*Chef,* did you put a protective detail on Miss Labelle?'

'Yes, it was the first thing I did, even before I left the hospital this morning.'

'Did you get the report to confirm what I said when they pulled me out?'

'It will be delivered to my home. I've decided to work on this myself from home to keep our findings away from prying eyes, and for confidentiality. I collected everything from Garcia's room and have put it all up on the wall in my study.'

'Good thinking.'

'There is something else I need to tell you which I doubt you know about.' Leonard looked over his shoulder to make sure no one else was in earshot and moved closer to Favre.

'What? Did you uncover something else?'

'No, there was a near-fatal stabbing which is, or could be, directly related to this case.'

'What? Who was stabbed?'

'Cynthia Gonzales, present at the first shooting.'

'*Mon Dieu!*' Favre became very agitated and tried to sit up.

'Take it easy! Stay quiet you're going to rip out the tubes.'

'Is she all right?'

'No, she's fighting for her life – here in this hospital. I'm looking into it as a connected crime. I spoke to her father last night, and it didn't look good. She was still hanging on this morning after I saw you.'

'I should have protected her. The curfew her parents imposed wasn't enough. It's all my fault,' Leonard saw tears flowing down Favre's cheeks, on the verge of passing out.

'Come on now, breathe. Just breathe. Stay with me.'

'*Chef?* … uhm … Yes, I'm here.' Paul regained consciousness and moved painfully on the bed.

'No, you did everything possible – you were on the right track from the beginning. No one could've done more than you. So, stay calm and get better as soon as you can. I need you to tie up the loose ends and solve this case.'

'Have you seen who Garcia suspected of being the mole?'

'Not yet, but I think it's in all the printouts he had. I will only discuss this with the Intelligence Branch.'

'Thank you, Sir.'

'I'm going to leave you now to rest. I'll be back tomorrow morning, hopefully with some news.' Leonard touched the shoulder of his detective, then turned to leave before his concern showed. Again, he stopped for a moment at Garcia's bed and said a prayer.

On his way out, he enquired if Mr and Mrs Gonzales were still in the hospital. The nurse directed him to the family waiting area on the other side of the nurses' station. The parents sat huddled together. Very little hope showed on their faces. Leonard was loath to approach them. Though, he knew they would wonder what progress had been made on their daughter's case. He quietly entered the room.

'Bonjour, Monsieur et Madame Gonzales.'

'Bonjour.' They said in unison as they looked up enquiringly.

'I'm Captain Leonard, I spoke to you last night.'

'Oh, yes. I remember.' Arthur said something to his wife in Spanish ooand she nodded. 'Do you have news? Have you caught the person who stabbed our daughter?'

'Unfortunately, not yet, but we have a lead. We know who it is. We are hot on his trail. Please rest assured that he will be brought to justice. How is your daughter?'

'Well, not good. But as doctor said, there is always hope. They're in there with her now. I'm going back in when they're finished. She's still fighting,' Mrs Gonzales said.

'Is there anything you might have remembered about that day? Where she was going or, who she was with? The slightest fact could be the one that solves the case.'

'I don't remember,' she said. Just then, the nurse came over to say they could go back to their daughter's bedside. 'Sorry, I must go. You can speak to my husband.' She left without another word. The men watched her leave.

'We should never have come to Switzerland.'

'Why would you say that?'

'What do you say to a mother who might lose her daughter?' Arthur Gonzales asked.

'What do you say to a father who feels he didn't protect his daughter? This is a relatively safe country. This kind of violence is very rare. There is no way that you could have foreseen this.'

'I feel so guilty for exactly that reason. As a father, that is the only – and most important – job you have. Do you have children, Captain?'

'Yes, I have, and cannot imagine how I would react if they were taken away from me in a violent way. In my profession, we often come across loss. Although, to personally experience it is something we try not to think about.'

'I feel that I might not be completely innocent in this whole affair.'

'Why do you say that? What do you know? Have you done or seen something that caused you to make a remark like that?'

'I … I… well, I don't really know. Perhaps. No, I spoke out of turn. It's nothing.'

'Mr Gonzales, please don't stop. Whatever it was that made you say that could help us solve your daughter's case. You obviously know something, the importance of which you might not even realise. So please, let us help you, talk to us. Your regret in moving here seems to be at the root of your dilemma.'

'Well, okay. I brought my family to this country to expand my lucrative business in the gem trade. I must admit that sometimes I bend the rules a little. You know, I push the envelope and might short-change someone. Of course, in Colombia, it doesn't really matter, it's part of business. You make enemies, while at the same time you help them to do the same to one of their customers. Here, it's a different story,' Gonzales hesitated.

'Go on.'

'At first, I didn't think anything about the shooting where the young man was killed – even though Cynthia dated him. I thought it was life, things happen. You know, where we come from, it is not unusual for a shooting to take place. That's why I agreed to the curfew the police insisted upon. However, since then, another event made me rethink.'

'When, and what other, event was this?'

'About a week ago.' Arthur rubbed his hand over his face. 'We had a sample shipment of emeralds coming in by courier from Colombia.' He got up and paced around the room. 'I have to confess something.'

'Mr Gonzales, does this involve a crime? Do you need to come down to the station?'

'No, I don't want to leave my wife and daughter, they might need me. I'll tell you everything here. Then you can decide if it would be necessary for further action.'

'Fine, we'll play it your way. Still, I'll keep the possibility of questioning you officially open. We do have information from Interpol on some of your dealings. Please go ahead.'

'Yes, I know. Your officers told me about you checking up on my business affairs. Nevertheless, I'll continue. The shipment came in two parts. One which we declared officially, and the greater part of the shipment we hid in a secret compartment of the hand luggage the courier carried. Incidentally, she knew nothing about that.' Arthur stopped pacing and sat down again. 'We sent an employee, one of our secretaries, to the airport to meet the courier. She saw a man, who she later recognised from a photo your detective showed us, intercept and hurry our courier away in a taxi. To date, we've not been able to trace her.'

'I take it all of you – everyone involved – made statements regarding the interception of the courier? Though I doubt you mentioned the hidden compartment filled with stones.'

'You are correct. Our statement concerned only the loss of the declared samples; we never mentioned the concealed stones,' Gonzales ran his hand over his face.

'What else is there, Mr Gonzales?'

'Well, at the time, your detective asked me if I thought there might be a chance that the shooting was personal. In other words, that the real target of the shooting could've been my daughter and not the young man. Also, he wanted to know if it could've been a warning to us opening our business here in Europe.'

'So, what do you think now?'

'After recent events, I have no doubt that everything that happened was because of me expanding my business to Europe.' He looked defeated, glancing towards the room his daughter occupied. 'So, you see I'm guilty. I'm to blame for putting my daughter in that bed fighting for her life.'

'I wouldn't go that far, Mr Gonzales.'

'Nevertheless, your two detectives are also in critical condition because of something I put in motion. I should never have come here.'

'Before making any changes or pleading guilty to a hypothetical crime, I think you should concentrate on your daughter, and let us get to the bottom of this. You might have been the catalyst, but not the criminal in this instance. Please, allow us to solve this case. All you need to do for the time being is to take one step at a time.'

'I don't know how to do that. Nevertheless, thank you.'

'I'll leave you now. When I visit my detectives, I'll look in on your child, and keep you up to date with our investigation. In the meantime, good day to you. I hope you get good news soon.'

Leonard saw the will to live had seeped from Arthur Gonzales as he took the lifeless hand in greeting. Greed had turned into guilt, destroying a man who thought he could give his family what they wanted, not what they needed.

*

Alex saw Mrs Ginet through the peephole and opened the door. They had arranged to do shopping together at the Migros.

'*Bonjour!* Would you like a coffee before we leave? Or shall we have one there?'

'Let's have one there. I haven't really been out with the heat, and it's so much cooler there than in the building.'

'Good thinking. Let me get my bag.' Alex was silently pleased as the heat in her apartment had become unbearable. She had hoped that the evening storm would bring cooler air, but it only increased humidity. If only the night-time temperatures came down, it would help; except they stayed high, so everyone suffered.

Both sighed with relief as they entered the supermarket. The cool air had an immediate effect on them. With revived enthusiasm, they decided to have a fruit juice at the cafeteria before shopping and end their visit with a cup of coffee.

Elated Mrs Ginet sipped her fresh orange juice – to make it last, she said. Yet with the heat, Alex had an unquenchable thirst and downed half a bottle of mineral water before starting on her carrot juice. Secretly, she dreaded the moment Mrs Ginet might ask her about "their two detectives" – as she had begun to refer to Detectives Favre and Garcia. The older woman's liking for Detective Garcia, she found "sweet" – the only way to describe it. It bordered on a mother's protective attitude, yet not far removed from a teenage crush; she couldn't stop talking about how charming "her" Detective was.

Her neighbour had no idea that Garcia had been injured in the bomb blast, and she really didn't want her to find out. Moreover, she herself had been worried about his condition.

Nearly a week had passed since she last spoke to Paul. With no news from him, she began to wonder if she might have said something wrong which kept him from contacting her. The message she had left for him at the station yesterday, went unanswered. She pushed the thought aside and smiled at Mrs Ginet, who continued chatting away about nothing in particular.

The phone's ringtone brought Alex back to reality. It was a number she didn't recognise, and decided to ignore it. A minute later, the phone pinged to announce a message had come through; she glanced at the notice but decided that, as Mrs Ginet was still talking, it would be rude to interrupt only to listen to a voicemail. However, as time went by, she became impatient to know who left the message. As soon as her friend broke off her chatter to take another sip of orange juice, she took the opportunity to hold up her hand, asking for a moment to see who called.

Surprised, she listened to the message twice to make sure she had heard correctly. It came from Captain Leonard – Favre's superintendent in the Force – asking her to contact him urgently. With near panic, she got up, looking around for a private corner while explaining to Mrs Ginet that she had to responded immediately to the message. She moved away and pressed the recall button. After only two rings, the captain answered the call.

'Miss Labelle, thank you for calling back so promptly.'

'No, problem, I'm sorry I didn't answer your call. I didn't recognise the number.'

'I understand. There are a lot of unwelcome calls from telemarketers now. Look, to come to the point, we will be posting security in front of your building again, as well as a uniformed officer at your front door.'

'But why? And no, I don't want a policeman standing guard in front of my door! I thought the danger was over.'

'Well, not exactly. It is imperative that we place a guard at your door because there has been a direct threat against you.'

'By whom, for heaven's sake?'

'The suspect in the shooting in front of your building. Unfortunately, he is still at large, and we have not managed to track him down.'

'Where is Detective Favre? I haven't heard from him. Did he tell you about the threat? Is he in charge of the protection?'

'No, he has been injured in a motor vehicle accident and is in hospital. And yes, the suspect threatened you directly to him. He was unable to do anything about it at that moment.'

'What? He's in the hospital? Is he seriously hurt? Can I go and see him?' Questions spilled from her.

'Not advisable. Since there is a threat to your life, we cannot allow you to visit the hospital. You should stay at home. Where are you now?'

'At the Migros, to do shopping.'

'Which Migros? I will meet you outside and take you home personally. You have a maximum fifteen minutes to buy whatever you need. I'm sending you a photo of myself and my badge so that you do not leave with someone else. I'll be with you in a quarter of an hour. This is important, Miss Labelle – you must not go with anyone who says I sent them – wait for me!' Without another word, he cut the call.

She stood stunned; looked over to her neighbour, who had just finished her juice. This is a disaster! If only she had come shopping alone. How could she get her friend to buy what she needed in such a short time without arguing? How could she explain the police presence in front of her apartment without Mrs Ginet asking questions? What should she say to set the older woman's mind at rest to avoid panic? Mrs Ginet would never leave it alone until every single fact has been uncovered. How could she make her understand that they needed to keep quiet and not discuss the situation with anyone? Alex replaced her phone and went back to the table where her neighbour watched her approach.

'What's wrong, my dear?'

'I'm sorry, but I have to leave. Would you like to come back with me? We could do a very quick shop, then go home.' Alexandra saw that Mrs Ginet had various questions and continued immediately. 'Or you could take your time, have a leisurely cup of coffee as planned, and make your own way home. Why don't you do that? It would be so much more pleasant in the cool than getting back to the heat. What do you say?'

'You haven't told me what's wrong.'

'Nothing, just that I have to get back immediately.'

'Okay, as you say, my dear. I'll do as you suggest and take my time. I'll cool off and pop in to see you later. Then you can tell me what's troubling you. Is it that nice detective?'

'Now, don't worry about that. I must go now, buy something, and get home. You sure you'll be okay on your own?'

'Of course, my dear, run along now, I'll be fine.'

Alex grabbed her bag, practically ran through the supermarket picking up the essentials, paid, and arrived outside just as a white VW Jetta pulled up to a stop. A man got out. She looked at her phone, compared the photo. He walked over to her, showed his badge which she checked against the image on her phone. Satisfied, she held out her hand in greeting.

'Miss Labelle, I'm Captain Leonard, pleased to meet you.'

'Hello. Pleased to meet you. Can you tell me more about what this is all about, please?'

'Definitely. If you don't mind, could you please get into the car? I do not want you to be on the street so openly.' He held open the passenger door.

'This is ridiculous! This threat can't be that serious.'

'My dear Miss Labelle, you have no idea. Please get in and I'll explain.'

She got in, fastened her seatbelt while he walked around to the driver's side, got in, fastening his belt as he turned the ignition. Within minutes, they were on their way. She listened intently as he began by telling her how badly Favre had been injured and that he was not yet stable. However, the doctors thought he would pull through if no complications set in. Again, she asked to go and see Favre, and had difficulty understanding that, at present, it would not be possible. He looked relieved when they reached her address, and more so when he found a place to park.

She noticed that he scrutinised the area before he opened the door for her. He took her shopping bag, leading her quickly to the entrance of her building. He seemed to relax slightly as they entered, going up to her flat. Inside her home, she took the shopping from him and asked if he would like a cup of coffee. She put her bag of purchases on the counter and filled the kettle, plugging it in the socket.

Leonard was on the phone when she brought the coffee through to the lounge and set it on the table. They both sat down. Alex immediately asked him to continue and explain as promised. He began by setting out the sequence of events from the day of the shooting up to the car accident, which put both Garcia and Favre in a critical condition. He included the bomb explosion in which Garcia was critically injured the first time and the fire at Favre's apartment. When he came to the near-fatal stabbing of the girl whom she saw standing next to the young man bleeding in the street below, she could hardly believe her ears. However, the worst shock was the car accident which nearly cost the lives of both detectives. He explained that the suspect taunted Favre before driving off. One of the taunts was a direct threat to harm her. That was the reason they were not taking the threat lightly. He hoped she understood, he said.

Alex couldn't get the image of the scene below in the street out of her mind. Even though it had happened nearly a month ago, it felt like yesterday. Without warning, the image changed to a prostrate Favre lying in a pool of blood. She virtually choked on her distress.

'Are you okay, Miss Labelle? You're shaking. Would you like a glass of water?'

'I… yes, no… just a minute… are you sure Detective Favre is alive?'

'Yes, he is critical, but alive, and so is Detective Garcia.' He looked at her with concern. 'You're sure I can't do something for you?'

'No, I mean yes, I'll be fine. So, Detective Favre's apartment burnt down? And the arsonist was this man who caused the accident, and threatened me?'

'Yes, no question. That's why we are not taking any chances.'

'You're absolutely convinced that this suspect's threat to harm me is real and that I need someone outside my door?'

'Definitely. The only problem I have is to find the right person. We need someone we can trust implicitly.'

'Why is that? Surely, any one of your officers would be suitable?'

'We cannot be too careful. I don't want any leaks on our movements. We don't know who is watching.'

'Okay. What about Mrs Ginet? She won't let this rest.'

'You mean your neighbour?'

'Yes, and she will definitely speak to anyone who might be able to give her information. She is insistent and will find out what has been happening.'

'Well, you know her. I leave it to you to explain. Tell her what you think she needs to know or can handle. Leave out the rest. You could say that the guard would be here for both of you until the case is solved or the suspect captured.'

'That might work. She hates being left out of things. And being called in to give a statement was an excitement which highlighted her existence. She felt important talking to the police – helping to close a case, as she put it.'

'Do you feel a bit better?' Leonard watched Alexandra carefully. She looked pale and fragile. He hated the idea of leaving her, except he needed to get to the Intelligence Branch as soon as possible. A few of their officers could stand guard, and their expertise would be necessary to trace Olivier's vehicle.

'Yes, thank you. I'm still a bit shaky. It was a shock to hear about everything that had happened after the shooting. It seems as if this man, the shooter, has a vendetta against everyone involved in the investigation. I cannot wrap my mind around that. Why? Why would he go after your detectives like that?'

'From our information, we are dealing with a trained killer who is a full-blown psychopath. Therefore, nothing he has done or will do would make sense to you or me. He is very dangerous because his reasoning goes beyond our understanding.'

'I understand.'

'Could you please stay indoors until I arrange an officer to be stationed outside your door? I'll introduce the person and his relief to you myself. So do not open the door to anyone else. I think the best would be if you call Mrs Ginet over. Keep her here with you until I return. That way she will also know not to open her door or speak to anyone except me. You should tell her that you shouldn't even strike up a conversation with the guarding officer.'

'Oh, that'll be difficult as she would want to give them coffee and feed them.'

'Please emphasize the importance to her of not discussing what is happening or speaking to anyone besides yourself, and, of course, me. Do you think you could handle it?'

'I'll definitely try. I'll keep her here for as long as possible, maybe offer her dinner and to suggest watching TV together.'

'That'll be a great idea. I'll try to get here with the officer as soon as possible. Probably around ten o'clock.'

'That's so late, what about your wife?'

'Rest assured, she understands and would reprimand me if I didn't check up on you!' With that, Leonard got up and said goodbye. Alex walked him to the door, locking it behind her. She leaned against it for a minute before going into the kitchen to pack away the fruit and other purchases. The routine movement helped her organise her thoughts.

It wasn't long before she heard Mrs Ginet open and close her door. She gave her fifteen minutes before she phoned to invite her over. The older woman tried to interrupt with questions. However, Alex did not give her a chance, managing to convince her that they would talk when she came over. Mrs Ginet wanted to know if she could come right away.

'Of course! Come over now, we could chat while I prepare our dinner.' Alexandra chuckled at her friend's eagerness to find out why she had to leave in such a hurry earlier.

'Do you need anything, could I bring something over?'

'No, thank you. I have everything. Of course, if you have some of those dark chocolate ginger sticks, I wouldn't say "no"!'

'Done – I'm coming.' Mrs Ginet was as good as her word. Within a minute the doorbell rang. Through the peephole Alexandra saw a smiling Mrs Ginet and let her in with an equally broad smile. Though, her own smile could be described more as amused, than happy.

'So, what happened today, why did you have to leave so suddenly?'

'Okay, sit here at the counter while I prepare our dinner. Would you like to have a glass of wine in the meantime?'

'That would be lovely. But I think you are avoiding my question.'

'No, not exactly. I need a glass of wine while I tell you, I think you would appreciate one as well.'

'Why? Is it bad news? Are you in trouble?'

'No, well, not really. Though, I need protection. I mean, we need protection. There's…'

'What? Are we in danger?' Mrs Ginet interrupted.

'Hang on; give me a moment to explain.' Alex placed a glass of wine in front of her friend and repeated a sanitised version of what Captain Leonard told her. She watched the reaction her words brought. Fear and confusion showed on the older woman's face which turned into concern. As expected, her first question after she listened was to enquire after Detective Garcia.

'Are you sure he will pull through? I must see him.'

'No, we cannot go to the hospital. We must stay here under guard. You do understand that? Also, we cannot talk about this to anyone, you realise that don't you?'

'Oh, yes, sorry, I forgot. Well, I'll bake him some cookies. Captain Leonard can give it to him when he visits the hospital.'

'Yes, that'll be a good idea. Captain Leonard will be here much later – round ten – then you can meet him. I know it's late for you, but we'll watch a movie to pass the time.'

'That'll be lovely. What are you making? Which movie are we going to watch?' Virtually without letting a breath pass between questions, her thoughts jumped back to her pet subject. 'Poor Detective Garcia, do you think he's in much pain? I wish I could do something for him. He must feel so helpless and alone in that hospital bed.'

'Be patient, you'll know soon enough.' Alex tossed the salad. 'I think Detective Garcia's in good hands, and the captain will take a message to him if you want. His priority should be to get better. His wife will be with him soon; if she's not there already. So, he won't be alone at all. His bed is most probably next to Detective Favre's. They would keep each other company.'

Dinner prepared and ready to be served, Alex couldn't wait to get the evening over, so she could relax, collect her thoughts, quietly go over everything that had happened. Moreover, for the sake of her friend and neighbour, she hoped she had succeeded in hiding her fear, and suppressing her panic.

'Do you want to eat at the counter or the table?'

'Let's eat at the table.' Mrs Ginet's request didn't surprise. Alexandra took out tablemats, cutlery, and condiments, placing them on the table.

*

Captain Leonard arrived around nine-thirty, saw the relief on Miss Labelle's face when she opened the door. As she introduced Mrs Ginet, he immediately realised the difficulty they were facing. The older woman immediately overtook the conversation with questions, general comments, and advice on how they should proceed with the investigation. More importantly, her constant interest in the wellbeing of Detective Garcia caused him to carefully weigh his words. His stress level rose as she tested his resolve to not discuss the case or give away any facts which could jeopardise their investigation.

'I'm very pleased to be able to tell you both that everything is in place. You are safe, and there will be a car outside with two officers and one outside your apartments.'

'Thank you, you explained it clearly. You are very kind, Captain.' Mrs Ginet smiled.

'I'm glad you understand the importance of not discussing this with anyone and always doing what the officers say. If you need to go to the supermarket or church, please tell them. They have instructions to drive you there, and one officer will always accompany you inside the shop.' He looked from one woman to the other.

'These are officers I seconded from a completely different section of the Department. They aren't involved in the case and have no details about the investigation's progress. You can rely on them—ask for help if needed. However, please don't pepper them with questions, as they don't know anything, and please respect their privacy.'

'Of course not! But I can give them a cup of coffee and some biscuits, can't I?'

'Better not. Also, you'll have to go outside if you want to give the two officers in the vehicle something. That means that the one guarding the door had to leave his post to accompany you. You do see the dilemma, don't you? You will be putting Miss Labelle in danger.'

'Oh, I see. Yes, Captain, I know what I'll do. When they take us to the market, I'll give them their cookies then.' Satisfied that the problem was solved Mrs Ginet nodded, crossing her arms across her chest: no more to be said on that matter.

'I suppose that will be acceptable.' Leonard shook his head, no point in arguing or trying to explain any further. 'I'll walk you to your apartment.'

'Not necessary, it's just next door.'

'No, it's best I see you safely home.' He bid Miss Labelle good night, holding the door for her neighbour, who seemed reluctant to leave. The look of relief on the younger woman's face showed her approval. He left as quickly as possible. He still had a lot to do before turning in. Tomorrow would be a long day.

CHAPTER EIGHTTEEN

Two days later, when Leonard visited the hospital's ICU, he saw across the room that Favre was sitting up, eating. Garcia was awake and off the critical list, although not yet stable.

He stopped to reassure José that his notes were in good hands, and that he personally had made progress in finding the mole. He wished to confirm his findings and held up a copy of a photo on which he had circled someone. Through the oxygen mask covering José's face, the captain could see a slight smile. When Garcia nodded, Leonard reciprocated, confirming the verification.

'I'll have the name and badge number of the person on my return to the station. It won't be long before we'll have all the pieces.' He gave a three-finger salute and moved on to Favre.

'I'm pleased to see you look better. I suppose they'll move you to a general ward now that you're eating.' As usual, Leonard offered no formal greeting. Though, after a moment, shook hands with Favre, a subconscious indication of his concern.

'Thank you. I'm beginning to feel more like a human being, and they said later this afternoon they'll move me.' Favre put the knife and fork down and pushed the tray aside, He found every movement painful because of his cracked ribs. The neck brace made it difficult to move his head from side to side. 'Have you managed to get the Intelligence Branch to track down the vehicle with the partial number plate I gave? And what about the mole?'

'Gosh, you don't waste any time. What's with all the questions without giving me a moment to pull up a chair?'

'I am eager to wrap this case up and put Olivier behind bars before he can do more damage and hurt another person.'

'I am completely in agreement with you. We are getting closer. With the help of the IB we have found the car, and they have posted officers around the building. When he emerges, we'll get him!'

'Has anything happened at Miss Labelle's building? Is she safe?

Olivier must be working with someone else. He could easily have sent another to harm her.'

'We are keeping a very close watch over her. No one is getting near her. We're vetting all visitors. She wasn't very pleased at first but understood. She has been telling her friends that she won't be available for a while. Her neighbour gives us some trouble, but with Alex's help, we have managed to keep her in line so far.

'I'm going back to the station now to tackle the problem of the mole. At first, I didn't want to believe it. Then, in two different prints, I saw a face which could be the same person. Granted, in one, the person is virtually next to Olivier, and in the other two, the face is much more indistinct. However, after careful scrutiny, there is an eighty percent possibility that it is the same person.'

'Who is it? Someone from the station?'

'Disappointingly so – I still find it difficult to believe. If it was one of our female members, I would say that she fell under the seductive spell of Olivier, but this is not the case.'

'Please, who is it? I cannot stand the suspense any longer.'

'Bonavita, a Deputy Desk Sergeant; been on the job twelve years; an average officer on all counts; no special commendations – married with two children – one with learning difficulties. Besides that, nothing in his file stands out indicating a reason for betrayal.'

'No, not Bonavita! I cannot believe it. I've spoken to him often. He always had a smile and kind word for those who came in.'

'Stop shaking your head, it'll aggravate your concussion. I know, it's incredible, but it seems to be true. I have ascertained that he will be on duty this afternoon, when I'll ask him a few questions.'

'And if he doesn't arrive to take his shift?'

'Then I'll go to his home. If he's not there, I'll ask Intelligence to track him down. Let's hope he tells us what we need to know, because so far, we only have circumstantial evidence against Olivier. He made sure of that.'

'Oh, *chef,* I forgot to tell you. With my concern for Alex, I mean, Miss Labelle, I omitted to tell you that Olivier mentioned he calls himself Alpha, and as such, presented himself to the person who hired him for the job.'

'I remember you mentioned that his nickname was Alpha. Was there something else you remember?' Leonard took out his notebook.

'Yes, it's very pertinent to the case. He mentioned that the "Boss" who gave him the assignment was the "Godmother of a Dynasty". He said when this is all over, the woman wouldn't even realise that he had taken over the gem trade. Furthermore, he would head up the organisation.'

The nurse came in, at that moment, and saw an excited Favre.

'Will everyone please calm down? Captain, if you keep on upsetting us, we shall be forced to ask you to leave.' Leonard had to smile, why do medical staff use the first-person plural when referring to their patients?

'Sorry, just a few more minutes.'

'Detective Favre, you must calm down; otherwise, we will not be moving you out of the ICU. Understood?

'Yes, nurse, it was my fault. As the Captain asks, just a few minutes more.' He was relieved that the nurse in charge of his care was not the one who spoke in CAPITAL LETTERS! He watched as she checked his monitors and straightened the covers, then, turning on her heel, went to check on Garcia, who seemed to have fallen asleep again.

'Favre, who do you think he was referring to? You've been close to the case from the beginning and must have an inkling.'

'The only person that sprang to mind was Bescutti's mother. She has ruled that family with an iron hand. What do you think?'

'Did she control that part of the business?'

'*Chef,* according to the Crime Unit, she used to rule the family. She stepped down many years ago. This corresponds with what her son, Bescutti, said. Although, I gathered that she was much more involved. He protected her by diminishing her role.'

'So, you think there's truth in what Olivier hinted at?'

'Yes, I do. I think she has kept her son in the dark because he wanted to legitimise their businesses. I don't think she was prepared to relinquish control over that vast empire and continue behind the scenes.'

'But how does Gonzales fit into the whole scenario?'

'When he arrived in Europe to expand his gem trade, she perhaps saw a threat which had to be eliminated. A surefire way to make someone give up and run, would be to threaten and attack their family. Only a woman would have the idea of going to the heart of the family, the daughter. A man would've been more upfront and gone after the actual threat, Arthur Gonzales himself.'

'Fine, I'll work on that presumption.'

'I'm impatient for Garcia to regain stability. We need his input. He might have another hypothesis – I value his instinct and analysis more than you know.'

'You and me both. Let's hope we can brainstorm with him soon. At least he's heading in that direction. Let me not tire you. I'll leave you now, and come back later when you are in the general ward.' They said goodbye, and as he left, he saw Doctor Stein tend to Garcia. Leonard stopped to ask for an update.

'Well, Sir, we are cautiously optimistic. He is showing signs of getting stronger. He regained consciousness last night. Although he floats in and out, we don't feel it's necessary to put him under again. The natural healing process should be taking over as soon as he has stabilised – which, by the way, we feel would be in the next twenty-four hours.'

Leonard left with hope and a much lighter heart, especially when he met Maria, José's wife, in the passage. He felt relieved that his detective would not be without support. They exchanged pleasantries, and he updated her on her husband's condition.

'When will we be able to come back? Living on the run and hiding from people we don't know, is taking its toll.'

'It's nearly over. We are closing in on the suspect.'

'Who is it? Please tell me who are we supposed to look out for? The children are getting restless, they're asking questions about their father, and I don't know what to tell them. They want to come home to their friends, and school holidays are nearly over, they'll need to go back to school when it opens.'

'Yes, I know, and I can assure you it will all be over by the time the new school year begins. We estimate another week. I will keep you informed when you can return.'

'Captain, I trust you, please make sure we'll be safe.'

'Mrs Garcia, that is my sole aim.'

'Thank you, Captain, I'll go in to see my husband now. Goodbye for now.'

Leonard nodded, leaving to find Gonzales and the latest on their daughter's condition.

*

Code blue rang out as he approached Cynthia's room. Medical staff scurried in all directions. The Gonzales couple stood in an embrace, consoling each other. The mother's sobs shook both of their bodies, and emotion spilled over into the area. The noise emanating from the room was deafening to Leonard. The sense of urgency contrasted with the stillness from which he had just come, amplified the sound. With nurses and doctors dashing into action, the intense situation surrounding him made him sidestep, flattening his back against the wall to allow free access to whatever or whoever was needed. He watched, stunned.

'Charge. Stand clear.!' Cynthia's body bucked, relaxed. A minute passed.

'Again. Charge to two-hundred. Clear!' Doctor Stein's voice cut through the quiet.

Both parents turned together, not letting go of each other. They watched as their daughter's back arched and fell back down. The doctor checked the monitor, paddles in hand. On the screen, a flat line showed as he waited for a beep. Everyone around the bed waited, holding their breath. Nothing changed. 'How long has she been under?'

'Ten minutes.'

'Once more, charge to two-fifty. Ready? Clear!' Again, the fragile body bucked. Doctor Stein stepped back, setting down the paddles. No one moved. They waited. The line stayed flat. Nurses looked at each other, turned their attention to the doctor. Anticipation transformed into defeat and surrender.

The doctor readied himself to call the time of death when a small kink jumped in the monitor's flat line. It repeated. A wave came along. Then a 'beep' pierced the stillness of the room. A second "beep" cut into the air.

'Wait!' The doctor with everyone else held on. The sound became regular.

'We've got a rhythm! She's back. Good work everybody. Let's get her stable.' With a glance towards the parents Doctor Stein nodded. He spoke to the resident and left the bedside to speak to Arthur and Anna.

'Mr and Mrs Gonzales, as you saw, your daughter arrested, but we managed to resuscitate her. She has a good rhythm now, and we are watching her carefully. You do understand that her condition is critical. This was the third time she has arrested, and we don't know if her body could take another round of shocks. Be that as it may, we are optimistic. She came through this, and she is a fighter. Hang on to that.'

'Can we go in to see her?' The parents asked simultaneously.

'You can sit with her. Talk to her, but make sure you keep her calm. She needs to hear your voices and reassurance. She won't wake up for a while. Though, we are convinced she can hear you.'

'Thank you. Thank you, Doctor.' Anna let go of Arthur and rushed over to Cynthia's side. Arthur watched her go – hesitated – keen to speak to the doctor, though not wanting to waste one minute by not being at his daughter's bedside.

'Chérie c'est Mama. Reveilles toi. Pour moi, s'il te plaît.' Anna's desperation, not knowing what to do or say, was evident. She looked over to where her husband was still in conversation with the doctor.

Leonard saw panic grip her. He could imagine all the questions flooding her mind: *'What are they saying? Is Cynthia dying? Is there no hope? Why don't they include me in the conversation? Do they think I cannot bear losing my only child? Well, they'd be right. I couldn't bear losing her.'* From experience, he knew the agony mothers go through and have heard these same desperate questions over and over. There was nothing he could do to help. In this instance, he was completely helpless.

He moved towards Arthur Gonzales. The girl's father's shoulders sagged, though he still tried to offer a grateful smile to the man who had saved his daughter's life. Leonard waited until Gonzales shook hands with the medic before he approached.

'Salut, Mr Gonzales, I am so sorry about your daughter and pleased that they managed to pull her through.'

'Oh, hello Captain. You saw that?'

'Yes, I arrived just as they called the "Code Blue". Did the doctor at least reassure you? Will she recover?'

'We don't know yet. He said it could go either way. I don't know what to tell my wife. It would devastate her just knowing that our child might not live.'

'I think she knows. Could we talk for a moment?'

'Sorry Captain. I need to go to my daughter. Could we do it later?'

'Look I won't take too much of your time, but it's important if you want us to apprehend your daughter's attacker.'

'Okay then. But make it quick. My wife needs me to be there.'

'Let's sit down.' Leonard indicated the chairs behind them.

'Mr Gonzales, have you had any dealings with the Bescutti family?'

302

'No. I told your Detectives that.'

'In your effort to expand your gem-trade business in Europe, did you come across a woman who could be a competitor?'

'I have had dealings with a young woman in Zurich who deals mainly in Colombian emeralds. However, she's been a client of mine for many years. I dealt with her father first. She took over the business when he fell ill. He died two years ago.'

'Do you think she would want to take control of the organisation trading in gems?'

'No. She, like her father, never wanted a large organisation. They prefer to remain small and exclusive. That way, they control pricing and who they deal with and sell to.'

'You have not come across any other woman in the trade, specifically one who would be on the darker side of the trade?'

'You mean shady or illegal trading?'

'Yes, exactly. You have your ear to the ground, and therefore, hear things which we might not. Any ideas?'

'None that I can think of. Only I need to get to my family. I cannot think now. Contact my partner, Eric Pichat, he could find out for you.' He glanced over to his wife and daughter. 'Please, I must go now. Could we speak later?'

'Yes, sure, I'll contact your partner and keep you informed. Good day and good luck.'

'Thank you. Goodbye.'

Leonard watched Gonzales quickly walk over to Cynthia's bedside, bend down, planting a kiss of her forehead before taking her hand, and with the other reaching over to take his wife's. The captain only hoped the desperation he saw on the parents' faces would turn into confidence for the future. He left to follow up on Eric Pichat.

*

A half-hour later, Leonard had all the information needed regarding Pichat from the database. After reviewing the interview Favre had conducted, he was ready to call and ask the relevant questions. He knew he had to tread carefully. People with access to this kind of information lived close to that dangerous world. He didn't want to scare Pichat into silence or tempt him to disappear. He needed cooperation and openness. He couldn't expect total honesty, but he hoped this man would at least trust him with as much detail as possible. He wondered if Gonzales had warned Pichat that Leonard wanted to ask questions, though he doubted the worried father had the opportunity. Gonzales didn't seem to have anything on his mind except the wellbeing of his daughter.

'Mr Pichat, would it be possible for you to spare me a moment? I can be at your offices within twenty minutes. Your partner, Mr. Gonzales, told me to contact you.' With an affirmative reply, Leonard made his way to their offices.

On arrival, they introduced themselves, sat down, and within minutes the secretary brought in coffee. Leonard updated Pichat on the condition of his partner's daughter and the direction the investigation had taken. Pichat's reaction to the suspicion that the stabbing was related to the initial case intrigued Leonard.

'Mr Pichat, you don't seem surprised that there might be a connection between the various events.'

'Well, to tell the truth, not really. It was one of the scenarios that I ran. I only began to put it all together when our shipment of emeralds was intercepted.'

'So, you know who is behind it all?'

'No, not yet. However, I have my theories.'

'Pray, tell.'

'What? You want me to share everything with you?'

'That's the idea, unless you think there are things which would force me to arrest you.'

'No. No, it's just there are some confidential details, which would come out if you submit your report.'

'Let us begin with the non-confidential part. That is to say, you have your ear to the ground. Though, you know quite a bit of what's going on in areas where, how shall I put it, we don't have easy access to. Is that a fair assumption?'

'Uh, … well, I suppose. What did Mr Gonzales say?'

'Actually, he directed me to you. He mentioned that you might have heard something.'

'Fire away.'

'Have you heard anything about a woman who controls the gem trade

– by that I mean dealings which would be in direct competition to you? Someone, let's say, who might feel directly threatened by your presence here?'

'Nothing directly. Then there is the possibility of a couple of groups, but as for a woman, that I'll have to confirm. Years ago, Mama Bescutti ran their gem operation – the mother of Georgio Bescutti, that is. However, I've not heard of her taking up the reins again.'

'Do you think you could try and find out who the woman responsible for the atrocities might be? Maybe contact all your informants?'

'I'll put my ear to the ground. Can't promise anything, of course, but will do my best.'

'Don't forget this is to find the perpetrator who stabbed your partner's daughter.'

'Definitely not – it has become personal, she's a nice girl, spoilt, but nice. Leave it with me, I'll be in touch.'

'You do that. Here's my mobile number, phone me directly or leave a voice mail to call back, no information on the message, please. I'll call back immediately. Don't hesitate, I reiterate, call me with anything you might discover. '

'Will do, Captain. Thank you for stopping by.'

'Good, we need to pin this person down – don't forget she was the one who gave the order to eliminate Cynthia. The shooter in our first case, we believe is the perpetrator who stabbed her. If that's the case, we have completed the circle and eradicated the threat and made everyone safe.' Without another word Leonard left.

*

The officer on desk duty stood to attention as Captain Leonard entered the station. Without reacting to the officer's quick salute or returning the gesture, Leonard demanded Bonavita be called to join him in his office without delay.

'Oui, chef!' The young officer quickly picked up the phone to pass on the message. Three minutes later, Bonavita arrived, knocking on Leonard's office door.

'Entrez.' Leonard heard the greeting but continued to study the file in front of him. He turned over a page, then carefully closed the folder. Only

then did he look up.

'Take a seat, please.' He studied Bonavita sliding into the chair on the other side of the desk. Nothing obvious stood out, yet Leonard got the impression that the officer was tense. Although, various possibilities existed for this state; he suspected passing information on to a prime suspect, could be the prime reason. He noticed the officer shift in his chair, clasping his hands together. Leonard remained silent for a moment longer.

'Anything I could do for you, *chef?*' Bonavita finally broke the silence, clearly showing his discomfort. The captain let a couple more moments pass while scrutinising the officer's reaction.

'Actually, yes. You know we are shorthanded with both Favre and Garcia in hospital. They'll most probably be out of action for quite a while.'

'Yes, Sir. I'm aware of that. By the way, how are they?'

'Not doing very well, I'm afraid.'

'They say it was a car accident. How did it happen?'

'Yes, an accident.' Leonard ignored the question. 'Are you *au fait* with the case they have been working on?'

'The shooting of a young man a few weeks ago? Yes, I am.'

'Well, that investigation has developed, and I need your help gathering further evidence so we can close the case.'

'Whatever you need, *chef.'* Bonavita visibly relaxed. He sat back and dropped his hands into his lap. 'Where and when do you want me to start? Do we have a suspect?'

'We have a couple of people in the frame – nothing substantial or supported by evidence. That's where you come in. We need to eliminate persons of interest and get to the real perpetrator. I need you to get out there and talk to all the informants we have. Find out what they know: who they've seen acting suspiciously in the area at, or near, the time of the shooting. Also, while you're at it, see if anyone knows of mercenaries active in the city.'

'Do you think a mercenary could be involved?'

'As we don't have the shooter, I'm throwing out every possible angle. Why? Do you disagree? Do you have a feeling that I'm going down the wrong path?'

'Oh, no, sir. It's just very farfetched, don't you think? I don't want us to waste our time. It was only the shooting of a young nobody, not a celebrity or politician.'

'Bonavita! Every victim of a violent crime is a celebrity or politician as far as this department is concerned. Understood?'

'I … I'm sorry, sir. I didn't mean it that way. I spoke out of turn. I apologise.'

'Yes. Apologise to that poor boy's parents! They're devastated over losing their only son – in fact, their only child. Do you have children?'

'*Chef,* I'm sorry. Yes, I have two, a boy and a girl.'

'Imagine one of them being killed like a dog in the street. Wouldn't you want to find the killer? Think about that.' Leonard opened the file and casually looked at the contents. Then, he looked up at the officer, who wiped perspiration off his brow. 'Enough of that, let's get on. Are you ready to work on this case?'

'Definitely. I'll gather whatever information I can, and report directly back to you.'

'Good. So, get on with it.'

'*Oui, chef.'* Bonavita got up and hurried out of the office and down the hall, to fetch whatever he needed to get on the streets to fulfil the command.

Leonard picked up his mobile, hit a couple of buttons. 'He's on his way, just left my office. Discreetly please. And don't forget we do need photographic evidence and if possible, audio. You have his mobile number. Monitor his calls. Remember, this is highly sensitive.' He cut the call and replaced the phone in his inside pocket.

*

Alpha stood on the corner, watching the two officers in the vehicle in front of Miss Labelle's building. For the last two days, he had surreptitiously followed the movement in and out of that block. The young woman and her friend – the older one – were always accompanied by an officer, and driven by the two officers wherever they needed to go.

Mince alors! He could kick himself. He should have come the day he shot out the tyres of the two pigs! Nevertheless, at least he satiated himself thoroughly with a streetwalker. She surprised him, was even better than the last. In fact, she lasted the whole afternoon and only began pleading for mercy early evening. Why did she complain when he used his gun on her? It brought her to a height she had never reached before, of this, he was sure. Her screams of ecstasy proved it. She screamed louder and bled redder than the previous one.

Perhaps he should have come here first and not waited to celebrate. Not to worry, he'll find a moment to get Favre's tart, even if it meant he had to get rid of the old lady and this policeman as well. Three for the price of one. Quite a bonus, and the stakes weren't too bad either! How to do it, raised a few questions, but it wasn't impossible.

Anyway, it was a great sight watching that car roll - better still when he managed to speak to Lover boy. Reliving that moment gave him such pleasure. Furthermore, the pig didn't like it when he spoke about his tart – he wanted to burst out laughing. Yes, all he had to do was to replay the whole scenario in his mind to feel that thrill again. Well, now he could concentrate on the lovely Miss Labelle. Her name said it all. He was sure Lover boy never even had the courage to take her to bed. A chap like that could never satisfy a woman – they don't know how! And this man was a real wimp.

Well, back to reality. Information from his inside man still hadn't come through for the day. Yesterday's news brought both good and not-so-good news. Both pigs were still in ICU. The fat one remained on the critical list, but Lover Boy's making progress. He had really hoped that it would take longer before their suffering diminished. Those two deserved long, drawn-out pain, and lots of it – perhaps with a handicap later – for costing him his bonus.

Impatiently, he tapped his phone. Why was the required information late? You can't depend on anyone except yourself, that's a fact. So far, this man has been on the dot every time, even though he is a plod.

Hanging around in front of this building was boring. The only distraction was the two friends who came out of the building with their guard, and a young man exiting from the next block walking a tiny, slightly familiar, dog. Oh well, that wasn't what was important now.

He sighed, shifted on his feet, and waited. The image of the emeralds gave him patience and, at the same time, gooseflesh. The lustre of emeralds cannot be equalled by any other gem. They have a sparkle that soothes, doesn't cut into you like a diamond. And to think the whole market was now his. However, this was only the beginning – the first step to control the whole gem market: semi-precious and precious stones. What a future at his fingertips! Lost in his reverie, he jerked when, twenty minutes later, a vibration into his thigh muscle brought him back to reality. It took a moment for him to realise that it was signalling a call, not a message.

'Yes. ... You're late. Where were you? ...' Alpha laughed. *'You're joking! You? ... Well, what do they want you to do? ... Interesting. ... Well, keep them guessing. We'll feed them something: get them off the trail. Though I'm more interested in where they are on the case and what their next step will be.'* ... He listened for a moment. *'What? You want to meet? Face to face? Why? ... Are you worried about payment? You shouldn't be. ... Oh, you want to meet the mastermind. In that case, why not? It'll be fun, we could grab a beer. What do you say? ... Great, let's meet tomorrow at six, then you can update me at the same time.'* Alpha touched the red button to end the call and put the phone away.

He found the call interesting. Meeting one of their own officers for a beer would be fun – rubbing their noses in it! They were all such imbeciles. This confirmed his opinion of the police. The mere fact that they asked his inside man to be their eyes and ears on the street for this investigation! An investigation into him by his own paid informant – what a laugh! The informant's ignorance of his actual connection to the case also tickled him. As far as the plod was concerned, he was merely an interested party, writing a book on crime and how the department would uncover and follow a suspect. Where does the police department find their servicemen? They were all clueless. Or were they so innocent or just stupid, thinking that crime only happens in other countries? Either way, they were no a match for him, not with all his years of experience.

This gave him another opportunity to have some fun.

Soon everything would be in place. Then he could begin to send his inside man on a bit of a wild goose chase. That would really confuse the constabulary!

Every time he cleaned up after an operation, it presented great possibilities to practise his craft. He still regretted how he disposed of his two lookouts after the shooting. The Boss's anger infuriated him – he never took authority well – and this affected his cool headedness. If the Boss hadn't insisted on getting rid of them for good, he wouldn't have pushed to see if she would follow up on her threats. Sending them away was not what she ordered – she tasted blood. Disappointment was not in her vocabulary, nor was it an accepted norm. Nevertheless, they were now far away in one of those godforsaken, no-extradition countries in South America. Yes, clean-up duty had its promises. He still had a lot of fun to look forward to here in the City of Calvin – and don't they know it! His mouth watered with the idea of how he would test the endurance of his informant.

The changing of the guard brought his attention back to the building he had been watching. A patrol car pulled up next to the parked police vehicle. One officer got out and entered the apartment block. The driver spoke through his open window to the occupants of the parked car, then reversed a car length allowing the other to manoeuvre out, and waited for the officer guarding the door to arrive. The patrol car took the place of the vehicle on the point of departing. It took only three minutes for the replaced guard to exit the building and get into the first-shift vehicle. They left with a quick wave, and the road returned to its previous quiet state. Evident that nothing further would happen during the rest of the evening, Olivier turned and made his way back to his own apartment.

*

Leonard sipped the coffee his wife had brought him earlier. It was lukewarm, not her fault, as he hadn't taken it when she placed the cup next to him. Since he left the dinner table, he had been holed up in his study, going through everything he had learnt so far. The picture was becoming clearer, the trail easier to follow. Unfortunately, still no concrete evidence. His phone rang.

'Leonard. ... Yes, right. You have news? ... Excellent. ... And the proof as requested? ... Very good. Bring everything here to me at home first thing in the morning with your verbal report. ... Fine. Oh yes, good night.' He cut the call and ran his free hand over his face, more in relief than frustration. Things were opening up. At last, the first pieces of evidence which would stand up in court, proving Bonavita had passed on information to a person of interest in an ongoing criminal investigation. Further, the domicile of Olivier, whom they have followed discreetly for the last three days, was now ninety percent confirmed. The apartment was registered under another name; he must be sub-leasing or squatting. From the observations, they verified only one person, Olivier, entering or exiting the place.

What remained now was for them to apprehend the man – hopefully in the process of cleaning up loose ends, one of those: probably Bonavita. Then, they needed to find the woman who ordered the original shooting.

Ideally, they would confess to the crimes. Except, Leonard knew they were experts in their fields of criminal activity, especially Olivier, and would be difficult to crack. Moreover, a confession would be the last thing coming their way easily.

His wife called down to him. He closed the file. Sleep was needed to be fresh for the arrival of the officer from the Intelligence Branch in the morning.

*

Antonio couldn't understand why Cynthia wasn't answering her phone. All his texts had also remained unanswered. What did he do to merit this silent treatment? As far as he remembered, they left on reasonably good terms. Two days of absolute silence from her wasn't normal. Even if she was mad at him, she would respond to his text, if only to tell him to shove off and leave her alone. Yet, he was convinced he hadn't given her a reason to be mad.

He could still see her walking into the coffee shop – sizzling hot – her small body moving with such rhythm. She made the music of South America come alive in this northern hemisphere, adding to their current heatwave. It automatically ran through her whole being. Just like hot Latino blood which fired up passion. Was it the samba or salsa rhythms emanating from her every move? Never mind – it was intoxicating. No matter how hard he tried, he couldn't get his emotions under control. One thing he was sure of – they had to get back together. They belonged together, no matter what their parents said. Once he was back on the team and captain again, he would be in a better position to get her to date. He was convinced he saw a flicker of what they had between them before, in her eyes. Their connection had survived and would continue to survive.

This wasn't normal. He was getting worried. Where was she? He decided to pop out to Starbucks in Plainpalais, just in case she was there with some of her friends. He knew that two of them have returned from holiday. He put his tablet away, picked up his phone, slipped into his trainers, tied them, adjusted the knee brace, and grabbed his crutches.

On the way out, he saw his mother on the phone with her back to him. She sounded worried. He could only hear snippets of the conversation as he waited to attract her attention – she would be furious if he left without telling her.

'... *What!* ... *When?* ... *She was stabbed?*' ... Just then, his mother turned and saw him standing there. Immediately, she pressed the phone to her chest to prevent him from hearing what the other person might say.

'Mom, I'm going out. See you later.'

'Uhm … uhm … fine, come back soon, I want to talk to you. Be careful.'

'Okay, will be. Bye!' He hoped that whatever his mother wanted to talk to him about wouldn't be more of the same: avoiding Cynthia. With that he left.

Suddenly, a remnant of conversation he overheard struck him. He wondered what the phone call was all about and who had been stabbed. Was that what she said? Did the person die? He couldn't imagine any of his mother's friends or acquaintances being in a position to be stabbed, they were all so ordinary.

Numerous questions competed for attention in his mind, but all were pushed aside by the thought of getting to Starbucks to see if Cynthia was there. That could be it, with her friends back in town, she's been too busy to reply. However, that was no excuse. He felt disappointed, hurt even, to be ignored like this. Oh well, he was on his way now, so he might as well confront her when he saw her.

At the coffee shop, he saw no one he knew – and Cynthia was not there. He decided to hang around; ordered a latte to while away the time, and took a seat where he could see the entrance. He didn't have to wait long before one of their fellow students came in, saw him, and immediately joined Antonio.

'Hey man, how are you?' The new arrival called out. He came over, and the two young men fist-bumped. He slumped into a chair opposite Antonio.

'Hi, every day better. I'll soon be back on the field. What're you doing?'

'Ah, just hanging, seeing who's around.' He looked from one side of the room to the other, scanning for other familiar faces. 'Hey man, did you hear what happened at Starbucks Rive? Man, it was rad. Everyone's talking about it!'

'What happened? I haven't heard anything.'

'There was a stabbing - and get this - it was where we used to all hang out. Also, you would never, ever believe this: it was your ex who got knifed, man! You sure you didn't know?' He smiled and slapped the table as if the crime was the greatest excitement he's ever had.

'What? Cynthia got stabbed! What are you talking about? Are you sure it was her? How do you know about this?'

'Hey dude, chill! You must slow down. Of course, it was her. Two of her friends - you know, Debbie, Suzanne, and Suzanne's sister - were there. They saw it all! Debbie told me they were going to the movies when it happened. They all freaked. They think she's dead. The ambulance took her away.'

'Where is she now? Are you sure she's dead?'

'Look man, I don't know. Debbie thought she was dead, but perhaps she's in hospital.'

'I have to go,' Antonio looked at his phone. Still nothing from Cynthia, and now he knew why. He had to get home and speak to his mother. It might have been Cynthia she was talking about on the phone. He got up and nearly forgot his crutches in his rush to get back. He had to know if she was dead. His heart sank at the thought.

Not prepared to wait for the bus to Cologny, he called an Uber and virtually fell through the front door when the car dropped him home.

'Mom? Mom, where are you! Is it true?' Antonio's shout echoed through the hall.

'I'm here. I'm in the kitchen.'

'I heard that Cynthia has been killed.'

'Come and sit down.'

'Mom! Cut wasting my time! Tell me what's going on! If you don't, I promise you I'll go out that door and never come back. I'll never speak to you again!'

'Fine, calm down, I'll tell you what I know.' Manuella dried her hands on a dishcloth, took off her apron and pulled out a stool at the counter. 'You'd better sit down as well.'

'So, she's dead, isn't she?' He threw down his bag and half-stood, half-sat on the other stool, turning to face his mother.

'No, she's not dead. She's been stabbed and is fighting for her life in hospital.'

'When did this happen? When did you know? Why didn't you tell me? Is it one of your tactics to keep us apart? You do know you won't succeed, don't you? We're destined to be in each other's lives.'

'Now, slow down and keep your head. I only heard about it this morning. That was the call I was on when you ran out to meet friends.'

'Oh, I heard you said something about a stabbing. I never connected it to be Cynthia – I thought you were talking about one of your friends.'

'That's the trouble when we eavesdrop or only hear snippets of a conversation. The danger is, we often jump to conclusions.'

'Can I go and see her?'

'No, not while she's in ICU. You could send her a card or something like that. You cannot go there – it would only upset her parents.'

'Well, Mom, tell me what happened. I heard it from a fellow student, and it was like it was the greatest thing ever! He thought the experience was like the circus coming to town!'

'Very insensitive of him! Is he a good friend of yours?'

'Not really, he's just one of the blokes at Uni on the second team. We don't mix much, except at practice sessions. He's waiting for a spot on my team, so if I can't make it back, he'll be standing in line to take my place.'

'He doesn't sound very nice.'

'Oh, he's a jerk. Let's forget about him. Mom, tell me exactly what you know, please. And can I go and see her in the hospital?'

'You're right. He's not worth our time. All I know is that she was stabbed at the Rive Starbucks. Luckily, there were quite a few people around who knew what to do. An ambulance arrived soon after and managed to stem the blood flow. She was taken to the Cantonal and is in the ICU being taken care of.'

'Who told you?'

'Your father phoned. Everyone's helping the police to find the person who did this.'

'My father's helping? That's the last thing I would've expected you to say, seeing that he's so adamant I stay away from her.'

'Yes, he and her parents are helping the police. They think it's connected to the shooting Cynthia witnessed. Now you understand why we didn't want the two of you to see each other. It could be dangerous.'

'Is that why both of us have been under curfews?'

'Yes. We thought if you were home in the evenings, it would minimise the risk. Unfortunately, it looks as if we're dealing with a much more determined criminal. So, whenever you're out, please be careful and don't take any chances. If you think you are being followed, let me know and come home immediately.'

'Okay, Mom. I just don't understand why you couldn't tell us to begin with. It would've helped, and we most probably would have done what you asked instead of sneaking off behind your backs to meet up.'

'Well, we all thought we were protecting you. We didn't want to scare you. It's no joy to live by looking over your shoulder all your life.'

'Is that what you had to do with my father's family?'

'Not exactly. I never knew what they did for a living, after he left: and the way he left made me ask questions. I thought I was married, and then suddenly, without warning, I wasn't. I was so hurt and lonely but could do nothing about it. That was the way he wanted it, and he paid for everything. I accepted his decision. Although I pieced some things together and realised there must have been a very good reason for him to leave his son. The mere fact that he insisted I raise you under my maiden name, made me look up his family name, and I came across dubious and vague information. That's when I realised the information wasn't dubious, it was the family who was in dubious business. So, I made sure we lived well and respected your father's wishes that there would be no contact from then on.'

'You should have told me this before.'

'Well, he strictly forbade me from telling you about him. He didn't want you knowing who you really were, and furthermore, he kept you away from his family – for your own good. They don't know you exist. In the end, it was for the best – he made the right decision for us.'

'Do you really think so? Even though I would've liked to have a father in my life, I don't think I can forgive him for hurting you and leaving you alone all these years to manage on your own.'

'I haven't been alone exactly, I had you.'

'You know what I mean - like the other kids. Their fathers came to games and were there to talk to and give advice.'

'When did you ever take advice from someone? You even knocked heads with your coach. Tell me I'm wrong.'

'I know, I know. But still, it would've been nice to know that he was around.'

'My son, you haven't done too badly, have you?'

'Well, if you look at it like that. We are good, the two of us.'

'Yes, we've had a good life.'

'Could you tell me about him please? What does he look like? How did you meet? You must have loved him if you married and had me. Do you still love him?'

'All these questions. Could we leave it at that for the time being?'

'Only if you promise to tell me everything.'

'Fine, I promise, now let me be.'

'Mom, could you help me send Cynthia a get-well card and some flowers?'

'Do you think it's a good idea?'

'Definitely. I want to do it with or without your help.'

'Okay, fine. Go to the credenza and look through the cards I have – choose one.'

'Thanks Mom.' Antonio had a spring in his step as he left the kitchen.

CHAPTER NINETEEN

The two-bed ward was bright and, for the present, only occupied by Favre. He woke early, feeling better and impatient to get back on his feet, though breathing was still painful. The doctor had just left, satisfied with his progress, and removed the neck brace. However, he would be closely monitored, as he was not out of danger. Doctor Stein advised that later that afternoon, they would help him to get out of bed, to sit in the chair for a while. His spirits rose with the promise – depending on how he felt – that a physiotherapist would soon give him various exercises, instruct him on the use of crutches, and help him to walk for ten minutes. With his right upper arm and shoulder immobilised, and his leg in a cast, he was curious to know how he would be able to use crutches. Well, he'd have to rely on the physio's expertise, he told himself.

Determination drove Paul to get better and stronger as soon as possible. He wanted to get back on the case. For the time being, his brain power – the only part of him which still worked more or less as before – would have to suffice. Unfortunately, he experienced excruciating headaches whenever he concentrated for a long period of time, a remnant from the concussion. He had to persevere and suppress it because the investigation needed a clear head. Further, frustration crept in because every scrap of information came to him second hand from Leonard, who in turn got it from Intelligence Branch. He wanted to interview, personally follow-up on every scrap of information, get the feel for it, turn it over, and chew on it. He always worked with Garcia at his side, and he felt impatient for things to be as they should.

Thinking of Garcia, he realized no one has updated him on his partner's progress. He was eager to know if his partner was finally off the critical list. With nothing to do now but wait for Leonard to come by; he lay back and dozed off.

'Favre.' A hand on his shoulder brought consciousness back. 'Favre.' The voice repeated. He opened his eyes, turning towards the sound. His Captain stood over him. 'Favre, how are you?'

'*Ah, chef.* Sorry I must have dozed off.' Paul tried to pull up into a sitting position, failed, apologised again, leaning back into a half upright state. 'I'm getting there slowly, hopefully faster than the doctor has in mind.'

'Now Favre, I don't want you to rush things and retard your full recovery.' Leonard pulled the chair nearer the bed and settled in.

'No Sir, any progress? Have you got firm evidence?'

'You'll be pleased to know I have received some interesting pieces of information this morning from IB. I put Bonavita in charge of gathering intel from informants.'

'But he's the mole!'

'Exactly, as lead investigator, he would have free rein. Don't forget, at this moment we only suspect him to be the mole. We have no evidence to support our suspicions. I thought the easiest way to obtain such evidence would be to set him loose, have IB monitor his mobile phone, and follow him.'

'Oh, I see, good thinking, *chef*. And did you get something?'

'Well, you wouldn't believe it. Or perhaps you would! The first call he made was from his personal phone to a burner. Even though we were ready for it, we couldn't believe our luck. They pinned the location and recorded the discussion. No names were mentioned, except the location: the corner of the block where Miss Labelle's building is situated. And since we were on the tail of Olivier, Alpha as he wants to be known, we connected the two because Olivier received a call at the exact time Bonavita made his call. Apparently, they arranged to meet today at six. Bonavita is expected to be paid – we imagine – for the information he's passed on so far. Olivier also inquired about the wellbeing of you and Garcia. It seems he's not finished with the two of you yet.'

'Nothing seems to stop him.'

'That's why I've arranged for plainclothes officers to be placed at certain unobtrusive vantage points for both your protection.'

'Did you get anything further on Alpha?'

'Well, they trailed him from where he took the call to the same premises that we are now sure is his domicile. It's registered to another person, who we have found is on an extended holiday in Ibiza. She advised she will be absent for another two months and under no circumstances did she sublet her apartment to Olivier or any other person.'

'What have you heard about the young girl, Cynthia?'

'I'll go there when I leave you to pop in to check on Garcia.'

'Please come back here afterward, as I have no news of my partner's condition, or the girl's. They won't tell me anything.'

'As for the girl, yesterday she was in a very bad state, they had to resuscitate her. Her father said it had happened twice before since they brought her in. I hope for the parents' sake she pulls through, but at present it is not looking good. They're hoping she rallies and gets at least fifty-fifty chance.'

'I'm sure the parents would be relieved when we arrest Olivier. We are sure he's responsible for stabbing her, aren't we?'

'For the moment, the only thing on their minds is wanting her to survive, to be able to take her home. And to answer your question, we received the CCTV footage late yesterday. Pichon and Borel are going through it now. They are optimistic. Borel says he has a feeling they'll find the same image as on all the other videos. I think he's trying to intimidate the two of you!' Leonard chuckled.

'Whatever. I'll take their "feelings" and add it to Garcia's and mine as long as we can catch this guy. His path has been violent, and unless we catch him, it won't stop. It looks as if he's even more ruthless than his Interpol jacket.'

'I agree with you there. We have to get him off the streets.'

'I would like to be the one to put him behind bars. How will our evidence stand up in court? He did threaten to harm a civilian. Wouldn't my testimony be enough?' Favre reached over and took the beaker of water next to his bed.

'The problem is, there were no witnesses, and you were quite banged up. With a good lawyer, he could argue that you imagined it all, trying to pin the crime on him to increase your arrest record.'

'That's nonsense, and you know it, Sir.'

'I do. But don't forget we are dealing with a highly intelligent psychopath. In any case, as far as other evidence goes, we have nothing concrete or any substantive proof. Nevertheless, we have enough to get a warrant to search his flat. With the photos and audio, we got yesterday, it's more than we had the day before. Unfortunately, they didn't mention any specifics: names, an event, or an operation. But it's a start.' Leonard hesitated before continuing.

'We have received notification from the hospital that three prostitutes came in with serious injuries. Besides being beaten – presumably with a fist, or perhaps, more seriously, the butt of a gun – they were also cut. The cuts weren't very deep, but drew blood, which made it impossible for them to work for at least a week. From what the medical staff gathered, one of their Johns treated them violently. Viciously would be a better description. Apparently, this client was a first-timer for each one of them, and as far as they were concerned, would be the last time they ever allowed him near them.'

'What has that got to do with our case?'

'The interesting fact is the timing of each attack, if that's what you want to call it. The first one came the night of the shooting, the second when your apartment burnt down, and the third when the girl was stabbed.'

'Oh yes, that is a strange coincidence. Or is it synchronicity? Though, I wonder why there's a gap of no complaint between the first and second attack. Do you think we'll find another injured streetwalker out there? You know, from the day of the bombing at the station when Garcia was injured?'

'Could be. The hospital contacted us when the third victim came in. They found it suspicious, and sufficiently serious to get us involved. We sent an officer round who interviewed the woman. He got the information of the previous two patients as well. At first, they refused to talk to us at all, but when they heard there were at least two other women injured, they were more cooperative. Here's what's interesting: each described a very handsome and charming man. He asked for rough sex, which they agreed, using a safe word. Except, what awaited them wasn't the norm. He took great pleasure in tormenting and torturing them each time they used the safe word. All three said they pleaded for him to stop. He showed no mercy; instead, he only became more vicious. They also said he had dead eyes. He enjoyed hurting them – revelled in it. He sneered and laughed the more they suffered and used the safe word. He took great pleasure in their pain.'

'Well, that's how we have come to know him.' With Favre's headache back in full force, he breathed deeply a couple of times, and took more water trying to control the agony.

'The physical description they gave fits Olivier exactly. Therefore, we can bring him in on Afflicting Grievous Bodily Harm to begin with and go from there. It will give us time to gather more evidence and stop him from cleaning up loose ends. We need Bonavita alive to give us as much on this

Alpha as possible.' Leonard moved in his chair.

'You sure Bonavita doesn't know his contact is, in fact, our prime suspect?'

'I cannot believe he does. I doubt very much he would have passed anything on if he knew exactly who the recipient was. Don't you?'

'No, I agree. I don't think he knows who he's dealing with. He isn't the brightest of our officers, but I doubt very much he would knowingly betray a fellow officer. You know we do have a code – we have each other's backs.'

'I know. It doesn't get any less so when you go up the ranks.' Leonard shook his head. He knew full well how ranks close when a colleague was threatened. He saw Paul's eyes clouding over. 'Look, I'm going to leave you to rest, and check in on Garcia and the Gonzales family. Don't worry, I'll pop back to give you an update just before I leave, rest for a bit.' He gave the detective a small wave, Favre caught his attention.

'How is Alex? I mean Miss Labelle. Is she safe?'

'Yes, don't worry about her. She has around the clock protection, as I explained. Now concentrate on getting stronger and get some rest.' Leonard turned and disappeared into the corridor for the elevator bank.

On the ICU floor, he pressed the button for the hydraulic doors. They opened with a hiss and a sigh. A nurse whom he hadn't seen before stepped out from behind the reception desk and asked who he was looking for. Once he explained his presence, she let him pass.

Garcia looked peaceful, with fewer tubes going into and coming out of his stocky body. This was a good sign. Leonard crept quietly forward and stood next to the bed. Relief spread through him: José breathed on his own. Through a mask, oxygen still flowed silently, speeding up the healing process. José's colour had improved. Leonard jumped when a voice behind him brought him back.

'He looks better, doesn't he?'

'Oh, *bonjour,* Maria. Yes, he does. What does Doctor Stein say?'

'Hopeful is about the only thing he has said. The nurses, however, were not as guarded and were very optimistic, believing he had turned the corner.' Maria didn't move. She just stood there, a step behind and to the side of Leonard, with a paper cup of coffee in her hand.

'What do you think? You know him and his strength to rally best of all.'

'Yes, that's true. He's as strong as an ox. Still, even an ox has its limits.' She moved forward and touched her husband's feet with her free hand. 'I think he won't survive another assault like this. He was lucky this time. He made it, and I believe he will get up out of this bed, if only to solve the case.'

'I agree with you. He's a man driven, and this investigation touched his family. He won't forgive that transgression.'

'Have you caught the man?'

'He's in our sights. We're closing in.'

'You had better. Forgive me, but I'm not prepared to allow this type of threat to my family be repeated. We've been living in hiding for weeks now, and the children are getting more and more restless. They want to go home, and I agree. I want my family all in one piece, back in our own beds.'

'I hear you, Mrs Garcia.' Just then, José stirred, opened his eyes, and looked from one to the other, confusion apparent.

'What happened? Is everything okay?' He pulled the mask off his face. 'Maria, where are the children? *Chef,* what are you doing here?'

'*Chéri,* you've been sleeping. Don't you remember we talked about your accident last night? You're better now, though still have to stay in bed.'

'Oh … uh … yes. I remember now. Sorry, I hope I didn't scare you.' José looked at Maria and then turned his gaze towards Leonard.

'No, not at all, you were only slightly disorientated,' Leonard added.

'How is Favre?' Both José and Maria wanted to know.

'He's much better and in a general ward – still being watched carefully. He's allowed to sit in a chair for a short while as from today, and tomorrow they'll help him to walk on crutches for about ten minutes.'

'Good old Paul. As determined as I am. We'll be ready to get that bastard, and his accomplice before you know it! Did you get the mole? Was it Bonavita, as I suspected?'

'I don't want to discuss this now.' Leonard looked towards Maria.

'No, *chef,* you can discuss the case in front of Maria. She knows as much as we do.'

'Oh. I see, good. I gave him a task which would confirm and give us evidence of his disloyalty.'

'Disloyalty? More like treachery or treason! Whichever, the strongest description of his deceit towards the uniform should apply.'

'Calm yourself, dear.' Maria smoothed the covers over his body.

'You're right. I would like to charge him with treason. Nevertheless, I spoke to Favre, and he feels Bonavita doesn't realise who he is dealing with. He thinks that Olivier flattered him into believing he was only passing on irrelevant information. For what we only assumed could be under the premise of something inoffensive.'

'Well, I can believe that. He's not the sharpest.'

'That was exactly what Favre said. So, I asked Bonavita to gather intelligence from all corners. We've already had him contacting the recipient of the information. We've got photo and audio, which we presume is Olivier, as he received a call on his burner the exact same time.'

'Therefore, evidence is piling up.'

'Definitely. We also have the possibility of bringing Olivier in on a GBH charge. It'll give us time to grill him and prevent him from tying up loose ends.'

'That could be an idea.' Garcia was fading fast, his eyelids drooped.

'Maria, I'll leave to give you time with your husband. Get well soon, Garcia.' Without another word, he left to seek out the Gonzales family.

The parents of Cynthia sat dejectedly on each side of her bed. Her mother held her daughter's right hand, and her father held the left, careful not to interfere with any needles or tubes. With their free hands, they clasped each other's across Cynthia's body. All the tubes and IVs would confuse everyone except the medical staff. The monitor emitted its usual rhythmic beep, which brought a sense of confidence to the room. Leonard knocked softly on the door jam. Both looked up, recognised him, and smiled weakly. Mr Gonzales nodded to his wife, got up to speak to the captain.

'How is she doing?' Leonard asked: as usual without preamble.

'Good morning. She's hanging in there. At least she didn't arrest again.'

'Yes, that is good news. Surely it means that she's getting stronger?'

'Well, the doctor said that, although weak, her heart rhythm had regularised slightly, which gave grounds for a positive outcome.'

'I'm very pleased to hear that. Let us hope she continues to improve.'

'She's a fighter, takes after her mother. Me, not so much. I throw in the towel and begin again. In business, it's the most cost effective. I like things easy, things that can be negotiated without a problem, or solved with a couple of strokes of the pen.'

'I spoke to your partner. He hasn't come back to me yet. Have you heard from him?'

'Oh, he called late last night, said he heard some rumours, and would contact you today. Don't worry. He'll give you whatever he found. He is dependable. Look, I would like to get back to my daughter. Is that okay?'

'No problem, I only wanted to find out how you were doing and check on your daughter's progress. I sincerely hope she improves.'

'Thank you, have a good day.'

'Thank you. The same to you. Please don't hesitate if we could help you with something – anything.' Gonzales nodded, and Leonard watched him turn to join his family.

He felt anxious to get back to the investigation. However, he should stop at the station before going home and back to the files. He hoped to receive a report from Bonavita. It would be interesting to hear what he had come up with. Still, he needed to be careful not to show his hand. Bonavita might not pick up on it, only he was convinced when his officer reported to his contact, i.e., Olivier, the latter would demand a word for word repetition and suspect their deception.

The meeting between the two was also planned for late this afternoon. He had to make sure at least three undercover IB officers were present at the rendezvous. He sincerely hoped those officers in IB were trustworthy. It would be a disaster if they also had a mole amongst them. Ideally, he could be there 'by chance,' but he might be seen by Bonavita. He doubted Alpha would recognize him, but he couldn't risk it.

Now, another thing nagged at him. Favre had brought it to his attention – the time gap of violent maltreatment towards prostitutes. If the hypothesis that each attack happened after Alpha committed a crime was found to be sound, there would be one woman who never reported the abuse, she disappeared or could be dead.

His mobile phone rang as he got in his car. *'Leonard. ... Oh yes Mr Pichat, I only just left Mr Gonzales. ... She's a fighter. ... Look, could I stop by your offices now? It's on my way back to the station, and it would save time if we could sit down face to face. ... Good, I'll be there in fifteen minutes.'* He ended the call and slipped the phone into the cup-holder between the seats. 'Right, perhaps a couple of puzzles could be solved,' he mused.

Exactly fifteen minutes later, he pulled up in front of the hotel where

Gonzales had offices and handed his keys over to the valet with strict instructions for the car to be near at hand. He took the lift to the appropriate floor and gave the receptionist his name. She immediately showed him through to Eric's office and left to bring them coffee.

'Pleased you could see me so quickly.' Leonard took a seat where Pichat indicated.

'No problem, I have heard some rumours which might be of interest. Nothing definite you see, except there are a few strange ideas floating around. It might lead us to the right person.' As the door opened, Eric beckoned the receptionist in with the coffee.

'Good, there's something I wanted to ask you as well.'

'Go ahead, anything – if I'm able to help.' He handed a cup to Leonard and took one before he settled back into his chair.

'Have you heard from your courier yet? I mean the young woman who disappeared with your sample emeralds and intercepted by one of our suspects.'

'In fact, now that you mention it, we haven't. With everything that's happened, it slipped my mind completely. No, we've had no sight or sound from her.'

'Have you heard anything concerning that incident?'

'No, none of my informants mentioned the young woman, where she could be, or have knowledge of stolen emeralds.'

'Okay, we will revisit that aspect of the inquiry later. For now, what can you tell me?'

'Well, from the word on the street, there are three women who might be heading the dubious gem trade and who might specialise in emeralds. They are Bernita Coertze, who holds dual nationality of Belgium and Switzerland who has been in that line of work for about eighteen years; another is Chao Li, a Chinese national who has been operating in Switzerland, mainly Geneva, for the last twenty years; finally, we have Mama Bescutti and the Bescutti family who as we know have been operating here for at least fifty years. Although Mama B, as she is known, controlled the gem trade branch in the past, everyone says that, far as they know, she had left the business many years ago for her sons to run. Apparently, they had decided to stop dealing in gems about ten years ago. Anyway, she must be pushing eighty-five by now.'

'We know the name Chao Li. She's had a couple of brushes with the law, but nothing related to the gem trade – mainly suspicions of money laundering, which we could never prove. We'll look into Bernita Coertze; the name doesn't ring a bell, though we wouldn't typically deal with that type of violation.'

'What about Mama B? Are you dismissing her as a possible operator?'

'Actually, no, I'm going to cover all possibilities. In your opinion, could she have reinstated the old trade without her sons knowing?'

'According to the rumours, she's a very astute woman. No one could ever put anything past her. Her sons tried to pull the wool over her eyes several times, only she always caught on, and put a stop to whatever they did which she might not have agreed with. She controlled everything with an iron hand. Apparently, her sons would never cross her for fear of her retaliation. The story goes that she could be vicious and unforgiving.'

'Fine, I'll investigate her from that angle. That'll be all for now, let me know if something else comes up. Oh yes, could you please give me full details, and a description of the missing young lady – your courier?'

'Will do, just give me a moment. We have all the details at reception with a photo for recognition at the airport.'

'Thank you.'

'May I ask you something before you go?'

'Of course.'

'Why don't you ask Georgio Bescutti what his mother has been up to?'

'That's my next stop.' Leonard collected the information on the missing courier and left for the WTC Building, where Georgio Bescutti had his offices. *'Begin with the least obvious and see where that leads,'* he thought.

Since the station was on his way, he stopped to check if Bonavita had reported in. He had not. Therefore, the Captain left word that he should be contacted as soon as Bonavita came in and that he should be kept at the station until Leonard had spoken to him. In the eight minutes it took to reach the WTC, his mind couldn't set aside the condition of his two officers. He parked, went up to Bescutti's third-floor offices, where the secretary announced his arrival and, led him through on Mr Bescutti's request.

'Good morning. Captain Leonard, is it?'

'Yes, you've dealt with Detective Favre. He's indisposed at the moment, so I've taken over the investigation.'

'Pleased to meet you. Whatever you need, I'll be prepared to help.

326

Please, take a seat.'

'There is one thing I'd like to discuss with you. It might seem strange, but's it come to our attention that the shooting a few weeks ago had its roots in competition over the gem trade – specifically emeralds in this case.'

'Really, a connection to the gem trade?'

'Yes. Furthermore, it came to our attention that the person behind the whole incident was a woman. Apparently, she brought the gunman to town specifically to eliminate her competition.'

'I don't understand, what did the young man have to do with the gem trade? Was his family in that line of work?'

'No, not at all. The shooting, as we've gathered, was a warning to a competitor to get out of town. Unfortunately, the target moved, and the young man was shot instead of the girl.' Leonard carefully watched Georgio's reaction.

'But your detective told us the girl is the daughter of Arthur Gonzales. I know he does trades in semi-precious stones, though I doubt he could be a serious rival. Was he the target of this violent warning? Who on earth would be so cruel as to kill the child of a rival? That, I cannot understand. And you say it could be a woman who orchestrated the crime?'

'Yes. We received intel which told us there could be three possible suspects: a Bernita Coertze, Chao Li and your mother, Mama B, as she's known on the street.'

'Is that why you're here? You want to know about my mother?'

'Correct, could you tell me if she ever dealt in semi-precious or precious stones?'

'Well, yes. At the time, she controlled that branch of our organisation completely. However, about ten years ago, she decided to abandon that side.'

'Could you tell me why she closed that side of the business? Also, do you think she might resurrect it without your knowledge?'

'As far as I remember, the official reason was she considered the market not lucrative enough.'

'Could there have been another reason?'

'Oh, wait. You're right, it wasn't that. The suppliers we had betrayed us. I remember now. She became so angry; we stayed out of her way for the next three months. They overcharged, and I think they sent inferior gems. Also, there were no other suppliers left who would do business with the

Bescuttis. If you knew my mother, you'd understand – something like that would never be acceptable. She wouldn't drop you not just with penalties; it would cost you your whole business, from which you'd never recover. She would eliminate your whole family – she could be brutal.'

'In that case – could you answer my question?'

'Sorry, I forgot the question. Oh, you mean would she resurrect the gem trade? I doubt it. She withdrew from the business because of that setback and handed over the daily run of the organisation to us. She wasn't very pleased with how I handled it then or now. I refused to bow to her authority.'

'What do you mean?'

'Well, I've tried to change the manner in which we do business. I closed various sections that I felt didn't comply with trade law. As I said, she didn't … in fact, she still doesn't like it. We've not been on full speaking terms for the last ten years – we only meet on her birthday and at Christmas. I keep my own counsel as much as I can. As I'm sure you know from my interview with Detective Favre, I kept my marriage and my son hidden from her and the family. I don't want my son to get entangled in this life.'

'Somehow she found out – you do realise that don't you?'

'I didn't, until your detective pointed out the possibility. I do not want to ask her, because that would draw attention to my son. His anonymity would be destroyed, and she would insist on being part of his life, drawing him into the organisation and control him.'

'So, what do you think? Could she take back her place in the gem trade without you knowing? If so, in your opinion; could her method of establishing herself as a leader stretch as far as ordering the killing of a competitor's child?'

'I suppose it's possible, she is vicious. Don't forget, even though she's getting on, she's still as sharp as she's always been. Perhaps my brother might know. Should I ask him?'

'Could you ask him without alerting your mother to our inquiries?'

'No, they're as thick as thieves. That's why I have such trouble in keeping this organisation legitimate.'

'Perhaps he's helping her re-establish her role. Okay, don't do anything just yet. Let us do our thing first. We must check on the other two as well. I think that's all for now. Please don't hesitate to call me directly on my mobile if you think of or hear something.' Leonard got up to take his leave.

'Good day, Captain Leonard.'

'Another thing, could you give me your mother's address? Further down the line, we'll need to speak to her.'

'Sure.' Georgio nodded, wrote the address on a yellow post-it, and handed it over. He watched him go. When the Captain turned in the doorway, looking back, he saw Bescutti shake his head and turn towards the window, his reflection clearly showed his concern.

Leonard sorted through the pieces of information in his mind during his drive back to the station. While talking to Bescutti, he had received a text message from the duty officer that Bonavita had arrived and was available. He wondered what Bonavita would offer him and how to find the truth behind it. He doubted there would be much to work with, but their primary purpose was to prove that Bonavita transgressed.

*

Favre fidgeted in the bed, pushing the lunch tray away. He had no appetite. It felt like the sheet was strangling him, holding his body in a vice. The nurse had untangled the sheet and straightened the covers twice already, warning him to quiet down, not to move so much. Yet, he couldn't lie still; but at the same time, he felt he couldn't move. More importantly, he couldn't calm his mind. Impatient to get out of bed, sit in a chair for a change, and walk, added to his irritability. More than anything, he wanted to visit Garcia, speak to his partner, and assure himself that his friend would recover.

Leonard's visit had disturbed him. He felt completely lost and helpless. So many things had happened, and just as many awaited his getting better to stop Olivier and put him behind bars. Alpha's words haunted him. He tried to doze, only visions of Alex kept popping into his mind. He was terribly worried. He saw her gunned down, lying in the street next to the body of the police officer who was supposed to protect her.

Desperation clouded his mind. He shook his head to clear it. Without waiting any longer, he picked up the phone by his bed, and dialled the number which he had memorised. Before the call could be answered, he replaced the receiver. Confusion set in. Was it a good idea? Yes, he had to know if she was okay. He took the phone again and redialled. This time he waited until he heard her clear voice, though, he detected a slight hesitation.

'Alex? Are you well? I'm so worried. Sorry, this is Paul, Paul Favre, the detective who came to see you.'

'Of course, I know who you are! I'm so pleased to hear your voice. I tried to come to the hospital to see you, only Captain Leonard said it would be putting your life in danger.'

'He's right. No matter how much I would like to see you, it would put your life in danger as well. Do you have the protective detail with you? Is there one with you in the flat, or at your front door? Is there a car outside watching your building? You must do exactly what they say, even if you don't like it.' He realised he was rambling, but it was so good to hear her voice. He only wished he could see her, hug her.

'Yes. No. ... Ah yes. Yes. And finally, I am – in response to all your questions. I think that was the order in which you asked them! Calm down, I'm fine, and making sure I stay that way. I'm more worried about you; you sustained terrible injuries.' She returned to his last question. 'Mrs Ginet is giving them grief, questioning everything and treating every officer like her own valet.' She tried to hide her anxiety; he must focus on himself with getting better, not worry about her.

'Yes, I had heard she's giving orders around there.'

'She's standing at the window with binoculars and is convinced there's a man on the corner watching. She complained that he's been there for three days now, and no one has checked up on what he's doing. She insists that they should take it seriously – though I think they don't believe her. I haven't seen him.'

'Could be one of our men watching our men watching you! Don't worry about it. I'll mention it to Captain Leonard.' Personally, his concern mounted. He knew Leonard hadn't placed any other officer on protective duty besides the two in the vehicle and the one guarding Alexandra's apartment.

'Thank you for checking up on me. Everything is fine here. Let me know when I can come to visit you in hospital.' Paul heard a slight hesitation in her voice, but she didn't say any more.

'No problem. Keep safe. I hope to speak to you soon again.' He replaced the receiver, realising that he had inadvertently ignored the fact that she wanted to visit him. Or was it on purpose? With his headache gaining strength, his confusion spread – he couldn't be sure of anything.

The only thing he knew for sure was that he had to follow up about the stranger Mrs Ginet said she saw watching the street and building.

He picked up the receiver again. This time he dialled Leonard. A couple of ring tones later, the call went through to voice mail. *'Captain, I spoke to Miss Labelle. She said Mrs Ginet saw a man watching them from the corner. Is it one of ours? Please call me back when you know.'* With a sigh, he finished the call and lay back. He couldn't do more than that for the time being. He turned his gaze towards the door, wondering: who would be the next victim?

No, he couldn't leave it like that. Who knows who else was on the Alpha's payroll! He had to go to her. Through the doorway of his hospital room, he could just see the shoulder of the uniformed officer Leonard had placed on guard duty. Was he there to keep Favre safe? There to guard against intruders or to keep Paul from leaving? He tried to get up. Pain wracked his body, his head throbbed, and vertigo overtook him. He crumpled back onto his injured leg, his arm impeding smooth movement. With a groan, he realised that he wouldn't be going anywhere soon. He had to rely on others. But the person he trusted most lay pinned down with serious injuries a couple of floors above him. Frustrated, he thumped the bed with his good arm. He was truly helpless, fast losing hope of ever being able to keep Alex safe.

Thoughts stampeded through his unsettled mind. If Leonard had men tracking Alpha, he must know that Olivier was staking out her building from the corner. Why didn't he say so? Or was it another officer? He wasn't convinced. Who was watching Alexandra's building? Why had Leonard not told him he suspected something sinister like that? Did it mean the IB officer trailing Alpha was one of Alpha's men and that he is stalling the investigation? How many people did Olivier have spying for him? Who would know?

The nurse came in and reprimanded him for trying to get up. She helped him into the chair beside the bed.

'Detective Favre, please get comfortable. I'll be back in fifteen minutes to get you back into bed.'

'Could you please tell me how my partner is?'

'You mean Detective Garcia? You know I cannot give out information to anyone who is not a family member.'

'But I'm his partner. That's like being married!'

'Yes, I know. And in this case, I have been given permission to keep you up to date. He is making progress, and they are hopeful that he will be leaving ICU soon.'

'When? Will you put him in this room please?'

'Well, yes, that's the idea. So be patient, he'll be with you sooner than you think.'

'I doubt that. I would want him here now, today, this afternoon!'

'Perhaps tomorrow, so keep the faith. That's all I can say.'

Favre leaned back into the chair, trying to calm down. At least the possibility of Garcia being with him soon cheered him slightly. The nurse handed him his medication, which he took without objection. The sooner he got back in form, the sooner he could get out of here to protect Alex.

He wondered how far Captain Leonard got with finding out the identity of the woman Alpha worked for. Which woman would have the audacity and cunning to find a person like Olivier, and hire him for such a cruel job? How many women were known to deal in gems? A Chinese national had been suspected of illegal dealings some years ago. However, those charges were dropped due to insufficient evidence. Perhaps she had started up again. He racked his brain, trying to think of who else could be interested in taking over that specific trade. Could it be Bescutti's mother? She used to deal in gems about thirty or so years ago. If so, the question remains where and how did she find Olivier? If she's been out of the family's business for so many years, surely, she wouldn't have the contacts. There could be a completely new player, one who hasn't been picked up on the radar of any law enforcement agency. Unfortunately, his hands were tied. He had to wait for Leonard to bring him IB's information. Then he could begin analysing all the evidence.

Alpha's voice still reverberated in his mind, with the same sinister effect as when it had cut into his consciousness at the crash site. Chills ran up and down his spine. How could such evil manifest itself in the timbre of a person's voice? Was it acquired or always there? Surely no one was born with such malice. The infuriating thing was that Alpha's voice could also be very soothing and charming – far from menacing. People were lulled into a comfortable state by his voice; he knew how to gain their trust. If not, how could he convince an officer of the law to spy for him? Though, as they now knew, Bonavita wasn't very smart. Fine, they didn't think much of his police work. However, his problem wasn't being sharp; he was too much of an innocent. He trusted too easily, and in this line of work, trust can only go so far. You must use common sense with your instinct.

At that moment, Leonard walked in. Immediately, Favre's attention left ruminating on Olivier's voice to the possible news Leonard might have. He tried to get up from the chair. The effort sent sharp pain through his body, so he sat back and waved Leonard to take a seat on the edge of the bed.

'*Chef,* you're back so soon! I didn't expect to see you until tomorrow, perhaps, the earliest this evening.'

'Good to see you sitting in the chair. Have you been sitting there long? It's much better talking this way, than you on your back. Strangely, you seem more intimidating than when we talk with you lying prostrate in bed!'

'Odd thing to say – I would never have thought that. Anyway, what have you found out? Did Bonavita give any useful information?'

'I let him talk. Nothing useful came out of it. I didn't think he would shed light on the case, yet I encouraged him to keep on meeting with his various informants and report back on a regular basis.' Leonard shifted on the bed, then continued. 'Concerning the possible female gem trader, IB gave me three names: Bernita Coertze, Chao Li, and surprise, surprise - Mama B, better known to us as Mrs Bescutti, the mother of Georgio Bescutti.' The captain then told Favre everything they learnt about each of them so far and the progress investigating each one.

'Who gave you the names? Have you spoken to Georgio Bescutti?

'Arthur Gonzales's partner, Eric Pichat, put the word out for information, and these were the names he received. He knew of them but never worked with any of them. After my visit to their offices, I went directly to Bescutti's offices. He wasn't much help. As far as he was concerned or knew; his mother hasn't been in business for at least twenty years and left the gem trade behind thirty years ago.'

'Do you believe him?'

'Well, I'm going to meet with her tomorrow. There are a couple of things I would like to check before going into the lion's den.'

'Since the nurse helped me to sit in the chair, I've been wondering if Mama B could've been the one. I had no proof, just a hunch. I saw the possibility but discarded it because of her age and because family is very important to her. I don't think she would give the order for another person's child to be killed.'

'I suppose you're right. However, I'm not overlooking her. I have some questions that might shed light on the whole trade - questions which only she could answer. Though, I got the feeling that Georgio avoided his mother as much as possible, if that's anything to go by. Not exactly being afraid of her, though definitely treading lightly where she is concerned.'

'I hope she talks to you. What's your feeling about the other two, *chef*?'

'Choa Li sounds a possibility. I know nothing of the other one, Coertze. I'm waiting for IB to get back to me. It could also be that the Yakuza has a woman trading, which we don't know of.'

'I thought of that as well.'

'I'll look into that angle again.'

'Sir, I need to ask you something. Did you place an officer on the corner of the block to watch the building, as well as protection detail guarding Miss Labelle?'

'No, why do you ask?'

'Mrs Ginet – you know, the elderly neighbour also under guard – she mentioned seeing a man watching them from the corner. No one seems to have taken her seriously. I'm therefore worried that it's Alpha, which would mean the officer from IB following Olivier could either not be reporting Olivier's true movements; or the man on the corner is another of his minions he had posted there to spy on Alex's movements. Do you trust IB completely?'

'Well, I trust them as much as possible. Don't forget, they are men just like us. If Olivier could find someone amongst our people to work with him, then I can't discard the notion that he couldn't find someone there as well. I have checked them out, yet nothing is infallible.'

'Will you look into it please Sir?'

'Definitely. I wonder why they've not taken the sighting seriously?'

'Perhaps because it came from Mrs Ginet and not Miss Labelle. Apparently, she nags them constantly and treats them like her personal errand boys.'

'How do you know all this? Did you speak to Miss Labelle?'

'Yes, I couldn't suppress the worry about her safety, and had to speak to her personally. She told me what was happening, assuring me she was well-guarded, and felt safe. I told her I'd mention it to you.'

'Good. I'll find out as soon as I get out of here. I'll pop upstairs to see Garcia and get the latest on the girl, I won't stay long, because this is very important. In fact, I'll phone as soon as I get into my car.'

'Could you come back here again to tell me how my partner is getting on?'

'Of course, see you in a bit.' With those words, Leonard left.

*

Antonio stood outside the Intensive Care Unit, holding a card and flowers. His mother didn't know that he had planned to deliver the flowers personally. She had given him the money for the flowers, and he told her he would like to choose which flowers himself. Without argument, she accepted his reasoning – she was like that. The importance of a personal touch always counted in her eyes.

He looked through the glass, wanting to press the button for the doors to swing open. But he couldn't find the courage – he was both scared and excited at the same time. His hand reached out, then he withdrew it again.

Down the passage, he saw two men talking. One looked like he could be Cynthia's father - short, with an olive completion and dark hair. The other looked Swiss, tallish, and fair, and older. From an alcove, a nurse appeared, walked towards him. The doors opened, and she stepped out, asking if he needed help.

'I would like to see Cynthia Gonzales. These are for her.'

'Only family allowed. What's your name? I'll tell them you came to wish her well, unfortunately, flowers aren't allowed in the ICU. You could leave them with me, and I'll find a good home for them.'

'I have a card also. Oh, I'm Antonio, a friend.'

'That I can take to her. I'll put it next to her bed.

'How is she?'

'Look, you know I cannot give out information except to family. I'm sorry. You'll have to ask her parents.'

'Oh, I've never spoken to her parents. Couldn't you ask them if it would be possible for me to visit?'

'I'll tell them. She's not awake yet. It'll be best if you contact them directly.'

'Oh, okay then. Thank you.' He craned his neck to look over her shoulder towards the two men still in conversation further down the corridor. He turned. With a tentative move, he took a few steps towards the elevator, looked back, then left, determined to try again another day.

*

Garcia was half-sitting up in bed when his superior arrived. The tubes had diminished; only an IV, heart monitor wires, and oxygen remained. Leonard felt such relief that, for the first time ever, he greeted one of his men with warmth and a chuckle. Startled, Garcia straightened his back as much as possible and extended a hand in greeting.

'Is this what I think it means? You are making better progress than initially thought? Besides the remnants of bruises, which are now beginning to show their age, giving you a technicolour look, you definitely seem to be on the mend.'

'Oh, that's for sure, sir. Doc said that I could be joining Favre in his room as from tomorrow. They all think I'm a marvel and have earned the admiration of every staff member. I can't wait to chew the fat with my old friend. I hear you have some news.'

'Who told you that?'

'Maria visited Paul. You know women, they are inherently curious. She had to know what was going on. He shared what he knew, and she told me.'

'Oh, good, I see you're getting your sense of humour back. However, there's much more. Let me tell you what we know so far.' Leonard laid everything out, finished by telling Garcia to rest until the next day, when he'd visit both the detectives together.

'So, we're getting somewhere.'

'Yes, and we'll keep on until we have every single one involved under lock and key.' With a wave he left an excited, though, exhausted José to get the latest on Cynthia Gonzales.

A few minutes later, he stood at the door of the young woman's room, watching her parents as before, seated on both sides of the bed in prayer. Their daughter lay in the same position as he had seen her before. He could see no improvement. She was still intubated and attached to all necessary wires and tubes keeping her alive. Yet, he hoped for the parents' sake that the situation would change soon.

It took only a few moments for Arthur Gonzales to realise that Leonard stood watching them. Arthur got up, greeted the captain quietly, leading him away towards the small waiting area.

'What is the prognosis?'

'Doctor Stein said she needed to be kept under an induced coma for another day before they'll be able to say if she'll come out of it well or with permanent brain damage. It's a great worry. Nevertheless, we are hopeful our Cynthia will come back to us as she was before. It is what we pray for.'

'My thoughts are with you. I have heard she's an intelligent young girl who is studying law.'

'Yes, that's what she wanted to be since a child – arguing is her greatest asset.'

'Let us hope she becomes a great lawyer. Now, I wanted to let you know what your partner, Eric Pichat, told me and get your opinion. Do you think you could spare a moment to help us? I don't want to keep you from your family.'

'Let us get on with it. The sooner we finish our conversation, the sooner I can get back to my daughter's bedside.'

'Good.' Leonard didn't waste time and told him everything, including how they wished to proceed. 'Could you give me your opinion on what I just told you?'

'I've had dealings with Bertina Coertze before I came to Switzerland. She was in fact, the person who encouraged me to expand my business to Europe while being based in Geneva. I doubt very much that she would have anything to do with this situation.'

'Okay, that rules out Coertze. What do you know about Chao Li?'

'I've heard the name and some rumours, nothing good. They say she's the epitome of the supposed Chinese talent for cruelty when one crosses her. Other than that, I've never had personal dealings with her and cannot give you an opinion.'

'That leaves the third woman, known as Mama B – Georgio Bescutti's mother. What do you know about her?'

'Even in Colombia, we've heard of her. Not recently, mind you. However, the stories circulating about her in the trade, were terrifying. When I took over the business from my uncle, they told me she was already retired. I therefore cannot tell you anything about her. She must be ancient by now. How old is she, by the way?'

'Don't know exactly, but definitely in her eighties.'

'Do you think one of these women could have orchestrated all this?'

He waved towards his daughter.

'Well, as you know the information received was that a woman ordered the hit.'

'I'm sorry. I keep on forgetting what had happened before. I'm very worried and frustrated with the whole situation.'

'Understandable. So far, I don't really know which one. I'm not dismissing anyone or anything. They all look guilty. For the time being, I cannot pin it on anyone. We need more time. There might even be another person of whom we know nothing about. One thing is certain, we are not letting this go, and will follow any, and all leads to the end. Please be assured of that.'

'I trust you will. To think that I might be the cause of my daughter fighting for her life is unacceptable.' Gonzales ran his hand through his hair. 'Well, as I mentioned, I doubt if Coertze would be the one.'

'I think you are right. She would have discouraged you from installing here. Well, that leaves two – Li and Bescutti. In any case, I'll keep you informed. And if you hear anything further, please contact me directly.'

'Thank you, I will. Now if you'll excuse me, I must get back to Cynthia and Anna.' They shook hands, and each went their separate ways.

Leonard felt his mobile vibrate. On his way to the exit, he opened his phone. It was a message from Borel requesting him to come to the station as soon as possible. He popped into Favre's room just to say that Garcia would be joining him tomorrow. Further, according to plan, he would visit the two around eleven the next day.

*

At the station the duty officer told him Borel and Pichon waited at Favre's desk, which was where he found the two staring with concentration at the computer screen in front of them.

'Ah chef, regardez ça!' They said in unison.

'Qu'est-ce-que ça?' Leonard came round and looked at the screen over their shoulders. 'What am I looking at?'

'As you know, we followed Olivier from the area where the shooting took place, noting where he went. We've picked up him on CCTV footage at two different addresses he visited regularly – besides Paquis, where we assumed he looked for prostitutes. The first, as we mentioned before, seems to be his domicile. We checked that out as per the report we forwarded to you: the apartment which he sub-lets from a woman. The second one he recently only went to twice. However, the interesting fact is the building at that address, belongs to the Bescutti family.'

'What? Really, this is interesting. Who lives there? Does any of the Besuttis have a domicile in that building?'

'From the Canton's *Control des Habitants* office, the Penthouse is occupied by the elderly mother of Georgio Bescutti. There is another registered at that address. It is the daughter of Fernando, Georgio's brother, Claudia Bescutti.'

'Olivier went there twice recently, you say?'

'Yes. We went back roughly four weeks before the shooting. We found he visited that address at least three times before, making a total of five visits.'

'Anyone else he might have called on besides Bescutti family members?' Leonard's mind raced. The recent visits didn't coincide with the dates. However, it could conceivably be when Alpha reported on his progress and then, the last time, to receive payment, because that visit fell on the day after the girl's stabbing.

'It could be nothing. Nevertheless, we thought it might be important.'

'Good work, you two! This is very good news. We might just have our link.'

'Link, sir? What do you mean?' Borel couldn't keep his curiosity at bay.

'Well, you know, we wanted to know where he went and who he saw. This means we can finally lay out his movements exactly. Oh, I haven't told you about a report I received from the hospital which Head Office is dealing with.'

'On what, Sir?'

'Three prostitutes were gravely injured by one of their customers. It turns out their description of the John corresponds with the Interpol and Europol photos, as well as the person we're tracking on the CCTV footage. In fact, you captured him on camera in Paquis on the relevant dates. The point of interest here is the abuse coincides with events we think we can attribute to Olivier.' He explained his reasoning.

'Unbelievable! Sir, it must be him. I'm convinced it's him! We've never had any violence like that reported in the past, but I'll check – just to make sure we haven't received a similar report before.' Without waiting, Pichon went over to Garcia's computer and fired it up to check on old cases.

'Of course, it took some persuading for the prostitutes to report the various incidents. Yet they do talk amongst themselves, and perhaps these three could find out if others had a similar experience. Although, when they were interviewed, all three said they had never come across any of their colleagues who complained or mentioned that type of injury. Apparently, they warn each other about dangerous clients.' Leonard pulled out a chair and sat down. He felt exhausted. Running from place to place and keeping the investigation under wraps, has taken its toll. He wanted to bring them up to date with every piece of information he had so far received. Except, for the time being he couldn't risk it.

'Keep looking. So far, at best, we only have circumstantial evidence – nothing that would stand up in court for a conviction,' Leonard continued. His mind raced. The fact that Olivier visited the Bescutti building at various times gave him a reason to go back to Georgio. By the sound of things, he would need his help to get a meeting with Mama B.

'*Chef,* we have been called to do duty at the Gay Pride parade this weekend. Do we go or should we stay on this? We don't mind checking more footage.' Borel said hopefully.

'I'll advise Head Office that you cannot be spared. Still, I'd like you to keep an eye open for him at the parade. It would be just like him to rub our noses in it by being out in the open so conspicuously. I'll get the authority for you to watch the security cameras live. That way, if he's there, you could immediately notify the foot patrol, and we could grab him on GBH. That's all we have at present.'

'Great idea.' With renewed enthusiasm, the two officers looked at each other.

'Okay, I've a few appointments. Carry on. Let me know if you come up with something and if constructive.' Without another word, he turned and left, pulling out his phone. He spoke for a few seconds. Georgio had agreed to a meeting and expected him.

On the drive to the WTC, he tried to formulate the way to approach Bescutti. The possibility that the woman orchestrating the violence could be the mother of the man he intended to ask for help was going to be tricky.

He parked the car and went up to Bescutti's offices. The receptionist welcomed him with a cheery smile, saying her boss was waiting and that she'd bring in coffee directly.

Déjà vu, the captain thought as he found Georgio again standing at the window, his reflection clear in the glass. At the sound of the door closing behind Leonard, Georgio turned, greeted the captain, and waved him to a chair.

'There must be something serious if I have a visit from you twice in one day.' Bescutti settled behind his desk, straightening his jacket.

'Well, I didn't want to waste any time, and something came up that I would like your help with.' Leonard watched Georgio carefully.

'Anything. Just name it. I feel this has all gone on long enough without a conclusion.'

'Yes, on that I agree. It is rather a sensitive matter. You know from our previous discussions that we have a suspect under surveillance.'

'Yes, you told me. Did something else happen?'

'No, it's not that. We've been following him on CCTV footage all over the city. So far, we have pinpointed the places he frequents and his domicile. The disturbing thing which I'd like your help with is one address which he visited various times. We have no explanation on why he went there.' Leonard shifted in the chair, leaning forward, elbows on his knees, with hands clasped between them.

'So how can I help if you don't even know?'

'The address in question is a building owned by your family, and according to the *Control des Habitants,* your mother and niece occupy the penthouse.'

'Oh, you mean the building on Quai Gustave Ador, just off Rive, near the Jardin Anglais? Yes, my mother lives there. That building has been in our family for many decades - in fact more than fifty years.'

'That's the one. Well, the suspect, Olivier, visited someone in that building at least five times over the last six weeks.'

'Are you sure? That's the building he called on?'

'Oh yes, no doubt about it. Do you think you could arrange a meeting with your mother? I need to ask her a few questions, and considering her age, I would appreciate it if you could be there when I do.'

'As I've said before, I try to avoid contact with my mother. Well, fine, I'll do this only to get it all over with. Did you find something which points towards her? Do you now think she is involved? I mean, she is a very difficult woman and was in the trade before. I thought about it since you left earlier and ran through various scenarios, but I can't believe that she could be behind this whole story.'

'My first question to her would be who else lives in the building. That would be the only way to rule out possible suspects.'

'I'm not sure she'll know.'

'Who manages the building? We would need a list of all the occupants with their coordinates. That would include business or commercial entities as well. We need to pin down the person or persons he met with.'

'I'm sorry, I don't have those details. We'll have to ask my mother. Okay, I'll arrange a time to see her which would suit everyone. When will you be available, Captain?'

'You give me a time, and I'll make myself available.'

'Fine, let me call her.' Georgio picked up the phone, dialled, and after a few seconds greeted the person, asking to speak to his mother. To Leonard he said: 'That was Claudia who answered, she's calling my mother.'

'Bonjour Mama, c'est moi Georgio. Comment allez-vous ?'... Bien, merci, tout va bien.' He continued, *'I would like to pop around to see you. Do you have a moment to spend with your son? ... Tomorrow morning for coffee would be perfect. Shall I come by at eleven? ... Perfect, I look forward to seeing you, Mother. Goodbye and have a good evening.'* He turned to Leonard.

'So, it's set for tomorrow morning at eleven. Would that suit you?'

'No problem at all.'

'Where shall we meet?' Bescutti asked.

'I'll wait for you in front of the building. I won't keep you any longer – until tomorrow morning.' On that note, Leonard left.

He looked forward to spending one evening in the uncomplicated and calming company of his wife. Further, he couldn't wait to take a long shower and wash off the hospital smell which, after so many days of visits, seemed to have stuck to the surface of his skin, and permeated wherever he went. Also, one evening without having to go through loads of reports or do paperwork would not go amiss. He sighed: respite for at least one night.

*

Alpha sat at the counter. He never found barstools comfortable; except he told Bonavita he would be waiting there. He saw a corner booth open,

342

hoping it would stay that way until he needed it. Keeping one eye on the entrance, Alpha followed the rivulets in the condensation on the side of the glass. The cold beer tasted good, and he wondered how many beers he would have to buy his informant to get what he wanted.

At that moment, a smiling Bonavita bounced into the bar, waving a greeting. Immediately, Alpha picked up his beer and waved to the officer to join him as he moved to the corner. He beckoned the barman to bring another beer over to the booth. Alpha wondered how long he would have to put up with this idiot.

They settled in, and he supported Bonavita's small talk which was to insist on discussing the weather – the violent storms with lightning and thunder which made people jump, and the heatwave. The officer hoped that the Gay Pride parade over the weekend would be drenched. For Alpha, it felt like an age until the beer arrived. Pleased, Olivier took the opportunity to interrupt the officer and asked what had been happening on the case.

'Oh, nothing much. As I said, they asked me to gather information. It's a step-up for me. They've never asked me to do anything like this.'

'Congratulations, they're finally seeing your worth.' Alpha choked. His comment stuck in his throat like a bone. As a disguise, he cleared his throat. How could this man be an officer of the Law? How did he ever pass the academy? Well, Alpha reminded himself, it will all be over soon.

'Do you have many contacts on the street?' Another thing Alpha thought: he must sound interested.

'Not really. I mean, not yet. I'm trying to cultivate some. A person has to start somewhere.' Bonavita said, grinning from ear to ear.

'Good, you have the right attitude. So, what have you found out so far?' The officer's enthusiasm sickened Olivier, like a puppy eager to please.

'Well, no one really knows anything for certain, though someone said they saw the person who did the shooting at Navigation. The case seemed to have taken on a life of its own with the explosion at the station, where Detective Garcia got hurt, and then the fire at his partner, Detective Favre's, flat.'

'What do they say about this latest accident which injured both? And, by the way, how are they doing?'

'First off, not many have mentioned that accident – they seem to think it's not related and well, both are making progress. Still serious, but I hear that Garcia will be moved out of ICU tomorrow.'

'That's good news, not so?'

'Well, yes. However, no one can tell me when they'll be back at work, if ever. Their injuries seem to be grave – perhaps even putting an end to their careers. I hope not, they are really good at what they do, and would be missed.'

'It sounds as if you admire them, even hero-worshiping them!' Alpha laughed to deflect any chance of Bonavita uncovering his disdain and real motivation.

'No, nothing like that. They're just good at "detecting" and should be respected for that.'

'I get you. This is going to make a good story.'

'Do you think you have enough, or should I keep on giving you details?' Bonavita took a mouthful of beer, then, remembering something, nearly slammed down his glass in his eagerness. 'Hey, did you hear about the stabbing of a young girl? It would be an interesting bit for the book, don't you think?'

'Oh, I think I read something about it. Is it one of your cases? She died?'

'City is handling it. Apparently, she's fighting for her life at the Cantonal Hospital.'

'So, she didn't die? From the newspaper article, it sounded as if she died on the spot.' Olivier hid his disappointment.

'No, they managed to get her to hospital, and she's been operated on. Do you think it would be interesting to get more information on that as well for you?'

'The more I know, the more interesting the book will turn out to be. Just think, you'll be instrumental in getting a bestseller on the shelves. To use authentic material eludes most writers, so I'm very appreciative. Make no mistake, you will be mentioned in the book, you know, in the acknowledgements for the invaluable support and information you supplied, making the book possible.'

Alpha wanted Bonavita gone – spending another minute in his company took all the patience he could muster. Moreover, the man was boring. Though, he had to keep him on retainer to get the information he wanted. So, he told himself to ignore the irritation, concentrate on the possibilities which would ensure that he walked about free of any accusations or convictions, and get on with trading. In other words, leave him to get rich beyond all and any expectations.

'Let's have another drink, then you can tell me all about the reasons which made you join the police force.'

'Great, I'll get it.'

'No, the drinks are on me. Don't forget you're giving me valuable insight into the mind and workings of Law Enforcement.' Olivier got up and went to the bar. It took only a few minutes for him to return with two more pints.

'Thanks, Mate. This is great, spending time with an author, really gives me the inspiration to read more. My wife's nose is always in a book. I've never really taken to it. But my experience with you is tempting me to change my habits.'

'My pleasure. Let's enjoy the time we have to spend together.'

'*Salut!*' Bonavita lifted his glass to touch that of Olivier.

'Yes, thank you. Good cheer and long life to you, my friend.' Alpha felt like puking. He had other plans for this good fellow. Perhaps it's time to plan how he would amuse himself with this one. He found it amusing how easy it was to recruit members of the so-called law enforcement in this city, not with money, but with flattery. They fell for it every time! He chuckled silently.

First, he had to make sure that the Boss didn't find out the target was still alive. She'll be spitting with fury. Somehow, he had to get into the girl's room to finish her off as soon as possible. He could inject her with an empty syringe, creating a bubble in her bloodstream – undetectable but certainly fatal, and of course, the easiest.

When that's done, he'll get back to watching Miss Labelle's movements. He only needed a moment to get near the delectable Miss. That was unfinished business which has given him an itch he needed to scratch as soon as possible.

CHAPTER TWENTY

Leonard accepted the cup of coffee from his wife. Refreshed from the first good night's rest since the explosion at the station, he appreciated her attention and smiled up at her. He wondered what he would do without this good woman by his side. Her support for his work and unpredictable hours had never wavered. Even when he missed so much of the children's upbringing, she never complained. In fact, she was the one responsible for them turning out to be valuable members of humanity.

He finished his coffee and croissant, got up, and gave his wife a peck goodbye, promising to be back for dinner. He wanted to stop at the station to find out how far Borel and Pichon had got. With their earlier collection of social media videos, they now had access to a much wider field to check. He wondered if they had managed to track Olivier to any other addresses. Also, if they had picked up the IB tail he arranged. If they did, it meant Olivier could be aware of it as well. On the other hand, it would mean that they were doing an excellent job in analysing the different videos and CCTV footage. No matter what they found, he needed a clear head – he shouldn't get stuck in the quagmire of it all.

The meeting scheduled for later needed careful planning. The last thing he wanted was to show his hand, as it would derail the investigation if Bescutti's mother suspected that she was being looked at as a person of interest. Known as a real battle-axe, his curiosity about what she would look or be like, couldn't be repressed. The only thing he knew about her was that she came from the traditional Mafia family organisation and kept their rules and conditions alive within her own family. She had ruled with an iron fist while her husband was alive and took over after his death, where she became even more ruthless. Since her handing over to her sons – or as they described it – her retirement, nothing has come to light about her activities. According to Georgio, this happened about fifteen years ago. However, rumours he should not overlook, were her intelligence and her uncanny ability to sum up a person. It made him apprehensive and, deep down, anxious about the meeting.

He found Pichon and Borel, and asked without preamble, how far they had gotten with scrutinising the footage of various cameras. Both jumped up, greeted him with an air of expectation. Though the disappointment on Leonard's face when they told him that they had found nothing new, made them apologise profusely. The captain waved it off.

'Don't let this discourage you. Keep going, I'm sure we'll get him soon.' He turned to leave, looked back. 'I've arranged for you both to be there watching the security surveillance live during Gay Pride – so enjoy.' Their goodbyes fell on deaf ears as he disappeared from the bullpen for the meeting with Bescutti.

He left the car in a loading zone near the Jardin Anglais, with the sign 'POLICE' clearly visible. As he turned the corner into Quai Gustave Ador, he saw Georgio already waiting for him in front of the building's entrance, the residence of the feared Mama B. They shook hands in greeting.

Without another word, they entered and took the lift to the penthouse. The doors slid sideways with a quiet swish, opening directly into the entrance hall, decorated with a large antique mirror, and an arrangement of a variety of fresh flowers in a large Chinese vase. The flowers' fragrance softened the otherwise austere ambiance. From there, an arched opening led into the living room.

The high ceilings gave a feeling of sorely needed space. The solid Italian furniture, heavy, deep-red brocade curtains framing the large windows, and the plush old-rose padded sofas gobbled up every inch of breathable air. The oriental carpets and rugs dampened the sound in the room. However, it was the portraits and paintings – encased in ornately carved gilt frames – adorning the walls that left virtually no empty space to hang another item, which overpowered the place. No specific colour dominated the room, though whatever was there flowed into the other, making ebony prevalent. Irrespective of how much light flowed into the space, it remained sombre and oppressive.

Leonard always envied those who could afford to live at this or any address on the Quai. The impressive constructions had housed, and still housed, royalty and aristocracy from every corner of the world. These were palaces in the centre of town. It crossed Leonard's mind that in any other ambiance, the Bescutti's apartment would be rich and varied, resembling status with a welcoming warmth. But here it turned into an overbearing and dictatorial atmosphere – no arguments were accepted. He suspected it might resemble Mama B's character.

Georgio gave Leonard a look which said, 'Now you see why I haven't been here in years.' With a slight shake of his head, he led Leonard further into the apartment to a smaller reception room where Mrs Bescutti sat ramrod straight in an armchair. Superiority emanated from her. She was thin and bony, however, all you were aware of was her iron will.

'*Bonjour, Mère, comment ça va?*' He bent over giving her a kiss on the cheek.

'*Mon fils, bonjour – fatiguée, mais bien, merci, et toi ?*' Her upturned face looked impassive. Whatever his reply would have been didn't really interest her. When Georgio introduced Leonard, she shook his hand, giving him a look which confirmed what he always imagined as "the evil eye."

'Mother, this is just a courtesy visit by Captain Leonard. He has a problem, and would like your opinion, and perhaps advice on who to approach.' The furtive look he threw towards Leonard clearly stated: 'Go with me here.'

'*Madame Bescutti,* please excuse my ignorance. As your son said, I really do need your help and would appreciate whatever you can tell me.'

'I don't know how I could help the police. I don't waste time with police matters, as you can see, I'm not young anymore. Time is running out for me.' She looked at her son, 'and what do you have to do with the police? Are you mixed up in something?'

'Please, Mother. To answer your question: no, I'm not in trouble. We won't be long, but it's important.'

'So, what is this unsolvable problem of yours?' She clenched her jaw and looked out the window. She obviously found her visitors irrelevant.

'With respect, Mrs Bescutti, years ago you were in the emerald trade, and I wondered if you could educate me in who was, and could still be, in this market.'

'Why do you want to know this?' She stared at Leonard, who felt her eyes boring into him. He had never felt this small. The last time the same feeling overtook him, was when his six-grade teacher caught him writing a letter to a girl he was crazy about.

'Well, I cannot discuss the case. However, I can tell you that a shooting took place, which is connected to the emerald trade.'

'You are wasting my time. Georgio, you should know better than to come to me with this nonsense.' She turned away, dismissing both.

'All we ask is your help by giving us a direction to follow or perhaps a couple of names.' Georgio threw his hands up in surrender.

'Why do you want to know? Are you going into the trade? Is that why you are asking, you want to eliminate the competition with the help of the *gendarmerie*?'

'No Mother, you misunderstand. I only suggested to the captain that you might know more about the trade than I ever would, and you would be the best person to ask. I brought him here in good faith hoping you would steer him in the right direction.'

'Well, I'm not interested. You can go now.' She stared at them when they didn't move, then waved them away. 'I said go. Leave me alone. I've said what I wanted to say.'

'Goodbye, Mother.' He turned away. 'Sorry, Captain. We'd better go. She won't change her mind.' Georgio took him by the arm, leading him towards the lift. Leonard could only mumble a goodbye.

At street level, they paused. 'Well, let's go somewhere and have that coffee we didn't get upstairs to gather our equilibrium.' Georgio sounded more apologetic than Leonard expected.

'Yes, I can do with that. However, I cannot stay long.' The captain didn't want to admit how badly he needed a coffee just then. 'That visit was ominous to say the least. She really didn't take to me, did she? I didn't expect her to ask us to sit down, or offer us a cup of something, but still.'

'Don't take it personally. She likes no one! And since I tried to make the family business legitimate, the rift between us has widened. To say the least, she now tolerates me because I'm blood. I'm her eldest son, which means something traditionally. I suppose that's why I've not been disowned or banished.'

'It must be difficult and frustrating, to say the least.' They stopped at the nearest café and ordered their coffee which they took to an outside table.

'Yes, it is. She tries to block me at every turn, even though she's not in the business any longer. She uses my younger brother to do whatever she feels necessary.'

'Do you think he could be the one pulling the strings on her behalf? Our suspect said the boss was a woman, but I suppose your brother could be acting on her behalf.'

'Anything is possible. However, to come back to our time with her, I agree with you, more was said by her avoiding the issue. I hate to say this, but I do think you should look deeper into her possible involvement in the case. She is my mother, though I'm perfectly conscious of the fact that she always used violence to control her minions, and as I said, she's ruthless, or should I say heartless.'

'Nevertheless, do you really believe she could be that cruel by targeting the child of a competitor? I mean, this is serious business, so think carefully before you reply.' Leonard finished his coffee, and he paused. 'I'll have to leave soon. I want to stop by the hospital and see my two men, but would like to continue our conversation.'

'Oh, I forgot to ask. How are they doing? It was a terrible thing that happened.'

'They're doing better. Favre seems to be out of the woods. We are still hoping for Garcia's full recovery. We'll know more in a few days.'

'You believe it's connected, don't you?'

'Yes, we have proof that it's the same person. He so much as admitted it.'

'What? So why isn't he in custody?'

'The comment was made to Detective Favre at the scene of the accident. Favre was in and out of consciousness when the suspect made the comment. Therefore, he's not a reliable witness as far as the courts go. We need definite proof, not only circumstantial, which is all we have at present.' Leonard got up to leave.

'I wish you well, and good luck with the investigation. Please let me know if I could help any further, and please keep me informed.'

'Will do. We still have to interview the other two women and see what comes from that. It would've been helpful, confirmation in fact, if your mother had given us any names.'

'Yes, I know it was frustrating. I'll keep my ears open.'

'Of course, I am sure I do not have to remind you that our discussions are confidential. Please don't discuss it with anyone.'

'No, I understand. I'll be careful when I speak to my brother.'

'Okay. Well, I must go, let me know what comes up.' Leonard left Georgio Bescutti, feeling his eyes on him as he walked away.

*

Traffic to the HUG was light, because most of the residents had left the city for their annual holiday. The exodus to the South was legendary, with so many Portuguese and Spanish nationals living and working in the Geneva area. On top of that, many Swiss escaped to the South of France, or other sunny Mediterranean destinations. Nevertheless, tourists swelled the pedestrians to the normal body count in the City of Calvin during this period.

Leonard's spirits rose when he neared Favre's room. He could hear that Garcia had joined his partner, and both sounded much better. The captain wasn't sure if their improved state of health was based on physical improvement, or merely the fact that they could be together and converse. He nodded to the officer doing guard duty and stopped before entering to watch the two patients. They looked and acted like an old married couple: comfortable in each other's company, used to bickering and teasing, with complete trust in each other's instincts.

'Good to see the two of you are at it already.'

'*Bonjour, chef!*' The two detectives said in unison, pleased to see him. Favre sat up in bed, though Garcia still lay propped up against the pillows. His attachment to IVs and other medical paraphernalia had reduced drastically.

'Any news? Have you spoken to Bescutti's mother?' Favre couldn't hide his impatience for a progress report.

'I just came from a meeting with him and his mother. In fact, he arranged the meet and took me up to see her. I doubt she would have received me if I requested a meeting on my own. He paved the way.'

'Didn't that restrict you a bit? Obviously, he would've tried to steer the conversation away from the possibility that his mother was Cruella.' Garcia, who had not met Bescutti, felt there was too much history in that family to blindly presume Georgio's impartiality.

'Cruella?' Leonard looked from one to the other.

'A character in a film: a cruel woman who murders puppies,' Garcia explained.

'Oh, well. Yes, I suppose the name would fit. Georgio sided with me. His mother as much as disowned him when he began to legitimise the family business. I've never seen such cold maternal instincts. The surroundings didn't welcome us either. She never even asked us to sit down.'

'Did you learn something to help us? Is she the one behind it all?' Favre asked.

'We learnt absolutely nothing. However, we both felt there was more to her refusal to help in any way. He is going to discreetly find out if his brother knows something – incidentally, his daughter lives with Mrs Bescutti.'

'Georgio's niece? Did you meet her?' Garcia's curiosity could not be tempered.

'No, she was nowhere to be seen. Although I had a feeling someone else moved around in another part of the enormous penthouse. I trod very carefully. I only asked the mother to delve into her long experience and help us with possible names to approach in connection with the emerald trade, or her opinion on how to go about finding out. Neither Georgio nor I mentioned dubious or illegal trade.'

'I take it she didn't fall for your flattery,' Garcia said. He pushed the oxygen mask off his face.

'You can say that again. Her attitude could be described as openly hostile. I'm sure she gave me the evil eye at one point. Cruella, you say? I think you've labelled her correctly. But – and it is a big BUT – we have no proof that it's her.'

'So, what you're saying is that we must rely on Georgio to get us the intel on his mother. Are you sure we can trust this pigeon?' Garcia shook his head incredulously and took a deep breath of oxygen from the mask. 'It's a known fact that the actual culprit would involve himself with the investigation, and sometimes the investigators, just to find out how far they have gotten in solving the case.'

'I hear what you are saying, except in this case, I feel we can trust him. We had coffee afterwards and spoke for a while. My feeling is that he's sincere. He wants to clean up the family business and she's standing in his way, or as he put it: so far, she had blocked him wherever she could. He doesn't agree with her methods at all, and definitely not the way she uses violence to control people.'

'When I met him, he seemed helpful, though a little reticent. Perhaps that was only because he wasn't sure how the shooting of the young man affected his own son, whom he wanted to protect as far as possible. I got the impression that he was devastated to find out that we knew about Antonio. He wanted to know how we found out. I explained about researching Antonio and found Manuela. By tracking the name Vicario, we came across the marriage certificate. I also told him the rest were assumptions, which brought us to the truth. I'm not sure he knows that his mother had uncovered his secret.' Favre tended to agree with Leonard concerning Georgio.

'He never brought up his son, and I never mentioned him either. If you didn't tell him, I doubt he's aware she knows about Antonio.' Leonard finally pulled up a chair between the two beds and sat down. 'How do you know that his mother knew?'

'When we interviewed Gonzales, he admitted they had the information already but never saw an opportunity to use it. He asked his partner how they found out – he seems to be the person with his ear to the ground where these grey-area jewels are concerned. Apparently, when they researched the European and International emerald trade, there were rumours, yet nothing concrete. They shelved the information.'

'Yes, I read your report. I've been in contact with Eric Pichat. He's reaching out to his informants to find out what they know about Mama B, Chao Li, and Bertina Coertze. So far, he has given me little information which could help us nail this Olivier. Nothing that was worth much. We're slowly getting there with the help of Georgio Bescutti, Arthur Gonzales, and his partner.'

'Favre told me his girl, Cynthia, was stabbed and is fighting for her life a couple of doors from where I was in ICU.'

'Yes, that's correct. I didn't want to burden you with the news until you were better. We think it was Alpha, Olivier, who stabbed her – trying to finish his mandate. Before your paranoia kicks in again, I only want to add that all three of these men are not under suspicion and are doing their utmost to help get our suspect behind bars, especially after he stabbed the girl. None of them have any mercy for Olivier. Furthermore, we need the woman behind it all. And for that, we can use their help. As we have no confirmation of who in the precinct is collaborating with the suspect, I am limiting all contact to only Borel and Pichon. I'm also being careful with IB. So, you can see these three are our only means of getting real help. I also feel they will not talk out of turn, given the sensitive aspect of the case.'

'Nothing further from Bonavita?' Garcia asked.

'Not yet, though I think things will soon heat up. We expect Alpha to make an appearance at the Gay Pride parade tomorrow. Borel and Pichon will be watching the live security feeds and alert the foot patrol to detain

Alpha on GBH.'

'Oh yes, Favre told me about that. I suppose it would be a start and give us some time to get to the bottom of everything else.'

'One thing is for sure; we'll be able to legally take his fingerprints and DNA to compare with what we've gathered so far. That'll give us the concrete proof we need to put him away for good.' Leonard got up. 'I'm going up to see the Gonzales family, hope the girl's doing better.'

'Please let us know if she has made progress?' Favre asked.

'WHAT DO WE HAVE HERE?' The charge nurse – who spoke in capital letters – on duty when Garcia was brought in the first time stomped into the ward. 'YOU HAVE BEEN HERE BEFORE AND SHOULD KNOW THE RULES. YOU HAVE TO LEAVE NOW. VISITING HOURS HAVE NOT YET BEGUN.' Leonard's body visibly shrank, and he apologised profusely. Apparently, after a week off, this nurse came back on duty. Leonard sheepishly looked at his men, who in turn apologised, trying to explain that it was a police matter. However, she would have nothing of it. With arms akimbo, she stood waiting for the captain to leave.

'When something new comes up, I'll let you know.' He turned towards the door, looked nervously in the direction of the nurse, then hesitated, decided he would take a chance. He turned back. 'Look, this is your case, therefore the two of you had better get well soon; we need to close this investigation. I don't want to do it without you.'

'Au revoir, chef,' Favre said. Garcia waved him out as he put the oxygen mask back on his face. With the charge nurse watching over them, both detectives felt rapped over the knuckles with nothing further to say.

*

Leonard saw Arthur Gonzales pacing the floor outside his daughter's room and approached with apprehension. He also noticed that the uniformed officer guarding the door was nowhere to be seen.

'Are you all right? Did your daughter take a turn for the worse? What's happening?'

'No, not for the worse. We really don't know what to do. She's not improving, and the doctors want to operate again.'

'What do they think? Why is it necessary to operate?'

'They repaired her spleen when she was brought in after the stabbing.

354

She was so lucky that the knife only made a very shallow cut in her heart muscle, which they repaired easily, except the spleen took the brunt of it. Now they say it is imperative to remove it completely. My wife is beside herself.'

'Why do they want to do that?'

'They say she's bleeding internally again. Doctor Stein and his team believe it's the only way to save her life. They assured us that she could have a normal life without a spleen. My wife is worried that it might not be true.' He shook his head in anguish. 'The medically induced coma was supposed to give her body the opportunity to heal, only it seems not to have worked. I don't like all the sedatives and drugs they have already given her, and now it will be another anaesthetic. Where will it end? How will her little body cope?'

'Have you spoken to your family doctor? I'm sure he will be able to give an opinion which could put your mind at rest. At least he knows your daughter and her medical history.'

'That is a good idea. Thank you, Captain. He'll most probably be able to calm and reassure my wife of the possibility of life without a spleen. I'll call him immediately. His surgery is just across the road.'

'Good. I hope it'll give her peace of mind. Look, I won't keep you. I only came by to tell you that we've begun to trace the three women who are rumoured to be involved in the trade of gemstones. Your partner has been helpful. We'll keep on working with him and keep you informed.'

'Thank you, Captain.'

'Please give my best to your wife. I'm thinking of your whole family, praying for your daughter's recovery.'

He left for the nurses' station to find out where the officer had got to, and if he had given them a reason for his absence from guarding the young girl. No one had seen or heard from him. The captain immediately pulled out his phone, texted IB to find out if the officer was recalled or if they had counteracted his instruction.

Without delay, he arranged for another uniformed policeman to be stationed to guard the girl and decided to wait until he arrived. The captain had a deep-seated fear that if Alpha heard that Cynthia was still alive, he would not rest until he rectified the situation in his favour. Could Olivier have gotten to this officer as well? He wondered if they would be able to stop Alpha's path of terror in time.

Once the replacement guard arrived, Leonard opted to go home for lunch, giving him the opportunity to contact IB in the privacy of his home study. He also needed the latest on their progress without anyone listening in on the conversation. True, they were closing in on Alpha. However, he personally couldn't wait to detain Alpha before he could afflict any more injuries to his officers or any civilian.

*

At that moment, Alpha would never know to what extent he disturbed Leonard's peace of mind. His own mind, occupied with how to surreptitiously reach the ICU, kept every other thought at bay. Singular in his aim to finalise his mandate from the Boss before she became aware of it, he rushed through the hospital foyer. Frustrated with himself for not concluding the job successfully at the time, he now wanted it over quickly. He needed to get back to concentrate on Miss Labelle. Yes, he could kick himself. He had to leave his post for this! He only hoped that he had not missed his only opportunity to grab the detective's little whore and take her to his place. It would really rile up that twanker Favre. Oh, how he now wished he had done a better job with them as well. How much rosier would life be if they both had kicked the bucket in that accident? However, that wasn't his plan at the time.

Well, no time for remorse and asking: "what if?" One step at a time. Now, the next step was that spoilt brat. He had managed to get rid of her watchdog. The ICU floor lay before him as he stepped out of the lift with no one in sight; he pressed the button to open the security doors. With a hiss and sigh, the doors allowed him in. He passed a supply room and slipped in, rummaged through the shelves, pulling down everything he needed.

Yes, step by step. Now, the next would be to get into her room. Obviously, her parents would be hanging around. Still, he was sure he could get past them dressed in scrubs. A medical person with a syringe would not seem out of place. He'd pretend to check her chart first, then quietly ask the parents to move aside for him to do his work. As they stepped away, he would, with his back to them, inject directly into the spot where the IV's needle goes into her hand.

Ready, he slowly opened the supply room door and peered out, first right, then left. No one could be seen in the corridor, which he entered quickly, closing the door behind him. As he rounded the corner into the hallway in front of the section where the girl's and other ICU wards were, he caught sight of Leonard, the captain who Bonavita had told him was overseeing the case. He had to hand it to that idiot old Bonnie, as he called him. The description he had given was spot on – he would have recognised the captain anywhere.

He swore under his breath, he had not planned on this and stepped back out of sight. Luckily, the captain was texting, concentrating on his phone. Alpha turned back, nonchalantly walked back towards the elevators, saw the toilets, and decided to wait in there until the coast was clear.

Ten minutes had passed before he poked his head out into the corridor again. The coast was more-or-less clear. He saw Leonard step away to speak to a uniformed officer a bit further down from the girl's room, obviously a replacement. Leonard must have been on his way out. He saw his chance and slipped into the room. Casually, he picked up the chart. Both parents looked up enquiringly at him. His request for them to please give him space to work drew nods from both. The mother didn't want to let go of her daughter's hand, whispered some words of reassurance to the girl and reluctantly let go.

Alpha stepped forward towards the side of the bed. At that moment, two doctors, one in a white coat, the other in civilian clothes, with two nurses, sailed into the room, talking non-stop, basically took over the room. Alpha was forced back, handed over the chart without a word, and took his leave. He shoved past the officer without being recognised. That, he felt was the only good thing about this whole effort. Damn, this is not good! He had it all in hand: so near to finish it all off.

Now forced to come back later, his frustration turned into fury. With cold rage, he stomped back to the supply room where he had stuffed his clothes in a box. He pulled the scrubs off his body and changed, ready to leave and reclaim his lookout spot from where he could watch when, and how he could get his hands on Miss Labelle. He still wanted to go to the Gay Pride Parade, but his plans had all gone awry. Oh, well, that was only for amusement.

'Wait. Don't waste your time worrying about missing this opportunity. Think of what you can accomplish when you get your hands on Labelle.' His mind raced with anticipation. 'The little bitch in hospital can wait – she's not going anywhere!' He caught himself muttering, which he had never done before. This incident had derailed his plan, furthermore it vexed him. It made him talk to himself! It had to stop. Uncharacteristically, he had lost his temper during very calm conditions. He continued to berate himself all the way to the spot. He knew he shouldn't act until he felt calmer, before his next step.

Alpha took his place where he could see the entrance to the building, and still unseen by the police in the front of it. He leaned against the wall, weight on his left leg, his right bent and hooked behind his left ankle. He felt the knife in his pocket; ran his fingers across the handle, and felt the button which would release the blade. How great that felt, smooth, sedate, and at the same time, ready for action.

Hidden in the shadows, waiting. Already calmer, just the feel of the instrument relaxed him. Further satisfaction came from the pressure of his gun in his lower back. He visualised the sheen of the metal, remembering how he had caressed that last prostitute's body with the barrel. Oh, even now the force emanating from it had the power to give him an erection. He remembered how she squirmed with anticipation. And when he used the knife and gun together, one in each hand, her passion knew no bounds. He smiled. The memory, and the feel of both instruments, gave him instant gratification. He looked forward to applying the same method on Miss Labelle, to bring her to her highest sexual pleasure. The fantasy running through his nervous system increased his heartbeat, heightening his circulation.

It nearly made him miss his target, as he only saw her after she was a hundred metres from her building without a bodyguard. Again, opportunity had passed him by. Because a minute later, a policeman came running out and joined her with long strides.

*

For once, Favre had the last word. To be exact, Garcia had fallen asleep, either from the medication, or because he was bored with arguing with his partner. How to convince Alexandra to go on a date with him had become the issue, the case set aside for the moment. Not that the case was of lesser importance – no, it was that Favre desperately needed help in the field of romance. At least that was Garcia's opinion. He accused Favre of not having a romantic bone in his body, and too hung up on what he did wrong in his marriage. The main argument held by José remained that Paul's ex-wife had been in the wrong. He maintained the failure of the marriage was neither Paul's fault, nor losing custody of his daughter. To José's exasperation, various suggestions and lessons in seduction fell on deaf ears. He wasted his precious experience about love and passion on Favre. As an example, he used his three children and Maria, his wife. Favre agreed Garcia had 'moves', though still argued that Alex wouldn't fall for the usual seduction – it had to be different, special.

He picked up his phone and selected Alex's number, touched the green telephone icon. The ringtone made his hands break out in a sweat. He found being nervous to call a woman at his age laughable and was tempted to cut the call. Too late. She responded with a *'Hello'*. For a moment he was tongue-tied but recovered in time with a similar greeting. After the usual pleasantries, he returned to his most important concern.

'Is that man still on the corner watching? ... Has Mrs Ginet seen him again? ... Yes, I asked Captain Leonard. He said he would look into it. ... Good, just be careful when out.' ... How I wish I could sit in your kitchen at this moment, having one of your famous omelettes. ... Well, I didn't say I missed your neighbour's biscuits. ... Though to see you without her hanging around, would be great. ... Yes, I would even put up with her if I could get out of here. ... Would love to see you and hope it'll be soon ... Enough of this; please be careful and have a great day.' Paul reluctantly finished the call, and upon returning the phone to its cradle, lay back. He tried to rest, except his mind kept going back to their conversation and her voice. He felt a smile on his face and quickly checked if Garcia was watching him. To his relief, his partner seemed fast asleep.

'Finally, you learned something from me,' José said without opening his eyes.

'You were listening to my conversation! That's really, really, bad manners. I thought you were asleep,' Paul said, surprised at how embarrassed he felt.

'Just dozing. Your effort on entering the field of romance kept me from falling deeper into the arms of Morpheus.'

'Well, go back to that realm – I don't need any further comments from you about how I should approach my personal life.'

'You mean your love life.'

'Go to sleep, you need to rest and get your strength back, we have a case to solve.'

'Oh, I've solved it, that's why I can rest easy.'

'Okay, Big Guy – spill – you've solved the case? So, who is behind it all?'

'No, no way. I'm not making your life easy. You must use your own brain power. I'm injured, don't forget.'

'I'm also injured!'

'I have more serious injuries, and I need my rest. You need something to keep you busy, instead of hobbling off after Miss Labelle before you're completely educated in the art. I haven't finished giving you guidance on that score.'

'Well, I'll have to put that on the backburner for the time being. It'll be too dangerous to get side-tracked before we have Alpha behind bars.'

'You're right there, Mate.'

They discussed the various aspects of the case, until Favre realised he was talking to himself, because Garcia dropped off to sleep again. The only option for him was to take a short nap as well.

*

Alexandra felt invigorated after speaking to Paul – elated even. His unexpected call brought possibilities. She admitted that she had not felt this excited about seeing a man since her disastrous relationship with Denis.

Suddenly, apprehension made her want to withdraw from the possibilities she had just felt, back into that safe place, At the same time, she couldn't wait to see Paul, if only to confirm that he was on the road to recovery. It was as good a reason as any. Why not go now? Slip out, get past the officer. She could pick up a taxi at Navigation, it would be easy. She ran her hands through her hair, looked in the hall mirror, and satisfied with what she saw, grabbed her bag and keys.

With great care she opened her door a sliver. Perfect – the guard, in conversation with her neighbour, didn't notice her. Alex slipped into the passage, softly closing the door, and made for the stairwell. She could hear Mrs Ginet and the policeman, their voices fading as she descended, until completely inaudible when she reached the front entrance of her building. Across the road, the two officers on watch were chatting, not looking her way. Without hesitating, she made a dash for Navigation.

In the corner of her eye, a movement flashed. It could be the man Mrs Ginet mentioned. He was moving. Concentrating on her get-away, she took no notice, continuing her quest. The man came towards her, stopped, hesitated, turned away. At that precise moment, the voice of the policeman calling her to stop, broke her momentum. She ignored him, then realised she had no option except halting her course. With a sigh of resignation, she stopped and waited for the guard to catch up with her.

'Miss Labelle, please, you cannot leave without me. Where are you going? I'm here to accompany you wherever you wish to go.'

'I'm so sorry. I thought I could just pop out to the hospital to see Detective Favre. I didn't think there would be a problem, seeing I would be in the company of another police officer.'

'That would not be a problem, except getting there. You would be unprotected on the bus, tram, or taxi. We cannot take any chances; this is a very dangerous situation.'

'I understand. Nonetheless, I would like to go. Could you take me then?'

'Of course.' He led her back to the car, opening the door for her to step in and take a seat. She heard him address the two officers in the vehicle, giving them instructions to take her to the Cantonal, and for one to accompany her to Detective Favre's room. He would stay there with Mrs Ginet, guarding the apartment in the event the suspect tried to attack the old lady, set fire, or do other damage to Miss Labelle's home.

Alex felt embarrassed. Her foiled attempt at escaping exposed her feelings for Paul. It was the last thing she wanted people to be aware of. In any case, she's on her way there now. So, there's nothing further to do besides getting there and see Paul. She sat back and relaxed.

*

Paul looked over at a sleeping José. He worried about his partner. Would he ever get back to his usual self – physically, that was? Emotionally and mentally, he had no doubt. José was strong in those categories. He had his wife and children to bring him back to normal. José, he felt, was a very lucky man.

He wondered if Leonard had notified his ex-wife and daughter. He didn't want his ex to storm in here where she had no reason to be, and neither did he want his daughter to see him in a hospital bed. In fact, he had forgotten about them completely. Was that a sign that he was ready to begin anew? Start afresh? He really hoped so. He thought he had found the right person to venture into the future, would she feel the same? He closed his eyes, decided to rest for a short while.

A soft touch on his shoulder gave him a start. His eyes flew open. A vision from his daydream. He blinked, saw Alex standing next to the bed, smiling. It couldn't be – it wasn't a vision.

'Oh, hi. How did you get here?' The words tumbled out. He tried to pull his body upright, began to stutter.

'I can leave if you want me to.'

'No! No, that's not what I mean! I was just surprised. Aren't you supposed to never come here, and further, not alone?'

'I couldn't wait any longer, and I'm not alone. A guard-dog has been right on my heels all the way here. I'm perfectly safe, and you as well. We now have two officers outside the room on watch.'

'You are a sight for sore eyes; that is for sure. I was thinking of you and wondering if the captain had everything under control in and around your building when you walked in.' He deflected his real feelings.

'Rest assured; he has everything under control. So far, he's been the only one who could get Mrs Ginet to be quiet for a while. She's taken over the "guarding" duty of our guardians – if you know what I mean.'

'I can just imagine. She is a force of nature.'

'How is Detective Garcia doing?' Alex nodded in the direction of the adjacent bed.

'He is doing better. However, his determination to get back to his physical strength is unsurpassed. Mentally, he is as astute as ever. As far as he is concerned, he has solved that case.'

'That's good news. I cannot wait for us to lose the watchdogs and move forward.'

'I hope, when you say that, it means what I'm hoping it would mean.'

'That depends, what are you hoping for?' Alex avoided looking him in the eye.

'Let's not talk in riddles. When this investigation is all over, I would like to take you out on a date and discuss the various possibilities we have.'

'Well, let me say this: I'm open to listen and consider all possibilities. Further, I look forward to beginning a new stage in my life – to leave all those old negative memories behind.'

'That sounds promising. I agree the past has passed. It cannot be changed, so we'll just accept it for what it is. It is time for me to do the same. So, you see, we already have common ground.'

'Sounds good, though we'll discuss that later. I don't want to overstay my welcome around here, only I would like to know how you are doing and not the "I'm fine" routine. I want the truth, and when do you think you might be able to get out of here.' Alex blushed. He found not only the blush, but her concern attractive. In turn, it made him sensitive, wanting to open up to her without delay, except he couldn't decide how.

'As soon as I'm back on my feet, we'll get together, have a good night out, and talk until the early hours.'

'So, you intend to keep me up through the night, are you? A girl needs her beauty sleep. I'm sure you know better than to interfere with that unless your intentions are honourable.'

'I assure you; my intentions are honourable. However, I suppose I'll have to prove it.'

At that moment, Captain Leonard walked in, surprised to see Alex. Agitated, he looked around, didn't see the officer he placed at the door, neither the one allocated to guard Alex. He stopped in the doorway, looking at each in turn.

'Miss Labelle, what are you doing here? I told you it was too dangerous for everyone concerned if you ventured out and came here. Favre, where is the officer who guarded your door? And Miss Labelle, where is the one who was supposed to always be with you?' Leonard moved towards Paul, nodded a greeting, and turned back to Alex.

'*Salut, chef.* The officer accompanied her. As far as I know he is outside with the one guarding my room.'

'I didn't see either – I'll have to find out where they are. However, they ignored my instructions. They will be reported for insubordination.'

'I'm sorry, it's my fault. I slipped out and he caught up with me, saw my determination to visit Detectives Favre and Garcia. He had no choice. I had to make sure they were both okay.'

'As you can see, they are both making progress. The fact remains that the officer who accompanied you, and the other who was supposed to be standing in front of this room, are now both out of sight. Who is now guarding either one of you? Now, if you don't mind, I think you should say your goodbyes and be off. I need to speak to Detective Favre.'

'I understand. I'm sorry if I created problems for them.' Alex looked at both men. 'I'm pleased that I could see you and Detective Favre. Please give Detective Garcia by best wishes for a quick and complete recovery. Goodbye to you both.'

'And you don't say goodbye to me directly?' The voice came from under the covers of the bed to Paul's right.

'Garcia! How long have you been awake? Have you been eavesdropping again?' Horrified, Paul turned towards his partner.

'Long enough to know that you suck at seduction.'

'Gentlemen! I'm leaving now – you can carry on arguing once I'm not in the room.' The smile Alex gave them engendered a flutter in Paul's stomach. Her wave to both detectives and nod to Leonard made him want her to stay.

'Miss Labelle, please hold on for a moment until I find the two officers. I'll walk you out. Then I insist you stay put at home until I advise that the coast is clear.'

Favre couldn't take his eyes off the sway of her hips as she left with the captain. His imagination went to how her skin would feel under his fingertips – like satin. Yes, he had no doubt, and couldn't wait for the moment when that became reality. The reverie consuming him abruptly came to an end when her voice broke in. Even her voice sounded like a melody to him. He shook his head. It must be the medication, as he heard her talk to his boss.

'Yes, sir. Please keep me informed about these two.' Alex left the two law enforcement officers to catch up and discuss the case from their hospital beds. The third accompanied her to the corridor, where he handed her over to an apologetic policeman. The captain re-joined his two bedridden men.

'Now, have either of you come up with an idea of how we can nail this Olivier with solid evidence?'

'I've been running the events of the accident through my mind, especially when he came over to talk to me,' Paul began, looked over to his partner who painfully turned over, pulling himself more upright in the bed.

'What do you mean? Could we find his DNA at the scene of the accident or any other proof that he was there?' Leonard pulled up a chair.

'I was completely out, so can't help you there,' Garcia said.

'Well, when he came over, he stepped on the back of the car, rocking it to push it over the small cliff. However, I think we could have his prints when he bent down to speak to me. He placed his hand on the side of the car, for balance I suppose. His fingerprints would definitely be on that part of the vehicle.'

'That's good; it could prove he was there and caused the accident. Also, prove your statement that his threat was not a hallucination, but real.'

'Would a lawyer be able to argue he only passed by to assist the injured?' Garcia wanted to know.

'A good lawyer would always twist whatever is available to twist. Make no mistake; he'll find something to distort.'

'Did Borel and Pichon confirm his residence by tracking him on CCTV?' Garcia wanted to know. 'Can't we grab him there?'

'We'll snatch him wherever we can, and I'm hoping it would be today.'

'Have we narrowed down the suspects behind the whole thing – the woman I mean? Are you sure it's Bescutti's mother?' Paul could not accept that it would be that easy.

'No, she is one of them; we have eliminated the Belgian woman, the Chinese is still being investigated. It seems that Mama B is the most probable. Nevertheless, I have nothing to confirm that. Something doesn't fit. Okay, she's a cruel heartless woman, but it seems far too pat. We shouldn't jump to conclusions.'

'You're right. There's more behind this than the obvious.' Garcia's instincts locked in.

'Good, we're getting back to normal.' Favre slapped the bed with his good hand. 'Now, who do you think we should concentrate on, old man?'

'We keep Bescutti in the frame and look deeper into others who might operate around her and the Chao woman,' Garcia offered, then added, 'and not so much of the old!'

'I agree with that,' Leonard interrupted the detectives. 'Now before I go, if you two feel up to it, please think carefully on how to present the evidence so there would be no doubt of his guilt in these crimes. You let me know if you need any of the case notes or photographs.'

'Actually, could you take photos of the documents I was working on, please?' Garcia wanted to carry on with his investigation that he began in the hotel room.

'I think I can do better than that. I took everything home and created a crime board – well, now a crime wall – in my den. I will photograph that and make large prints for you both. That would include the latest information we have on Alpha's movements.'

'Fantastic!' The two detectives said in unison.

'Good, that's it then. See you later this evening with news of a sighting.' Paul watched Leonard turn to leave for the ICU to check on the progress of the Gonzales girl as well as her family.

Favre half-turned to his partner. 'Okay, what is it that you didn't want to say in front of our boss?' When Garcia shook his head, he pressed on. 'No, no, I know you better than that. I can smell when you are chewing on something. You might think we wouldn't take you seriously or laugh it off. Not this time, mate. I always value your instincts, so spill.'

'I know it's just so out of the ballpark that it's not worth mentioning. Nevertheless, if you really want to know, I'll lay out my thinking.'

'Of course, I want to know.'

'Perhaps we should wait until we get the photos from Leonard's crime wall.'

'Sure, that could give us more clarity, but nothing stops us from ruminating on it now, does it?' Paul couldn't understand Garcia's reticence – it was so unlike him. 'What is making you doubt yourself?'

'It's as I said – it's far out.'

'Okay, we'll wait until we have Leonard's up-to-date info. In the meantime, let's concentrate on Alpha. What unbreakable evidence could we possibly submit at this moment besides the prints on the car?'

'Can you tell me exactly what you remember he said to you at the crash site? I need to know word for word.'

Favre repeated each word as he remembered it. He set out every movement of Olivier as he recalled the moments before he passed out and regained consciousness again in the care of the First Responders. Garcia interrupted a few times for clarity and then remained silent, considering each word and action.

Before they could go any further, the nurse came in with their medication and news that the doctor would be passing by shortly. Then, the orderly arrived with their dinner. Both men complained about having dinner that early and more to the point they now had less time available to do their work than before the accident. There was nothing to do except accept the routine thrust upon them.

Alpha left the area from where he chose to survey the comings and goings at the apartment of Miss Labelle. When he saw her coming his way, he stepped forward to intercept her. He swore under his breath. His disappointment when the Officer came running after her, clouded his mind. Profanities poured from him. Another chance lost! He tried to control and erase his frustration completely. It didn't help if he let it direct his actions.

At first, he followed Alex and her bodyguard, saw them turn back to the two officers in the car, where she got in and they pulled off. The bodyguard returned to the building, obviously to guard the old lady.

He found his vehicle and followed the car. The surprise that they made their way to the hospital, brought new hope. He could perhaps kill two birds with one stone: grabbing Favre's piece and ending the brat once and for all. As he settled into the seat of the car, the skin on his back pricked. He leaned forward, twisted his arm to touch a spot.

The tattoo of the latest leaf itched. It had not yet healed. A tree ran along his back – its trunk the full length of his spine. Roots touched a point ending just before reaching his coccyx – in the crack of his buttocks. The top reached the base of his skull. Various branches shot out, covering most of his back. Each etched leaf marked one of his kills, with the date and place edging the green. The top-most leaf represented his first kill, his most important – his father. This last one made forty-one in all, and most probably would increase in number as he went through life. Perhaps he should have waited with this latest addition. The brat isn't dead – at least not yet. He didn't intend to immortalise the young man; he was only collateral, not his mark. Although, the kill did happen by his skill. Well, the more the merrier. He decided to take this one for him, and once he finished the girl off, add hers.

The police vehicle stopped at the HUG's main entrance. He saw Miss Labelle with her watchdog leave the car and enter the building. Alpha went down into the car park. He wouldn't be leaving soon – he could therefore just as well park in the cool underground parking garage. He turned into and descended the slip-road, careful not to be picked up on the cameras. He kept his baseball cap on with his head lowered as much as possible, pressed the button on the control box. The box whirred, printing a ticket. He pulled it and waited for the boom to rise, never lifting his head when he entered the building, or all the way to the lifts and up to ICU. Even so, he doubted they would be looking for him here at the hospital.

He reached his destination, paused in front of the automatic doors, looked through the glass partition, then left and right. With the coast clear, he pressed the button. The doors swished open. He took several quick steps, ducked into the same storage room he had used before, donned scrubs, arming himself with a syringe. With confidence he strode towards the girl's room. Surprisingly, he saw no one guarding the door, and the parents were also absent. What luck! He looked towards the nurses' station. The mother was deep in discussion with the nurse on duty, their attention elsewhere. The father was nowhere to be seen. He slipped into the room.

His spirits rose; things were looking up. With the end in sight, his heartbeat quickened. Once this was finished, only Bonavita had to be dealt with. The conclusion of this final episode in his plan: clean-up. His persona enlarged as he imagined the most important part of his grand scheme – amassing money, and she was the key.

The girl, unmoving, looked very pale – already dead. This was going to be easy! He drank in the scene – couldn't help himself, taking those extra minutes. The results of his attempt at Starbucks clear to see. Pity she couldn't feel anything in her comatose state. It would have been so much more rewarding if she squirmed with pain. Nevertheless, her stillness and near-death look gave him some satisfaction. The added anguish of the parents was further gratification. The more they were touched by his actions, the better. Chaos all round – what a blast!

Alpha cherished the moment and slowly pulled the syringe out of his pocket, broke it out of its protective sleeve. He felt the smoothness of the plastic cylinder between his fingers; it had taken on his body's warmth. It felt part of him now – he shared that inner heat with an inanimate object. It was intimate, the same sensation he felt every time he pulled his knife out of his pocket or rubbed his gun against his body. He couldn't resist running his thumb along the length of the syringe and felt his erection growing. Uncharacteristically, with gentleness he picked up her hand, held it for a second, moved his own further towards the IV entry point. He felt a thrill overtake him as he pulled out the IV and inserted the needle of his syringe into it. Time stood still as he gazed down at her, his thumb on the plunger.

*

Antonio could not say his emotions were all over the place as his mother suggested. He knew exactly how he felt and what he had to do. Of course, he worried about Cynthia; hearing someone stabbed her shocked him to the core. Why would anyone do this to her? Perhaps his mother was right – except his feelings were not at all confused about Cynthia; they were crystal clear. The emotion he felt towards that person who hurt her, had become the problem. He wanted to get his hands on the guy who did this to her! Wow, perhaps it's one of her jealous girlfriends! Even so, he intended to make them suffer. Only deep inside, he couldn't decide what he wanted to do to him or her, except that he wanted to hurt them, and hurt them bad.

The depth of his feelings for Cynthia came to the fore the moment he had heard about the stabbing. He couldn't escape the fact that he felt more for her than only teenage infatuation or a crush – he truly loved her. The vision of Cynthia walking out of Starbucks the last time they spoke, had stayed with him. There always appeared to be movement in her form, a type of rhythm, even when she sat quietly in front of him. Especially when she was angry at him, he found her hot. He had never met anyone like her, and he refused to accept their parents' decision to keep them apart. Okay, neither Cynthia nor he had taken them seriously about the danger, but he was not convinced the cause came from them seeing each other. It must be something else – that's another thing he'd get to the bottom of. From now on, he would not minimise the possible danger, he would protect her with his life!

He got off the bus at the hospital and made his way to the ICU, hoping no one would stop him as before. People milled around in the reception area for visiting hours, and he managed to pass without any problem. The Intensive Care Unit, on the other hand, seemed quiet. With no one in sight, he entered and saw Mrs Gonzales talking to the nurse. He silently slipped down the corridor to Cynthia's room.

'How is she? Is she getting better?' He asked the male nurse standing over his girlfriend.

'Oh, just checking up on her,' the nurse replied, suddenly pulling away.

'You can carry on with what you were doing. I won't be in the way,' Antonio said, not wanting to interfere with Cynthia's treatment.

'No, don't worry I'll come back later.' With head lowered, and not looking at Antonio, he turned away, leaving hurriedly.

Antonio went over to the bed and picked up her hand. It felt cold and light as a feather. He bent down and planted a soft kiss on each finger. He couldn't believe how ill she looked – in fact, she looked like death. Despite this impression, the regular beeping of the machines measuring her physical state reassured him.

'Cyn, it's me, Antonio. Sorry I couldn't get here sooner. But look, I'm here now. It would be great if you would wake up and talk to me. I've been so worried; you cannot imagine. I freaked out when I heard. I couldn't believe what happened, and when I came to see you, they wouldn't let me in. Not family, you know. But you know me, I wouldn't let anyone stand in my way from seeing you.' As he spoke, he intently watched the still figure. The desperation in his whispered words echoed, jumped off the walls, and hearing it, he suddenly felt embarrassed. But he had to make her believe that he would never abandon or ignore her.

'Look, what I want to say is: I'm here for you and won't leave unless you want me to.'

'How did you get in here?' The voice of Cynthia's mother broke into his conversation. Antonio jumped up, turned towards the sound.

'I'm sorry, Mrs Gonzales, I just had to see her. I needed to make sure she's okay.'

'You're not supposed to be here. She's critical, and only family members are allowed. You had better go.' Anna shook her head. 'Okay, you can stay with her for a little while, and I'll let you know how she's doing.'

'But could I come and see her again tomorrow, please?'

'I don't know. I will have to ask my husband and the doctor. It depends on how she responds without the respirator.'

'How long has she been off it?'

'Since this morning. The good sign is that she's been breathing on her own. Now we are waiting for her to wake up.'

'Is there nothing that I could do to help? Please, Mrs Gonzales, I cannot stay at home doing nothing. All I do is worry about her.'

'Perhaps talking to her would help. Her father had to go to the office, and I would like to go home quickly to have a shower and change.'

'Oh, I can watch her. Please Mrs Gonzales, let me do this for you. I'll make sure she's okay, and if she wakes up, I'll phone you immediately.' The concern and eagerness in his tone touched Anna.

'Fine. I'll tell the staff that you have been given permission to visit.' Anna moved closer to Cynthia, gave her a kiss on the forehead. 'I'll be back in a bit, *ma, chérie,*' she said to her daughter.

'Oh, there was a nurse here who was going to give her an injection, but left when I came in. Do you think you should tell them he could come back now?'

'What nurse? You said "he" did you?'

'Yes, a male nurse.'

'Just a minute and don't leave her side. And don't let anyone come near her – not even a nurse until I get back.' Without another word, she turned on her heel and left for the Nurses' Station.

'Okay.' Antonio pulled up the chair and as he sat next to the bed, took Cynthia's hand, and began whispering to the still form. He could hear Anna's voice rise in anger and frustration. He wondered what was going on, except he didn't want to take his attention off Cynthia.

*

Captain Leonard walked onto the floor of the ICU. Immediately, he noticed again the absence of the officer in front of the girl's room. He also saw Mrs Gonzales in a heated discussion with the staff nurse. Approaching, he heard them arguing about a male nurse. Now, what's going on? He wanted to rip into the officer for his absence – if he could find him. However, this argument he heard caused further concern.

'Good afternoon, ladies. What seems to be the problem? How can I help?' The two women began explaining at the same time.

'One at a time, please. Now, what happened, Mrs Gonzales?'

'We know all the staff who are supposed to care for our daughter. They have been individually introduced as per your recommendation.'

'Yes, that's correct. For security reasons, we wanted only approved staff near your daughter. Why are you upset?'

'Well, a male nurse was in her room a minute ago. He left as soon as Antonio Vicario walked in.'

'What? Is Antonio here? Who gave him permission to visit?' Leonard was upset.

'Well, I told him it's okay to stay with her and not let anyone near her, not even staff. She's okay for the time being. But the problem is no male nurse has been vetted, and that was the one Antonio interrupted.'

'I know, no male nurses were approved. What did this man look like? Did Antonio tell you?' The urgency in Leonard's tone did not escape Anna.

'Let's ask Antonio. I'm sure he could give you a description of the man.' Anna went directly to her daughter's room, Leonard following.

'Antonio, Captain Leonard would like to have a word with you.'

'I'm sorry, Captain, I know I came without permission, but Mrs Gonzales said it was okay to be here.' Fear and consternation were clear in Antonio.

'Calm down, son. You're not in trouble. I only want to ask if you could describe the male nurse who you saw in the room earlier.'

'Oh, yes of course. Although I didn't really see his face, but I'll give it a try.'

'What made you say he was a nurse?'

'He had on like, that blue uniform.'

'You mean scrubs.'

'Yes, I suppose that's what they're called.'

'And had a syringe in his hand.'

'What did he do with the syringe?

'I don't know, I only saw him put it back in his pocket.'

'Perhaps it would help if I showed you a couple of photos.' Leonard pulled out a file from his briefcase and laid out various photos. One of Olivier, the others those of Tweedle Dee and Tweedle Dum and the last of Bonavita. 'Tell me if you see him here.'

'Well, let me see. As I said, I didn't see his face clearly, he turned away from me, but out of these five, this one is most likely the one.'

'How sure are you – say from one to ten: ten being one hundred percent.'

'I would say seven. Yes, seven. The chin is the same, the build and colouring: definitely. I couldn't see his eyes. He was looking down. This guy in the photo's eyes look like ice. Was this the man who stabbed her? I wish I could get my hands on him. I'll kill him!'

'Not so fast, tiger. Calm down – if he's the one responsible, we'll get him and see that he is punished to the fullest extent of the law.'

'He deserves more than that. He needs to suffer like Cynthia's suffering – and her parents. This is a nightmare for everyone concerned!'

'We know and are working on it. Two of my detectives are in this hospital by the same hand. So, you can imagine how seriously we are taking this. We have placed a protection detail in front of this room to make sure she's safe, so rest assured we are doing whatever possible.'

'Well, I basically walked right into this room with no one guarding the door. Mrs Gonzales was talking to Staff Nurse, and I just walked in! So, someone is sleeping on the job, don't you think.'

'Yes, I agree. And make no mistake, they will be reprimanded severely. Now, I think I had better get working. I need to check the hospital thoroughly for this man. If he's around here, no one will be safe, including you. Please stay put, I'm calling in reinforcements.'

'I wanted to go home to shower and change. Could I do that?' Anna interrupted.

'I would prefer if you could stay here until we catch this man, or at least confirm that he has left the premises,' Leonard said before he left to make various phone calls. He came back after a few minutes.

'Antonio, stay with Mrs Gonzales until I give the all-clear. Phone your mother and tell her where you are. And Mrs Gonzales, please contact your husband, and ask him to be vigilant when he leaves the office to come here. We are not going to take any chances. I'll get back to my detectives to check on them as well.' Just then, two armed officers appeared at the entrance of the room.

'Captain Leonard? We're here as per your request. Where would you like us? There are four more men at the entrance of the ICU.'

'Good. Two of you could relieve the officer who was posted here. The staff nurse has photos of all the vetted staff members allowed to enter this room, and/or minister to Miss Cynthia Gonzales.'

'*Oui, chef.* The others are awaiting your orders.'

'Well, Mrs Gonzales, Antonio, I'll be leaving you in their good hands. I'll check in again tomorrow.' With a nod, he left to post two of the four fresh officers in front of Favre and Garcia's room, and the other two with the two just relieved to search the building. He accompanied the officers to his Detectives room.

The fact that Olivier dared show his face in the hospital and came in close contact with the girl was disconcerting. He realised the bravado of this killer should not be underestimated. He was fearless, making him more dangerous than anticipated. Ice ran through his veins.

He discussed this new dilemma with Favre and Garcia. They needed to take this latest development into consideration. He bid them a good night and left to obtain all CCTV footage from the hospital's security cameras. This was a job he wanted to do personally and hoped to be able to go through everything before going to his office in the morning.

*

Alpha swore under his breath. Not again! He had to get out quick. He stole down the corridor and backed into the storage room. He double-punched the wall out of anger, leaving bloody knuckle prints on the white paint. The pain went unnoticed. He could not believe the bad luck he's had trying to get to this brat. By now, Miss Labelle must have left the hospital as well. Both targets lost. It was not his day. He'll have to start all over again tomorrow. However, his frustration brought him to boiling point. He wanted to beat the hell out of someone. Like a caged animal, he circled the small space, constantly swearing, then suddenly turned and retraced his steps. He could pull the hair out of his head from aggravation! His pacing continued for several minutes. The situation infuriated him. Why couldn't they just stay out of his way?

Virtually tearing the scrubs off his body, he threw them down with force. He donned his own clothes, pulling his baseball cap firmly on to cover most of his face. Now he needed to get out unnoticed. From further down the corridor, he heard the brat's mother's voice rising. That she was furious about something, came over loud and clear. Alpha couldn't be sure why the woman argued, except that she had rushed into the girl's room just prior to her outburst. The staff nurse also came out from behind her desk in a rush. Obviously, the young man overstepped and shouldn't have been there. Again, unforeseen bad luck preventing him from doing what he came to do. He hung around, the door at a slit, waiting for a moment to slip out.

This plan was also thwarted as he saw Leonard walk through the doors. The captain quickened his pace as he became aware of the heated discussion further down the corridor. Alpha realised that unless he left now, it would be impossible to escape, convinced that the captain would lock down the hospital without delay once he spoke to the young man.

Alpha followed his own counsel and quickly left, taking the stairs to exit the building. In the stairwell, he passed the officer he saw before guarding the girl's room, chatting to one of the nurses. He kept his head well down and with a muttered '*salut,*' left them to their conversation. When he reached the next level, he exited the stairwell and took the elevator down to the parking level, his plans for this escapade abandoned for the day.

CHAPTER TWENTY-ONE

Leonard saw Borel and Pichon at their allocated desks, noting their surprise when he purposely strode into the bullpen. He paused, punched something into his mobile phone. He supposed they didn't expect him so early; neither did they expect him to walk directly over to the printer without a word. Leonard waited a moment, then retrieved some printed sheets of paper and placed them in a folder. He had planned his day to be able to supply as much information to Favre and Garcia as possible.

'*Bonjour, chef, vous êtes la!*' Borel said. Leonard, as usual, only nodded as he pulled out a chair to join them in front of the bank of computers they were scrutinising.

'I hope you have made progress.'

'Well, we picked him up near Navigation, except we lost him and never saw him again until late afternoon when he arrived at Paquis. Probably to look for a prostitute,' Borel offered.

Leonard looked at each man in turn. 'Yesterday, late afternoon, we had a suspect enter the hospital room of Cynthia Gonzales. I am convinced it was Olivier, according to the identification by the young man who saw him.'

'What? How did that happen? Where was the officer on duty? Which young man?' queries poured from Pichon.

'All good questions. Firstly, the officer appeared a few minutes later and was well reprimanded. I relieved him of his post. However, before he left, I instructed him to join the floor-to-floor search for the suspect.'

'Did they find him? Are you sure it was Olivier?'

'Well, I showed the young man his photo, and even though he couldn't say for sure, he felt it could be a definite possibility. The man posed as a male nurse, and when disturbed by the young man, left abruptly with head lowered, not looking directly at the boy. By the way, he is the son of Bescutti.'

'What was he doing there? I thought they were being kept apart for safety's sake?' Borel asked, confused.

'Yes, that was the idea, but obviously he wanted to see if his girlfriend was okay. I suppose he heard so many stories, most probably thought she was dead. Enough of that, I obtained the security footage from the hospital and went through it last night.' Leonard pulled out the discs he retrieved.

'Did you see him?' Borel took the discs and inserted the first one into the computer.

'Well, I identified one person who made sure no camera captured his features. You will see that it is the same person the cameras picked up on the way from the time he entered the parking garage to the ICU, and then back out again. Obviously, the cameras are only at the various building entrances, the reception area, and in the elevators. The two of you are better equipped to recognise this man from his body build and other features, and would most probably recognise him in your sleep. Also, could you check the car's registration plate of the driver acting suspiciously? I made a note of it.' He handed his notes to Borel and Pichon.

'This Olivier is really pushing the envelope and daring us to nab him,' Borel said.

'That's the actions of a psychopath, and we know he is one,' Pichon added.

'We agree on that. So, I will leave this with you to get on with. Let me know when you have an opinion, and in your estimation, when can we get this man off the streets.' Leonard turned and left without another word.

*

At his next stop, he hoped to find answers to some of the questions on the table. He found Bescutti in his office, deep in contemplation while watching planes landing and taking off from the airport. Startled out of his mesmerised state by his secretary's voice announcing Leonard's arrival, he spun around. A sudden smile transformed his previous pensive expression.

'Ah, bonjour, Capitaine. Comment allez-vous?'

'Good, good. I've come to find out if you have had any further news, or any communication with your brother or the rest of the family. Could you give me any information?'

'Yes, well, let's sit down and have a coffee. I'll run through everything I've learnt so far. Please sit.' Bescutti gestured towards one of the easy chairs. He took a seat opposite Leonard. The secretary hurried out to get the

377

coffee, and the two men exchanged niceties until she returned with a tray of coffee, cream, and sugar. They remained silent until she had left, closing the door behind her.

'You cannot be too careful. I do trust her. However, I prefer if the family remain ignorant of the fact that they are under suspicion. They have long arms and, with that, reach far and wide throughout the business. They like to know as much as possible, which of course I am opposed to.'

'I understand. I do hope I've not given anything away by mentioning your brother and family. I can believe it is a sensitive matter.'

'No, not at all. It is sensitive, yes. We cannot be too careful.' Bescutti took a sip of his coffee, replacing the cup and saucer on the table between them.

'So far, I have not uncovered any startling revelation, although some information has been discovered. It all seems rather strange, or rather conflicting. I cannot get to the bottom of it, also I cannot vouch for its credibility. Even so, there seems to be some light at the end of the tunnel.'

'Why so cryptic? I am intrigued.'

'That Chinese woman, Chao Li, had contact with the family, however, not with my mother. Perhaps someone spoke to Chao on behalf of my mother, though that is only a supposition. In other words, I have not yet found out exactly who spoke to Chao, and why. It is also not clear if she instigated the contact, or a member of my family had. So, you see, there lies the reason for being careful on why and how I phrase things.'

'Have you located her? Chao that is?'

'No, my investigator has not yet discovered her whereabouts. We'll let you know as soon as we find her.'

'Good, we would need to speak to Chao Li urgently to clear this up. However, could you keep on digging on your end and keep me informed. On our side, we have not been successful in either finding her, or the woman who gave the order for the shooting. Once we find out who is behind the scheme and have Olivier arrested, we would be able to close the case completely,' Leonard finished his coffee.

'No problem, I would like to know who this woman is as much as you do. In a strange way, I'm hoping that my mother, or one of the family, would not be involved. I suppose I still hope for them to come over to the legitimate way of doing business.'

'Oh, on the matter of our main suspect: a man acted suspiciously at the bedside of the girl, Cynthia Gonzales. We believe it is Olivier. He was disturbed by Antonio Vicario.'

'What? My son? What was he doing at the girl's bedside?'

'Well, he slipped in, obviously couldn't live without news of her well-being. Though, except for him, she might have died.'

'For his safety, he wasn't supposed to frequent her. I made that clear to his mother.'

'My own children have left home, but I can assure you no one can stop a teenager, or rather a young adult, from following their heart. Especially in this case where the girlfriend has been injured. He would have moved heaven and earth to personally find out if she was okay.'

'Yes, I suppose so. In the eyes of my son and Gonzales' daughter, we didn't act practically, or logically, by keeping them apart. How is she doing, by the way? And how are the parents holding up?'

'At the moment, she is holding her own. One good thing is that they've taken her off the respirator and she's breathing without outside help. The parents, as you can imagine, are still very concerned. At least they can now take alternate absences from her bedside to go home, shower, and change.' Leonard got up to leave.

'That's good to know. Please give them my best. As I said, we'll keep each other appraised.' They shook hands and Georgio accompanied him to the door.

Back on the street, Leonard looked in the direction of the airport, wondering whatever happened to the courier Arthur Gonzales had hired. After her interception by whom they now know was Olivier, what had happened to her? Where could she be? Why had she not surfaced? There were so many facets to this case that he sometimes felt as if the loose ends were taking over, unravelling their progress. Bonavita sprang to mind – another of Olivier's loose ends which he most probably would want to deal with. What lay in store for this officer?

He reached his car, shook his head, and only wished he could trust more people. He was tired of carrying this all alone with his two best detectives – the only ones he really trusted – out of action. The fact that it had become imperative they put Olivier behind bars as soon as possible, could no longer be ignored.

He decided to call on the offices of Gonzales, hoping they could perhaps shed light on some of the questions still to be answered.

Eric Pichat received him and showed him into Arthur's office. 'We can talk in here.'

'I've been wondering if you have any other information about the courier who disappeared,' Leonard opened the conversation.

'Such as?'

'Has she made contact? Have you found her? Do you know if her return ticket has been used? You bought it through your travel agent, I presume, therefore they could check. At this moment, I do not want to involve official avenues because, as you are aware, we are trying to keep this on a need-to-know basis.'

'To answer you, no, we haven't found her, and I've not asked our agent to check. I'll do so immediately.' Eric picked up the phone and gave the secretary instructions to do so.

'Thank you. Now, the other thing I would like to know, is if you've discovered who could be your possible competition in the gem trade.'

'We've made very little progress, except that the Belgium woman you mentioned is completely out of the picture. She deals only with her established suppliers. The Chinese one apparently passed on an opportunity and went into partnership with another group.'

'Are you sure about that? Have you found out who this other group could be?' Leonard asked.

'Not hundred percent, no. All we could find out were vague rumours which suggested Chao Li was approached and declined, because she didn't trust the prospective partners. Except, whoever those "prospective partners" could be, we have not yet uncovered.' Eric pulled a folder nearer and opening it, handed a sheet to Leonard. 'These are the typed-up notes of what we learnt.'

'Thank you, I'll go through them carefully. It might throw light on another aspect of the case. An unexpected crumb to show us the way forward, would be welcome. It is difficult to tell what could change a case or how things would turn out. So, we always look at every detail, no matter how trivial.'

'Well, you're welcome to whatever we have; you only have to ask.' Even though Eric proposed this, Leonard realised that he might not want him to take up the offer. There were too many features to their dealings which might raise suspicion. Luckily, the secretary knocked and came in with her notepad, saving Pichat from further commitment.

'Yes? You have the information we need?' Eric welcomed the interruption.

'Sir, they phoned the airline under the pretext of asking for a partial reimbursement of the ticket.'

'And?' Both men watched her expectantly.

'The airline advised only a portion would be refunded, as the ticket would now be considered as a single fare. The agents wanted to know what we want them to do.' She looked down at her notes again. 'Sir, what should I tell them?'

'Tell them to go ahead with reclaiming whatever balance remains. Thank you; that'll be all for now.'

'That would mean the courier never left Geneva, or if she did, it was not by air,' Leonard said, looking at Pichat with concern.

'That seems so. I dread to think what could've happened. Where do you think she's now? She didn't have any relatives or friends here in Switzerland, that much we know. The only person in Europe she mentioned was her aunt in Spain.'

'Well, that tells us we have another loose end to tie up.' Leonard got up. 'I had better get back to the office with this possible missing person. Could you please come down to give us an official statement?'

'What do you mean "give an official statement"?'

'We would need a statement that you have had no news from her; that she could be missing; with a description and her full details for us to be able to open a case file on her possible disappearance.'

'I could do that. Would that be attached to our statement concerning the missing gem samples?'

'Exactly, we would look at the initial statements by you all as part of the missing woman's case. It'll give us more to go on – a motive, where to begin as well as bringing an urgency to finding the woman.'

'I see. No problem. Would you need Arthur to come in as well?'

'No, I don't think so; your statement should be enough. I don't want to worry him excessively, not with his daughter still in a critical condition.' Leonard slipped the typed-up notes into his inside jacket pocket, got up, shook hands, and left Eric with a worried look on his face. Leonard presumed it would be about all the small details which he might have to cover up and eliminate, before more in-depth investigations into their business dealings were made. Though he didn't want to think about that – he had too much on his plate as it was.

*

Despondent that so little progress had been made, Leonard drove to the hospital in a melancholic mood. He had hoped there would've been more concrete evidence to use for the conclusion of the case. Nobody seemed to know anything! If the underworld of Geneva could not get the information needed, who could? Was the Intelligence Unit in the loop or were they also as ignorant as his own men were? Looking at the results of both Bescutti and Pichat's enquiries, the end did not look even remotely within their grasp.

So many people have been seriously hurt since the fatal shooting of Marcus Stephens, that it was impossible for him to shake off this feeling of helplessness and sadness. The fact that Garcia might never be the same again, and Favre's injuries could keep him from active duty for months, brought him to the parents of Cynthia Gonzales. No one knew if she would pull through, and if she did, would she be incapacitated in any way – mentally or physically? He only felt relieved that he had not been present at the interview of the Stephens couple. Their grief would have been unbearable to witness.

Nevertheless, he would bring his two detectives up to date, and give them the enlarged printed photos of his crime wall and confirm by phone with Borel and Pichon on their findings. That should be enough for them to carry on with the investigation from their hospital beds. He depended on them to see what he had missed, perhaps nothing. Except, at that moment he felt tired, overwhelmed by worry, and therefore, could easily have overlooked or misinterpreted a crucial piece of evidence.

On his arrival at the hospital, he forced himself to shake off the heavy feeling and straightened his shoulders. It would not be good for his detectives to sense his despondency. Though, they lifted that sense when he saw them in a jovial mood, both much better than the day before. He nodded to the two officers now posted outside the room, forced a smile, and entered.

Garcia noticed him first, giving a small salute. Favre turned, doing the same. Leonard shook hands with both, and pulled up a chair between the two beds, extracting from his briefcase the folder with photos of which he had made two sets.

'*Chef,* you seem to have news for us. We are ready to work, even though it would be from our hospital beds,' Favre offered.

'Yes, we can't wait to get our teeth into the case again.'

'That's excellent news. Here's what I have.' Leonard gave each a set of photos and copy of all the notes he had accumulated. He ran through the information while they perused everything.

'This is good; we can work on this. Look, Favre, this is exactly the way I laid out the crime board in the hotel room. *Chef,* this is great! You've added to this, and it makes sense now! You see where I picked up an "insider"? You said it was Bonavita, where are we with that now? What concrete evidence do we have against this Alpha?' Garcia couldn't contain his excitement in getting back into the investigation.

'Okay, slow down, cowboy! Let the captain finish – give him time to answer one question at a time.'

'Yes, despite the lack of evidence that Mama B was behind it all, I have a strong feeling that we're on the right track. It's someone in, or close to that family.'

'I agree. Do you think Georgio is definitely above board? Perhaps, he's holding something back to cover for someone close?' Garcia didn't hold back on his distrust.

'Be that as it may, I cannot find any indication that he is withholding information. So, for the time being, I tend to take whatever he says for what it is. Though, I've saved the best for last.'

'Don't keep us in suspense. What have you uncovered?' Again Garcia.

'The bravado of Olivier seems not to have any bounds. He ventured into the ICU yesterday, again attempting to put an end to the young girl. I suspect the two of you would have been on his list as well. The fact that Miss Labelle was also to be found in the hospital at the same time; it could have been that his plan was to eliminate Miss Gonzales, Miss Labelle, and the two of you during one visit to this establishment.'

'There seems to be something missing here. Why isn't he in custody? Is that why we now have two officers at the door?' Garcia found the latest news incredulous and frustrating.

'But you said "attempting" – what do you mean by that? Sounds as if he didn't succeed. I don't understand. Who prevented him from doing what he came to do?' Favre sat up straighter.

'Well, yes. Firstly, that is why I doubled the guards. Secondly, he managed to slip right past us – as slippery as an eel, he is. The officer guarding the door left his post, and Olivier, dressed in scrubs posing as a nurse, managed to get into the girl's room. He was at the point to administer something through the IV line, when the boyfriend – Antonio Vicario – walked in asking how she was doing. This saved her, as he turned and with an incomprehensible mumble left the room.'

'Wait a minute – I thought that young man wasn't supposed to come near her? At least that's what the parents ordered.' Favre wanted to know.

'That's true. Obviously, you cannot stop young love. In this case, it turned out to be a blessing. Mrs Gonzales was talking to the staff nurse, and Antonio slipped in, disturbing Olivier in the act. At first, the mother was furious to find Antonio there, didn't want to hear any excuses. However, when I arrived minutes later in the midst of the argument, he apologised for interrupting the nurse.

'This statement changed the discussion abruptly. Concern replaced anger, and more questions were thrown into the mix. No male nurse had been allocated to the girl's care – as you know, everyone was vetted carefully. Antonio gave a vague description as he couldn't see the face clearly, but pieces began to fall into place. I immediately asked for backup and a lockdown, only he managed to get away yet again. Nevertheless, I procured the CCTV footage for what it's worth from the hospital, and Borel and Pichon will try to track him from there.'

'They would if he took a taxi, Uber, or the bus. Except if he got here by car, do we have his plate number?' Garcia's concern showed.

'From the video of all cars in and out at the time in question, we have managed to track a possible person who made a concerted effort to hide his features with the same estimated build. I know it sounds vague, only it's all we have, and from that we do have a registration number to follow. If it pans out, we could follow him further. Hopefully, we'll close in and arrest him.'

'And Bonavita? How does he fit into this scenario?' Favre was concerned.

'Well, I've asked a young officer to follow him and radio in his movements. Bonavita has not yet brought me up to speed as to his next meeting with Olivier. Though, I suspect that after Olivier's close call at the hospital, he would want to tie up loose ends, and of course Bonavita is one. I'm confident we will be able to avert the demise of our colleague. Of course, it would be ideal if we could catch Alpha in the act of trying to eliminate him.'

'Is that why you have an officer track him?' Garcia asked.

'Yes, as well as another avenue to find Olivier. As you could see from my notes, I'm also trying to trace the missing courier, seeing her return ticket was not used.'

'Any news on that sir?' Favre wanted to know.

'Well, I've asked Eric Pichat – Arthur Gonzales's second in command – to come into the Station and lodge a formal Missing Persons statement. We'll go from there, but so far it doesn't look promising.' Leonard looked from one to the other. 'I am going to leave you now to get on with looking over the data I brought. Let me know if you get an idea.' He got up and placed the chair against the wall.

'Leave it with us, Sir, we're going to analyse everything immediately and will let you know whatever we find – or any idea which might come up.' Favre awkwardly shuffled the papers with one hand into a neat pile.

As Leonard left, he saw Favre turn towards his partner. He knew he could always count on these two, no matter what their condition. Was he pushing them too far? Were they physically up to it? He knew they would never shrink from their duty or step back. However, was it fair taking their attitude for granted? In any case, that was all he had, and quick and certain closure was necessary.

*

Favre moved with difficulty into a position in which he could spread the documents Leonard brought. He had become impatient for the casts on his arm and leg to be removed. The constraints made him irritable. Convinced that his complaining had forced Doctor to give in, the doctor insisted on at least another week after which a removable cast could be used. Be that as it may, he couldn't wait to be more mobile.

His blood boiled. The photos of the crash site brought his trapped feeling back. The smell of dust, fuel, oil, and blood filled his nostrils as if it had happened yesterday. He shook his head and studied the pictures of

Leonard's crime wall. The timeline and route mapped out from the CCTV footage confirmed what he thought. To catch Alpha, they would need to outwit him. The fact that he had the audacity to come to the hospital, attempting to finish off his contract, strengthened their assumption that Alpha was a force to be reckoned with. He turned to Garcia.

'Hey, Partner, how do you think we should nab this guy?'

'Well, you see all those visits to Paquis? I think that would be our best bet. He pays visits, or shall we say, goes to look for company, every time something goes down. What do you bet that he was on his way there yesterday after his foiled attempt?'

'Okay, but that was yesterday. How do we know he'll go there again today?' Favre respected Garcia's intuitive approach.

'Of course, we could get him at his home; except he would anticipate that move, so I would suggest we get him where and when he least expects it. That would be Paquis when he looks for a prostitute.'

'What do you think about when he meets with Bonavita?'

'That could work. Although he might use Bonavita as a hostage if he realises what we're up to. To my way of thinking, he might, after the next meeting with Bonavita, go to Paquis. I also think it would be their last meeting, after which eliminating our officer would be first on his mind.'

'Okay, I'll go with that. Let's see how we should get him without endangering bystanders.' Favre scratched his head. 'The best, if possible, would be to follow him in real time, and not on CCTV after the fact. Such a pity we couldn't get him at the Gay Parade.'

'From what I understood, he never went. I wonder, what kept him away? There's only one officer following Bonavita, we'll have to ask the captain to add a second.' Garcia suggested.

'You are thinking that there might be a possibility to catch Olivier in the act of trying to get rid of Bonivita?'

'Yes, we need to be there!' Frustrated, Garcia continued. 'Well, I don't mean you and me – I know that's impossible for the moment, but the Force should have a stronger presence besides only one officer. That would also be an opportunity to put a tail on Olivier – if those idiots from Intelligence don't lose him again!'

'I agree, that would be a good opportunity. I suppose we could put our own people on it, as we have now pinpointed the leak.'

'Do you really think Bonavita is the sole informer?' Garcia was not convinced.

'The captain seems to think so, although I understand why he's playing it safe and not taking it for granted. Alpha had proved to be such a clever dick that he most probably has various people, and not only at our station, but in Intelligence as well.'

'Good, let's set out our suggestions, see what the captain thinks. I doubt he'll disagree.' Garcia pulled a note pad nearer, scribbling a couple of notes. 'It's now or never – we have to get him without wasting any more time.' They discussed the possibilities.

'The captain should still be in the building. Do you want me to phone and ask him to get back here asap?'

'Yes, let's get this over and done with.' Garcia leaned back into the pillows.

*

Surprised, Leonard took the call from Favre – he had left them only a short time ago. Then again, he shouldn't be surprised, as his two best detectives would not leave any stone unturned to get back to solving this crime. He finished off his check on the various officers he had placed on guard and briefly spoke to Mr and Mrs Gonzales, pleased to hear that their daughter's condition had stabilised. He was anxious to get back to Favre and Garcia to find out what they wanted to share so urgently.

The animated conversation he saw the two were having when he entered their room, lifted his spirits.

'So, you called. What have you got?'

'Sir! Pleased you could come back so quickly.' Favre said.

'Yes, luckily, I was still here. The Gonzales girl has stabilised – not out of the woods yet – though it looks a bit more promising.'

'Good to hear,' Garcia said and turned to his notes. *'Chef*, we've listed some of our suggestions. The only thing is we will have to move fast. Except, with the two of us laid up, we are not sure who will be the best to execute the plan.'

'Leave it with me. I think Borel and Pichon have proved themselves capable as well as trustworthy. What do you think of bringing the two of them over here for the five of us to go through it step by step?' Leonard suggested.

387

'I think you're right, sir. We can work with them. Both have accompanied me when I visited Bescutti and Gonzales. They are still green, I know. Nevertheless, they showed promise and know the movements of Olivier better than anyone. How long will it take them to get here?' Favre's enthusiasm rose.

'Yes, I agree they would recognise him in a crowd before anyone else. So, this is what I suggest: if they leave the station now, we will have about twenty minutes to go over your suggestions and streamline them before they arrive. What do the two of you say? You agree?' The captain looked from one to the other.

'Oh, definitely. That gels with me!' Garcia sat up straighter in bed.

Leonard phoned Borel and Pichon, instructing them to come as soon as possible, and to bring whatever they had concerning the case. He pulled a chair between the beds and, huddling together over different photos and notes, they discussed the various options on how to pin Olivier down.

The minutes passed quickly and before long, one of the protection-detail knocked and entered, advising that two officers from Servette Station were asking permission to enter the room. Leonard gave consent, got up to make room. Borel and Pichon nodded to Leonard with a mumbled *'chef,'* greeted the two detectives, and waited for instructions.

'Good, grab those chairs and gather around the beds. We have a lot to discuss. Also, I want to emphasise that what we decide here, must be kept under wraps if we want to succeed. Only those we choose to work with us, will be privy to our plan.'

'Oui, chef.' They said in unison and pulled two more chairs around the bed.

'First, may we ask how the two of you are doing?' Pichon ventured.

'As you can see, we are making progress – of course I'm stronger than my partner here and will be back at work before Favre even has an inkling of hobbling back!' Garcia quipped.

'That's what you think! Once these casts come off, I'll be back at my desk, going full steam ahead, leaving you to lick my heels!'

'Enough, you two – save your strength for the fight we have on our hands.'

'You're talking about Olivier, are you, sir?' Borel wanted to know.

'Yes, we must grab him as soon as possible. We are all here to set that plan in motion, and I need your full attention, not to mention commitment.

If you have any doubts about any part of the plan, you should speak up immediately.'

'We are ready, captain.' Pichon and Borel agreed.

'Did you find anything further on the tapes which we can use? The captain said you looked at the hospital tapes and the latest surveillance,' Favre wanted to know.

'Well, yes. We both agree that the person trying to hide from the cameras in the hospital was Olivier – the build and stance match perfectly. We also picked him up in Paquis as suspected later yesterday – that is, early evening. According to the time stamp, he must have gone there directly after leaving here. Couldn't resist getting company.'

'I suppose we'll have to look for an injured and abused prostitute again. He seems to have this insatiable desire for a violent sexual encounter after every gratifying or frustrating life occurrence,' Garcia mentioned.

'That would give us more ammunition. I mean another crime to add to the list we are building up.' Favre looked at the photos spread out on the bed. 'Though, what we need is the finger- and palm print match on my car, not lengthen the list of offences.'

'Oh, yes. We have just received that from forensics.' Borel drew out a report.

'Well, give it to us, man, don't waste time!' Impatient, Leonard grabbed the page from Borel's hand.

'What does it say? Is it the proof we need? Can we use it to nail him?' Garcia asked.

'Not so fast! Let me see. Yes, it gives us definite proof that he was at the site. The prints are a seventeen-point match to that from Interpol. This will confirm what Favre said at the time.' Leonard was cautious.

'But this is the evidence we were looking for! Couldn't we go ahead and issue a warrant for his arrest now?' Favre wanted to know.

'I think we can. However, I want to make absolutely sure he cannot slip through our fingers, due to a loophole in the law. Give me a moment to confirm with the Attorney General. If he says it will be enough, we'll go ahead without delay.' Leonard took out his phone and moved to the corridor to make the call.

'While we wait, why don't we hash out a couple of things?' Garcia asked.

'You're right. You've been following Alpha for a while now, on CCTV that is; now we need to step up and track him in real time,' Favre explained.

'You mean put someone on him to actually trail him?' Borel wanted to know.

'Yes. However, here is the tricky part, the officers we put on this duty should not be from our station. In other words, they should not be known to those at Servette,' Garcia said.

'But why? We wouldn't get the collar if he is caught by another station. Couldn't we do it ourselves?' Pichon asked.

'Let the Captain explain,' Favre said as Leonard walked back into the room with a satisfied grin.

'The Attorney General has agreed to issue the warrant.' Elated, everyone high-fived.

'Captain, we began to explain the time had come for Alpha to be followed on foot, and it should be done by another station's officers. Pichon wanted to know why, we prefer if you explain further.' Favre handed Leonard their page with notes.

'Good. This is what we've got to so far in this investigation.' Leonard settled in his chair and continued. 'The two of you are some of the very few who know exactly what Olivier has done – how many crimes he must answer to. What you most probably are not aware of, is that one of our own has been feeding him information.'

A collective 'What?' escaped Borel and Pichon.

'Let me explain. We realised that Olivier was always one step ahead of us, and with the diligent study of the different crime scene photos, we picked up a possible informant. We did not jump to conclusions here – I want to assure you. We also picked the same officer up on one or two of the CCTV footage you scrutinised.'

'But we didn't see anyone,' Borel defended. 'We would have picked up a familiar face. Are you telling us we messed up?'

'No, not at all. You were only looking for Olivier, never anyone else. Also, in your defence, as you're temporary, you don't know everyone at the station that well. So, you are not to blame for missing the connection. However, we have looked for persons other than Olivier, and found the mole whom we have approached with the pretext of contacting all his informants for anything new about the initial shooting. We didn't mention any of the other incidents – only the shooting of the young man.' Leonard looked from one to the other for a reaction, seeing none he continued. 'We put someone he wouldn't recognise, hence an officer from Intelligence, on the mole's trail. To date, this Intelligence officer has reported about the mole having one meeting with a person who fitted the description of Olivier. This corresponds with the mole mentioning he had a meeting with one of his informants and would have their next meeting due later today.

'This is where our possible chance comes in. We want to double the number following the mole. We now have one IB officer on Olivier and intend to have two others in the Bar waiting to trail Olivier in the event of us not having the opportunity to get to him. Though, these two would be standing by. This way, when the mole meets Olivier later, we would have at least four officers on hand to execute the arrest warrant.'

'How sure are we that we can nab Olivier then?' Pichon was sceptical.

'Who is this mole?' Borel wanted to know.

'Okay, firstly, we have confirmation that the meeting is going ahead as planned, and the mole is Bonavita.'

'No way, not Bonny!' Pichon and Borel chorused.

'He always gave us a friendly greeting,' Borel added.

'Oh! I see! Even though we never said much, he always came over to chat. He could see the crime board! That's how he kept up to date with the case. We might have given him information inadvertently,' Pichon was shocked at their lack of judgement.

'Don't blame yourselves. But yes, unfortunately. However, we doubt he realises what he is doing. Olivier most probably spun him a tale and Bonavita, innocently supplied information on the case,' the captain put things in perspective. 'I suppose now you understand why we are looking for officers who are not known by anyone at Servette. So, who do you know outside of our Station?'

'Well, I have my friends from the academy, and Borel has others as well. They are spread over the Canton, and I doubt Bonavita would know them. He did his training long before we were there.'

'Good, get four of them over to us immediately. You think you could manage that?'

'Definitely. Where should we meet – surely not at Servette, someone could see them.' Borel's worried look at his partner said it all.

'Could we meet here, at the hospital?' Pichon asked.

'No way! You want to get us in trouble with the nurse? She hates our guts as it is, and that would put her over the top. She would most probably refuse to feed us!' Garcia said, horrified just thinking of the reaction the nurse who spoke in CAPITAL LETTERS would have.

'It's a pity we can't meet here, but you're right. It would be best if you all came to my home. You know where that is, don't you?' They nodded. 'Good, I'll warn my wife to expect you at one pm. That will give your friends enough time to get there.' Leonard shifted in his chair. 'We'll loop the two of you in on video-link here in the hospital during the briefing.'

'You can video-link?' Garcia couldn't believe his ears.

'Of course – I might have been born long before you lot, but I'm not a dinosaur and have kept up to date. I will connect my phone to the TV, which would give us a better sound quality and screen size. That way you could interject whenever necessary. Will that do?'

'Captain, that would be perfect! We'll be part of it all – be able to communicate – a video conference call would work perfectly.' Garcia's enthusiasm had no bounds.

'Yes, I need your input even though you might not be there in person. Make no mistake, you are an integral part of this investigation, and we cannot conclude it without you.' Leonard got ready to leave. 'We also have to have an alternate plan in case this proposed meeting between Olivier and Bonavita does not happen.'

'I suggest we have at least three officers following Alpha,' Favre said.

'Yes, I thought of that. Borel, Pichon, where do you think we would be sure to pick up Olivier's trail? We have ruled out the apartment he is using, because it's too obvious, and he would most probably expect it.' Leonard pushed his chair out, waited for the reply before leaving.

'In that case, the most frequent and predictable spot would be Paquis. He has been there various times – in fact, initially we thought he might live there – except we noticed certain days he did not go near that part of Geneva,' Pichon explained.

'Fine, I'll expect you all at one pm.' Leonard turned and left without another word.

*

'Could the two of you stay for a minute to hash out a couple of things to tell your academy colleagues?' Favre asked. Both Borel and Pichon nodded.

'Let us first contact them and get them here ASAP,' Borel suggested.

'Please stress how dangerous this man is. They should take all precautions,' Favre warned.

'Thank you, we will. One thing we picked up, or rather did not pick up: we lost him for about an hour on CCTV. We don't know what he was up to or what it means – if anything. Only we saw him in Navigation Square when he left his car yesterday afternoon; lost him for an hour; then he appeared again in the square, got in, and drove off.' Pichon sounded apologetic.

'You say yesterday in Navigation? Could he have gone to stake out Miss Labelle's apartment building?' Favre wanted to know.

'Could be, though there is no way of knowing, as we don't have cameras at that spot or any that capture that area. And if he knows where the cameras are, it'll be easy to avoid them,' Borel said.

'I ask, because Miss Labelle's neighbour noticed a man watching the street from one of the corners just out of sight of the patrol car outside the building.'

'That could've been him, except, as we've said, we lost him. It could've been that he drove from there to the hospital. We'll have to check to see if we can pick up his car between the two points: that'll be easy and quick.' Borel pulled out his laptop, tapped in a couple of keys. The screen lit up and with a couple of further keystrokes, he had the video ready, scrolled through and with a 'voila' turned the computer towards Garcia and Favre.

'That's him there! He's clearly visible in the driver's seat. This gives us confirmation of his car's registration number. Oh no! Look, it seems as if he is following the squad car in which Miss Labelle is being driven.'

'So, he did follow her to the hospital. The make and model, as well as the plate, correspond to the car entering the hospital parking.' Favre turned to Garcia. 'We must finish this, and now!'

'Okay, Mate, we've got what we want. He was here with the intent to do harm. Let's not waste time and get this show on the road.'

The four law enforcement officers sat discussing various aspects of the case until Favre and Garcia were satisfied that the others knew everything they would need for a successful outcome. Just in time, as the nurse came in with their medication and hustled the two visitors out, Police business or not.

Bonavita looked forward to his planned meeting later with his writer friend, Sebastian. In fact, he couldn't wait. Convinced he would be mentioned in the book, become famous, and finally earn the respect of his colleagues, he knew he could add some other juicy aspects, especially to this latest case, which seemed to be the main thread the book was based on. Further, the promise of sharing in the financial gains once the book was published, delighted him. He could take the family on that holiday to Thailand they've wanted for years.

Bonavita found the guy so interesting and charming. Everyone seemed to be his friend, or at least he made friends easily. They looked at him as a hero, a real adventurer. Well, to be honest, Sebastian was formidable, and as Bonavita seldom found anyone impressive, it meant something. He deemed it fortunate to be called a friend, as the guy said last time. This collaboration meant everything. It would change his whole world, not to mention his life!

Well, not long to wait. However, he had a scheduled meeting with the captain this morning, in fact, in half an hour. He had nothing to report as none of his informants had given him any info. He was not letting slip the hour of his meeting with Sebastian this time. The captain seemed far too interested in how many, and who he had as snitches. Unusually, Leonard asked for names and how they came to be informants. He could kick himself when he mentioned Sebastian, not as a snitch, but as a person who had a knack of getting information others could not. He'd say nothing this time. He didn't want to jinx anything. Hopefully, the captain wouldn't remember what he had said at their last meeting. He'd inform the Higher-ups when all was said and done, and once he had received the advance.

In the meantime, he would finish off this call, it wouldn't take long, domestic disturbances usually could be resolved there and then. At the station he'd write the report and have his meeting. All would fall into place. He was sure of it.

All the way to Servette, Leonard mulled over the various options they had discussed at the hospital. Only one aspect of this present situation pleased him: the progress his two detectives were making on the road to recovery. They really showed their determination to get back on their feet. He found it reassuring and very welcome. It had been exhausting working without their full competency. His wife would also be pleased to know of their improvement, as it would give him respite from the pressure he'd been under.

Though, first he needed to meet with Bonavita. Hopefully, this officer would be ignorant of the tail they had put on him, and especially that they expected him to lead them to Olivier. Now he had to choose two extra men to trail Bonavita. Leonard needed this trap to be faultless.

At the station, he instructed the officer at reception to find Bonavita and send him to his office directly. He passed the bullpen and, with Borel and Pichon – recent fixtures behind the desk of computers – now absent, it felt empty despite the couple of desks being occupied by old-timers. Leonard felt the two young policemen were an asset to the Force and invaluable in this case. With more guidance and experience, they might be able to fill the shoes of Favre and Garcia when the time came. With a sigh, he reached his office, sagged into his chair, wondering how long before Favre and Garcia would be back. His thoughts were interrupted by a knock, forcing him to look up. Bonavita waited to be acknowledged.

'Good, you're here. You have an update for me?'

Bonavita stood, expecting to be given permission to sit down. It didn't come, so he kept standing in front of the captain's desk.

'*Oui, chef.* I spoke to a couple of informants. None had any information, that is to say; nothing useful.'

'Have you met with everyone? Is there still another who might have something? I seem to remember you mentioned a meeting with one later today.' Leonard saw the man in front of him shuffle uncomfortably.

'No. Yes. Perhaps. No. I mean, I doubt he has anything to say, that's why I'm not including him.' Nervousness clearly got the upper hand as he clamped his hands together, released them, and clamped again.

At that crucial moment, Leonard's mobile rang. The caller's identification made him pick up the call immediately. *'Hold on one second,'* he said into the phone.

'Bonavita, I need to take this call, wait outside for a moment.'

'*Oui, Chef.'* He got up and once he left the captain brought the phone back to his ear.

'I'm here, sorry I wasn't alone. Go ahead. What do you have to report?'... Where? ... How long have you been on the trail? ... Good, is this the first time he's gone there? ... I see. ... Why wasn't I informed before? ... Fine, I understand. Has the officer in the patrol car noticed him? ... Yes, I agree, they might be aware. ... They have no orders to intercept, only protect. ... Give it another ten minutes, report back if he makes a move.' ... 'If not, in another ten minutes, and he's still there, radio it in and ask for backup, anticipating immediate action.' Leonard ended the call with the officer from Intelligence, went to the door and called the waiting Bonavita back in. He continued their conversation as if there were no interruption.

'I would've liked to include what this man found out. However, I will leave it for you to judge. I don't have to include him in the report. So, you are still meeting him later?' the captain didn't want the officer in front of him to suspect any undue interest.

'Well, yes, but as you say, it's not important to include him. Anything else, sir?'

'No, that'll be all. Report back to me when you uncover something new.'

Leonard turned his attention back to the file on his desk, forcing Bonavita to retreat without verbal dismissal. With the office now occupied only by himself, the captain didn't hesitate, and dialled Favre's number. The question now was: should he instruct the extra bodies arranged by Borel and Pichon, to go directly there with telephonic instructions, or keep to the arranged meet at his home to familiarise them with the tentative plan on the case? Except, the opportunity presented was too good to be missed. Nevertheless, he wanted his two detectives' input. They might have another idea on how to ensure success. He updated them with Bonavita's news as well as the information the Intelligence officer gave him.

Predictably, Garcia wanted to act immediately, Favre advising caution. True, there would be at least three officers available to arrest him. However, Olivier's ability to evade them so far should not be taken lightly. He could easily slip out of reach and then be forewarned. Too great a risk, according to Favre, unless they could get more men on the scene immediately. This would mean that Olivier must stay put until they could put the other officers in place. But would he?

The captain was aware that the successful completion of the whole case depended on his decision at that moment. Too many aspects existed which could derail their plans. The most important: Olivier acting the way they wanted him to. Unfortunately, no guarantee of that existed – ever. Though, a decision must be made now and not later. Leonard got up and paced around his office, one hand on his hip, the other either smoothing down his hair, or with his fist pressed against his mouth. Time was running out. He should act now, the ten minutes he had given the Intelligence officer tailing Olivier was nearly up, and Leonard could not be seen as indecisive. He was still pacing when his phone rang. Decision time.

'Leonard. What's happening?' ... *Exactly what is the situation?* ... *Fine, continue and let me know the result.'* He tapped the red icon on the phone to end the call. He ran his hand over his face, took a deep breath, and dialled Favre's number.

'On my way,' is all he said and cut the call. He grabbed the file on his desk and left for the HUG.

*

The captain walked into the room where his two Detectives occupied their hospital beds. It was less than an hour since he last saw them, but it felt like a full day. He nodded to both, and they greeted him with curiosity.

'We didn't think we would see you so soon. What's going on?' Garcia asked.

'I had a report back from the officer tailing Olivier. About five minutes after I gave him the order to standby, observe, and report back in ten minutes, one of the officers in the patrol car exited the vehicle. He looked in the direction of Olivier, spoke on his radio, and began moving toward the rear of the vehicle. This must have spooked the suspect, as he slowly turned and walked away. The Intelligence officer was still on his trail, but we have lost that opportunity. Unfortunately, this means that Olivier is very aware of what is going on. We will have to be much more careful if we want to nab him during his meeting with Bonavita.' Leonard resumed his pacing, only this time at the foot of the two beds where the two detectives lay, silenced by disappointment.

'A pity losing the opportunity,' Favre commented.

'What the hell did that patrol officer use his radio outside his vehicle for? What an idiot, he ruined everything!' Garcia's impatience had no bounds.

'Who was he on the radio with? Did he know of our plans? Who alerted him?'

'Favre, slow down with the questions. On my way here, I contacted dispatch and spoke directly to the officer. The radio call to the patrol car was their routine check-in, nothing to do with our scheme. His getting out of the car was coincidence. He went to get water from the trunk. Bad luck, or timing on our side.'

'Bad luck or timing! What a crock! We lost a great opportunity to take the bastard down!' Garcia would not let it go. He thumped the bed with his fist.

'Okay, I understand your frustration. However, we still have a chance when he meets with Bonavita. I am sure his vanity would not let him miss that opportunity. Alpha had flattered him, and he'll want to see how far he could stretch it. I had better get going. I don't want to be late at the house when Borel and Pichon show up with their pals.' The captain walked to the door, turned, and with a look over his shoulder, nodded and left.

*

Leonard pulled into his driveway, and still deep in thought, entered his home, calling out to his wife. He needed to warn her of their pending visitors and the need for her not to hang around. He knew she would want to fuss over the young officers and offer lunch. Well, he supposed that would be necessary as they were not given the opportunity for any nourishment. They had to drop everything and come to Geneva without delay.

'*Cherie! Ou es-tu?*' He put down his briefcase and took off his jacket. 'I'm home,' he called out again. 'Ah, there you are,' he said as she came out from the kitchen, wiping her hands on her apron.

'Hello Darling. I didn't expect you so early. Am pleased, then we can have lunch without rushing.' She approached and kissed him.

'Good, except, we won't be alone. I have colleagues coming over for an urgent and confidential meeting. What do we have to feed about eight of us?'

'Oh, well, you're in luck, as I've just begun to prepare a meal for the Women's Group. We can have that, and I'll cook up something else for the

Women's Group. That meeting is only for the day after tomorrow. I only wanted to get a jump on it. So, we're all set for today, and we could eat in fifteen minutes.'

'Great. One thing, I will need you to make yourself scarce while we discuss.'

'How long have we've been married? You don't need to remind me; it goes without saying. When you work, you need to work without me interfering.' She smiled.

'Thanks, you are one in a million. What would I do without you?'

'Don't let me start! The list is too long.' With a playful punch, she left, returning to the kitchen to finalise the lunch.

Leonard went through to his office, moved the two-seat sofa to the side, brought in extra chairs, and generally prepared for the arrival of the expected people. While copying certain documents, the doorbell rang.

He went to open and found Pichon with two unknown men on the doorstep. He saw Borel pull up behind Pichon's car, piling out with him were two other men. Everyone was dressed in civilian clothes, only their bearing confirmed their training. These men were obviously the best the academy had produced. Stepping aside, he held the door open in welcome. He waited for Borel and the other two to enter. Mrs Leonard came through, and introductions were made.

'Please make yourself comfortable. We'll be eating shortly. If you want to wash up, the bathroom is down the hall. As soon as I've laid the table, you can all come through to the dining room. In the meantime, I'm sure my husband would be able to keep you entertained.'

The mumbles of '*Oui, Madame, merci,*' were heard from each one of the visitors.

Comfortable in his own home, Leonard made small talk while he waited for the invitees to take turns using the bathroom. He learnt that Pichon and Borel were very highly regarded by their respective friends. This gave him a renewed estimation for his two young officers and confidence in his previous feeling that they could easily be trained to one day take over from Favre and Garcia. As he looked around at each one, his spirits lifted for the first time that day. Perhaps they did stand a chance to close the case today. He smiled to himself as he heard his wife call '*A table!*' from the dining room. Good, he thought; lunch was ready, soon they could get working.

As the group entered the dining room, Mrs Leonard placed a large bowl of mixed salad and a cut baguette on the table. A jug filled with water and an open bottle of red wine were ready for the visitors. She placed a large casserole dish in the centre of the table. The aroma of *Coq au Vin,* which Mrs Leonard – an excellent cook – had prepared for the Women's Group, made everyone lick their lips in appreciation. Pichon's request to pop round more often to sample her cooking raised laughter and similar requests from the others. The captain finally brought the joviality to an end by stating that the time had come to do some serious work. He agreed that they could take their coffee in the den, where they would be working without any other interruptions.

With everyone seated in the captain's den, he detailed every aspect of the case, explaining their idea of how to bring the investigation to an end. He found all were keen to refine and execute the plan flawlessly. The importance that Olivier, aka Alpha, must be captured alive, raised questions.

'If he is such a dangerous psychopath, shouldn't we take the kill shot when it presents itself?' one of the newcomers asked.

'We should not ignore another – perhaps the most important – side of this case, which is that Olivier was a hired killer in this affair. That first assassination brought our attention to the devious and vicious intentions of the person behind it all; the one who gave the order. Now, to this day, we have not found out exactly who this is. We have narrowed it down to a couple of suspects, but the real culprit has not been pinpointed. We hope Olivier would give us that name.'

'If he is such a hardened criminal, would he divulge it?' one of Borel's friends asked.

'Not unless we offer him something in return.'

'What could we possibly offer him? If convicted, he would be in for life. I doubt any judge would give him less than fifty years – deal or no deal, and that would be for the murder, four counts of attempted murder, arson and terrorism, perhaps even kidnapping,' Pichon was upset.

'We could offer him thirty years in a medium - secure facility with the possibility of parole. That would mean he might get out in twenty and serve out his time in reasonably comfortable accommodation – not in a maximum-security prison. He could still have a life after incarceration.'

'But he's a psychopath – he'll never change his ways. He'll still be dangerous when he's released,' Pichon insisted.

'I agree. At least at that time we should be able to keep tabs on him much easier. And if he makes a misstep, we'll be there to arrest him. He would never be set free. Ever again.' Leonard looked from one to the other.

'So, what do you all say? Are we ready to do this? Are we going ahead with this plan? If so, and none of you have any other suggestions, let us get ready to streamline our steps.' They looked from one to the other and finally at Leonard – all nodded agreement. 'Good, let's get started.' Leonard pulled out copies of the schematics of the area around the bar where the meeting would take place, plus the layout of the establishment itself, handing each a copy.

While the Captain laid out the plan in finer detail, those in the room nodded in understanding, asked a couple of questions for clarification, and finally, acceptance. Time had passed quickly. Everyone got up, each with documents and jackets in hand, straightened their backs. They were ready for action. The hour to take up position ninety minutes away, enough to discuss amongst themselves over a cup of coffee at a café well-placed from the targeted bar.

Leonard walked the posse to the door. As he turned to kiss his wife goodbye, his phone rang. Eric Pichat began talking as soon as Leonard announced his name. He requested the captain to pass by his office as soon as possible. His tone made it clear that he didn't want to discuss the matter on the phone. Even though Leonard wanted to be near at hand when the men executed the plan to arrest Olivier, he could not wait to hear what Eric Pichat had uncovered.

Hastily, he told his wife not to expect him home before dinner, went through to the den, and gathered his papers, which he stuffed into his briefcase. Now armed with all relevant details of the case, he grabbed his keys and set off for the offices of Gonzales.

*

The traffic to the Beau Rivage didn't hold him up, and he got there in record time. Leonard needn't have given his name, as when he arrived, Gonzales and Pichat's secretary immediately showed him into the office where Eric waited.

'Glad you could come so quickly, Captain.'

'Yes, so what is so urgent and confidential that you couldn't tell me over the phone?'

'The information we got concerning the possible competitor in the gem trade gave me cause for concern.'

'What do you mean? Surely the competitor is the person we are concentrating on?'

'Captain, that is what I'm worried about. Our sources say it is as we have suspected, a woman. She is known as "Princess" and based here in Geneva. They also said it is rumoured that there is doubt it being Mama B going under a pseudonym.'

'Okay, let's say it's not Mrs Bescutti. Who is this "Princess" then? Did they give any further information? And why is it giving you such concern? I would have said it was good news, narrowing the field and giving us an avenue to follow.'

'I don't know, it was something in the way it was reported to me. Sinister and cruel. This "Princess" is not someone who you would want to cross paths with, or, in any event, toy with.' Eric seemed genuinely unsettled, even afraid.

'So that is your personal feeling. Have you spoken to Arthur? What was his response?'

'No, I haven't informed him – not yet anyway – he has a lot on his plate. And yes, it is my personal feeling. It was a feeling I got when our contact gave us the information. In no uncertain terms, he told us to lose his number. He didn't want anything further to do with this matter or with us, he said. Except, it was the way in which he said it. And he couldn't get away quick enough. I've known this man for many years, and I know he doesn't scare easily. This is the first time I've felt fear ooze out of him. I do think we need to take his reaction into consideration and move with caution.'

'I hear you, Eric. We will take every precaution possible.' Leonard began to get impatient. 'Now, can you tell me anything else: anything that may allow us to pinpoint this "Princess"? I would love to put her behind bars for orchestrating it once and for all.'

Eric, sensing the captain's frustration, tried in vain to clarify the sense he got from his informant. They discussed various nuances and possible clues which could be drawn from the details given by the contact. The indications pinpointing a certain person were too vague, and the two men gave up trying to identify the woman. Leonard resigned himself to being obliged to drag the information out of Olivier. That, of course, if they were successful in arresting him later.

Anxious to know what was happening elsewhere in Geneva, he cut his discussion with Eric Pichat short. The fact that he had sent out his men on an operation which might prove dangerous laid heavily on his mind. He left to re-join Borel and Pichon overseeing the men on the point of trapping Olivier.

*

Pichon tapped the earpiece hidden in his ear to activate the connection between him, Borel and the men strategically placed, ready to approach Olivier during his meeting with Bonavita. It was crucial the latter remained ignorant of their intention. Therefore, the men were unknown to most in the City of Geneva, as they were based in other towns of the Canton or they were Vaudois or Bernois.

Borel and Pichon sat at the café out of sight from the suspect's proposed meeting place. At an outside table, they slowly sipped coffee. Here, the six men had discussed the finer details of the plan, after leaving the captain's home. They had agreed that no names would be used; Olivier would be referred to as "A" and the officer meeting him as "B". Other details were also covered to ensure the two groups moved in concert. Further, radio contact was established with the original IB officer following Bonavita to instruct him not to intervene when they moved to intercept. The one following Olivier was told to stand by.

Borel and Pichon saw Leonard approaching, began to stand up out of respect for a superior, but sat down again as the captain gestured them to stay put. He brought a nearby chair to their table, joining them with a nod. Borel handed him an earpiece, which Leonard inserted. The communication link was complete.

A voice spoke into Pichon's ear: 'B's approaching.' Borel, given the code name "Stick", nodded.

'Any sign of A?' Pichon asked the disembodied voice.

'Not yet. B's taking a seat in a booth.' Came the reply.

'Stand by.'

'*Chef,* do you think that Olivier caught a whiff of our plan?' Borel asked.

'Possible. Though, we have kept it under wraps. Besides myself, only the six of you knew of the plan. I am convinced that it is his training, and usual anticipation of our next step which has kept him out of our grasp. He would be wary at this stage after we nearly trapped him at the hospital.' The captain scratched his head.

'He most probably arrived much earlier and is nearby, watching if Bonavita was being followed,' Pichon said.

'Clearly, that would be his modus operandi. However, the IB officer knows to follow at a discreet distance. And as the meeting place was known, he would not be seen within a block from there, though within eyeline.' Leonard hoped that he assumed correctly.

The voice in the earpiece came to life.

'Someone of the description given is approaching.'

'Watch him.' Pichon's reply.

'He's checking to see if he's being followed. Now entering the bar. I'm moving to cover the back exit of the bar. "Tailor" out. Handing over to "Tinker," already inside.'

'"Candle" here, moving closer. "Maker" entering the bar as backup.'

'Good. Stand by, keep at the ready until we give the order,' Pichon said. They waited, listened anxiously.

'"Tinker" here. "A" scanning interior, satisfied, approaching "B" – "A" sliding into booth. Jovial greeting.'

'"Maker" here, taking seat at counter on way to toilets opposite end of "Tinker"'

'Good, "Stick" joining "Tailor" at bar's rear exit. The rest will join to guard the entrance. IB to enter bar and assist in arrest. Five minutes, everyone.'

Within five minutes, each gave word that they were in place. Pichon moved to the entrance to back the other two up, and the captain opted to support those at the Bar's rear exit. He had dialled the IB officer on his cell phone, and on the open line, the officer heard the order and the countdown.

'Everyone ready? Now at the count of three, move in and arrest "A".' Pichon breathed deeply. 'One, two, three – go!'

In a casual movement, the three officers stepped towards the booth in which Bonavita and Olivier sat in conversation. Olivier glanced up in suspicion, jumped up as the three closed in on them. Bonavita was completely confused and looked bewildered. The officers drew their weapons, identified themselves, and told Olivier that he was under arrest for murder, and to stand with his hands clearly visible.

One of the officers showed his police ID to the barman, who had pulled out a baseball bat to protect his patrons. The officer announced who they were, calming the staff member to avoid confrontation.

They told Olivier to put his hands on his head and turn around. Outnumbered, he did as he was told. Even though they had the upper hand, the three officers felt chills run through them as they saw Olivier sneer and burst out laughing. With no regard for his comfort, they handcuffed him roughly.

One of the three pushed a protesting Bonavita, who tried to intervene, back down into his seat. One said, 'we'll deal with you in a minute.'

'"Tinker" here. Suspect in custody. Assistance required.'

The Captain, Pichon, Borel, and the other officers, all entered the bar from their posts and surrounded the cuffed suspect. They were not taking any chances that he might try to make a run for it. Bonavita they took by the arm and strongly steered him out of the bar, disgust on their faces.

Leonard took out his phone and dialled an important number. As far as he was concerned, it was imperative that he made this call immediately.

Without preamble or waiting for confirmation that he had the right number, he said: *'We've got him!'* the captain closed the call – no other word was spoken.

*

Favre received a call which made him shout out at the top of his voice, thumping the bed. Favre's strong reaction made Garcia look over at him.

'Hey mate, don't keep me in suspense. What's that call all about?'

'They've got him!' Favre could hardly get the words out because elation took over.

'Alpha? Great! Fantastic news. Now we can pile up the charges against him.'

'Yeh, yeh. The list is getting longer with every stone we overturn. I only hope that he doesn't slip through our fingers.' Favre became pensive.

'What are you getting at? Oh, I know you – you are thinking this arrest was too easy.'

'From what we've learnt dealing with him, he's a slippery character and we should not underestimate him. He might have something up his sleeve.'

'Besides making a deal with the Justice Department, I doubt he'll be able to get off easily. Look what he did to us!' Garcia was getting riled up.

'I know, I know. However, can you imagine how far they'll bend backwards for him to pinpoint the person who ordered the hit in the first place? They're desperate to nip that illegal gem trade in the bud. Especially if it is run by a ruthless and cruel person.'

'You mean they might let him off completely?'

'No, except if he spills, they might deport him with the proviso he never set foot on Swiss soil again and that would mean he would only set up shop in a neighbouring European country and orchestrate his evil deeds from there. And I want him behind bars for the rest of his life to pay for every crime he committed!'

'I'm with you there, mate! Let's make sure the captain understands our point of view for him to convince the Federal Court.' Garcia shifted uncomfortably on the bed.

'First things first, now that he's in custody they'll get a warrant to search the car he used, and the apartment where he has been staying.'

'Let's hope he was less careful there, so that more trace evidence can be found to nail him. In fact, I would like to see him leave in a box!'

'I understand your sentiment completely. Though for my part, I would like to see him suffer, and if he's dead, he won't feel a thing,' Favre said.

'You have a point. Did the captain say he was on his way here?'

'I doubt we'll see him before ten o'clock, if at all. He would want to personally be present when they book Olivier. And I suppose he'll do the initial interview. So, we can relax because Alpha is in custody and wait for full details later.'

'I don't think I'll be able to sleep!'

'Patience partner, patience. I personally want a blow-by-blow account of how it went down rather than the abbreviated version. So, let's get some rest.' Favre settled back into the pillows and closed his eyes.

CHAPTER TWENTY-TWO

Leonard's shirt and suit showed twenty-four-hour wear, his tie loosened, and top shirt button undone. However, his tired face carried an ear-to-ear grin as he entered the hospital room at ten o'clock the next morning.

'*Bonjour, mes amis!*' His out-of-character greeting made both detectives sit up.

'*Bonjour, chef!*' Favre and Garcia said in unison.

'You look as if you fell under a bus,' Garcia remarked.

'In a way, I feel like it. I've been up all night interrogating our special friend, Olivier, and our colleague Bonavita. Nevertheless, I am relieved that we have come to a point where we can say: we are ready to close the case.'

'Did he give up the name of the woman?' Favre wanted to know.

'Not yet, he wants to make a deal.'

'What did I tell you, Favre! I don't trust that slippery bastard. He'll get away with it.'

'Don't jump to conclusions – the Attorney General is considering what deal to offer to ensure Olivier confesses to all other crimes committed in Geneva, and he gives us the information we require.' Leonard pulled up a chair and sat down facing the two detectives before continuing.

'The charge sheet only noted the shooting, and the attempted murder on the two of you, which of course would carry a very heavy penalty. With the agreement of the AG, I omitted the other charges for the time being, so that we would have something to nab him on after the deal is struck. I made sure that the AG understood that immunity should only be granted for one of the crimes on the initial charge sheet.

'This morning we received the Justice Department's official permission to exclude the other charges now, and later issue a fresh arrest warrant for all the crimes. They realised we are still uncovering more crimes. Therefore, no matter what, he will be going away for a very long time.'

'That's good news. Does Olivier know how much we know? I mean, does he have an idea of what charges he will finally face?' Favre asked.

'No. I specifically only mentioned the two. As far as he is concerned, that is all we have on him. Though, to cover us, we added that the situation might change as the investigation continues. I imagine his lawyers would have a field day if I didn't mention anything, and we suddenly spring it on them.' The captain took a deep breath. 'Oliver seemed very smug when we set out the two charges, which gave me the impression that he did not suspect what we know – especially, not how much more. I didn't let on, but let me tell you how everything unrolled yesterday.'

Leonard leaned forward. With his elbows on his knees, he gave his two detectives a detailed account of the arrest, the involvement, and actions taken by each officer. Olivier's reaction and arrogance when interrogated, drew sniggers from the two patients. Leonard told them of Bonavita's astonishment and protests when he was arrested as well. He was shocked when he realised, he had passed on information, giving Olivier the means to stay one step ahead of the investigation, thereby committing crimes against his colleagues. Leonard described how Bonavita deflated in front of him with disillusionment when he informed him that the persona and the name, Sebastian, were not real. No book project existed, and being a writer was a ruse to get information on the movements of the detectives working the case. It appeared that the greatest betrayal in Bonavita's eyes was that Sebastian was a pseudonym. After nearly an hour, the captain sat back, satisfied that everyone was now up to date with events.

'There you have it. You now know everything. Olivier will be transferred into Federal custody later today.' The two patients immediately began to protest.

'Don't be concerned, it's only for security reasons. We don't want him to influence or pay someone to help him escape. The case remains ours, and we will be in charge of every step. The decision was made only because there had been too many leaks, and besides Bonavita, we think Olivier might have convinced others to work with him. We all know how charming he can be when he thinks the situation warrants.'

'That's a relief! I thought we might have gone through all this pain and suffering for nothing,' Garcia said.

'When do you think the case will come before the courts?' Favre wanted to know.

'Due to the gravity of the charges, the AG is not going to waste time, and Olivier's lawyer has argued for a speedy trial, obviously to avoid any further items to be added. As you are aware, we are ready with many more crimes. If he gives us the name of the woman behind it all today, we can move immediately.' Leonard suddenly stopped and looked at both detectives.

'Oh, I nearly forgot! So many things have happened since I saw you last. Eric Pichat discovered that the woman is known as "Princess," and the information gleaned pointed away from Mama B. Although the connection to the Bescutti family, though there, is not yet clear. Further, the cruelty and heartlessness were confirmed. Eric's contact appeared terrified and refused further contact with either party for fear of life-threatening reprisal.'

'When will you be talking to Olivier again?' Favre asked.

'Just after lunch. He's being processed by the Federal Police at this moment. Once they are finished with the formalities and he is in his cell, I'll call his lawyer and the AG to be present for the deal to be presented and signed. The deal is that Olivier must divulge the woman's identity and full details of his mission. It would take us the rest of the day to confirm his allegations. Once everything is checked out, and we have this "Princess" behind bars, the documents would be officially lodged with the Justice Department.'

'When will the other charges be drawn up, and added to his indictment?' Favre asked.

'Most probably tomorrow. At the latest, the end of the week. Borel and Pichon are formulating the arrest warrants as we speak, which will list everything we know so far: the explosion, arson attack, kidnapping, and disappearance of Gonzales's courier, including the assaults on the three prostitutes.'

'Bet that last one would be a surprise for him! I'm sure he doesn't rate physical abuse as a crime against humanity!' Garcia chuckled.

'Has anyone uncovered further information on the courier? Perhaps she could shed some light on why she was intercepted, where she's been all this time – and what she's been doing. Olivier might have paid her a large amount to hand over the sample of emeralds and disappear,' Favre suggested.

'Could be. Or he could just have gotten rid of her,' Garcia said.

'You always see the worst!' Favre interjected.

'Well, we have no proof of that. We are still looking. As yet, she hasn't surfaced. Forensics are going through his car and apartment as we speak.

They'll let me know whatever they find, and if there's any sign of her being there, they won't delay advising me.'

Leonard slapped his knees and got up to leave.

'Good, will keep you informed. Though firstly, I need to get home: kiss my wife and have a shower. I think my wife thinks I've deserted her.'

'I only wish that we could get out of here and be part of this interrogation, being laid up like this is no joke. I feel fine, and sure Maria will be pleased to get home and have the family all together.'

'Be patient, it won't be long now. Both of you have some rehabilitation that awaits. Be good little soldiers. Do what the doctor says, and you'll be back on your feet in no time. I, for one, cannot wait for the day when we welcome you back at the station.'

'Same here. See you later, Sir.' Favre said as Leonard walked out.

*

At home, Leonard gave his wife a hug when she came hurrying out of the kitchen, concern on her face.

'Are you okay? You mustn't work so hard; you're not thirty anymore! Go and clean up; then you can have some lunch.' Her scolding made him smile. He knew she would have something ready for him to eat. True to form, she had prepared an early lunch. She'd never change – and he loved her for it.

'*Ma cherie,* I'm tired, but fine. And thank you, I won't be long. Then I'll tell you how Garcia and Favre are doing.' Another thing he appreciated was that she never asked him about a case. This gave him confidence to discuss certain aspects of an investigation with her. She gave him a different insight, and her questions quite often brought an aspect to light which he might not have thought of on his own – or only reached much later.

A little later, refreshed, he sat down with his wife, enjoying a much-awaited meal when his phone rang. He got up from the table and took the call out of earshot. The conversation was short. With a set expression, he went back to finish his meal. His only comment to her was that he had to be in Court at three-thirty the afternoon; therefore, couldn't stay as he had to prepare before then.

Twenty minutes later, he said goodbye to his wife and went directly to the station. Borel and Pichon were, as usual, in front of the computer screens, this time scouring the footage to pick up a possible destination of Olivier, other than the apartment or Paquis, where he usually picked up prostitutes.

'*Bonjour, chef.*' Both men said in unison as they looked up.

'We have work to do. I just had a call. Olivier will appear in court at three o'clock for his arraignment. It is sooner than we expected. However, I want us to be there and be prepared.'

'Why does his lawyer want to rush this? It sounds suspicious,' Pichon asked.

'I'm sure they have something up their sleeve, but what?' Borel added.

'Yes, I agree. That's why I want to be there to see if we could have a quiet word with his lawyer.'

'I doubt he'll divulge anything. He doesn't have an obligation to inform us of what he has uncovered from his client. In any case, if it's something that might incriminate him, it'll fall under client privilege. If he told us, he would risk being struck off.'

'So, what do you think we'll discover, sir?' Borel asked.

'You never know. Let us begin by analysing the lawyer's body language. Perhaps he is as distrustful of Olivier as we are. Who knows, he might let something slip.' Leonard himself wasn't sure of what they would learn, except he knew every iota of information, and the smallest sign might help them in the conviction of Olivier. It was at times like these when he needed his two best detectives. They saw what others never did.

'Whatever you say, sir.' With that they prepared for the arraignment.

*

The legal proceedings at the court were nothing new for any of them, though seeing the small smile on Olivier's face as he stood in front of the judge, gave the three law enforcement officers, chills and uneasy feelings.

Just as the Judge stated that he had accepted the documents placed before him with a plea of guilty on the attempted murder charge, and the deal the AG had offered concerning the murder of Marcus Stephens, Leonard's phone vibrated with a message.

Discreetly, Leonard looked at the screen. With a sign to his two officers, he left, leaving them to observe and note when the trial date would be. Outside the Court, he slid his finger over the phone's screen, tapped the

411

message just received to call the number. It was answered immediately. *'Leonard. You called with an urgent request to contact you. What's this all about?'*

'We are here at Cornavin. The Railway Police called Head Office. They were advised to redirect all recent suspicious events to IB as per your request. You had better come immediately. We found something.'

'I'm on my way.' Leonard cut the call and left without looking back at the Court House.

It didn't take long to reach Cornavin Railway Station. When he arrived, he was directed without delay to the self-storage lockers. An area was cleared and cordoned off by yellow tape. A group of three members of the Railway Police, two Cantonal Police Officers, and the IB officer were standing in deep discussion. One of the men noticed him, stepped out of the circle to greet him, and ask him for identification.

'Yes, I'm Captain Leonard. What do we have here?' Leonard showed his ID and waited for an explanation.

'Sir, we have something which might be relevant to your case,' the IB man said.

'Captain.' The most senior RP pointed to a medium-sized duffle bag in the centre of the group. 'We were alerted by one of the cleaners about a strange smell coming from this area. We believe the smell could be due to decomposition.' He shuffled from one foot to the other. 'It could be anything, from meat left in the locker to a dead pet. People leave strange things in these lockers. Once we found ...' The man was interrupted.

'What do you mean? Haven't you opened it?' Leonard asked.

'No, when we pinpointed where the smell came from, we only opened the locker and took the duffle bag out. We didn't want to touch it in the event of it being dangerous or something to do with a crime.'

'Fine, and any one of you?' Leonard gestured to the other officers standing around, 'did you touch or open it to look inside?'

'No, none of us felt we should. We thought it better if you took on that responsibility, seeing the importance of the case you are working on, and the strict instructions you left,' the IB officer added with nods of agreement from the CPOs as they looked from Leonard to each other and back again. Leonard wondered if any one of them had the guts to take on any responsibility, or if it truly was concern for the successful termination of a case.

'Good. Let's get to it then. You have gloves? Okay, open it.' He stood back, holding his breath. The others did the same.

The senior RP bent down and unzipped the black bag. He jumped back, losing his balance. His backside hit the concrete floor with a bump. Various "ugh," "oh no," and "yuk" were expressed by those in the circle. Everyone took a step or two back turning away from the offensive smell coming from the receptacle. Some turned back tentatively to look at the contents. Leonard stepped nearer. Everyone had either a hand or handkerchief in front of their noses. The contents revealed a small-sized decomposed body tightly stuffed into the bag.

'Get the coroner and forensics over here immediately,' Leonard barked. 'I want an identification, cause, and TOD as soon as humanly possible. We cannot lose time. It is essential that we get this information without delay.'

'Sir, they're backed up. It would take at least two days,' one of the CPOs said.

'Use my name. And if necessary, get the AG's approval, tell him it's for me. But you get it for me now!' He turned, left the group pulling out his phone at the same time.

'*Eric, I'm at Cornavin. I'm coming over now!*' He didn't give Eric Pichat a moment to reply or recover before he cut the call, replacing the phone in his pocket.

Five minutes later, he walked into the Gonzales's place of business. Eric was waiting for him at reception. Without pausing, Leonard walked past him into the office they had used previously.

'What's wrong? What's so urgent?'

'What did that girl, the courier, wear when she arrived? And how big was she?'

'Wait, ah, I can't remember. What's this about? I'll have to ask our girl who went to the airport to meet her.'

'Call her in right now. I need to have all the information.'

'Okay, just a minute. She might be out of the office.'

'Find her wherever she is, we need that information immediately.'

'Okay, okay, sit down, please.' Eric picked up the phone and spoke to the secretary. It took only three minutes for the girl to walk into the office. However, Leonard could not sit down; he paced crossing the office. His anxiety affected Eric.

'You called for me, Mr Pichat?' The girl timidly asked.

'Yes, this is Captain Leonard, he has some questions.'

'Can you tell me what the courier was wearing when you saw her being intercepted at the airport?' Leonard interrupted the niceties.

'Oh, hello. Oh, I can't really remember.'

'Well, try, girl, we don't have all day! It's important.' Leonard was losing patience.

'Think back to that day. You were waiting at the airport, at Arrivals. She came out, and you were going over to her. Then a man came and took her by the arm, leading her away.' Eric tried to calm the situation, helping her to recall that day.

'Oh, yes.' Tentatively, she nodded. 'Yes, she looked so small against this man – just like a child.'

'Okay, okay, that's good. Now, what did she wear? A dress, jeans, or shorts?' Leonard wanted to know.

'Shorts. I remember because I still wondered if she didn't find it cold on the plane. She was coming from their winter to our summer.'

'Fine, were they white, a colour, or denim?' Eric prodded.

'They were like Bermuda shorts in denim, with a bright pink t-shirt and denim jacket. I can't remember if she wore sandals or sneakers.'

Leonard sank back in one of the chairs. 'Thank you. I'm not sure, but I think we found her. From what I saw briefly, it could be her.'

'What do you mean, you think it's her? Couldn't you speak to her, ask her where she's been, and what she's been doing all this time?' Eric had all these questions.

Leonard gestured for the girl to leave before he said anything further. Eric thanked the girl, waving her out. Once they were alone, Leonard explained what they had found, were awaiting confirmation of identity, and time of death. Both men sat in silence for a while. Eric got up and poured both a strong drink.

'Wait until we have confirmation before telling your partner. He's most probably with his daughter. This can wait for a day or two.'

'You're right. He would take it personally. It was at his request our possible suppliers sent someone over with the samples instead of using DHL or FedEx. He really doesn't need more guilt.'

Both sat in silence, sipping their drinks. Neither realised the time passed.

'Mr Pichat, do you require anything else?' The secretary's voice brought both men out of their ruminations. Perplexed, they looked up at her.

'Sorry, what's that?' Eric asked.

'I apologise for interrupting. I only want to know if you required anything else, or could I go home?'

'Oh, I didn't realise the time. Sorry, yes. I don't need anything further. Good night.' Eric was apologetic. Leonard shifted in his chair.

'Is that the time? I had better leave, things to do. I still would like to stop at the hospital and update Favre and Garcia.' Reluctantly, he got up, shook hands with Pichat, and left, not looking back.

*

Visiting hours at the HUG brought all shapes and sizes out to visit someone laid up in one of the wards. Most carried either flowers, fruit, chocolates, or candy to soften the enforced stay away from their home, or as a token of the visitor's concern for a loved one's wellbeing.

Leonard made his way to the ward where Favre and Garcia were. He hesitated at the door, giving the two officers guarding the door leave to end their shift. Now that Olivier was under lock and key, they could lessen the guards at the various points. Although he was not completely convinced that Olivier hadn't engage someone else to do his dirty work, he thought halving the guard should be safe.

Then, before entering the room, he glanced at both Favre and Garcia. He was pleased with the progress they had made – proof of their determination not to be left behind. Their injuries had left multi-coloured bruises on their faces and body parts not covered by either a bandage or cast. Favre's plaster casts had been replaced by a temporary one on his leg, and a special support for his arm. The captain realised that he didn't want to – no, couldn't lose his two best men. They were essential as examples for the next generation of law enforcement officers. When Garcia noticed him in the doorway, he entered.

'*Chef!*' Garcia called out. 'What are you standing there for? Come in!'

'I suppose you have had your dinner.' Leonard walked over, pulled up the chair, and sat down. 'I have news.'

'We're ready Sir, what can you tell us? What happened at the arraignment?' Favre wanted to know.

'That went according to plan. Olivier has been charged with attempted murder on two law enforcement officers and accepted a deal for the murder of the young man. However, I've come to tell you that we might have found the young girl.'

'Which young girl?' Garcia asked.

'The courier Gonzales employed to carry samples from South America to Geneva. You remember she was intercepted by Olivier.'

'Where? When? What does she say?' Questions tumbled from Garcia. Leonard explained who had contacted him, what they found, who was present at the opening of the holdall, as well as what he saw, and his impression.

'We don't have definite identification yet. Nevertheless, my gut tells me it's her. The employee at Gonzales's office gave a description of what the girl wore as she remembered it. From what I saw glancing at the body in the bag, the clothes match. I'm waiting for the coroner and forensics to confirm.'

'That'll take forever!' Garcia protested.

'I've put a rush on it. We should have some news this evening.'

'Not long to wait then. It's already evening,' Garcia commented.

'Yes, you're right. With everything that's happened today, time has run away from me, except waiting for the results, which made it drag.'

'Will you let us know as soon as you hear, please, sir?' Favre asked anxiously.

'Without a doubt. Keep your phones close. I'm just going to ICU to tell the Gonzales family about the arraignment, and then off home.'

'What about the courier? You going to tell him that she might have been found?'

'No, Favre, not yet. Both Pichat and I decided to wait until we had positive identification. He has enough to worry about at this moment.'

'Sounds good to me. I wouldn't want the anxiety of wondering if it's true or not. He would have her fate on his conscious in any case. Worry before knowing would be extra strain,' Garcia empathised.

'Agreed, so I will be in touch. Get some sleep so that you can get back to work.'

'*Bonne nuit, chef.*' Their words landed on the captain's back as he left their room, the Gonzales family already on his mind.

The ICU was quiet, and the two officers guarding the room watched him approach. The latter stood up and nodded to their superior. Leonard returned the nod and asked where the parents of the girl could be found, as they were not at their daughter's bedside.

'In the office at the nurses' station with the doctor, sir.'

'Carry on, in a couple of days you may return to your usual duties. But for now, you remain at this post.'

'Yes, sir.'

Leonard walked over to where the parents and Doctor Stein were in discussion, their demeanour, promising. A smiling Arthur Gonzales saw Leonard approach and excused himself to meet the captain.

'Ah, good evening, Captain. You have arrived just in time to hear the good news. Our daughter had a bad spell yesterday. However, she has turned the corner, and the outlook is very promising indeed. The neurologist has tested her reaction, and it seems that her brain function is normal. They are going to bring her out of the coma first thing tomorrow morning. They believe one more night would be beneficial. We have full confidence she will wake up tomorrow and recognise us. Besides that, we are convinced she'll be back on her feet in no time.' Gonzales couldn't stop talking. The joy the change in his daughter's condition brought, spilled over.

'Very good news.' Pleased for the parents, Leonard had no other words.

'What brings you here besides checking up on Cynthia's progress?'

'Well, that was the primary reason. However, I wanted to tell you that Olivier's arrest and arraignment went according to plan, and we'll advise you of further developments.'

'Further developments? By that, you mean him being accused of attempted murder on my daughter, besides his other crimes. You are going to make sure he pays for what he did to my little girl?'

'Yes, exactly. We want to make sure everything will be ironclad, with no way for him to get out of paying for every wrongdoing here in Geneva. Make no mistake, the stabbing of your daughter is high on the list. We will not let him get away with it.'

'Good. Because if you don't. I'll be forced to make sure he answers to me.'

'Now, don't take matters in your own hands. We want to nail him, and if there were to be interference from any other quarter, we might lose that opportunity.'

'Well, we'll wait and see. I trust you can bring him to justice. Lock him up and throw away the key!' At that moment, Mrs Gonzales approached them.

'What's this about a key?'

'Nothing, my dear, just talking about justice which should be done.'

'Mrs Gonzales. Yes, the suspect has been arrested and arraigned, he's not going anywhere soon, except to be transferred to maximum security.'

'I'm happy to hear that. Did my husband give you the good news?'

'*Oui, Madame,* he certainly did. I'm very pleased for you and want to let you know that the officers guarding your daughter's room will return to their usual duties in two days.'

'The danger will be over by then?' Anna wanted to know.

'In fact, it is already behind us. Nevertheless, we are playing it safe, just in case he had accomplices. I reiterate my relief and share in your joy about your daughter's progress and bid you a good night.'

'Good night, captain, and thank you for keeping us informed.' Both parents turned as one and went to their daughter's bedside.

Leonard nodded to the officers and took his leave. He couldn't wait to get to his car to phone the coroner and check on what forensics had found from the remains and the duffle bag.

When he had settled in the driver's seat, he pulled out his phone, activated the selected number, and put the phone on speaker. After the eighth ring, the coroner answered.

'*What took you so long? What news do you have?*'

'*Sorry, Captain. As you requested, we are doing the autopsy of the young victim,*' the coroner sounded tired and harassed.

'*Yes. So, what have you found? Do you have and ID and TOD?*'

'*The only thing I can tell you now is that it is a female, around her late teens, or early twenties. Dental work denotes possible South American origin. Time of death is a little difficult to determine exactly – I estimate between fourteen and ten days. Cause of death still to be determined. However, from first glance, it looks like she's been beaten, tortured, and repeatedly raped. I will know more after a more detailed examination.*'

'*Nothing else?*'

'*Forensics would most probably be able to tell you more with the analysis of the clothing and bag in which she was found.*'

'*You mean the definite origin of the girl, and where she met her death?*'

418

'Yes, the trace elements on both would pinpoint a more exact provenance of the clothing and bag, as well as retracing where it had been before the railway station locker. On my side, I need more time for a more precise cause of death, age, and nationality.'

'Okay. How much more time would you need?'

'As much time as is necessary, captain. So, may I please get back to work?'

'Good. Yes, I'll leave you to it, let me know as soon as you've uncovered anything more.' Leonard closed the call. Pensively, he sat in his car for a while before turning the ignition over. He pulled away on route for home.

CHAPTER TWENTY-THREE

Alexandra woke with a smile. Her conversations with Paul the last couple of nights gave her renewed hope. He would be out of hospital tomorrow, and they could start their life together or at least begin to get to know each other better. Already she had certain menus in mind for when he came for dinner. They always said the way to a man's heart was through his stomach. Even if it wasn't true, she wanted to make him dinner – not only once, but often. If possible, that is! Alex told herself not to take things for granted – take it slow. There were two people in this scenario.

He also said the case was nearly over. That would mean she would have free movement again and would not be watched or forced to be accompanied wherever she went. She knew Mrs Ginet would miss chatting and handing out biscuits to the officers. However, she would not miss any of it.

In a day, Paul would be out of hospital, and Garcia's wife would collect her husband as his family would be back in Geneva. Everyone hoped life would get back to normal from then on, Alex most of all. Both detectives would be on sick leave while doing their rehab and allowed back at their posts once cleared for duty – most probably behind a desk at first – until they were declared one hundred percent fit for active duty.

Until then, she had a lot to do. She wanted to clean her apartment completely and stock the cupboards, make the final adjustments of the planned menus, and decide which would be served first. For the last time, she'd do her shopping accompanied by the officer appointed to keep her safe. She'd get Mrs Ginet to go as well, he could carry their bags for them. They could even stop for a cup of coffee – treat him for giving them such protection! Alex sang as she prepared to go out.

*

'When will Maria arrive to take you home tomorrow?' Paul Favre couldn't wait to be discharged, and he knew José Garcia felt the same. Both were getting impatient. They had received no news from Leonard yesterday, except for a message saying he'd contact them as soon as concrete information came his way. Frustration overwhelmed any other emotions they might harbour, pouring icy water over the joy their intended release from hospital should bring. Perhaps something would change now that three days had passed since Olivier had been arraigned.

'She said she'll be here at eleven. Doctor Stein will have passed by then to give us permission to do the rest of our recuperation in the comfort of our own homes.'

'Fine for you to say, I still don't have a home. Remember that my place was burnt down! I'm living in a hotel.'

'At least there you'd have full service and a restaurant available. What did the Insurance company say? Surely, they'll cover your accommodation for a while longer.'

'Yes. Except, I don't know for how long. The possibility of finding an apartment in Geneva is so difficult, I'm not sure how soon I'll find something. As you know, the housing situation is stretched to the limit with very few apartments available for rent.'

'You'll have to buy something. I know the prices are exorbitant here, but in my opinion, that would be the only solution.'

'Well, we'll see how things develop.' Paul didn't want his partner to get the wrong idea about what was on his mind. He worried that even though the deal had been struck with Olivier, he still had not given up the name of the woman behind the whole affair. True to his psychopathic personality, Alpha had talked in circles, giving clues here and there. But not enough for them to pinpoint her identity. He still held back her real name. That she was known as "Princess," he did at least confirm. In the face of this, Leonard refused to guarantee low-security incarceration until every item in the deal had been met and the woman arrested. Rightly so, Favre thought.

In the meantime, Paul worried about Alex. The guards at Cynthia's ICU room and theirs had been reduced to the original one officer, and tomorrow, those at Alex's apartment would be withdrawn completely. Without the protection detail, she would be vulnerable. The danger that one of Alpha's collaborators might get to her and carry out the threat aimed at Favre – that all those close to him would suffer – terrified him. Paul shivered. He wanted her to be safe. She had become one of the most important people in his life, and he would be crushed if he lost her before they could start their relationship on a deeper level.

Garcia need not know his concerns. He looked over at his partner. José had enough to worry about with his family threatened to the extent that they had to go into hiding. There would be great celebration when he got home with his family intact. Paul realised that since he met Alex, he had begun to envy José. Even when he had been married with a daughter, he never felt that warmth or closeness, which was so evident in the Garcia family. If he could have that with Alex, he would die a happy man. However, Favre's thoughts were interrupted by Leonard's arrival.

'Ah, bonjour, chef.' The detectives said in unison, straightening as much as possible on the beds.

'How come you are still in bed? Aren't you supposed to be up and about?'

'The nurse said we had to be in bed until Doctor Stein arrived and could only get up thereafter,' Favre explained.

'And you've seen her, *chef!* She's not one to argue with unless you are prepared to take your life in your own hands!' Garcia was quick to remind Leonard.

'Yes. I remember; I crossed paths with her a couple of times. In any case, I came to tell you that the forensic reports have been finalised and the identification of the cadaver in the duffle bag has been confirmed.'

'So, is it the courier Gonzales engaged to bring the samples through?' Garcia asked.

'Yes. It is the young girl. The forensic evidence retrieved is conclusive. Clearly, Olivier had a hand in her death, as well as stuffing her in that holdall. The evidence shows she had been tortured, severely beaten, and repeatedly raped before dying.'

'So, we can charge him with her murder. That is great news. What about all the other crimes? Did they find some proof of the explosion and fire in my apartment?' Favre asked.

'Well, that is still in the works. We cannot charge him with anything else, until he has surrendered the name of the person who gave the initial order.'

'Mince! Chef ça ne marche pas! No! We cannot let him get away with these terrible crimes. He must be held accountable!' Garcia was losing his temper.

'Wait, mate. I see what the captain has in mind. He will slap these charges on Olivier immediately after the woman has been captured. Isn't that right, Sir?'

'Yes, exactly. For the moment, he believes that he is in the clear and will only have to serve the minimum in relative comfort for the attempted murder charge against the two of you. That is how I would like to have it; with a surprise from which he cannot escape as soon as we have the woman.'

'You know best, sir. So, how far are we on finding out who this "Princess" is?'

'We are closing in. The connection with the Bescutti family has been confirmed. Though which one remains a mystery. Nevertheless, we are closing in.'

'Have you spoken to Georgio Bescutti again?' Favre wanted to know.

'I have a meeting with him at noon. I will then hear what he has uncovered, and let you know as soon as possible.'

'How is the young Cynthia doing? We haven't heard much about her progress. If she was the original target, I can imagine Olivier would be beside himself if she survives,' Garcia said.

'She's making progress and has been breathing on her own for three days now. Apparently, she woke up and recognised her parents. However, she's not out of the woods yet and drifts in and out of either a coma or sleep. I'm not exactly sure which. Though, her parents tell me Doctor Stein is satisfied, told them it was the natural healing process. He expects her to be fully awake not later than today.'

'Will you be able to interview her?' Favre wanted to know.

'I hope so. We still do not know how much she remembers of the attack. The doctor was adamant that we do not press her unduly; not until she is fully awake.'

'Yeah, well I suppose it would be difficult to interview her if she drops off every minute or so. I wonder if she remembers anything at all.' Garcia thought back to the accident. 'I had no memory of what happened just before the accident, or the accident itself. It took time for it to come back to me.'

'We'll just have to wait and see. In any case, I'll go and see her now; they might move her out of ICU.' Leonard shook his head; impatience had crept up on him. 'Good, I will see you later.' He turned and left just as the

423

doctor arrived.

'Good morning, gentlemen.'

'Doctor, can we go home? I don't think I can stay here a day longer. My family needs me.' Garcia didn't wait to say what was uppermost on his mind.

'The prognosis is good, and if it stays like that for the rest of the day, you'll be home with your family tomorrow for lunch. Last checks tonight and tomorrow morning. Mind you, if you develop a fever by then, we'll be forced to keep you a bit longer. So, don't disappoint me, gentlemen. I want you out of here as much as you want to leave. The nurses are complaining that the Police Department does not respect the visiting hour rules. And as you well know, we do not argue with the nurses!'

'Yes, Doctor, we'll keep our fevers down. We understand your respect for the nurses. They can be formidable and run the place very efficiently, I might add,' Favre commented.

'We would be lost without them; I can assure you. So, stay out of trouble and you will be home tomorrow.' The doctor bid them a good day, leaving to see to his other patients.

'I suppose the team didn't retrieve Gonzales's sample emeralds,' Garcia said.

'The captain would've said if they had. Though it must be somewhere.'

'If not in his apartment, where? I cannot see him having a safe deposit box at a bank, do you? He would be the type to have it next to his bed to admire and fondle! I doubt he would miss one day in which he would not look at each stone and relish the idea of having more.'

'José, I agree. An egoist such as him would want all his material possessions within reach. So, where do you imagine it could be?'

'Cap didn't mention anything about his gun or knife. Perhaps it's all together, and they are still processing it.'

'That must be it.' Favre left it at that. He wanted to go back to his ruminations about what Miss Labelle could be doing, and how he planned to deepen their relationship.

*

Leonard left the HUG after visiting his officers and the Gonzales family. The good news of the progress all three had made these last three days,

424

promised that everything would fall into place and turn out to their satisfaction. It was imperative that he maintained his present positive attitude and not fall back into despondency. They were too near the finish line – and bringing in negativity now would be counterproductive.

He pulled up outside Bescutti's offices. The Secretary announced Leonard's arrival. He found Georgio as usual staring out of his office window at the airplanes taking off and landing. Bescutti turned with a smile.

'Captain, welcome. Let us have a coffee. I've ordered a light lunch for us and would be honoured if you would partake with me.'

'That's very kind. Yes, I could eat something, and would love to stay for lunch.' With that, Bescutti called his secretary, giving instructions for the lunch, and coffee to be brought in.

'Shall we sit over here?' Bescutti gestured to the armchairs flanking the coffee table on one side of the room.

'Perfect. Let me update you while we wait.' Leonard recounted the salient features of events from trailing Olivier, his arrest, the deal offered, the arraignment, up to the discovery of the body in the bag. Georgio was surprised that Olivier was offered a deal. However, he understood the motive behind the action, thinking it a clever way to ensure Alpha's permanent incarceration.

'Now, what have you heard? From the information Eric Pichat has given us, have you found out who could be involved?'

'You said the rumours named a woman called "Princess." Well, with that in mind, I kept my ear to the ground whenever I visited my family. As my mother tolerated my presence, I was not included in any conversations and, strangely – or perhaps not so strange – they never spoke of business or anything connected thereto, while I was around.' Restless, Georgio stood up and walked over to the window again, from where he continued.

'It was not until this morning, when I had a call from my brother, that I thought we might have a clue.' He turned back to face Leonard. 'Incidentally, that's why I asked you to come over as soon as you could.'

'Yes, I had hoped that you had some news.'

'My brother chatted amiably about how pleased he was that I decided to spend more time with our mother and the family. Then he went on to tell me about their last family dinner, and how proud he was of his little "Princess." I asked if she had graduated with top honours or something like that. He only laughed and said his "Princess" is making a name for herself in the world of business.

'I asked what line she decided on, but he was vague and said that it was a start-up. He didn't want to jinx her chances of being a success by talking about it before it really got off the ground.' Bescutti came back and took a seat just as a soft knock on the door made him hesitate. 'I'll continue in a minute.'

'Come!' He called out, and the secretary with another young woman came in with trays carrying their lunch, a pot of coffee, plates, cutlery, cups, and saucers. They gave each a serviette, and the secretary asked if she should serve the lunch or if they help themselves. 'Not to worry, we'll manage. You carry on, thank you.' Silently, the two women left.

'Thank you for this,' the captain said, indicating the lunch. Each man helped himself to some green salad with cold chicken and bread.

'Not a problem, much nicer to eat with someone than alone, don't you agree?'

'Definitely. Hurried office lunches are not good for the digestion, my wife always says, and prefers if I could go home for lunch. However, times have changed, and we cannot spare the hour and a half or two hours going home for our midday meal.'

'I agree. In fact, I rarely take more than thirty minutes for a lunch break, unless I entertain business clients.'

'In my profession, it differs day to day. Crime controls our hours!'

'That must be frustrating, as you never know if you'll be able to have a break.'

'True, but then it is rewarding when we can close a case successfully.'

'That brings me back to our conversation.' Georgio put his cutlery down and poured coffee for both. The captain mumbled his thanks before his host continued.

'Even though my brother did not say his daughter was breaking out into the gem trade, the mere fact that he called her his "Princess" made me wonder. You see, the pieces fit: his nickname for her, her start-up, and making a name for herself.' Georgio shook his head. 'Not the name I would like my child to have, but then my family is rather different. And from the example they've set in the past, I wouldn't be surprised if his daughter inherited the heartlessness and cruelty, which my mother exhibited.'

'From what I've heard, she is worse. As I told you, the contact wanted nothing further to do with Pichat, Gonzales, or anyone vaguely associated with them. He trembled while sharing the information with Pichat, and according to Eric, nothing scares this man. That should tell us something,' Leonard said.

'Exactly. Then I thought back to the couple of times I saw her, and the last dinner we had together. She was charming and polite. I don't know her that well, seeing that I've been ostracised for many years. However, it came to me that her eyes were always cold and expressionless. She would be smiling, yet nothing expressed amiability. Her words always had a cut to them. There was a shallowness in her expression that made me uneasy. *Mon Dieu!* Do you think she is a psychopath?'

'Oh dear, not another one! It sounds possible. Psychopaths are usually very charming and obliging people when it benefits them. Though, they have a cruel streak to force people to pander to their every whim. Olivier would be drawn to her, and of course, she would seek out someone like him to do her dirty work.'

'Why?' Bescutti asked.

'Because they are master manipulators, and both get a kick out of cruelty. Life has no value in their eyes, except, of course for their enjoyment. I wonder if they value their own lives. They both use charm and seduce people; win them over, and when finished with them, get rid of them permanently. In fact, I suppose she would relish living vicariously through his acts of cruelty.'

'So, what do we do now? What should be our next step? Should I approach her to find out if she's interested in resurrecting our defunct gem trade business? That would be confirmation, don't you think, captain?'

'I advise strongly against that. It is far too dangerous. If she thinks that you might want the trade for yourself, you'll be in grave danger. You see, you'll become her competition. As events have shown us, she does not accept competition; she eliminates them indirectly. You don't want anything to happen to your son or wife, do you?'

'Hell, no! I've protected them for so many years and would die first before putting them in danger. No matter what you think of me, Leonard, my wife, and son are very dear to me. I think I've proven that by staying away from them all these years.'

'Yes, your sacrifice proves that.' The captain took a sip of his coffee. 'I don't want you to do anything. Stay away; in other words act as usual, anything out of the ordinary would raise suspicion. That is the last thing we need at this crucial stage. Leave it up to me. First, we need proof that she is the "Princess", they are speaking of. If it is confirmed, then I'll arrest her for ordering the assassination of Cynthia Gonzales by the hand of Olivier.'

'Except, the girl is not dead. Is she? I thought she was out of the woods.'

'Oh yes, she's on the mend. Except, I doubt Olivier had the time to tell the "Princess" that his last attempt had failed. So, as far as she's concerned, he had eliminated the girl and thereby Gonzales's emerald trade. I have asked Gonzales and his partner to keep a low profile and not, if possible, make a trade for a week. That should give us enough time to wrap it all up. That is, if we get our proof!' Leonard wiped his mouth with the serviette and sat back.

'It's time for me to go. I want to interview Olivier, and suggest that we know who the woman is hiding behind the code name "Princess". In fact, I hope that would threaten his deal and egg him on to give up her real name before I voice it.'

'Oh, I do hope you succeed. It would bring this ghastly affair to an end.' The sincerity in Georgio's voice could not be missed.

'I agree with you there. I'll keep you informed. However, do not forget, stay away from the family, even on the phone: don't be over-friendly with your brother or your mother.'

Bescutti nodded, clearly resigned to let the law take over irrespective of the outcome, or how it would affect his blood relatives. To be estranged from them was nothing new. They shook hands, and Leonard left, already formulating his interview with Alpha.

*

He touched base with Borel and Pichon at the station, confirming that the three prostitutes gravely injured by Alpha, would be prepared to lodge formal complaints. He added the two officers' reports and statements by the three women to his file. One of the prostitutes was not eager to testify. Nevertheless, the other two had strong cases and were ready to appear in court. After satisfying himself that the cases were solid, Leonard immediately went to meet with Olivier and his lawyer at the prison.

'My client wants to know when he will be moved to the minimum-security prison, as spending his time in general population until the trial, wasn't the agreement,' the lawyer stated.

Leonard looked at the arrogant Olivier slouching in the chair next to his legal representative. The sneer turned the smug look on his face into a blood-chilling threat. How could Bonavita not see who this man really was, he asked himself. How could he charm and mesmerize people to the extent that they did his bidding? His manipulation has won over his lawyer as well, who seemed to bask in Olivier's arrogance, which he most probably took for confidence. Leonard wondered how people could be so blind as to succumb to such false power and empty flattery.

'I'm here to arrange that.'

'Right, so what are we waiting for? I'm ready to go.'

'In fact, it all depends on what your client has to say in the next few minutes,' Leonard watched both carefully.

'What?' Olivier said with bluster.

'Well, the deal brokered was that you give us the name of the woman behind the crime, and so far, you haven't.'

'You plods are such idiots! I gave ...' Olivier was interrupted by his lawyer who put a calming hand on Olivier's arm.

'Captain, we have given you sufficient information to uncover who this woman is, and therefore, we have met the requirements of the deal.'

'Not exactly. Clues and indications do not conform to the precise requirement, which is: the name of the person. The NAME we asked for, not the nickname, pseudonym, or any other aka she might be using.' Leonard shuffled the papers in the file in front of him. 'And if that is all you have to give us, I will tell you who it is. And if we could have uncovered it without your help, and I say the name out loud before you do, you go back to the original charges.'

'That's not fair!' Olivier blurted out.

'Have it your way. I repeat, once I name the person responsible, your deal falls away.' Leonard looked at both and began to open the file slowly. 'You're ready? Good, here goes. We are on the way to arrest the woman known as "Princess" at her residence.' He looked at the first page in the file. 'Her name ...'

'Wait! Wait! I'll tell you! Princess lives on Quai Gustave Ador. Miss Monica Bescutti!' Olivier could not get the words out quick enough.

'Ah, just in time. So, you are confirming our findings that Miss Monica Bescutti, aka "Princess," the granddaughter of Mrs Bescutti – Mama B – as she is known; hired you and gave you instructions to murder …' Olivier began to protest, his lawyer objected.

'Eliminate,' the lawyer interjected.

'Fine. Eliminate the daughter of Miss Monica Bescutti's competitor for the trade in semi-precious stones, specifically emeralds, to threaten …'

'Influence and convince,' the lawyer interrupted again.

'Influence and convince the company Gonzales & Associates to relinquish their European trade in said gemstones. Does that come close to your assignment?'

Olivier turned to his lawyer and nodded. 'Yes, that conforms to the request made to my client by said Miss Monica Bescutti.'

'Could you please get your client to complete his revised statement with the information given and any other items he wishes to add.'

'Of course, you'll have it in fifteen minutes,' the lawyer offered.

'So, when are you going to move me?' Oliver clearly didn't appreciate being holed up with common riffraff.

'Hopefully, early evening, or at the latest first thing tomorrow morning. We must lodge your official statement, giving her name and all the paperwork with the officer of the Court. Then the Judge must sign off that all the requirements have been met. Our arrest warrant for Miss Bescutti, and details of her being booked for the crime, must be attached. We will expedite the paperwork to the best of our ability.' Leonard closed the file and stood up, nodding to both. He left without looking back.

Outside the prison's interview room, he pulled out his mobile phone and called Pichon giving instructions to immediately arrange for the arrest of Monica Bescutti with the IB officers as backup. His next call was to the Judge to ask for the arrest warrant to be issued without delay, as he was on his way to collect it.

The third call was to Forensics to find out if any further proof was found at the apartment Olivier had been using. They advised that the report was faxed to his office as well as sent via e-mail to his account. He instructed copies to be forwarded to Pichon and Borel and the IB officers involved. He let out a long breath, releasing the tension which had built up over the last month.

As he reached his car, he made his fourth call. Favre answered on the second ring. Leonard gave him the news. The elation coming through from the other end of the phone told the captain that the phone was on speaker.

430

His two detectives had received the news they were waiting for since the beginning of the case.

His final call was to his wife, telling her that he would most probably be quite late. Nevertheless, the cause was a positive one: the arrest of the woman behind it all. He wanted to be the first to interview her.

Olivier was last on his list. Alpha could wait until the morning to be moved – perhaps not to his desired destination, but he would be rehoused. Leonard would arrange for the lawyer to be present for not only the move, but for the surprise he had in store for them.

CHAPTER TWENTY-FOUR

At four-thirty the next morning, the captain unlocked his front door.

He unburdened himself, placing his briefcase in the den and tiptoed upstairs directly to the bathroom, where he attentively closed the door. Careful not to wake his wife, he undressed dropping each item of his clothing on the floor. With revulsion, he regarded the crumpled heap, deciding to ask his wife to either destroy the lot or send it to professional cleaners for deep purification. Vileness had impregnated his clothes, stuck to his skin, and he imagined black tentacles threatening to invade his mind.

Finally, he stepped under the shower. The hot water scalded his skin to a bright red before he added cold water. He wanted to burn off all traces of whatever tainted his skin. He took the loofah, scrubbed his body hard, vigorously massaged shampoo into his scalp until some of the foam burnt his eyes. The sight of Monica Bescutti had to be expunged. The need to rid himself of the malignancy and savagery emanating from that young woman was uppermost in his mind. It horrified him. In all his professional life, he had never encountered anything or anyone like that.

No doubt existed that this woman and Olivier were two peas in a pod. They were both merciless killers. They had no empathy; human life held no value for them. Olivier had at least tried to be charming during interrogation, whereas she showed her true nature – vicious and snarling. From different backgrounds: he a male who grew up on the streets of Marseille, an ex-soldier in the Foreign Legion; she a privileged young woman brought up in a reasonably civilised manner. Except, she used her femininity to fool everyone, her father most of all, of that Leonard was sure. To him, she was his "Princess" and could do no wrong. How could this Monica be so barbaric? Did she learn it from her grandmother? Perhaps Mama B moulded her. In either case, as far as Leonard was concerned, children learn by example and therefore, it was clear from where she got this cruel streak.

When they made the arrest, he was told the old woman appeared genuinely shocked at the charge. She defended her granddaughter, not believing that the sweet girl could ever be part of orchestrating a murder. She argued that it must be a mistake for her granddaughter to be accused of such an appalling crime. Was the old woman part of the scheme to resurrect her previous activity? Was it a ruse to deflect them? If so, for what reason? Questions crowded Leonard's mind.

Finally, he closed the flow of water, hoping that none of the negativity remained. He stepped from under the shower wrapping one bath towel around his waist. He took another. After rubbing most of the water from his hair, pulled it over his shoulders. For a moment, he stared at the steam-covered mirror; with the side of his palm he wiped an area clear. He could see his moisture-distorted face staring back at him – red and shining from all the scrubbing. Except, stubble was forming. He ignored it. He had no strength to shave. He would leave it until he had rested a while.

He tiptoed into the bedroom and sank down on the bed next to his wife. For a moment or two, he lay there – on his back staring at the ceiling. With deep breathing, he tried to let go of the day's stress. He turned his head and looked at his wife. She stared back and reached out a comforting hand.

'*Tout va bien?* Have you closed the investigation?' she whispered.

'*Finalement, ma chérie.*' He had hoped not to wake her, though not surprised that she was. He had often come home during the early hours of the morning, only to find her waiting for him. She knew not to ask questions. He would tell her what had happened when he was ready.

'Sleep for a while. I'll wake you at seven.'

'*Merci, chérie.*' He sighed, took a deep breath, covered himself with the honeycomb summer blanket, and turned on his side. He tried to clear his mind. Exhaustion took over, and he fell into a fitful slumber.

*

The aroma woke him. When he opened his eyes, the mug of steaming coffee stood on the bedside table. His wife had left the hot liquid to bring him back from sleep. Even though Morpheus didn't take him completely, he did feel better than when he arrived home a mere two-and-a-half hours ago. He moved his limbs. He ached all over as if he had run a marathon. He supposed his verbal wrestling with the Bescutti woman could be rated as such; it took long enough! He smiled at the thought that it might pass as sufficient training for the *Escalade* race through Geneva later in the year.

Slowly, he sat up. He took his time going to the bathroom to freshen up and shave. His pile of clothes had disappeared – his wife had taken care of it. The bathroom felt cleansed.

'I feel like a human being again,' he said as he joined his wife at the breakfast table, dressed and cleanly shaven.

'I must say you look better than the glimpse I got of you going into the bathroom after four this morning.'

'I thought you were sleeping. Did I wake you?'

'No, I was only dozing, waiting for you to come home.'

'You know you don't have to wait up for me.' He buttered some bread.

'I know, but you might be hurt or need something. So, I rest until you put that key in the door. I listen to your footsteps coming up and know if you are okay or injured.'

'How do you know that?'

'I'm a mother! I can distinguish your, and each one of our children's, footsteps, tone, or breathing which indicate your state of emotion or physical well-being.'

'That's incredible – don't you want to come and work for me? We can use someone like that.' Leonard finished his breakfast and stroked his wife's hand.

'I think every mother has that ability. Your loved ones are always part of you.'

'Well, seeing you don't want to come to the station and work for me, I'll take my leave and wrap up this case,' he said, smiling. 'I'll tell you all about it when everything is said and done.' Leonard kissed his wife, collected his briefcase, checked his pockets, and left.

*

Garcia and Favre were packed, sitting in the chairs next to their beds in Geneva's Cantonal Hospital; ready and impatient to get out of there. The reasons were numerous: not only to get away from being constantly prodded and probed; neither to eat good Italian food again; nor regaining control of their lives, but to breathe fresh air.

The main reason was the news Leonard gave them at nine that morning. As soon as Leonard had arrived at Servette Station, he phoned his two hospitalised detectives, updating them on the status of the investigation.

They argued that they wanted to be there, not in hospital.

Now, they sat conspiring on how to get to the station and join in on the action. They wanted to see Olivier's face when the captain charged him with the list of the other crimes.

Also, they wanted to be there for his reaction when he heard of two charges of murder against him: the first of the young man Marcus Stephens, and the second charge based on finding the courier's body in a duffle bag at Cornavin railway station, with her DNA, the bag, and evidence that she had been in the apartment he used.

The attempted murder by stabbing Cynthia Gonzales at Starbucks, Rive, confirmed by trace elements of his DNA found on her by Forensics.

Further, forensic evidence in the flat that he had built a bomb, matching the explosives' fingerprint planted in Garcia's car, as well as flammable materials which corresponded with that used to set fire to Favre's apartment.

Also, not only was his DNA found, but also a full and clear handprint on the vehicle Favre drove with his partner, proving that Olivier caused their accident. This charge was also of attempted murder.

However, the charge of GBH – grievous bodily harm – of numerous prostitutes would most probably tip Olivier over the edge: he regarded streetwalkers as no value items to be used as the mood took him.

Favre and Garcia imagined the objections the lawyer and Alpha would raise, arguing that the murder of Marcus Stephens and the attempt on their lives were covered in the deal which was struck. Obviously, they would vehemently insist that the deal was valid. However, they would conveniently forget the fact the deal was based on full admission and declaration of crimes committed. Thus, the deal had no bearing on the charges therein. He was given the opportunity to declare all, and any crimes committed in the Geneva Canton at the time of his arrest. Because of this omission, the judge would declare the deal null and void and issue the extended arrest warrant, which Leonard would serve on Olivier this morning at noon in the prison's interview room. Besides the Captain, Borel and Pichon would be there to see Alpha's reaction when this warrant was read to him in the presence of his lawyer. The last blow would come when they told Olivier that he would be moved to a maximum-security facility where he would be held with no possibility of bail until his trial.

Favre and Garcia were irritated, they wanted to be there. Instead, they sat next to stripped beds, waiting for Maria to first drop and install Favre at his hotel and then take Garcia home, where his family awaited. They had more than a few choice words to describe the situation, even though it fell on deaf ears. Except it didn't go unheard.

'WHY ARE THE TWO OF YOU SWEARING LIKE THAT? YOU SHOULD BE ASHAMED OF YOURSELVES. WE CAN HEAR YOU DOWN THE CORRIDOR.' Their nemesis, the nurse who spoke like Favre's old school principal, instilled fear in everyone nearby.

'Sorry ... Sorry, we didn't realise. We apologise,' Favre stuttered, and Garcia joined in.

'GOOD, NOW BEHAVE OR YOU WON'T BE GOING HOME!' she turned on her heel, muttering under her breath, 'Please just go home, I cannot put up with the two of you one day longer.' The two partners looked at each other and sniggered, desperately trying not to burst out laughing.

'I didn't realise that we got under her skin like that!'

'I suppose we were a little demanding, with the captain in and out at all hours, and the protection detail outside always in the way checking who comes in and out,' Favre suggested.

'Their jobs are not easy, that's for sure, mate. Still, did she have to terrorise us?'

'How long before Maria gets here?'

'Not long, about thirty minutes, maybe sooner.'

In fact, Maria arrived fifteen minutes later. She dealt with the required paperwork and got the two loaded into her SUV. She refused point blank to take them anywhere except their respective accommodation. Even Garcia's suggestion that Favre come home to celebrate their release from hospital with the family before she took him to his hotel, went ignored.

*

Borel and Pichon looked worse for wear. They had been with Leonard until four that morning. The captain didn't comment; he appreciated their presence, not only during the long hours of interrogating Monica Bescutti, but also their attendance at work at this hour. Before he approached them, he took a moment to watch as they prepared documents, copied affidavits, and arranged forensic reports. The two had proven their worth, and the captain decided to request their permanent assignment to his unit.

'Good. You are already preparing everything I need to present to the judge for the extended arrest warrant, listing all the crimes.'

'*Bonjour, chef!* We are nearly ready for you. Did anything happen after we left this morning?' Even through their tiredness, they sounded excited. Finally, the investigation was coming to an end. He knew they were also pleased to have had the opportunity to introduce their Academy friends, who assisted in the capture of Olivier. Borel and Pichon were definite team players and an asset.

'No, nothing new. I stayed to see that Miss Bescutti was securely behind bars, even though it was temporary accommodation.' Leonard moved back to his office.

'I've got to make a couple of calls. The two of you carry on and finish off so that I can get to the judge as soon as possible. If nothing changes, we'll meet at the prison just before noon. The lawyer and Olivier should be ready for us by then.'

Closing the door behind him, he sat in silence, looking around at the various framed certificates and citations hanging on the walls of his office. He picked up the in-house phone, dialled zero for an outside line, followed by Georgio Bescutti's place of business number.

'*Bescutti, Leonard here. I have news and thirty minutes before I need to leave. Would you like an update on the phone, or could you come over here as soon as possible?*' The captain replaced the receiver when he received the reply.

His next call was to Favre, who, as usual, put the call on speaker so that Garcia could join in. The captain recounted the events as from the afternoon when they set out to arrest the "Princess" up to the phone call he had just placed to Georgio Bescutti. Leonard pulled out transfer forms, called the Commissioner at HQ to verbally request the transfer of Pichon and Borel. Pleased with the tentative approval, he returned to the bullpen to check on the two newest members of his unit. All he could do now was wait.

In fact, he didn't have to wait long, as Bescutti walked in only ten minutes after he had called him. Leonard gestured for him to approach; he made them each a coffee before they went through to his office.

'Bescutti, I didn't want to say anything over the phone, until we had everything sealed.'

'You're right. I trust my people. However, as I mentioned before, the

437

members of my family are devious, and they would threaten loved ones or pay off my staff only to find out what I'm doing. So, I prefer that you speak directly to me face to face. That said, what do you have?' Georgio settled into the chair facing Leonard's desk.

'I'm not sure how to say this, except that I apologise in advance.'

'That sounds ominous.'

'Yesterday late afternoon, we arrested the woman known as "Princess" at her residence.'

'Yes? And? Who is it?'

'It is your niece, Monica Bescutti.'

'Really? So, we were correct in our thinking. Did she give up easily?'

'Your mother tried to intervene. I didn't get the impression that she knew what was going on. She seemed shocked and very distressed about the whole affair. Paramedics had to be called as she collapsed just before we took Monica away. I have heard that she is fine, recuperating in hospital. They'll most probably keep her for a couple of days.' Leonard studied Bescutti. 'I take it you haven't heard from your family.'

'No. No one has contacted me. I suppose I should find out how mother is.'

'If I were you, I would wait another day or two. Act as you normally would. You never contacted her every day, did you? If I remember correctly, you called her once a week.'

'Yes, that's right.'

'I would advise you keep to that routine. That way, they would not be able to implicate you in this torrid affair. We know you had nothing to do with it. However, her lawyers would use every trick to minimise her culpability by saying her father, grandmother, and even you were all complicit. I've never seen such malignity in one so young – and a female to boot.'

'As you said, Monica and this Olivier must be cut from the same cloth – both psychopaths. Such a pity. I feel for my brother; she's his only child. Now you understand why I severed all ties with my wife and son. I didn't want that evil to penetrate their lives or influence the way they saw others.' Bescutti ran a hand over his face. 'When you grow up seeing your father and those you look up to in the family, having no regard for human life, you have very little opportunity to develop it yourself.' Georgio was truly saddened by the whole affair.

'How did you get out from under it then?' Leonard found it ironic that Georgio, being of the same blood, had empathy and concern for his fellow man. From the start, he had done his best to stay within the law in his business affairs. To the extent of attempting to bring the rest of the family in line with legal practices.

'A strange story. My father kidnapped the wife and daughter of an associate as punishment for a deal gone wrong. This woman was given the task of being my governess – or I should say forced. My father threatened her daughter's life if she refused, or her husband intervened. The daughter was my age and became like a sister to me, and her mother; whom I love dearly, basically brought me up with her values. We became partners in hiding our true feelings and ideas from others and were aware my parents watched our every move. As soon as I could enter university, I chose Edinburgh because it was out of my family's reach.'

'But your brother? Didn't the same woman bring him up?'

'Oh no. A cousin of my mother, who had her values, took him in. Old Mafia values. So, you see, therein lies the difference.'

'Whatever happened to the woman who brought you up, and her daughter?'

'Another sad story. When she was only sixteen, the daughter was forced by "Mother Dearest" to marry a distant relative who was much older and cruel. The poor girl didn't last a year; she committed suicide to escape. When I left for Edinburgh, I convinced my parents that I would need someone to do my bidding, basically be my slave. They agreed, so it happened that I took the woman with me, and as far as they know she is still in my employ. She is independent and happy – as far as a mother could be who had lost a child. We keep in close contact just in case mother asks if her work is up to expectation and if she's looking after me in the manner that I am accustomed to. This woman and I have decided that the next time anyone asks after her, I would say that she had died.' Bescutti gave Leonard an anxious glance. 'Captain, I have not named this woman for obvious reasons. What I've told you must please stay between us. No one else should know about it.'

'Definitely. I fully understand. It is a strange story. All I can say is that I am thankful this woman came into your life. The mould has held.'

'Thank you, Leonard. To hear you say that gives me hope for my own son's future. You have no idea how much it means to me. They say, "like

439

father, like son," though I hope that my son would be a better man than I could ever be – even with the humane values instilled in me throughout those years.'

A knock on the office door interrupted them. 'I apologise. I see I'm needed. Please excuse me. It's time for the next phase. And please remember, play ignorant until such time as your family, or anyone else contacts you with the news, then act surprised or horrified – whichever you feel appropriate. From my side I will keep you informed. Enjoy your day.' Both got up, Bescutti leaving for his own business and Leonard to collect the relevant documentation to present to the Judge.

*

Ten minutes to noon, Leonard drew up at the prison, parking next to the car with Borel and Pichon. The Judge had no problem in issuing the new warrant, also keen to see Alpha safely off the streets of Switzerland. Therefore, armed with the relevant documents, the three law enforcement officers registered at the desk and were allowed to the interview room for their meeting with Olivier and his lawyer.

Leonard introduced the two men with him to the lawyer. They all took their seats at the table, waiting for Olivier to be brought in. As usual, when Alpha entered, he had a smirk on his face and a smart remark to the prison officer who uncuffed him. The lawyer and prisoner sat opposite the three men from Servette. The lawyer had his file ready on the table.

'Right, you lot. I'm ready to leave for better accommodation. And take note of what I say: I want no interference while I'm there so I can get back to my life and business.'

'Mr Olivier, good morning. Please take it easy. Let us get this done.' The lawyer tried to deflect the obvious disdain Alpha aimed at Leonard and his officers.

'Take a seat, this won't take long.' Leonard, matter-of-fact, pulled out his recording device and the file from his briefcase. He took his time taking out the arrest warrant with its supporting documents.

'You don't mind if we record this, not only for the official report, but for posterity?' Leonard asked, looking at both, his finger poised over the recorder.

'Fine. Get on with it!' Olivier was getting impatient.

'Please, Mr Olivier, getting annoyed will not speed up the process,' the lawyer tried again.

'Your lawyer is right. Good, here we have it. New documentation,' Leonard said while Pichon and Borel watched Olivier's reaction.

'Present on this 24th day of September in the year 2019, are the following: ...' Leonard listed all around the table and the purpose of the meeting, citing the original arrest warrant. With a short pause, he continued.

'That warrant has now been declared unenforced. It is hereby replaced by a new arrest warrant as follows.' Leonard took a breath. Olivier slouched in his chair, his lawyer listening attentively, making notes.

'Mr Olivier, you are hereby charged with two counts of murder, two counts of attempted murder, kidnapping, committing a terrorist act, arson and two counts of grievous bodily harm. All the supporting documents are here.'

'What! This was not the deal!' Olivier jumped up rattling the table. 'Do something!' he shouted at his lawyer. The latter sat dumbfounded and silent, then he recovered. The prison guard stepped forward and cuffed a protesting and struggling Olivier.

'Captain, this is highly irregular! We had a deal! Where are the supporting documents? I demand to see them immediately.'

'No problem.' Leonard handed over a copy of the list.

'You will notice the following:

- The two murder charges concern: Mr Marcus Stephens,
and the kidnapping and murder of Miss Juanita do Santos.

- The attempted murder charges concern: Miss Cynthia Gonzales and two Law Enforcement Officers, Detectives Paul Favre and José Garcia.

- The terrorist act concerns the planting of explosives at an official Government Building under an official vehicle allocated to Detective José Garcia.

- The charge of arson concerns the attack which destroyed the apartment of Detective Paul Favre and endangered persons and/or persons unknown.

- The charges of GBH concern the complaints by various Professional Women working in the Paquis area. Two of the complainants are Mesdames Rose and Christina, with others to be named.' Leonard set the warrant down and looked at the felon.

Olivier had tried to interrupt on various occasions. Leonard ignored his rantings and spoke through it all. The disbelief on Olivier's face made Leonard wish he had a video recording of the whole event. Alpha cursed all to a life of hell and worse, and disputed every point, finally exploding when the GBH was mentioned. However, his temper could not be controlled, as he was screaming, and shouting obscenities.

Leonard called for a second guard to enter the interview room to help the one present to restrain Alpha.

'Captain, please, we had a deal,' the lawyer tried unsuccessfully.

'That deal was declared null and void by the Judge when he realised that the basis of the agreement had not been met.'

'But, sir, my client gave the name of the woman who hired him for a mission and instructed him to complete said mission resulting in the events that followed,' the lawyer pleaded to no avail.

'With due respect, Maitre, the most important part of that agreement was that Mr Olivier declare any and all crimes he might have been involved in, in the Geneva area. You do remember that stipulation, do you not, sir?'

'Well, yes, but surely my client was not responsible for all these crimes. What evidence do you have? We will dispute and object to each point.'

'As is your right. I hereby submit to you all the information which you will require to defend your client. For the moment, he will be transported to another facility where he will be held until the arraignment for this arrest warrant be dealt with. A court date will be set by the Courts, giving you sufficient opportunity to prepare for trial.' Leonard, as cool as can be, handed over copy documents to the lawyer, and stopped the recording. He picked up his briefcase, put it on the table to replace the file and recorder. Olivier, even though restrained, lunged at Leonard, propelling the briefcase into the captain's midriff, knocking the wind out of him. His chair toppled over, and he hit the floor with a thud. Borel and Pichon immediately helped the captain up.

Olivier burst out laughing.

'Get the prisoner out of here immediately!' The authority with which Pichon gave the order didn't leave any doubt as to what they wanted to do with Olivier if he remained.

'Serves you right, you bastard! Make no mistake, you haven't heard the last of me!' Under protest and trying to fight them off, Olivier kept on sneering and swearing as he was led to lockup.

'Where will you be taking him?' the lawyer asked timidly.

'He'll be transferred to a maximum-security facility immediately,' Borel replied as the three policemen took their leave without a further word or thought of what would happen to Olivier until the trial, when they would all give evidence. For the moment, their work was done.

When they reached their vehicles, they broke the silence.

'Are you okay, sir?' Pichon wanted to know.

'Oh, thank you, yes. It took me by surprise that's all. No, I am fine really, very pleased it's now all over. I only wish we had a video recording of our time with our dear friend to show Garcia and Favre.'

'I agree – a pity they couldn't be there. Nevertheless, the voice recording would give them a good idea of our time together. Olivier is really something!' Borel said.

'You can say that again. What a vile character. Though, between the three of us, I think Miss Bescutti is slightly ahead from what we experienced last night,' Pichon dared to say.

'I think both are the worst I've ever come across in my long life in law enforcement. I really do not want to venture into rating either – it would give me sleepless nights. I do hope there are not many more of them coming our way!' Leonard said.

'I think I speak for Borel as well when I say, we are pleased that it's over. After yesterday and today, all I need as soon as possible is a hot shower and a good meal.'

'Yes, I agree. Before you do that, the final report awaits. See you at the office,' Leonard said as he got in his car waving them goodbye.

*

As soon as Paul had settled in the hotel room, he telephoned Alex. Her pleasure evident to hear from him, lifting his spirits and when she insisted on coming over to see him immediately, the pit of his stomach fluttered with excitement. At first, he objected, pleading tiredness, and her safety, which was not yet completely ensured. However, she would have none of it, she had to make sure he had everything he needed and was well. Her offer of bringing dinner brought him round, and he agreed, on condition it was Italian. The increase in his heartbeat told him his excuse was only a mental one. The sweating of his palms confirmed his emotional anticipation. Finally, he admitted to himself he also couldn't wait to see her, and she would be a welcome sight.

He moved with difficulty around the room with the temporary leg cast. Though, with one arm in a sling, he tried his best to put away his affairs which Maria had left on the chair. Then he arranged his shaving kit, toothpaste and toothbrush in the bathroom. The plastic bag with his damaged and blood-soaked clothing from the accident, reminded him of the moment he had looked into Alpha's eyes. He relived the chill he felt when Alpha threatened him. The days spent in the HUG, the pain, discomfort, and terror that there would be no end to the fear. He shoved the bag out of sight into the cupboard. His reminiscence was one thing, but reminding Alex of what could have happened, was the last thing he wanted, not at this juncture in their relationship. Shaking off his thoughts, he concentrated once more on making the room acceptable for visitors, he stretched out on the bed to rest until she arrived.

Paul opened his eyes at the sound of the knock, realising he must have dozed off. Despite his struggle to get up and answer the knock, he felt refreshed, and with a ready smile, he opened the door.

Two men pushed past him. He stumbled, fell, hopelessly trying to get out of their way. Pain seared through him. The cast hampered his efforts. One of the men grabbed his good arm, and dragged him further into the room, shoving him onto the two-seater sofa.

'Who are you? What do you want?' Paul managed to say through the pain.

'Where is our Boss?' The larger of the two asked, holding Paul by the throat with one hand and pressing a knife to Favre's cheek, threatening to cut out his eye.

'What are you doing here? How did you find me?'

'Just answer my question!' The grip around Paul's throat tightened.

'Let go of me! How did you get past Reception?'

'Answer, or you'll never ask another question!'

'If you let go, I'll answer.' From the corner of his eye, Paul saw a shocked Alex standing in the doorway, staring at the scene.

'Hey, the bitch is here!' The big man's partner also noticed her.

'Well, don't just stand there, get her.' His grip on Favre loosened somewhat, giving Paul the opportunity to wiggle from the hold. He pushed out his leg with the cast, trying to trip the smaller man who made for the door and Miss Labelle. However, the man only stumbled; he managed to right himself and reach for the door.

He saw Alex drop the plastic bags holding their dinner, turn, and run back towards the elevators. The next was the figure of a uniformed officer, on the spot where Alex stood a second ago, aiming his firearm into the room.

'Police. Step back and put your hands on your heads.'

The two men were so taken aback by the appearance and authoritative command of a policeman, that they did as they were told. The big man let go of Favre, dropped the knife, stunned, put his hands on his head. The other, stopping in mid-stride, glanced from the officer to his partner, and not daring to argue, did the same.

The officer activated his radio near his right shoulder with his left hand, the gun in his right never wavering. He asked for backup at the address as soon as possible for the arrest of the two men, stating they were armed and dangerous. Paul assumed Alex had alerted hotel security, who then arrived. They assisted the officer to secure the two intruders. Paul interrupted the arresting officer a couple times trying to ask questions of his two attackers, but the officer would not have any of it, and bundled them out as soon as possible. Paul's objections and insistence that he needed answers followed the group up to the elevators. The only request Paul managed to get through was that the men be taken to Servette Station. The sight of Alex silenced him.

Alex immediately came forward, rushing over to Paul. He saw the concern on her face as she helped him up and over to the bed, where she tucked the pillows behind him, lifting his injured leg onto the bed. Paul followed her every move. In between grunts, he thanked her, while rejecting her help. She trembled slightly, though otherwise had complete control of her emotions. He had to admire her for that, most women would be hysterical with such an experience. His pride conflicted with his emotions. He wanted her presence, but not her sympathy or charity. Then, as he touched her arm, he could feel her concern was something much more. He relaxed back onto the pillows. He didn't say anything, only watched as she went back into the corridor to picked up the plastic bags she had dropped before.

'Was that our lunch?' Paul asked.

'We'll see. I'm not sure we can salvage anything. Nevertheless, I am going to try as I don't want to leave you alone to go out for more. You said you're fine, but are you really? Did he hurt you? Are you sure you're okay? A good thing I arrived when I did.'

'Never mind me. I'm fine. You were in danger. I would never forgive myself if something happened to you.'

'Well, you can thank Captain Leonard. Yesterday, when I asked him to remove the guards, he insisted they stay with me for another couple of days.'

'That was really good luck with your protection right behind you. Remind me to thank him.' He shifted into a more comfortable position. 'If what you brought is spoilt, let's order in. There's an Italian who'll deliver, they know me.'

'Whatever you say, sir.' She said playfully, the ordeal already set aside.

While she checked the bags with food, he phoned Leonard to report the incident. The captain expressed his relief that, besides receiving a fright, they were both uninjured. He advised he would follow up and be at the station for their booking on charges of B&E with the intention to do harm. He added that he would interrogate them himself. Finally, he told Paul that he would inform Garcia of the attack and wished them *bon appetit* and a good afternoon.

With that, Paul turned to Alex, and said that the afternoon was theirs and he could not wait to eat food prepared by anyone other than the hospital kitchens. She laid out a rough picnic on the bed and brought their plates of *fritto misto* with salad and bread rolls over. She filled two glasses with water and placed them on the bedside table next to Paul.

'Just what the doctor ordered!' Paul said to her. 'How did you know that I hankered for some Italian seafood?'

'Just a hunch.' She settled on the bed next to him with her plate. A comfortable ambiance followed as they ate, talked, laughed, and teased. Their relationship forged.

*

Leonard's blood pressure rose. The call from Favre about the two men had unsettled him. The tale Alpha had spun had not run its course; it infuriated him. Even though he had expected others worked for Alpha, he had fervently hoped it was paranoia on his side. Now, this event proved otherwise. The traffic to the station added to his mood.

'*Bonjour, chef,*' the desk sergeant called out as Leonard walked past him to the bullpen. As usual, the captain only nodded, continuing without a break in his step. His two new men were, as usual, at their temporary desks. Both looked up and greeted him. Borel got up, following Leonard to his office with a bulging file in his hand. The captain moved around his desk, pulled out his chair, and sat down.

'What have you got there? Is it something I need to sign?'

'Yes, sir. It's the final report on the case. We have also tied the two men who were brought in a few minutes ago, to Olivier. They were more of his lookouts and did his clean up. They may have answers to the loose ends.' Borel put the file down in front of his superior.

'Good, let's get ready to interview them.'

'How do you want to go ahead? Should we separate them? Pichon and I could begin, soften them up, and then you could come in to put the final nail in. What do you think, Sir?'

'Good tactic. I don't think these two are very sharp. I understand they wanted to know where their boss was. Well, I think we should remain vague. Let them know the whereabouts of their boss will be disclosed once they tell us everything. You should do the initial interview with the two of them together, then separate them to unnerve them. They would become suspicious of our intention.'

'Great, sir. I understand, we interrogate each separately, you come in at a certain point and finalise. Sounds good to me.'

'Would you bring Pichon up to speed? I'll watch from the observation room. Let me know when you are ready.'

'Give us ten minutes.' Borel skipped out to his partner, eager to begin.

True to his word, Borel gave Leonard the signal, and they began the interrogations. The captain watched and listened, saw the consternation on the faces of the two arrested men when separated. He smiled inwardly at the vigour his two officers expressed as they continued the questioning of the individuals. The fear on the felons' faces when he stepped in made his spirits rise. These were the last of Alpha's troop, that became clear.

Leonard, finally closed the file in front of him, giving instructions for both offenders to be arrested, locked up and charged with assisting in the various crimes committed by Olivier, and some of their own. He went back to his office, satisfied. They now had more evidence against Olivier and further proof of the link to Monica Bescutti. There was no doubt of the expected outcome of the trial. Those involved would be locked up in maximum-security for many years. Leonard doubted the people of Geneva were aware they had been saved from further psychopathic criminal activity on the scale law enforcement had witnessed during the last summer months.

Time to go back protecting citizens from the usual criminal activity in the City of Calvin. He picked up a memo that another demonstration on climate change demanded all officers on standby.

EPILOGUE

Two young men, barely out of their teens, were not having much luck with their day of fishing on the lake. Their rowboat five hundred metres from the shore, just off Point Noir.

Except for the soft lapping of the water against the boat, only silence surrounded them, perfect for the fish to approach, but nothing took their hook. The youngest of the two, only seventeen, suggested they had brought the wrong bait. However, the older one, who had turned twenty the week before, insisted they had to be patient. Fishing takes patience. That was the secret to wisdom – at least that's what his grandfather always said. The younger couldn't understand what wisdom had to do with fishing. As far as he was concerned, you fished to get something to put on the table. They had been there for two hours already, with nothing to show for it, and he was getting hungry.

'Hey, I think I've got something!' The older shouted.

'Come on, reel it in! It's high time we get our reward for sitting out here!'

'It's big! I can feel it!' The pole bent in his young but strong hands. 'He's not struggling too much, except he's heavy to reel in. It must be a very big fish; most probably he'll start fighting when he gets nearer. The bigger ones are clever, you know. They can pull you right out of the boat!'

'I can help.' The younger was eager to bring it on board.

'Get the net ready; you'll have to hold it with both hands if it's as big as I can feel it to be. And don't rock the boat, or we'll both go over into the drink.'

The younger man crouched next his friend, the net at the ready. He watched the surface of the water with intensity. The catch should break the surface any minute. He could see the shadow just darkening the blue-grey of the lake.

'It's here, get ready!' With an enormous pull on the bending pole, he reeled in as fast as the cog would lock and release.

'Hey! It doesn't look like a fish, it's something else!'

'Don't be silly!' The older of the two said.

'No, look, it's sort of square. Hey, it's a suitcase!' The young one became excited. 'Let's see what's in it.'

'Ah, no, let's just leave it. It's rubbish someone threw away.'

'Who knows? There might be something in it we could use. Let's have a look; we can always throw it back afterwards.'

'Okay, if you want, but you'd have to pull it on board – it's heavy.'

The young man leaned over and pulled the suitcase, cabin size, on board.

'The seams have come apart in places. It must have been in the water for quite some time. The zip is still closed, but the stitching is coming undone.' The excitement in the young man mounted. The older one remained disinterested.

'There are women's clothes in here and a dictionary – Spanish to French.'

'What else? Is there something we could use?'

'Don't know – perhaps we could dry it out and sell it or give it to Caritas. Wait, there is something else here. The base of the case came apart. There are plastic bags with something wrapped in tissue paper.'

'Let's see.' The older took one of the bags from the younger's hand and opened it. His jaw dropped. He looked from the parcel in his hands to his friend.

'How many of these plastic bags are there?'

'It looks like about twenty or perhaps thirty. What's in them? Let me see as well. Could we use it or sell it?' the young man lifted the base further and peered into the corners. He ran his hand over the base, feeling for further bags. 'Yes, I think it must be more like thirty.'

'Oh, yes. We can use this! Look – you won't believe what we've found! I don't know much about these things except that I am sure and certain we could sell this for a lot of money. We'll only sell about ten at a time not to attract attention.' The older one opened his hand in which, on a bed of tissue paper, cut stones – deep green, with a shade of blue winked back at them in the sunlight. The oily sheen of each mesmerised the young men.